OUTCASTS

Born and raised in England, Martin Lake discovered his love of history and writing at an early age. He worked as a teacher and trainer before he decided to combine his two passions and write a historical novel. Since then, he has written over a dozen novels and several collections of short stories. When not writing, he can be found travelling, exploring interesting places and watching the world go by. He lives on the French Riviera with his wife.

Also by Martin Lake

NOVELS

Land of Blood and Water
Blood Enemy
Wolves of War
The Flame of Resistance
Triumph and Catastrophe
Blood of Ironside
In Search of Glory
A Love Most Dangerous
Very Like a Queen
A Dance of Pride and Peril
Outcasts
The Artful Dodger

SHORT STORIES

For King and Country
The Big School
The Guy Fawkes Contest
Mr Toad's Wedding
The Big School

OUTCASTS

Martin Lake

First Published in Great Britain

Copyright © 2012 Martin Lake

The right of Martin Lake to be identified as author of this work has been asserted by him in accordance with the Copyright, Designs and Patents Act 1988.

All characters in this publication are fictitious and any resemblance to real persons, living or dead, is purely coincidental.

All Rights Reserved.

No part of this publication may be reproduced, stored in a retrieval system, or transmitted, in any form or by any means, electronic, mechanical, photocopying, recording or otherwise, without the prior permission of the copyright owner.

ISBN 978-1727867015

Cover Design by Rachael Gracie Carver
Typeset by Jackdaw Books

For Adam

JERUSALEM 1185

The young man sprawled in the dirt, desperate to avoid the spears that stabbed towards him.

'Get out, you filth,' cried an old man from the edge of the baying crowd.

The spears prodded once more, driving the young man to scurry away like a crab in the sand. He turned, crouching low, and his powerful arms knocked away the points to prevent them harming him.

Beyond the spearmen a crowd of citizens watched in fascinated dread.

'This is shameful,' one man cried, his eyes wide in horror. 'He should be honoured for what he did, not reviled in this way.'

'You are right,' said his companion, an aged Greek merchant. 'But tell me Bernard, would you allow such as him to enter your inn?'

He turned to watch the bitter scene unfold.

'Get out you filth,' cried the old man once again and this time his cry was taken up by others in the crowd, their tight throats yelping like street-dogs.

The young man staggered to his feet, shielded his aching eyes from the burning sun. He saw a young woman in the crowd bend to the ground. She straightened, weighed a heavy stone in her hand and threw it at him. Her aim was good and the stone smashed into his cheek, tearing at his lacerated skin.

This seemed to act as a signal. Dozens of stones flew from the hands of the onlookers, pelting him with vindictive fury. He did his best to shield his head from the missiles and staggered out of their reach.

'He should be allowed to join the Order of Saint Lazarus,' said the inn-keeper. 'He was a soldier of the King.'

The old Greek shook his hand. 'True. But he was not a knight. Even lepers, it appears, are ranked by birth and blood.'

The young man halted a short distance from the crowd and stared back at them. One of the spearmen stepped from the ranks and approached him, flinging down a bundle of white linen clothing and a bell before hurrying back to his fellows.

'Get away from us,' cried the voices from the crowd. 'Get away, you filth.'

'I shall do so,' the young man called. 'I have no desire to live my life with you.'

He stooped to the bundle of clothes, and turning, limped off towards the desert.

The crowd hooted in derision.

CHAPTER 1
ARRIVALS AND DEPARTURES
The David Gate in Jerusalem June 1187

John and Simon Ferrier climbed up the steep track towards the city. John felt he might die at any moment. The sun poured out of a clear blue sky, an intense, implacable heat which seemed intent on beating him to his knees. He uncorked his flask and sipped at the water. It tasted of iron and gave no relief to the desert of his mouth.

'Nearly there,' he gasped to his cousin.

Simon gave him a blank stare.

The last mile was the worst. John forced his eyes to peer through the glare but no matter how often he looked he appeared to be no closer. It seemed the city would stay forever beyond his reach.

Could that be, he wondered? Was Jerusalem so holy a place that those unworthy would never attain its bliss?

The two men lurched together. The contact gave them renewed purpose and their pace quickened. Finally, they reached the city and stumbled into the deep shade beneath its walls.

'At last,' said Simon.

'Ten months,' John said. 'Ten months. But we've got here.'

Just outside the gate to the city a cistern had been placed for the relief of pilgrims and their horses. The water was brackish and oily, strewn with wisps of straw and dead insects. They plunged their heads into it and swallowed great draughts. In England it would have been too warm to drink; now it was like water from an icy stream.

Eventually they drank their fill and took up their staffs. Hearts hammering with excitement they strode into the city.

Crowds of people lined the road, jostling for position. The sheer numbers pressed the cousins back until their legs slammed against a stone shrine. The noise of the crowd was almost unbearable.

Two small boys squeezed behind their legs and clambered onto the shrine.

They yelled to each other in joy and excitement.

'What's happening?' John asked them.

'King Guy,' cried the youngest boy, 'King Guy is going to war.'

Almost immediately a trumpet called from deep within the city. A heavy and regular beat sounded in the distance. It grew louder and soon the reverberation jarred the ground beneath their feet.

A huge cheer rose from the crowd and the children shrieked with delight.

Riding down the cobbled street came two lines of knights, pennants high, bright armour glistening in the sun. The knights in the line nearest to them wore white coats emblazoned with stark red crosses, the others wore red surcoats with white crosses.

'Who are they?' John asked.

'Knights of the Temple and the Hospital,' cried the youngest boy. 'I am for the Templars but Claude-Yusuf is for the Hospitallers.'

'Gerard is too young to know better,' explained the older boy with a shrug.

Five yards behind the knights rode two men on great horses.

The older man was a red-head with rough beard and close-cropped hair. He sat forward in his saddle as if hoping by his stance to push it faster. His eyes were wide and shining and he glanced about him with an exultant look.

'Who is that?' asked John. He did not say but he was disturbed by the look of the man.

'Raynald of Châtillon,' said an old man in the crowd. He leaned closer. 'If you are wise you would make no comment about him, no matter what anyone says, good or ill.'

John and Simon exchanged wary looks.

'And the other?' John stared at the man who rode beside Raynald.

He was tall and slim, with thick, flowing hair and neat trimmed beard. His face seemed carved from stone; handsome and dignified, with full lips and a strong chin. His eyes were stern and imperious and he glanced about him at the crowd acknowledging their cheers with a nod of his head.

'That is Guy of Lusignan,' said the old man.

'King Guy, King Guy,' cried Gerard. 'Hooray for King Guy.'

The king, hearing the cry, searched out the owner of the voice and held out his hand. Gerard gasped and reached up for the king's hand. Guy took it, shook it in a sign of triumph and smiled.

Delighted, Gerard grinned at Claude-Yusuf. 'King Guy has shaken my hand,' he cried, 'King Guy has shaken my hand.'

Behind the king came a compact body of noblemen who looked neither to right nor left. They were followed by long lines of knights and foot-soldiers. The boys became even more excited and Claude-Yusuf began to yell at the top of his voice.

One of the soldiers heard his voice and turned, searching the crowd. His face lit up and he waved with wild enthusiasm. He called out to the boys but could not be heard.

'Goodbye, Father,' Claude-Yusuf cried, 'goodbye.' But his voice was lost in the tumult.

Eventually, the last company marched through the gate and disappeared down the road that had brought John and Simon to the city.

The huge gates were winched shut. The crowd, which moments before had roared with joy at the departing army, gradually fell silent. People turned and looked at their neighbours, elation fading from their faces. The throng began to disperse. Those who remained looked forlorn, almost embarrassed. A pained silence descended upon them.

John and Simon gazed at the crowd in confusion. It was the first time they had paid them any attention and they were shocked.

The men were swarthy and heavily bearded, a few with turbans. The women wore veils and their arms shimmered with silver.

They can't be our people, John thought. Since landing in the Holy Land the cousins had paid little heed to the locals. They had assumed that Jerusalem would be full of Europeans. It appeared they were wrong. The people here looked unlike anybody they had ever seen.

There was a sudden commotion behind them and they turned to see what was happening.

A priest with pale face and livid eyes had grabbed the eldest boy by the hair.

'You dare to stand upon a sacred shrine,' he cried, slapping the boy across the face.

Simon stepped forward. 'Leave him alone,' he cried. 'He's doing no harm.

'Infidels must not pollute this shrine,' said the priest.

'I'm not an infidel,' said the boy.

'Liar,' said the priest. He clenched his fist still tighter and shook the boy's head. 'What's your name, infidel?'

'Claude-Yusuf. My father is a soldier. He's just marched off with the King.'

The priest slapped the boy once again. 'A half-breed. Worse than an infidel. I'll have you whipped.'

'You can't do that,' said Simon.

'Can't I?' The priest held Simon's gaze. 'I think you'll find I can.'

'He's done nothing wrong.'

'He's a half-breed. Whelped on a Saracen mother. I'd slaughter the lot of them.'

Both boys began to wail.

John had not interfered until this point but he could stand by no longer. He stepped up to the priest but Simon saw and blocked his way, preventing him from reaching the priest.

'I have journeyed from England to Jerusalem,' Simon told the priest, 'and in all those miles I've never seen such unchristian behaviour.'

He prised open the priest's fingers.

The priest's eyes narrowed. 'I shall remember you, infidel-lover,' he said. He strode off, his curses carrying on the air.

The boys wiped their noses.

'Are you all right?' John asked the older boy.

'Yes.'

'I am as well,' said his friend. 'My name is Gerard. Are you pilgrims?'

John nodded. 'We are. We're from England.'

The boys exchanged looks, this news of much greater interest than the recent assault upon them.

'Is England in France?' Gerard asked.

John shook his head. 'Certainly not.'

Simon bent down to the boys. 'You seem to like soldiers. You were watching the army march past.'

'Claude-Yusuf is for the Hospitallers,' Gerard said once again. 'I'm for the Templars. I shall be one when I get older.'

'What about you, Claude-Yusuf?' John asked. 'Do you want to be a Hospitaller?

The boy did not answer. He stared at the ground and twisted his toes in the dust.

Simon shrugged and held a penny up to the boys. 'Thank you for arranging such a magnificent welcome to the city,' he said. 'We are going to stay at the Pilgrim Hostel. Do you know where it is?'

'It's a long way from here,' Gerard said.

'A long way,' said Claude-Yusuf. 'We know a better place.'

John raised an eyebrow, suspecting some trick.

'The best inn in Jerusalem,' Gerard continued. 'It's much better than the Hostel. Good beds, good drink and good food.'

'It's close by,' added Claude-Yusuf.

Simon laughed. 'Then let's take a look at this marvel of an inn.'

The two boys took the cousins' hands and led them into a maze of alleys. John feared they would soon be lost but in a few moments they found themselves at the inn.

'See,' said Claude-Yusuf, 'I said it was close.'

After the glare of the streets the inn looked dark. Better yet, it was cool. A large room stretched in front of them with rough tables and benches dotted around in an ordered manner. At the far end of the room a door led into a courtyard with small trees and shrubs. Along the wall ran a counter stacked with barrels of ale and bottles of wine. A woman stood behind this, cutting bread.

'We've brought some pilgrims,' Gerard called. 'From England.'

'From England?' The woman smiled and handed each of the boys a slice of bread.

'You're good boys,' she said, glancing over towards John and Simon.

Her face was oval, with olive coloured skin and dark brown eyes. Her hair was a tawny blonde, little darker than the colour of straw. Two dimples played on either side of a tiny mouth. John had never seen anything as lovely. He cast his eyes downward, seeking to banish the thought from his mind.

Simon smiled at the woman.

'My name is Simon Ferrier,' he said. 'And this is my cousin, John.'

'Welcome,' the woman said. 'You must be tired. Can I offer you food and drink?'

Simon nodded enthusiastically but John shook his head.

'Not yet, I beg,' he said. His eyes remained fixed on the floor. 'My cousin Simon may wish to eat but before I do I must climb the hill of Calvary and see where Our Lord was crucified.'

The woman gave a fleeting smile and then frowned, wondering how best to answer.

'To see that would indeed be a miracle,' called a man from the courtyard. He was of slight and wiry build, dark skinned with curly hair, a moustache and a wide grin. His apron was covered in red and brown stains, some of them still wet.

Perched upon his shoulder was a small girl about five years of age. He slid her to the floor and came towards them.

'There is no hill of Calvary,' the man continued. 'It was flattened and a church built around it.'

John was shocked. 'So we can't see Calvary?'

'Not a trace of it.'

'And the cross?'

'Oh you can see that; or a bit of it at least. It's in the church. There's a tiny fragment of timber buried in a cross of gold.'

John frowned. 'Gold?'

'The churchmen felt that Christ would have wanted gold.'

The woman sighed and shook her head as if in warning.

'The cross isn't in the church now, father,' Gerard said. 'The army took it and marched with it at the front of the column, the very front, just behind King Guy. The army took the cross to go to war.'

'Did they, indeed?' The man looked troubled. 'So they stake everything on this attack,' he said almost to himself.

The woman approached the two pilgrims.

'The Church of the Sepulchre is wonderful,' she said, 'but is locked at dusk.' She gave a thoughtful look towards John. 'Surely just your coming to Jerusalem will please God enough without the need to starve yourself.'

She saw his lips move, muttering troubled words to himself. The sight made her heart ache and without intending to she touched him fleetingly upon the wrist. He looked up and found her eyes staring into his. His heart lifted. The dark stain upon his mind began to thin as if by a morning breeze.

'Well if the church is locked that settles it,' said Simon, flinging down his pack. 'We'll take ale please. The road from Jaffa is very dusty.

They sat and watched while the woman poured two flagons with foaming ale. The dark man wiped his hands upon his apron, picked up a jug of wine and drew up a stool.

'Welcome to our inn,' he said. 'My name is Bernard Montjoy. We have good food and there's a clean chamber with a bed and window.'

'We brought them, father,' cried Gerard. 'Claude-Yusuf and me.'

Bernard smiled, tousled his son's hair and gave a wink to Claude-Yusuf.

'We want food and a bed,' said John.

'Excellent,' said Bernard. 'I'll see to your room and my wife will bring you food. Agnes is the best cook in the Kingdom of Jerusalem.'

The woman blushed and smiled.

John's heart sank. She was married.

They ate a meal of the finest bread they had ever tasted, a slice of ham, some sharp and salty cheese and a honeycomb. When Agnes came to clear away their plates, John told her of the incident with the priest at the shrine.

'It doesn't happen often,' she said.

'The priest called the boy a half-breed.'

'My brother Robert married a Muslim woman who had converted to Christianity,' Agnes explained. 'Claude-Yusuf is their child. They are accepted here in Jerusalem but some newcomers from the west despise them.'

She gave a curious glance at John who looked shocked at this news. He shook his head and mumbled to himself. Of course, he was a newcomer too.

'It sounds a little like England,' Simon said. 'Some of the pure-bred Normans think that John is a half-breed because his mother is English.'

'I don't understand,' Agnes said. 'Aren't you cousins?'

'Yes,' said Simon. 'But my parents are both of Norman stock which is why I am dark like your husband. The Normans think that John looks like a peasant, with his broad shoulders and hair like straw. He takes after his mother, you see, a Saxon woman.'

'I don't think you look like a peasant,' Agnes said to John. 'You look strong and thoughtful. And being English is a good thing, surely, no matter whether your mother is Norman or Saxon?'

John reddened and looked away.

There was an uncomfortable silence before Simon spoke again. 'Claude-Yusuf says he lives with you.'

Agnes nodded. 'Claude-Yusuf's mother went to Ascalon in the spring and fell ill. She has not returned. Now that his father has gone to war he stays with us.'

John and Simon had the best night's sleep since leaving home. They awoke ravenously hungry and wolfed down a breakfast of bread and hot pork.

'How long shall we stay here?' Simon asked.

John shrugged. Their funds were ample but not unlimited.

'We should find out how much the Hostel costs,' Simon said.

John nodded but then looked up and caught a glimpse of Agnes picking some herbs in the courtyard.

'I suppose so,' he said. 'But I think we should balance cost with comfort. I don't want to spend every night with scores of filthy pilgrims if this place is only a little more expensive. The facilities here are excellent.'

Simon's eyes slid towards Agnes. He smiled to himself but decided not to comment.

CHAPTER 2
THE HOLY CITY
Jerusalem

Gerard and Claude-Yusuf raced into the room and headed straight for the cousins.

'Shall we take you around Jerusalem?' Claude-Yusuf asked. 'We are most excellent guides.'

'Claude-Yusuf knows everywhere and everything,' Gerard said with pride.

'That sounds a splendid idea,' Simon said.

At that moment Agnes walked in from the courtyard.

'But only if your parents agree,' John said hurriedly so that she could hear.

'Agree to what?' Agnes asked.

The two boys ran to her, each grabbing a hand and looking up at her with pleading eyes.

'The English have asked us to take them round the city,' Gerard said. 'We will be their guides.'

'They have asked you?' she said, feigning surprise. Her eyes went to the young men.

'In a manner of speaking,' said John. He felt his face redden.

Agnes glanced away. 'If you promise not to be a nuisance to the gentlemen,' she said.

The two boys wriggled with excitement. 'We will, we will.'

'I'm sure you will.'

She smiled at the men. 'Are you certain about this?'

'We don't know the city,' Simon answered. 'We need experienced guides.'

'I must see the church first,' said John. 'That is essential.'

Ten minutes later Gerard and Claude-Yusuf dragged the cousins out of the inn and led them through a narrow alley way. They were soon in the middle of a warren of streets and alleys. They moved fast, darting up and down, turning corner after corner until the two adults lost any sense of direction.

After a few minutes they walked through an arch into an open space.

In the centre of the space was a vast church.

The Ferriers gasped. They had never in their lives seen such a building. It dwarfed anything they had seen or could have imagined.

'I've never seen a tree as tall as this,' Simon said.

'I think it's even bigger than Nottingham castle,' said John.

Simon's gaze went from one end of the church to the other.

'I tell you what; I think the whole of the Goose Fair could be lost inside it and the city church as well.'

John nodded, awestruck.

The Church of the Sepulchre was made of glistening stone. Its roof was covered with silver and two large domes with golden crosses appeared to float above the roof.

As John gazed upon it he felt as if he were being dislodged from his firm footing upon the ground, almost as if he dangled half-way between earth and sky.

He brought his eyes back to the ground, seeking for some sense of normality.

They were standing on the edge of the cobbled area in front

of the church. It was thronged with people and the tumult of their noise was overwhelming.

Some looked similar to the people they had seen when they entered the city. Most looked like pilgrims from the west, travel-worn, filthy, staring at the glory of the church.

'Well,' said John, swallowing hard. 'You've brought us here. Shall we go inside?'

He took Gerard and Claude-Yusuf's hands and stepped through the porch into the church.

John was staggered by what he saw. Every wall was hung with tapestries. Gold figurines crammed every surface and the ceiling appeared studded with precious stones. The clear light of day flooded the interior; it was as if he had stepped into the Heaven of his imagination.

His eyes followed the long nave and rested on a huge alterpiece. His heart lurched at the sight of it. He wiped his eyes, took a breath and started down the nave towards it.

The alter showed scenes from the life of Christ: his birth, childhood, ministry and sacrifice, carved from fine-grained dark wood. John stared at the many faces of Christ in the screen. He was overcome, believing this to be the very image of his saviour.

Beside the alter piece was a large plinth made of fine marble. It was covered in flowers and small dishes of smouldering incense. In the centre of it was a rectangular slit which had, by some miracle of craft, been incised deep into the marble.

'What's this?' Simon asked.

'It's where the True Cross usually rests,' Claude-Yusuf said. 'But King Guy took it with him in order to beat the Saracens.'

Simon smiled. John recalled Bernard's words about this and wondered at them.

'Let's go this way,' Claude-Yusuf said, tugging at John's hand. 'This is where dead people were buried.'

'Is the tomb there?' John asked. 'Where Our Lord's body rested before he rose again?'

Claude-Yusuf shrugged.

'There are bones there,' Gerard said. 'Lots of them.'

'Show me where Our Saviour was crucified first,' John said.

The boys looked blank. They had no idea that such a place existed in the city.

An old pilgrim had been listening to their talk from where he rested on a bench. He reached out for John's hand.

'The place you seek can be found in a chapel above us,' he said. 'Climb the stairs by the entrance to the church and you will arrive there.'

John thanked the pilgrim and turned to Simon.

'I pray you cousin, will you take the children away for a while? I need to see Calvary on my own and quietly.'

'Of course,' Simon answered. 'I understand.'

Simon bent down to the boys. 'I'd love to see where people were buried,' He said. 'And their bones.' He had hardly straightened before he was whisked away.

John returned to the entrance and climbed up the stairs which led to the place of the crucifixion. With each step his heart felt more deadened, his burden of guilt more heavy.

At the top of the stairs he paused, his hand upon the door.

Dare I go in? Am I so reviled, so lost that I cannot sully this holy place?

He closed his eyes and tried to calm his heart. He took a deep breath and stepped into the chapel.

To his left was a small rock on which it was said the three

crosses had been raised a thousand years before. He fell to his knees in front of it.

He cast his mind back to his act of sin and sacrilege. He felt once again his anger, still hot as the blood which swept his veins. He felt once again the sense of shame.

He needed more. He tried to force his thoughts to the sorrow, the contrition he knew he should feel at the horror of his deed. But instead they turned again to those screams of shame and rage.

He knelt in silence for a long time, his hands pressed to his forehead. It was useless. Salvation would stay forever beyond his reach.

Could this be, he wondered? Was Jerusalem too holy a place for one so unworthy? Was he damned, never able to attain the bliss it promised?

He struggled to his feet and leant his hand against the wall, propped up like a dead thing awaiting disposal.

A familiar blackness settled once more upon him. He made a perfunctory obeisance towards the place of sacrifice and left.

He found Simon and the boys at the foot of the stairs.

'Are you all right?' Simon asked.

John smiled wanly. 'Yes. But what I desire may not prove as easy as I imagined.'

He did not tell Simon his real thoughts. Simon had trod long and weary miles with him on the journey to the Holy Land and it was not fair to even hint that they may have been in vain.

Simon nodded but made no comment.

'Well I saw the tombs but one of the priests took a dislike to the boys. I thought it best to leave.'

As he said it he glanced at Claude-Yusuf for it was he who had aroused the anger of the priest. The boy must have realised it but seemed unconcerned.

'Shall we take you round the rest of the city now?' Gerard asked.

Simon nodded. 'That would be good.'

The boys led them back through the maze of alley ways, past the inn and then cut right along the David Street towards the Jaffa Gate by which they had entered the city.

Close by the gate the city walls continued in an easterly direction to enclose a vast citadel. Two huge towers loomed high above the citadel walls, impregnable bastions designed to throw back the fiercest assault. The cousins crept past the fortifications, feeling like mice trying to scurry past a watchful cat. They felt ashamed, for the two boys were unabashed.

'This is where King Guy lives,' cried Gerard with pride. 'He waved to me once and kissed me on the head.'

I don't believe you,' Claude-Yusuf said.

'He did. You can ask my father.'

'Why would he kiss you so?'

'Because he knows that I am to be a Templar knight when I grow up.'

'How could he know that?'

Gerard went to answer then realised he did not know and was forced to shrug instead and try to look superior.

John and Simon looked everywhere as they walked. With every step they appeared to be going deeper into a more foreign world. There were no Europeans here apart from themselves. They could not help but stare at the exotic appearance of the people with their dark faces and strange, bright clothes.

The locals, on the other hand, gave the Englishmen only the most cursory of glances. They were well used to the sight of pilgrims.

'Are these Saracens?' John asked.

Claude-Yusuf shook his head. 'No Muslims are allowed to live within the city walls. These people are Armenians.'

They strolled through streets and markets, past churches and shrines, through alley ways and little courts, startled by the bright and vivid colours. Their nostrils were filled with the scent of strange food: pungent spices, musky stews and fish both fresh and rotting. The noise was overwhelming for everyone talked at the top of their lungs.

After a few minutes the boys turned left and they entered a quarter of the city which was even more strange to their sight. The people were smaller than the Armenians and even darker of face. They wore clothes of bright and vibrant colours and every man was bearded. Small groups of men clung around tiny squares, locked in fierce discussion, their arms waving until someone said something amusing which made them roar with laughter. But as soon as they saw John and Simon they grew quiet and watched in silence until they passed.

'Are these Jews?' Simon asked.

Claude-Yusuf nodded.

'They make lots of pretty things,' he said. 'Mother and Aunt Agnes come here to buy their clothes.'

They came out onto a larger road. To their left was an open space crammed with people talking in close huddles. On either side of the street were tiny shops, most of them little more than booths. The cousins peered in as they passed. They did not appear to sell anything at all.

'Gerard,' called a figure sitting on a stool beside one of the booths. 'Claude-Yusuf.'

'Alexius,' they cried and ran over to him.

He was an old man, probably in his late fifties. He reached out for Gerard's ear and plucked a little coin from it. He then did the same to Claude-Yusuf. The boys were mesmerised and watched as he made a great show of biting on the coins.

'They are gold, most certainly,' he said, passing them to the boys who stood rapt, examining them. 'You boys have a gold-mine each in your heads. Don't let the Patriarch know or he will be after you.'

The man looked up at John and Simon and scrutinised them as if he were seeking to remember who they were. Finally, he seemed to have satisfied himself and grinned widely, showing a mouth filled not with teeth but with gold.

'Tell me boys,' he said, without taking his eyes from the adults. 'Who are your new friends?'

'They are English,' said Gerard, 'from France. They are staying at the inn and are my good friends.'

'Am I not your good friend?' the old man asked softly.

Gerard looked crestfallen for a moment.

'Of course you're our friend, Alexius, of course you are.'

He fell silent, biting his lip. 'But can't a person have more than one good friend?'

'He can indeed,' Alexius said. 'But he may, by definition, have only one best friend.'

'Claude-Yusuf is my best friend.'

'A good choice, if I may be allowed a judgement.'

He turned his attention to the Englishmen once more.

'You are pilgrims by the look of it.' He picked up a bag and shook it. 'And I am by calling a money-changer.'

He grinned and gestured them to sit on two stools next to

his own.

'My name is Alexius Kamateros of Constantinople. I can change any coin from east, west, south or north. As friends of these boys, I give you the best rate in Jerusalem.'

'We have English pennies,' John said.

The old man nodded. 'That is good. The English know how to make a coin.' He spread his hands. 'I have to say that the older the better. Since the Normans conquered the country the coins are not quite so fine.'

'But still good?'

'Oh yes, still good. Better than Frankish coins or German or Saracen.' He leaned close towards them. 'But not as good as those from the Empire of course.'

'Alexius' ancestor was an Emperor,' Claude-Yusuf said.

'Vespasian,' Alexius said. 'A long time ago. My people moved from Rome to Constantinople six hundred years ago.'

John and Simon exchanged glances, not knowing what to make of the old man.

'You doubt that I am honest?' he asked.

'No,' said Simon. 'I'm sure you are.'

'More honest than the relic sellers, at any rate.'

He leaned close once again.

'In the Street of the Palmers you will find only one honest shop,' he continued. 'The rest will sell you a part of a sheep's fleece and tell you it comes from John the Baptist's wild and woolly head. They will sell you a dried up old thorn and say it came from Christ's crown. They will sell you a rusty nail, or even maybe all three and claim you know what. Why I have even seen one sell a rock and claim that it was used to stone Saint Stephen.'

Simon laughed. 'We shall watch out for them. I have heard

that an Abbot in France has a golden casket where he keeps the fore-skin of Christ.'

Alexius threw his hand in the air. 'I can purchase half a dozen of the same, in the one street.'

'You say there is one honest shop?' said Simon.

Alexius rose from his stool and bowed. 'The shop belongs to he with whom you now speak.'

'Of course. I should have guessed.'

Alexius sat down once again. He sniffed, deciding what his next move should be. 'In the meanwhile, you want to change some money?'

'I would like something smaller than a penny,' John said.

Alexius produced a small scale as if from nowhere and placed three of John's pennies in one pan and adjusted a small lever on the scales. He opened a bag and poured tiny copper coins into the other pan until the scales balanced.

'This is the current rate,' he said. Then he poured more copper coins into the pan, causing it to sink to the table. 'And this is the rate for friends of friends.'

The noon bell rang and the old man plucked up his bags and scales and pulled down a shutter on his booth.

He turned to the cousins. 'Do you plan to stay long in Jerusalem?' he asked.

'We think so.'

The old man stared at them for a long time. 'Forgive me for saying, but I think you should not stay here too long.'

CHAPTER 3
SAINTS AND DEMONS
Jerusalem

Bernard heaved a barrel of ale onto the counter.

'Good news,' he said. 'The young Englishmen have decided to stay for a month.'

'Excellent,' Agnes answered. 'With the soldiers gone the city feels empty and our coffers are beginning to look the same.'

'Do you like the English?' he asked. 'You might be related.'

'My great grandfather was English,' Agnes said. 'That was a long time ago. In any case, these two are of Norman blood. And my great grandfather was said to be the son of the Normans' deadliest enemy.'

'But do you like them?'

She paused before picking up a cloth and polishing a tankard. 'I like them as much as any other guest. Why do you ask?'

'They've only been here, what, three days and the boys seem to have got attached to them already.'

Agnes looked troubled. 'Do you think it is a cause for concern?'

'I don't know. I think Gerard believes they will stay here forever.'

'Gerard's always excitable.'

Agnes came over to her husband and brushed her fingers through his hair. 'And what about you? Do you like them?'

He grinned. 'I do. That may be why I am asking the question.

I like them a lot, more than an inn-keeper should like his guests.'

'That is because they come from somewhere far-away and exotic. England sounds so exciting. Jerusalem is boring and you hanker for adventure.'

He grabbed her by the waist and stared into her eyes. 'I have all the adventure I need just living with you.'

Agnes blushed at his words and a tiny smile grew upon her lips.

'I like you saying this,' she said. 'But I sometimes wonder if you don't yearn for a little more adventure than I can provide.'

'Not in the slightest,' he said, pulling her close.

Later that day John sat in the courtyard enjoying the last of the day's sunshine. He closed his eyes and turned his face up to the sky, enjoying the warmth bathing his skin. His lips felt dry and hot and he licked them slowly.

He did not hear any noise but he suddenly became aware of a presence in the courtyard. His first thought was that it was one of the boys.

But then he knew. He knew it was Agnes.

He opened his eyes and turned to look at her.

She was leaning in the doorframe, a cloth and a plate in her hand. She must be enjoying the sun as well, he thought.

His heart quickened. Or perhaps she had been watching me.

'I didn't mean to disturb you,' she said softly.

He shook his head.

'You didn't. I wasn't asleep.'

'You looked very peaceful.'

He thought as if the breath was being squeezed from his lungs.

'I was just thinking, just dreaming, day-dreaming rather.'

She laughed, a little tinkling sound which almost made

him shiver.

'I do that,' she said. 'Or I do whenever I get a minute's peace. I'm afraid that isn't often.'

He gazed at her but did not answer. His mind struggled to find something to say but every phrase he formed seemed inane.

The sun had moved so that half her face was in full sunlight and half in shade. The branches of the old olive tree flickered shadows across her face. Almost like a bridal veil, he thought. His gaze was caught by the line where light and shadow met. Her features, normally so bright in his imagination, were dimmed there but more alluring for that.

'You look red,' she said.

He touched his hands to his cheek and blushed even redder.

'It's the sun,' he said. 'My skin isn't used to it.'

She smiled. He had no idea what the smile meant. He guessed she may have realised that the colour on his face came from within.

'John,' called a familiar voice from within the inn.

He ignored Simon's call, hoping that he would not find him and go away.

'John,' he called again. 'Where are you? I've got something to tell you.'

Still John ignored his call.

Agnes smiled and glanced at the ground before looking up at him once again.

'Aren't you going to answer your cousin?' she asked. 'He sounds keen to find you.'

John nodded and went even redder. He cursed his cousin.

'I'm in the courtyard,' he called.

Simon appeared in the doorway and took in the scene. A grin which looked knowing and lascivious broke upon his face.

'I wasn't interrupting anything?' he asked innocently.

Agnes shook her head.

'Of course not,' said John quickly. He got to his feet. 'What did you want?'

Simon put his hand to his mouth as if struggling to remember. 'Do you know, I've completely forgotten.'

He gave a courtly bow to Agnes, winked at John and went back into the inn.

Agnes turned and gazed at John.

'I'd better go after him,' he said.

'I think you had,' she answered. 'Before he gets any more strange ideas.'

John mumbled incoherently and walked into the gloom of the inn.

The next morning the Ferriers climbed up to the battlements by the Golden Gate at the eastern part of the city.

John had spent a restless night, tormented by the sight of Agnes in the courtyard and tormented even more by his thoughts concerning her. It was imperative that he find some sense of salvation, however feeble.

They walked north for a few paces until John stopped and looked towards the east. His hands grasped the stone of the walls as though he was holding on to them for fear of falling.

'The Mount of Olives,' he said, in a voice made thick with emotion.

The sun shone on the trees which crammed the slopes of the mount. It looked a rich and wholesome place. John felt he should avert his eyes from this and stare down instead to Gethsemane to try to snatch a glimpse of Christ's agony the night before the crucifixion.

He bent his head and gasped.

'It looks lovely,' he said in surprise.

'The mountain?' Simon asked.

'No Gethsemane. I thought it would look bleak and awful, tortured by the memory of Christ's anguish.'

'You seem disappointed.'

'I am.' He shook his head. 'I came to Jerusalem to seek redemption for my sin. How can I do this when the city is rich and pleasant, the sights a marvel and a wonder?'

Simon drummed his fingers upon the battlements. 'Perhaps you are misguided John. Perhaps you can get redemption from things of beauty as much as from the ugly and the bitter.'

John shook his head angrily. 'Beautiful things are a danger, the snares of Satan.'

'Yet God put them on the Earth.'

'As a test.'

Simon sighed and closed his eyes. 'I can't agree with you, John. Beauty is to be enjoyed and loved. Even Christ chose to spend his last night on Earth in the garden below. Who are you to be different?'

'I am a sinner. Christ was not.'

'We are all sinners.' He smiled. 'I for one would very much like to sin with a certain woman.'

John straightened. 'Who do you mean?'

'You know.' He paused and grinned at John. 'The lovely Agnes.'

John did not answer. His mind raced, his thoughts skittering like starlings in a flock. 'She is married,' he said at last, coldly.

'That does not stop her being beautiful.'

'You must not think such a thing. She belongs to another.'

'That does not stop her being beautiful.'

'She is the mother of two children.'

'That does not stop her being beautiful.'

'We are guests in her home for God's sake.'

'That gives me opportunity. And by the way, you just blasphemed.'

John was speechless with rage. He turned away from Simon. Christ help me, he thought, Christ help me. Simon agreed to come on this pilgrimage with me, he has been my loyal and constant companion. Christ help me, Christ help him.

His thundering heart began to calm. He turned back to Simon and held out his hand.

Simon stared at it. 'What is this for?'

'Take it.'

'You offer me your hand as if you had done me wrong.'

John hesitated, desperately thinking of something to say to hide the truth. 'I offer you my hand because I love you and I do not wish you to seduce the lady Agnes.'

Simon smiled.

John could not tell whether it was a smile of friendship or mockery. Or perhaps of gratification that he had guessed the state of affairs correctly.

After a brief moment Simon took John's hand.

They arrived back at the inn in time for the noon-day meal. They were accosted by a blind man sitting by the entrance. John pulled out his purse and began to search for a suitable coin. Simon took the opportunity to slip straight into the inn.

As soon as he entered Bernard called him over.

'I'm glad you're here, Simon,' he said. 'Some English pilgrims have arrived and they are drinking like they've never seen ale before. I've told them to quieten down but they don't understand. Will you talk to them?'

Simon strolled over and listened for a while before returning. 'I'm sorry,' he said, 'I don't understand them. They speak English.'

'But you are English.'

'Yes. But I only speak French. Both my parents are of Norman stock. John may be able to help, his mother was English. He can speak the language like a native though he pretends not to.'

Bernard frowned. 'Is speaking English something to be ashamed of?'

'It's nothing to be proud of.'

Bernard shook his head. He saw John walk in and hurried over to seek his aid. Simon could see that John was reluctant but in the end he agreed and went over to the Englishmen and spoke to them. There were lots of jeers and cat-calls but, nevertheless, they quietened down and even agreed to pay for the ale they had already consumed.

'Thank you,' Bernard said. 'Some of us in Jerusalem speak Arabic as well as French but I had not realised that it was the same in other lands.'

'England is a bit like Jerusalem,' John said. 'It was conquered by foreigners and now the English feel like strangers in their own land.'

'He always says this,' Simon said. 'But it doesn't stop him acting like a Norman when it suits him. Nor his brother Alan who is one of Prince Richard's right-hand men. And you can be sure that Richard has little time for the English.'

'So are you English or Norman?' Bernard asked.

'Our ancestor came over with the first King Henry,' John said. 'He was an ordinary man, a blacksmith. He never called himself

English though. His son, our grandfather was the first to do so.

Bernard shook his head and pointed out the loud party of English pilgrims. 'And what would they think of you?' he asked.

'They would think we were their betters,' Simon said.

'But they'd be wrong,' John said. 'We are no richer than they and have no greater power or influence.'

'But we speak French, cousin,' Simon said. 'And that still makes a difference.'

At that point John saw Alexius, the money-changer, and pointed him out, anxious to change the topic of conversation.

Alexius beckoned them over. 'Englishmen, if you have no other plans, please join me. I leave tomorrow for Constantinople and may not see you again.'

'Constantinople?'

'Yes, I go to an important meeting. I am part of a family enterprise which trades across the Empire and the Muslim lands. My brother summons us all to account every three years.'

Agnes brought two more plates containing a rich stew with a strange aromatic smell.

'What is this?' John asked.

'Goat cooked in spices,' she answered.

'It looks lovely.'

'I wonder what it tastes like.' Simon muttered when she had left.

'It tastes very good,' said Alexius. 'Agnes is a wonderful cook. And she has a lovely arse.'

John stared at him in astonishment.

'I can say this,' said Alexius self-indulgently. 'I am an old man and young people allow me liberties. Perhaps they shouldn't.'

Agnes returned and placed a jug of ale upon the table. 'Young people also have good hearing,' she said. She grabbed a lock of the old Greek's hair and shook it.

'Ah,' Alexius said, feigning dismay, 'I am found out.'

'You will be thrown out if my husband hears.'

Alexius chuckled. 'He comes now, Princess. Here, Bernard. I was just telling our English friends that Agnes has a beautiful arse.'

Bernard came over and gazed at his wife. Then he leant close to Alexius. 'She has. But unlike me, who can see her arse in all its naked glory, you can see it only through her skirts.'

'How do you know I have not seen her exactly as you do?' Alexius asked, his eyes narrowing.

'Because I know that you are a creature of lies and fantasies.' He tapped the old man lightly upon the cheek and took a sip of his wine.

Alexius laughed, his eyes, twinkling with mischief.

Bernard glanced at the Ferriers. 'How do you come to be eating with this old scoundrel?'

'He changed some money for us,' Simon said.

'What?' Bernard gave a sharp look at the old man.

Alexius opened his hands wide. 'The boys were with them. I realised they were your guests. They got a fair price.'

Bernard drew up a stool. 'See that they continue to do so.'

'Of course,' Alexius said. 'After all, they may be your relatives.'

'Relatives?' John glanced at Bernard.

'Not mine,' Bernard said. 'I'm a Frank through and through.'

He grinned and bent closer to them.

'But my wife,' he continued, 'is descended from an Englishman; her great-grandfather, Robert. He came to the Holy Land with a man called Edgar who claimed he was the rightful king of England. Edgar was the heir of the ancient Saxon kings but William the Conqueror stole the throne from him. Family legend says that Edgar was Robert's father, though he did not realise this.'

John and Simon exchanged quick glances. They had heard a similar tale themselves but had thought it a fabrication.

'And Robert settled and raised a family,' said Alexius. 'Here in Jerusalem.'

'He had a child,' said Bernard. 'Agnes' grandfather.'

He gave a self-satisfied smile.

'But that was not the end of the story,' said Alexius. 'Robert was captured by the Saracens. They must have realised he was the son of King Edgar even if his father didn't.'

'Whether or no,' said Bernard, 'Robert was killed for not renouncing his faith.' He made a cutting motion against his neck.

'He was true to his faith,' said Alexius.

'He was a bloody fool,' said Bernard. 'What does religion matter compared to your own neck? The Saracens would have welcomed him, a man of his blood. He might have even become an emir.'

Agnes had returned with a beaker of wine and a plate of food for her husband.

'That old story,' she said with a smile. 'That's all it is, a story.'

'Some stories contain a kernel of truth,' said Alexius. 'Is not your own brother, Robert, named for your ancestor?'

'If this story had any truth I wouldn't be running around cooking food for old men and a hungry husband. I'd be living in a palace and sleeping in a bed of finest feathers.'

She put the plate down in front of her husband.

'Wonderful,' Bernard said, wiping his hands upon his filthy apron and bending to his plate with enthusiasm. He blew a kiss at

Agnes who raised her eyes to the heavens.

'With a headboard of cedar wood,' she said as she went back to the kitchen.

Alexius passed Bernard a chunk of bread. 'What news, dear friend?'

Bernard looked around the room. 'It's quiet, very quiet. There are pilgrims true enough but it doesn't make up for the army leaving the city. My takings are down.'

'You know where to come if you have need.'

'Thank you.' Bernard dipped his bread in the stew, turning it slowly to collect the juices. He glanced up at Alexius with a questioning look.

Alexius raised his hand to stop him from saying more. He turned towards the cousins. 'And how do the English like Jerusalem?' he asked.

John paused. 'It is not as I imagined it to be.'

'And how did you imagine it?'

'I'm not sure now. More ancient, more holy.'

Alexius laughed. 'It feels more holy now than when the troops are quartered here. Much quieter at any rate.' He helped himself to more wine.

'You pilgrims think that Jerusalem is a place where angels fly and saints tread,' said Bernard. 'In fact it's where different worlds collide and it breeds both saints and demons.'

Alexius placed his hand upon John's arm. 'Bernard is right. As a pilgrim you must find grace where you can. It does not reside in the stone walls of Jerusalem. Perhaps it resides in your own heart.'

John felt his eyes moisten at the words and bent to his meal to hide it. Can he read my soul he wondered? Out of the corner of his eye he saw Alexius nod to himself as if he now realised the answer to a question.

'And what of your news, old goat?' Bernard asked.

Alexius stared out of the door at the streets. 'My scales are frenzied, Bernard. The exchange is in turmoil, prices careering like wild bulls.' He picked up his wine and peered into it as it seeking to find something within.

'This is just a symptom,' he continued. 'Rumour is bleak.'

'What rumour?' Simon asked.

'Of anguish and of wars,' Alexius answered.

'The day we came to the city,' Simon said, 'we saw an army leaving by the same gate. What was it?'

'That was the army of Jerusalem,' Bernard said. 'Every last warrior in the kingdom. Twelve hundred knights and twenty thousand foot-soldiers.'

John frowned. 'And where are all these men of blood going?'

'To defeat Saladin,' Bernard answered. 'Or be defeated by him.'

CHAPTER 4
THE END OF THE ARMY
The Field of Hattin

The Frankish nobles stared at the carnage.

The plain was covered with the corpses of men-at-arms. The loss of foot-soldiers was to be expected, if not on this scale. What horrified the nobles was that a thousand knights had also been slain.

King Guy glanced at the scatter of men close by. They were overcome by thirst, wounds and despair. They could fight no longer.

The sun tormented those left alive, especially the wounded. Their groans carried far across the plain. Only the carrion birds were not dismayed by the sound. They circled patiently, waiting until the dying gave up the struggle and the battle-field grew still.

There was one strength still remaining to the Christians. Raymond of Tripoli had maintained command of a few of his troops, a hundred in all, knights and foot-soldiers.

The King called across the heaps of dead, commanding him to attack the Saracen army.

Raymond looked across the field of dead; disbelieving, despairing. His dislike of Guy was deep-seated. He had long argued against his determination to force war upon Saladin. But he never thought the man's folly would lead to this.

He stared for a moment at Guy. He turned and looked at

Saladin's army and then at his own pitiful remnant of men. Then he laughed; a laugh of desperation and bitter scorn.

Raymond sheathed his sword and forced his men to harvest their courage and whatever weapons they could find.

'Mount up,' Raymond cried. 'Find a horse and mount up. Even foot-soldiers, even if you've never ridden before, mount up.'

The Saracen host, thirty thousand warriors, was drawn up in a crescent in front of them. Raymond took a deep breath and led his hundred men towards them.

The ground was strewn with Christian corpses. His men turned their heads when they saw they were about to ride over stricken friends or comrades. But Raymond increased the pace and the horsemen moved into a canter. The two armies were close now and he cried out, summoning his men to their final hopeless charge.

He drew his sword and aimed it at the nearest emir. But as he did so, with unbelievable skill, the Saracens veered away. A gap opened up allowing the tiny force to ride through the army unmolested to safety.

On the other side of the battle-field Balian of Ibelin realised that all eyes were on the charge of his friend Count Raymond. He seized this brief opportunity to lead his last four followers to safety.

The Saracen army reformed and came to a halt a furlong away from King Guy and the rest of the Frankish lords.

Two men, the leaders of the victorious army, walked their horses a dozen paces in front of their warriors and gazed upon their stricken foe.

Later, as the sun set, Saladin walked alone across the battle field. He glanced back towards his camp where two dozen nobles stood captive. They were the sole survivors.

All around him lay the corpses of the army of Jerusalem,

twenty thousand soldiers and knights, the entire defensive force of the Kingdom.

Saladin turned to the south, his eyes peering across the bleak hills. Now, finally, he could unleash the storm upon Jerusalem.

CHAPTER 5
BALIAN OF IBELIN
Jerusalem

Fear flooded the city like a plague. It swept down from the Church and through the streets to the citadel. It seeped into every home and every heart. The people of the city hurried towards the high battlements, desperate to glimpse what they were terrified to see. Bernard, John and Simon shouldered their way into the crowd and were carried along to the walls.

There were no soldiers left in the city anymore so there was no challenge to them as they climbed the steps to the battlements.

The sun was drawing close to the horizon, painting gold the plain beyond the city. A vast army, swollen to fifty thousand warriors, was marching into place. Even as they looked, the last formations hurried to close the gaps remaining between them.

The city was surrounded.

'Perhaps our leaders will attempt another parlay?' John said.

'It did no good last time and it will do no good now,' Bernard answered. 'The moment those fools refused to surrender, Saladin swore he would kill every Christian.' He sighed. 'Just as the first Crusaders killed every Muslim when they took the city.

'So we must put our faith in the Lord Christ.'

Bernard shook his head, wearily. 'Christ's representative Archbishop Eraclius leads us now,' he said. 'So if preaching and whoring are needed to defend a city we have just the man to lead us to victory.'

They gazed out at the army arrayed below them. Most were infantry but to the rear trotted legions of horsemen, their spears glittering in the light of the failing sun.

But what caught their eyes lay directly ahead. Scores of catapults and mangonels were already in place, loaded with huge stones.

'Surely they cannot conquer these walls?' said John. 'Not even with those machines.'

'The walls might be strong,' said Bernard, 'but there are no soldiers left to man them.'

Simon pointed. A small group of horsemen trotted forward from the foremost Saracen lines.

'Horsemen,' he said. 'Five of them.'

Intrigued, the three men hurried down the staircase to the gate. They waited with the crowd until a postern door slid open and the horsemen entered the city.

The leader of the group took off his helmet to reveal the lined and haggard face of an elderly warrior.

'Balian of Ibelin,' Bernard said. He turned a worried face towards the Ferriers.

'What's wrong?' John asked.

'In my youth I was one of Balian's sergeants. When he married Queen Maria Comnena I made some jest about him marrying for a crown. I received a flogging and my dismissal.'

'What has he come here for?' said Simon.

'His wife,' said Bernard. 'She's here in the city. I was wrong you see. Balian married for love.'

The man who stood by Balian was a tall man of about the same age. Where Balian looked worried he seemed calm and relaxed.

He gazed around at the city as if remembering good times he had experienced here. He raked his fingers through his hair and then stopped. He had noticed them watching him and a broad grin of recognition spread over his face at the sight of Bernard.

'You know him?' John asked.

Bernard nodded. 'Jerome Sospel. Balian's best friend and lieutenant.'

News of the horsemen had spread and a committee of churchmen pushed their way through the crowd. They were led by Archbishop Eraclius who rushed to embrace Balian.

'Praise God,' he said. 'You have been sent to save the city.'

Balian shook his head. 'No. I have come for my wife and children. Saladin gave me free passage to collect them. I swore an oath to stay in the city for one day only and not to take arms against him.'

A fierce cry of anguish rose from the populace at these words. Balian glanced around at the sound but clamped his jaw tight, determined to ignore it.

'But that was an oath to an infidel,' said Eraclius. He stepped closer as though about to whisper but he made his voice loud enough to carry across the crowd. 'It is in my power to absolve you of your oath to the Saracen.'

Balian gave him an angry glare. 'I have come for my wife. Where is she?'

Eraclius peered at Balian, his mind working swiftly. 'She is in the palace. Go to her. Be joyous in your reunion. I shall come to you there later.'

The next morning the people of the city were overjoyed to hear that Eraclius had absolved Balian of Ibelin from his oath to Saladin. Balian was now free to take charge of the city's defence.

'What do you think of this news?' John asked Bernard.

'I don't know.' Bernard fell silent and shook his head. 'Jerusalem is my home. Our delegates were mad when they refused Saladin's terms; it condemned the city to destruction.'

He glanced across at Agnes who was singing quietly to their daughter. 'I feared for my family,' he continued. 'But with Balian here…'

'You think there may be a chance?'

Bernard shrugged.

Simon strode into the inn, his face shining with excitement.

'Balian has asked for every man to join him in defence of the city,' he said. He gave a playful punch to John's shoulder. 'It will be a glorious battle.'

John's heart sank. This was what he had dreaded to hear.

'I came to Jerusalem to be a pilgrim,' he said. 'I did not come to be a soldier.'

Simon stared at him in astonishment. 'To be a pilgrim is a luxury at a time like this. The infidel is beating upon the gate.'

'I will not kill my fellow man.'

Simon stared at him. 'A Saracen is not a fellow man. He is an infidel, damned for all eternity. That is what the church teaches us.'

'I do not believe it.'

Simon opened his mouth to reply but Bernard raised his hand to silence him.

'Hush, both of you. We should not war amongst ourselves.'

'I do not want a war,' John said. 'With Simon or with the Saracens.'

'You may not want a war,' Simon said. 'But what if the other man wants one? What if the Saracen is determined to have one?'

Bernard turned towards John. 'No one wants to fight, no one

wants to kill. And no one here wants to make you take up arms against your will.'

'He may have sworn to be a pilgrim,' said Simon angrily, 'but he never swore to lie supine before God's enemies.'

John looked up, his blood swirling with rage at the insult. He checked himself. It was this rage that had made him come on a pilgrimage, this rage which he had to do penance for, this rage which he had sworn to master, for Christ's sake and for his own.

'Shall I fight the infidel alone, cousin?' Simon asked in a cold voice. 'Or shall I fight with you by my side?'

John said nothing.

Simon's face quivered with anger. He strode off but before he could reach it the door was flung open.

A soldier looked around. 'Is Bernard Montjoy here?'

Bernard looked at the floor for a long moment. Then he raised his hand.

'Lord Balian wants you,' said the soldier.

'No,' cried Agnes.

'He commands it,' the soldier said. 'He demands it.'

At Agnes's insistence, John and Simon accompanied Bernard to the citadel. They walked in silence, Simon still angry, Bernard fearful, John trying to quell the voices which rained down insults inside his head.

The citadel was crammed with men: Franks, Armenians, Syrians and Jews. To one side was a pile of swords, spears and cudgels. A line of men received weapons from one of Balian's sergeants before shuffling to where a churchman stood, his hand held high in blessing.

Bernard turned his head away. He had glimpsed Balian of Ibelin in a corner of the citadel talking with a veiled woman and half a dozen children.

At that moment the gate of the citadel was flung open. To the astonishment of the crowd a dozen Saracen horsemen rode in followed by four men carrying a litter. Balian kissed the woman goodbye and helped her into the litter. The bearers made swiftly for the gate, followed by the children and last, the Saracen escort.

'What's happening?' Simon asked. 'Where are they taking that woman?'

'She is no ordinary woman,' said Bernard. 'She is the wife of Balian. More to the point she is grand-niece of the Emperor of Byzantium, as Saladin well knows. Saladin has no wish to antagonise the Empire. Maria Comnena could dance naked through the Saracen army and none would dare to look upon her.'

'Somebody is looking at you though,' John said.

Balian's comrade, Jerome Sospel, was beckoning to them.

Bernard turned a worried gaze upon his friends and gestured them to come with him.

As they approached they saw Balian force his gaze from the gate where his wife and family had just departed and turn instead to examine the walls of the city.

Jerome placed his hand upon Balian's shoulder for a moment, the briefest of moments. Then he turned to the three friends as they approached.

'Bernard Montjoy,' he said. His voice pretended surprise.

Balian turned at his friend's words and stared at the three men.

Bernard flung himself upon the ground, arms prostrate.

'My lord, Balian' he pleaded. 'You summoned me.'

Balian kicked him in the side.

'Get up, Montjoy' he said. 'Stop making a fool of yourself and of me.'

Bernard rose, dusting himself down, and stood abjectly, his head to one side. 'Mercy, Lord, upon your former servant,' he pleaded.

Balian considered Bernard. 'I seem to remember that I once ordered a whipping for your insolence. I have no need to repeat it now.

'I do, however, have need of you. In your youth you were a good soldier; a sergeant, I recall.'

Bernard nodded.

'I have need of every man who can bear a weapon.' Balian put his hand upon Bernard's shoulder. 'Most of the citizens will be good only to stop a Saracen arrow. It is men like you who must make a fight.'

Bernard swallowed. 'I have a family, my lord. A wife and two children.'

'Then even more reason to fight. If we hold on long enough then succour may come from the west. And if it doesn't arrive, yet we fight bravely, Saladin may agree to honourable terms.'

He gave a shrewd look at the Ferriers. 'Are these family?'

'Friends, my lord.'

'Can you fight, friends of Bernard?'

'Just give me a weapon,' said Simon.

John did not speak. Balian stared into his eyes. 'Will you fight for the City?'

'I am a pilgrim,' answered John. 'I am a wrathful man. My penance for an act of violence was to come to Jerusalem and never harm another.'

Balian turned to his comrade. 'What a delicious irony, Jerome,' he said. 'The peaceable are lining up for weapons and this wrathful, violent man has sworn never to fight again.'

'Perhaps he can be persuaded,' Jerome said.

'I can absolve him of his oath,' said the Archbishop. 'Much good it will do though.'

Balian turned to him sharply. 'What do you mean?'

'These are just common men,' said Eraclius. 'We need knights to win battles.'

Jerome nodded.

'You think this too?' Balian asked.

'Yes, my lord,' Jerome said. 'The people may be brave but they need knights to command them. Only knights will be able to inspire them.'

Balian's shoulders slumped. Jerome's words confirmed the enormity of the task he had taken on.

Then he straightened. His lips closed as tight as a scar.

'You three, on your knees,' he cried.

Terrified, Bernard, John and Simon scrambled to obey.

Balian drew his sword, making them flinch. He touched them on their shoulders. 'Arise, Sir Knights,' he said.

Astonished, the three men climbed to their feet. Simon looked ecstatic, Bernard full of doubt. John looked mortified.

'There,' Balian said. 'Now we have three more knights. That makes seven in the whole city. It's a start.'

He turned to his comrade. 'Jerome, send for my sergeants, I'll knight those first. And then Bernard, go find me such of your fellow citizens as you think will make good leaders.'

'But there are no nobles left,' said Eraclius. 'Only their children. Perhaps twenty of them.'

Balian held Eraclius' gaze, considering.

'Jerome,' he said, 'I want you to knight every son of a noble old enough to bear arms in battle.' He paused.

'And I will knight any commoner that Sir Bernard recommends to me.'

He turned to Bernard. 'As many as possible, but only men who others will follow.'

Eraclius held out his hand to stay Bernard.

'My lord Balian,' he said. 'I do not think this is wise.'

'Why not? You just said we have need of knights. How else will we get them? Can the skeletons of Hattin be made to fight again?'

Eraclius crossed himself at these words.

'No indeed, my lord,' he said. 'But neither can knights be conjured out of rough-hewn men.'

Balian's eyes narrowed and it looked for a moment as if he would strike the archbishop.

Eraclius flinched but maintained his ground. 'What do you think, Jerome?' he asked.

Jerome licked his lips and glanced up at the walls of the city which stood empty and unmanned.

'I have never heard of such a thing,' he said. 'But I have never been in a situation such as this.'

He paused. 'What I do know is that whoever Balian chooses to knight is a knight. That cannot be gainsaid and cannot be undone.'

Eraclius glared at Jerome and shook his head. 'So be it,' he said. 'If Christ could make fishermen disciples then maybe Balian can make peasants knights.'

He raised his hand for a moment as if about to cross himself at the impiety of his own words then he thought better of it and blessed Balian instead.

Jerome hurried off followed by Bernard.

Balian turned to John and Simon. 'From your speech you are English?'

They nodded.

'I can make use of another gift from England,' he said.

He glanced across the square to where one of his sergeants was watching the handing out of weapons. He gestured towards the man and he hurried over.

He was a tall man with a mass of golden hair like the mane of a lion. He would have looked a mighty warrior save for one thing. His right hand had been severed and was now a stump.

Balian drew his sword and touched him on the shoulder.

'You're Sir William Esson now,' he said.

Esson held up his stump. 'Jerome said you were doing this, lord. But how can I be a knight with only one hand?'

'One hand is better than none,' Balian said. 'And you've got a sharp mind and a tongue. A tongue which speaks good Arabic.'

Esson nodded.

'I want you to get the treasure which Henry of England gave to the city as penance for his slaying of Archbishop Becket. If the priests are reluctant to let it go don't hesitate to show them your swords.'

Esson smiled.

'Once night has fallen take the treasure and go to the Saracen lines. Buy as many weapons as you can from them. You'll find plenty willing to sell if the price is right. Don't stint. We need weapons not treasure.'

'Gladly, lord, but I am limited with one hand.'

'Take this man with you, Simon Ferrier. He's English so I'm sure his King would approve of his actions. He'll carry the treasure for you.

'Yes, my lord.'

Balian watched Esson and Simon disappear from the citadel before gesturing John to come closer.

He examined him for a while in silence. 'Tell me your name,' he said at last, 'and of your violent deed.'

'I am called John Ferrier, lord.' He looked at the ground. 'Our priest, Father William, taught me my letters; I was grateful to him. Then I met his sister and started to court her.' He paused, struggling to voice the words which clawed at his throat but would not come out.

Finally he muttered, 'I found out William was sleeping with her. I became mad with fury and attacked him.' He fell silent.

Balian held John's gaze in his. There was no censure in his eyes. 'And what did you do to this priest?' he asked.

'I smashed his face and broke some ribs and his arm.'

Balian whistled. 'That must have been some fury.' He straightened up and spoke sternly. 'Priests should not lay with their sisters. I for one deem your fury to be a rightful one.'

John blinked. Nobody had ever said this.

Balian turned towards Eraclius. 'Be wary of Sir John, my dear Archbishop. He has no love for priests who break their vows and sleep with women.'

CHAPTER 6
THE SIEGE BEGINS
Jerusalem

The following morning the people of Jerusalem were woken by a sound that had not been heard in the city for almost a century. A clear voice floated from beyond the walls, a long and warbling stream of words which simultaneously thrilled and alarmed. Outside the walls Saladin's soldiers heard the call of the muezzin and readied themselves for prayer. The most important battle of the age was about to begin and prayer was an essential element of a victory which all longed for.

Balian and Jerome watched from the battlements as the vast army bowed in worship.

'Do you think the Patriarch would be as effective in leading our defenders to worship?' Balian asked.

Jerome gave a thin smile. 'No, my lord, I do not. And please don't ask me to fetch him to do so.'

Balian chuckled. 'We need more than prayers today, old friend. We need a heavenly host.' His eyes swept over the multitude in front of him. 'Several heavenly hosts.'

Jerome glanced up at him. He was Balian's man, always had been. He had never questioned his judgements or decisions and never would. Now, however, he wanted a reassurance he had never felt the need of before.

'What is your strategy, Balian?' he asked.

Balian glanced around quickly at the men who stood upon the wall. 'Strategy? I have nothing that can be graced with such a title. My only plan is to hold these walls for as long as we have men who can wield weapons.'

Jerome nodded. 'To what end, my lord?'

'To the end.'

Jerome frowned.

'No. Not to the end of every man here. I am not so fool-hardy, nor so profligate of life. I aim to fight such a battle as will daunt the Muslims and impress Saladin. He is a realist and a man of much honour. If we fight a battle of valour and hardship then he may give us terms which will be acceptable.'

'You hope to secure Jerusalem?'

Balian shook his head. 'There is no hope of that. The best we can hope for is to win the freedom of its people and the right of Christians to worship here. The city will fall to Saladin no matter what we do.'

Jerome nodded. 'I think that may be termed a strategy.'

Balian turned to him and his eyes sparkled. 'Thank you. But it's not one that I wish anyone else to hear. Not now, not ever.'

'It will die with me, my lord.'

Balian turned towards him. 'If that is the case I fear you won't have to keep your lips sealed for very long, old friend.'

At that moment, Bernard and John clattered up the staircase towards them.

'We've been all round the city walls, my lord,' Bernard said.

He held his hand against the battlement, gasping for breath enough to continue. 'All the men are ready.'

Balian nodded. 'Thank you, Bernard. Go to your post now. I want you on the wall opposite the Mount of Olives. Take this young man with you. Gather your friends and neighbours close.'

'But that is on the eastern wall and the Saracens are to the west.'

'I know,' said Balian. 'I am manning this side with brave young men. To guard the east wall I want brave men who are clever as well. Unless I place my wisest heads there Saladin may attack to the east without my realising in time.

He watched them thoughtfully as they made their way along the battlements.

'Bernard is a good man,' Jerome said. 'He will fight well.'

'I hope all those I knighted will do likewise,' Balian said. He placed his hands upon the wall and peered out at Saladin's army.

'I think they will,' said Jerome. 'Being chosen as knights has charged them with fervour. The people of the city will follow their own knights better, I think, than they would strangers.'

'I hope you're right, Jerome. For make no mistake I shall be mocked for this deed.'

'You will, my lord. Let's pray that only you will be mocked and not them.'

Balian straightened and pointed to the west. 'I think the time of mockery is past.'

Jerome looked where he was pointing. The Muslim army was on the march, filling the plain below the walls.

In its vanguard rode a solitary horseman upon a beautiful white horse.

Saladin was coming to conquer the Holy City.

CHAPTER 7
THE END OF DAYS
Jerusalem

The western walls of Jerusalem were most open to attack and they were thick beyond compare. The Saracens had found to their cost that they would take any amount of battering.

After a few days Saladin had given up his attempt to smash the western wall and moved his siege engines to the east, close to the Mount of Olives. Few in Jerusalem had expected attack from this difficult terrain. In fact the Saracens had only been able to deploy half of their mangonels. But it stretched the defences more thinly than ever and Balian and Jerome spent all their time hurrying from wall to wall to check on their repair.

Thankfully the walls were proving strong enough. So were the new-made knights. The morale in the city seemed to grow each day rather than diminish.

'Perhaps there will be no cause for mockery after all,' Jerome said.

Balian laughed. 'You are ever the optimist, old friend.'

John rubbed the tiredness from his eyes. He had lost count of how long the siege had gone on. He was so exhausted that he might well have been fighting for ten years without respite.

He sat by the eastern wall counting to himself.

'What are you doing?' Simon asked.

'I'm trying to count how many days we've been fighting.'

'Six,' Simon answered authoritatively. 'Or maybe seven.'

'It's nine days,' Bernard said. 'Or at least that's what Agnes told me this morning.'

John's heart leapt. Agnes' image filled his mind. He saw her smile upon him as she had never done in life.

He blinked his eyes to clear away the image and saw Simon looking at him with a knowing grin upon his face.

'Still dreaming of the lovely Agnes?' he said.

John glanced in the direction of Bernard. He had heard nothing.

'Stop your filthy insinuations,' John said. 'Agnes is a married woman.'

'And you are a man. As am I.'

Simon picked some bread from his teeth. 'She is a rare beauty and I'm not afraid to say that she visits my dreams too.'

John seized him by the arm.

'We are guests in her house. And we are friends of her husband. Now, of all times, you should not be thinking such thoughts.'

Simon shook his head. 'Now of all times I should be thinking them. Any one of us could be dead in a moment. And mark my words, if Bernard gets an arrow in his heart I shall follow you in line to comfort Agnes.'

John lashed out at his cousin, slapping him across the mouth.

Simon wiped his mouth and nodded. 'I see you've got it bad, dear cousin. And am I to play the part of the priest who you savaged for a woman?' He got up and strode away.

John bowed his head in shame. At that moment a Saracen arrow would have been a welcome relief.

Bernard crouched down beside his friend, Oliver the little Frenchman from Provence.

'What was all that about?' Oliver asked.

'What?'

'Your two English friends. The big fair-haired one has just slapped the dark one.'

Bernard turned and looked over to where the cousins had been sitting.

John was alone; there was no sign of Simon.

'John has a temper,' Bernard said with a shrug. 'I have seen it myself. I wish he would learn to master it.'

'I don't think he will,' said a figure lying on the other side of Oliver. 'I have seen such men. They can never tame the beast within.'

'You should know, Jurgen,' Oliver said. 'You can be a beast as well.'

'Only when I'm drunk.'

Oliver smiled. 'Then that is all the time.' He turned to Bernard. 'Jurgen's from Saxony. Everyone is drunk there; all of the time. The weather is so bitter they have to drink to fortify themselves.'

'Here they come again,' John called running in a crouch towards them.

The four men listened as the air hummed with the sound of the mangonels being released.

After three days of bombardment they had finally got accustomed to the noise. They were little concerned by the heavy thuds as the rocks crashed upon the walls.

'I think these walls must be just as strong as the western ones,' Jurgen said, reaching for a flask of ale.

The others nodded in agreement. Bernard opened a packet of food which Agnes had prepared for him earlier. He was famished and rubbed his hands together in anticipation.

A loud deep rumble sounded below their feet. The four men

looked at each other.

This last sound was very different; not a heavy thud but a sharp crack. They threw themselves to the ground.

They were only just in time. The sound was the noise of the final piece of foundation being mined from deep below.

With the roar of a summer tempest the wall above the blast shuddered and slid into the space that opened up beneath. Slabs of masonry fell back to earth followed by dust as dense as a desert sand storm.

John threw himself to one side just in time. A jagged piece of stonework smashed into the ground beside him. It would have sliced his head from his neck.

In front of them a huge cloud of dust momentarily concealed the horrifying sight from their eyes. It cleared and they saw the huge breach in the wall. They saw rank upon rank of Saracen warriors. A horn sounded and they poured into the city.

Within the hour Balian rode out of Jerusalem to negotiate surrender.

CHAPTER 8
BLOOD MONEY
Jerusalem

A gnes remained in her chair when Bernard returned.

'Saladin has sent his terms,' he said.

He hurried over to her and took her hand.

'He demands ten dinars for each man, five for each woman and one for each child.'

She did not answer for a moment, her throat was tight.

'How much do we have?'

'A little over one dinar in the safe-box.'

Tears sprang into her eyes. So little; not even enough for both of their children. Her mind whirled, a chaos of thoughts and terrors.

'I've got creditors though,' Bernard said, attempting a smile. 'And we can sell the inn.'

She forced a smile upon her lips. Both of them knew that the inn would be virtually worthless now.

'Saladin has given us time to raise the money,' Bernard said.

He hurried across to the ledger which was kept at the entrance to the kitchen.

'I'll start calling in our debts at once.'

Bernard trekked from house to house, from shop to shop and church to church. Some who owed him money were willing to pay and did so with good grace. As the pennies and solidi were pushed into his hands he allowed his hopes to rise.

But many, those who owed him the greatest debt, pretended they were not at home or refused him to his face.

'I've got to look after my own family now,' said one of his oldest customers, a man who he had always extended credit to gladly.

'But that's my money,' Bernard answered. 'You're buying your freedom with my money.'

'Go to hell.'

Bernard leant against the wall. 'Hell,' he murmured, 'I'm there already.'

At the end of the day he returned home, his heart heavy and black.

'How much?' Agnes asked.

Bernard slid the money onto the table.

'Almost a dinar,' she said, forcing a smile to her face. 'You've done well.'

Bernard shook his head.

'Not well enough. And I fear that I will do less well tomorrow.'

Neither said what they were thinking. That here was enough to buy the freedom of two children but no more.

'Did you have any luck in selling the inn?' Agnes asked.

'One Jew was interested and would have offered three dinars.'

'Three dinars? It's worth much more.'

He nodded. 'It was last month. But not now.'

Agnes took his hands in hers. 'Then take the money, however little. Go to the Jew now and take the money.'

'I can't. He suddenly took fright. He feared that the Saracens would persecute him if he was seen to own a place that once sold wine.'

Agnes put her hand to her mouth.

They remained in silence for long minutes, staring into a pit that neither could ever have foreseen.

Finally, Agnes rose and went to the kitchen. 'There's some supper here, my darling. You must be famished.'

Bernard nodded. 'Tomorrow. I'll go out again tomorrow.'

He had reconciled himself to the fact that he would not be able to buy his own freedom. He would not give up on buying that of Agnes.

The next day was even worse than the first. The first day he had been met by cooperation or, at worst, by indifference. This day he was met by curses and looks of contempt. One man, a customer who owed him a great deal of money, punched him in the face before slamming the door on him.

When he returned at night he had half a dinar only.

They sat and counted up the money time and time and time again. No matter how many times they counted it, the amount remained the same.

Finally, Bernard said the words neither had wanted to say. 'Still only enough to buy the freedom of two of the children.'

Agnes squeezed his hand.

Bernard wept.

It was the last day left for the Christians to find their ransom. It broke with a bright sun which normally would have pierced the gloom in anyone's heart. This day some, those who had managed to find the money to buy their freedom, were jubilant and exhausted.

Others, like Bernard, were filled with a bleak desperation which weighed down their hearts and minds.

If only Alexius had not left the city, he repeated to himself over and over again. If only he had taken the loan which the old Greek had tried so inexplicably to press upon him before he left.

Ten dinars he had offered, with no charge and no interest.

Bernard had been astonished by the offer and refused it straight away. Alexius had insisted time and again, had even tried to give it as a gift for the children. Time and again Bernard had refused.

The following day Alexius had left Jerusalem for Constantinople.

Two days later had come word of the disaster at Hattin.

Bernard drew a deep breath. There were still creditors he could approach again, still people who might agree to buy the inn for a fraction of its worth.

'I don't think you'll be able to raise the money,' Agnes said, stroking his face.

'I know. But I must attempt it.'

He began once again his hopeless circuit through the city streets.

Agnes sat alone in the courtyard. Her mind was a whirl of dread imaginings. Earlier she had been in such a despairing mood she feared it would scare the children and had asked the boys to take Eleanor to the market.

Now they had gone she regretted it bitterly. Every moment without them seemed to be an irreparable loss.

A familiar figure stepped into the courtyard.

'You look as though your heart will break,' he said.

She nodded, not able even to make a show of contradicting him.

'You are frightened for your family?'

'I'm terrified,' she said. 'We've been able to raise enough money to buy freedom for only two of the children.'

'Who will that be?'

She waved her hand at him, not even wanting to contemplate

the decision which they knew they must face this evening.

He stepped closer and touched her on the shoulder. She felt his fingers tremble as he did it.

'It doesn't have to be that way,' he said.

'What do you mean?' she glanced up and looked into his eyes.

He pulled a purse from his belt and upended its contents upon the table.

Her quick eyes counted the money.

'Eight dinars,' she said.

'Enough to buy your freedom and that of the children. Including Claude-Yusuf.'

'We have two dinars already.'

'You will need that when you start your new life. Take all I offer.'

Her hand reached out for the money and then she paused.

'Are you certain about this?' she asked.

He smiled like a cat who had trapped a bird.

'It is not a gift, Agnes.'

'A loan, of course. I will pay you back as soon as I can.'

'It is not a loan, either. It is for a purchase.'

Agnes blinked. 'For the inn?'

He laughed and ran his fingers through her hair.

'No, Agnes, it is to purchase you.'

She sat upon the bed and stared blankly at the wall. She pulled the sheet over her knees. She felt dirty. Dirty and disgusting.

As he left he had thrown the eight dinars upon the bed and she had startled herself by scrabbling for them and clutching them close to her breast.

'These are desperate times, Agnes,' he said. 'Be sure to put it inside your safe-box.'

She nodded bleakly at him as if he were her husband who could instruct her to do something.

'I thought our coupling would be good,' he said. 'But it far exceeded my expectations. So full of passion, so full of lust.'

He laughed as he walked down the stairs.

She sat there for an hour, his final words beating time after time upon her heart.

No, she kept thinking, it couldn't have been, it mustn't have been.

She knew the act had not been like that. It had been a feat of desperation, a trading of her body for the lives of the children. There had been no passion, no lust on her part. But his very words began to poison her soul.

Bernard came home later that evening and she held out the coins for him.

He shook his head in disbelief.

'How did you get it?' he asked.

She shook her head and placed her fingers on his lips.

A thought slithered into his mind but he thrust it away.

'It's enough to buy freedom for the children and for me,' she said. 'But not for you.'

He stared at her and thought his heart would split. Tears filled his eyes and she kissed them away.

She put the coins in the safe-box and held out her hand for him.

They climbed to their bedroom. They made love, tenderly, in an agony of fear and desire.

They sat awake all that night, talking and talking.

The next morning they went to get the strong-box. It was gone.

CHAPTER 9
MOST DANGEROUS MEN
Jerusalem

Days later Saladin watched as Jerusalem emptied of its people. They walked past his tent in two columns. Those who were rich enough to raise the money to buy their lives hurried past, sliding their eyes towards the Muslims, fearing treachery and death.

The second column, that of the poor, walked with heads bowed, contemplating the long days of slavery, knowing their lives had been stolen.

Amongst them were Agnes and the children.

At the rear of the column walked the thirty commoners who Balian had made knights. Their heads were not bowed. The spirit Balian had poured into them still survived, despite the surrender.

A man standing slightly to the rear of Saladin stepped forward at the sight of these men.

'Brother,' he asked Saladin, 'who are these who bear themselves with such courage?'

Saladin shook his head. 'I do not know.' He gestured for Balian to join them.

'My brother al-Adil and I are curious about the men at the rear,' he said. 'Those who, alone of all my captives, do not seem to feel themselves defeated. Who are they?'

'They are my men,' Balian answered. 'The commoners who I

knighted in order to resist you. The ones I told you of earlier.'

Saladin nodded. He remained silent and his face grew thoughtful.

Balian watched Saladin for a while, hoping for some sign. But there was none.

Balian bowed towards Saladin who now smiled and clasped him by the arm.

'Go in peace, Balian of Ibelin,' he said. 'You were the most worthy of adversaries.'

Balian mounted the horse Jerome held for him and the two trotted off towards the rear of the column.

Al-Adil stared at the thirty knights. He tapped his forefinger upon his lip thoughtfully for a while and then turned to Saladin.

'I have served you well in these wars, my brother,' he said, 'and never asked favour or gift. I ask one of you now.'

'Speak.'

'I would have these men to be my possessions.'

Saladin's eyes turned towards the thirty commoner knights.

'They are men of new-found valour, brother,' he said. 'As such they are most dangerous.'

'I understand. I would still have them.'

'As you wish. Is that sufficient?'

Al-Adil gazed upon the line of captives.

'Perhaps a thousand more captives, as slaves.'

Saladin commanded that the knights and a thousand of the people be given at once to al-Adil.

By the time they had been gathered together the departed columns were far distant, Agnes and the children at the rear of the line.

CHAPTER 10
BOUGHT AND SOLD
North of Amman

Agnes stumbled as she walked. Eleanor was heavy in her arms. The little girl had walked hand in hand with her mother for miles but in the end fell to the ground, exhausted.

Agnes gazed down at her as she slept. This should not be happening, she thought as she wearily gathered the child in her arms.

A few steps ahead trudged Gerard and Claude-Yusuf. Both were kept going only by their pride and by the desire not to be beaten by the other. They were strong lads but for how much longer would they be able to keep up this relentless pace? She did not have the strength to carry them.

She glanced up at the sun. Here on the plains it burnt hot and she pulled a cloth over Eleanor's face.

Her heart was bitter and hard. She had failed to protect them. All her hopes, all her soft thoughts had come down to this. All her deeds. The only thing she could do now was to keep on walking.

Thoughts of Bernard haunted her mind. Where was he now? He might be dead or undergoing some dreadful torture. She did not know which was worse. She could not stop herself contemplating both.

Her thoughts floated back to those last, lost days.

Agnes reddened as she recalled the final day of freedom

allowed to the citizens by the Saracens.

Bernard had raced from the inn the moment they discovered that the strong-box and all the money had been stolen.

She had slumped down on the table and stared at the wall. Everything had been for nothing then. Her sacrifice, her degradation, her act of betrayal.

A foot-step sounded beside her and she whimpered in fear.

'What's happened?' he had asked.

Her face burned in shame as she recalled what she did next.

She told John everything, all the things she could not have possibly said to her husband.

He had listened in astonishment, his face growing ever more stern, ever more disgusted.

She saw this but she could not stop herself. She told all in a torrent of shame and fury and ended with the fact that the ransom she had bought so dearly had been stolen from them.

He turned his face away from her and she felt even more degraded.

Then he turned back, his face steaming with tears.

He had been unable to speak but he touched her on the neck, plucked up his sword and rushed out of the inn.

She sighed heavily as she thought back to that moment and her eyes filled with tears.

'Are you all right, Mama?' Gerard asked anxiously.

She brushed his wayward hair.

'Of course, I am,' she said. 'It's just some desert sand in my eyes.'

CHAPTER 11
CAPTURED BY THE TEMPLARS
Ascalon and Beit Lahia

As night fell the thousand people who had been bought by al-Adil fell still and silent, terrified to think what special fate had been reserved for them.

The courage of the thirty poor knights, hitherto so strong, now began to wane.

'What do you think will happen to us?' John asked Bernard.

Bernard turned to him. His eyes were full of tears. 'Al-Adil is notorious,' he answered. 'Ten years ago he put down a revolt in Egypt and hanged three thousand of the rebels.'

The man next to him nodded. 'I've heard we are to be crucified.'

The prisoners nearby clamoured in terror at his words.

'Someone said they heard Saracens sawing wood for the crosses.'

The clamour ceased abruptly. Each man looked at the tent of al-Adil in silence, all hope squeezed from out of them. Then low noise began to reverberate from their throats. The noise of prayers or of curses.

A little while later Saladin and his brother walked slowly towards the crowd. Al-Adil climbed onto a dais. He gazed at the people who were now his possessions. A terrified silence descended upon the plain.

A dozen guards headed into the crowd to where the thirty

commoner knights were standing. They separated them from the others and pushed them towards the dais.

Al-Adil looked at them closely. 'In reward for my services,' he said, 'my brother, Sultan Saladin has acceded to my request that you be given to me.'

'What for, you fiend?' cried one of the men. 'So you can gloat as you crucify us?'

Al-Adil looked horrified at his words and shook his head.

'You have fought hard and valiantly,' he said. 'I honour you who led the defence of your city.'

The men looked at one another, doubt filling their hearts.

Al-Adil raised his voice and addressed the whole one thousand captives.

'Indeed, all of you fought to defend your home, a cause of high honour. Because of your courage, I release you from your captivity. All of you are free.'

The captives did not move, doubting his words, fearing some treachery. Saracen soldiers moved among them, cutting their bonds and giving them drink. Only gradually did the truth begin to grip them.

Al-Adil climbed down from the dais and, together with his brother, joined the commoner knights.

'Today, because I honour you,' al-Adil said, 'I give you your freedom. Some of my friends think me mad believing you to be filled with the lust of battle and maybe with the poison of revenge.'

He held his arms wide. 'That I cannot say. But I can say that you are brave and honourable men. I trust you to remember this in all your dealings, whether with Christians, Muslims or Jews.' He touched his hands to his brow, bowed and departed.

Grooms approached and gave fresh clothing, weapons and

horses to the knights.

'What shall we do,' one of the men asked.

'I know what I shall do,' said Bernard. 'I'm going after my wife and family.'

'And I'll come with you,' said John.

And once we've found them, he vowed to himself, I will go on my own journey. No matter where he may hide, I shall hunt down Simon.

They hurried through the camp, grabbing hold of anyone who had any idea of where the captives were going. There was rumour and counter-rumour but no one knew anything for certain.

At last they met an old man who claimed he had news.

'The captives have been taken to Cairo,' he said. 'They will be sold in the slave-market there.'

'How do you know?' Bernard asked, seizing him by the arm.

'I can see with my own eyes, can't I?' the old man answered. 'Besides, I can understand some Saracen and I heard one of the guards saying they were going to Egypt.'

Bernard stared into the old man's face. 'You are certain about this?' he said.

'As certain as I am of my own name.'

Bernard nodded at this and strode off.

John gave one last look at the old man and thought that he caught a fleeting look of uncertainty upon his face.

But then the old man nodded once again. 'I heard them say Cairo,' he repeated. 'The slave market in Cairo.'

John turned and hurried after his friend.

They plucked up some torches, chose two of the swiftest looking horses and trotted down the road that led west from Jerusalem.

'Where are we going?' John called.

'To Ascalon,' Bernard answered. 'It's on the road to Cairo. I have relatives there and they may have heard news of Agnes and the boys.'

They followed the captives' path until they reached a small pool. On the far side the single trail cascaded into a dozen more, east, west, south and north. The Saracens had taken their captives to the four corners of the earth.

Desperate, they searched for any sign of Agnes and the children, a personal belonging, a scrap of her clothing, anything. It was hopeless.

They rode until the torches were guttering and their horses tiring. Begrudging the delay they flung themselves to the ground and slept fitfully, desperate for the dawn.

The next morning they rose with the sun and headed towards the city of Ascalon, reaching it just after noon.

Bernard rode swiftly through the streets and came at last to a large house overlooking the port. They tied the horses to a large ring set into the wall and hammered on the door. It opened a crack and an eye peered out at them.

'It's me, Yacob,' Bernard said. 'Let me in.'

The door opened wider to reveal the face of an old Muslim man. He looked at them suspiciously for a moment, his eyes uncertain in the bright sunlight. Then he smiled and flung the door open.

'Bernard,' he cried, embracing him enthusiastically. He pulled back and glanced at John for a moment before staring once more at Bernard.

'You have heard then?' he said.

'Heard what?'

'That Farah has died.'

Bernard gasped. 'Dead? How?'

The old man shrugged. 'She fell ill with a fever and never recovered.'

Bernard shook his head and rested his hand upon the old man's shoulder. 'I am sorry, Yacob.'

Tears came into the old man's eyes and he shrugged once more but did not answer.

'How is Robert? And the boy? Has he heard news of the death of his mother?'

Bernard turned towards John, his face strained. 'Let us talk inside,' he said to the old man.

'Of course,' he answered. 'Where are my manners?'

He led them into the house which was cool and dark. He went into a little courtyard garden and gestured to them to take a seat. A servant came at his call and hurried back with cool drinks and a platter of dates.

The old man gazed at Bernard. His eyes became shrouded as if with a dark cloud.

'Tell me,' he said.

'I have heard no firm news about Robert,' Bernard answered. 'But he marched with the Christian army to Hattin.'

'Then he is dead,' said the old man. 'At least if the rumours I hear are true.'

Bernard did not answer. He did not need to.

'And my grandson, Claude-Yusuf?' the old man asked.

Bernard held his hand over his mouth. 'Taken as a slave. And my children and Agnes with him.'

He bent his head and wept.

The old man knelt at his feet and embraced him, weeping as well.

An hour later the three men sat at a table in a small but airy room. Yacob broke bread for them and they bent to a meal of fish and beans. Despite their hunger none of them found it easy to eat.

The old man shook his head sadly.

'If the captives had passed Ascalon I would have heard rumour of it,' he said.

'But we can't have passed them in the night,' Bernard said. 'If they are going to Cairo then they would have passed through here.'

The old man nodded and placed his untouched bread upon his plate.

'That is true. The desert roads to the east have no paths and no water to sustain such a multitude. If they were going to Cairo they would have come through Ascalon. So that can only mean one thing.'

Bernard gazed at the old man who shook his head once again.

'It means they are not on the road to Cairo.'

'But somebody told us that was where they'd been taken,' Bernard cried. He turned to John for confirmation of the fact.

John hesitated. The memory of the man's look of doubt came to his mind. He wondered whether to say anything but Bernard was already speaking.

'It's the only clue we have, Yacob,' he was saying. 'It's the only clue we have.'

'It's a long way to Cairo,' Yacob said. 'What if you're wrong? What if they haven't been taken there? What if they have been taken north to Damascus?'

'Then we'll go there,' Bernard said. 'But we're part way to Cairo now. Surely it would be best to pursue them now we're part way.' He was beginning to sound less certain.

'Perhaps you're right,' Yacob said. 'But it is a perilous road to

Cairo and a long one.'

'Then the sooner we leave the better.'

The old man nodded. 'Eat your meal and I will get my servants to pack up plenty of food and water. You will need both on your journey.'

A little later Yacob led them back onto the street.

His face was streaming with tears. 'I have lost my daughter and her husband, Bernard,' he said. 'Please bring Claude-Yusuf back to me.'

Bernard could not answer but nodded and embraced the old man.

They climbed on their horses and cantered through the streets. John glanced over his shoulder and saw the old man standing by his door, wringing his hands in despair.

They rode for the rest of the day, taking a road which followed the coast south, meandering here and there to take advantage of the contours of the land. It proved slow going. They searched the ground which was covered in sand. Both saw that there was no sign of anybody passing this way but both kept silent about it.

'Tell me about the old man,' John said to Bernard.

'He is a wealthy merchant,' Bernard answered. 'Agnes' brother did some business with him and fell in love with his daughter Farah. They wanted to marry but the priests would not allow it unless she converted to Christianity. She was reluctant but she agreed. Claude-Yusuf is their child.'

John frowned.

'I had not realised there was so much mingling of people in Jerusalem, of Christians and Infidels. They trade together, they work together and now you tell me they even marry and live together.'

Bernard turned to him. 'And what of it?'

'It is wrong. Wrong in the eyes of the Lord God.'

Bernard shrugged. 'Who is to say so, for certain?'

'Don't you believe it to be so? Or are you in favour of this mingling with the infidel?'

Bernard stopped his horse and turned towards John.

'Yes I am in favour of it,' he said. He held up his hand to stop John from interrupting.

'My family have lived in Jerusalem for almost ninety years,' he said. 'We took the land from the Muslims and we knew it. But over the years the hate and fervour dwindled and, for the most part, each people learned to live in accord with the other. I have no other country now, John, not like you. I am as much a part of the Holy Land as old Yacob and I am happy to call him my kin.'

John frowned, unable to fully comprehend this notion.

Bernard grabbed his arm and fixed him with an angry and intent stare.

'John, it is the newcomers from Europe, the likes of Guy of Lusignan and Reynald of Châtillon, who have upset this precarious balance. They and the Sultan Saladin have brought hatred and fury back to this land. And look where it has got us. Look what has happened to my family.'

He shook his head sadly and started forward once more upon his quest.

They were riding through parched desert now with huge sand dunes towering above their heads. The sun was hot and they had soon drunk more than half of their water.

'We should take the path inland a little,' said Bernard. 'We will come upon a village called Beit Lahia where the water is said to be sweet and good.

'How long will it take?' John asked. 'It's almost nightfall and we have no torches.'

'We won't get to the village in the daylight,' he answered. 'But there are some pools to the north of the village and we should rest there.'

The night came swiftly and they could barely see their way in the gloom. At last they came upon a small pool with clean and fresh water and slumped beside it.

They drank their fill and ate some of the food which Yusuf had given to them.

As John fell asleep the image of Agnes came to his mind. He doubted he would ever see her again.

The morning came at last and they ate some of the food given to them by Yacob, their eyes scanning their surroundings as they did so.

John blinked. Something had caught his attention and he grabbed Bernard's arm. A small party of horsemen had spied them from the top of a hill and now turned and cantered towards them. John loosened his sword, assuming them to be Saracens. In minutes the horsemen had reached them.

To their relief they were Templars, presumably from one of the castles to the south of Jerusalem.

'Who are you?' their leader asked.

'We have come from Jerusalem,' John answered, rising to his feet. 'We have been in the siege.'

'Rumour has it that the city has fallen,' said another of the Templars.

'The rumour is true.'

The leader looked at them suspiciously. 'I asked you who you are,' he said. 'Yet you did not answer.'

'We are knights of Jerusalem,' said Bernard, rising to his feet.

The Templar looked at him with contempt and then slapped him upon the face.

'We are knights, truly' said John, stepping forward. 'We were knighted by Balian of Ibelin to lead the defence of the city.'

'It takes more than the tap of a sword to make a knight,' said the leader. 'You are peasants, peasants with an exalted idea of your place, but still peasants.'

John drew his sword. 'We are knights and if you cannot give us your courtesy then we will give you our blades.'

The Templar laughed. 'There are five of us and only two of you. And we know how to fight.'

'So do we,' said John.

The Templar laughed once again and turned his back. John, surprised by this, lowered his sword. The Templar turned immediately and smashed him across his face, sending him reeling. The Templar leapt after him, two of his comrades by his side.

John just managed to keep his footing and frantically parried their sword strokes. But he was outnumbered and outclassed and in a moment his sword was knocked from his grasp and three sword points pressed against his throat. Out of the corner of his eye he saw Bernard slice open one of his attacker's hands before he too was overcome.

They were dragged together and thrown to the ground while the Templars stood with swords drawn, deciding upon their fate.

'Shall we kill them?' one of the Templars asked.

Their leader shook his head. 'We cannot slay our fellow Christians without good reason, no matter what scum,' he said. 'Tie them up and leave them.'

One of the knights pored over their gear and brought some of it to the leader.

'Saracen knives and Saracen mail,' he said. 'They are in the pay of the enemy.'

'We're not,' said John. 'We are Balian's men and were given these things by al-Adil, the brother of Saladin.'

The Templar leader frowned. 'Why would he give you such things?'

'As a sign of respect and honour.'

The Templars laughed.

'Well that is the only honour you will receive, Sir Peasant,' said the leader. 'You will get none from Christians.'

'Balian will prove our words to be true,' said Bernard.

'That you were knighted by him?' He spat.

'Even if that were true, which I doubt, it does not make you a real knight. You will learn to curse Balian, my friend, for he has given you ideas above your station. From henceforward you will be distrusted by your own people and despised by your betters.'

The Templars bound John and Bernard with tight cords, pulling their arms back behind their backs and tying them to ropes about their feet. They dragged them a hundred yards from the pool and the shelter of trees. They were in agony, could not reach their bonds and could not move at all.

The Templars took everything they had been given by the Muslims and departed.

The sun began to climb ever higher in a sky empty of clouds.

CHAPTER 12
A PARTICULAR DEVIL
Jaffa

A thousand eyes were looking at him. Most were furtive, some were bold, a few were brazen. They all suspected.

Simon Ferrier bent his head, as if to protect his face from the sun and dust, in reality to shield himself from the eyes.

Fifteen thousand people trudged along in a long, dispirited column, all those with enough money to buy their freedom from the Saracens. Many of the women and children had said goodbye to a husband or father who had been able to raise enough for his family's ransom but not his own. These men were now captive, commodities to be sold in the slave markets. The women's lips moved pitifully, praying they would one day be re-united. They knew, however, that only prayers from wealthy lips were ever answered.

Some men had been able to buy their freedom. But the cost had been higher than mere treasure; they walked with heads bowed, burdened by guilt. They had left behind friends and family, comrades they assumed would be lost for ever.

Simon banished such thoughts from his mind.

The tramping feet threw dust high into the sky. Those priests educated enough to have read their Bible thought bitterly of an earlier exodus, when God had led the Hebrews to the Promised Land. Today, their promised land had been snatched from them, their former lives annihilated. They were on a march to nowhere, at best to exile.

Simon listened to the murmur of lamentation around him. Children howled, women sobbed, old men walked in stoic silence save for an occasional cry from bitter chests. Yet, weaving in and out of the moans he heard a never-ending undercurrent of whispers.

There were three groups who did not appear to share the common despair. Two were made up of the handful of soldiers who had been left in the city when the army of Jerusalem marched to its destruction. Most were elderly servants and foot soldiers of the Hospitaller and Templar Orders, too old, sick or incompetent to be a threat to the Muslims. By the agreement of Saladin they marched with their weapons and standards.

Each man led a pair of donkeys bearing saddle-bags crammed with the wealth of the Military Orders. At the head of one convoy rode Terricus, Grand Preceptor of Jerusalem and Acting Grand Master of the Knights of the Temple. There were few left to bear him allegiance, the single old knight who had remained with him in Jerusalem and a score more holed up in castles dotted across the kingdom.

The second group consisted of the Hospitallers. There were only two sergeants left and the acting head of the order, William Borrel. He was a man who was friendly and kind to everyone, except for the Templars. Most of the people in this group were the monks and servants of the hospital.

The third group was made up of churchmen. All the lesser clergy led donkeys laden with treasures: coins, jewels, relics, books and the silver tiles from the roof of the Holy Sepulchre. There were two hundred thousand dinars worth of treasure all told;

more than twice the amount Saladin had demanded to free the whole population of the city.

At the head of the Churchmen rode Patriarch Eraclius. He carefully cradled a phial bearing the tears of the Virgin Mary. Beside him on a white palfrey was his companion, the widow Pasque de Riveri. For once she had to abide no grins and whistles, no urchins crying out 'Here comes Madame la Patriarchesse', no contemptuous shaking of heads. Beside her, on a pony, was Constance, their child.

Next to the columns of refugees trotted Saracen officers, their guards for the long trek to the coast.

As the hours wore on Eraclius and his followers pushed through the throng of common people who were weaker, more dejected and moved at a slower-pace. As he rode Eraclius happened to notice Simon on the edge of the crowd, head low but moving forward with determination like a man wading against a tide. A memory fidgeted his mind. Of course, he thought suddenly. He's one of Balian's creatures, one of the commoners he knighted at the start of the siege.

Eraclius studied Simon more closely. Yes, he recalled now what he had heard of the man.

It was said he had fought like a fury in the battles, always in the thick of things. He had shown a love for danger, a lust to be at the centre of events. It was almost as if he wanted to shine in the eyes of his superiors.

But now he was on the margin, totally alone.

Perhaps he has left a loved one behind.

What would the future hold for him?

Eraclius smiled grimly. The young man's path seemed clearly laid out. He could never be accepted as a real knight. He would seek for honour and companionship and find only contempt and dismissal. He was as much in purgatory as a soul departed without grace.

Balian had corrupted the man's heart without even realising it.

Eraclius leaned down towards his Deacon. 'Walter, were any of the men knighted by Balian able to buy their freedom?'

'The sons of the nobles, my lord. They ride in the first column, stripped of arms of course.'

'What about the commoners?'

'Two or three of the richer merchants tried but without luck. The rest were too poor to even make the attempt. Balian tried to buy them from Saladin but he refused.'

'Why?'

'He told Balian that he considered them too dangerous.'

'Too dangerous?'

'He said that men who have nothing to lose become like devils.'

Eraclius licked his lips.

Yet there's one of them here, he thought.

So how did this particular devil make his escape?

CHAPTER 13
THE MULE
Beit Lahia

The sun was close to noon. John squirmed, his fair complexion beginning to burn. It was hours since his last drink and his mouth felt like sand. He glanced up at the sun, praying that a cloud would come and shield him from it. There were no clouds.

He groaned and licked his dry lips with a tongue which felt like linen. His only hope was that night would come soon.

Bernard sat in silence, ignoring the heat. He could not keep the image of Agnes and the children from his mind. Every hour that passed increased the distance they would have travelled from him. He wriggled his hands once again to see if he could free them. It was futile; they were tied too tight. He cursed the Templar knights and vowed revenge upon them.

'Is there any hope?' John said.

'For us or for my family?'

'For both.'

Bernard shook his head. 'There is little hope of anything unless we can get free.'

'I might die before that. This heat is too much for me.'

'It is hot but it will not kill you. At least not today. When night falls you will be more comfortable.'

'And tomorrow?'

'Then it might kill you.'

Despite the agony caused by their bonds the afternoon sun made them drowsy and they began to doze. When the temperature was at its height they both fell into a deep swoon.

They woke at the same moment.

John held his breath and glanced over at Bernard. Yes, he too felt something. They were being watched.

John inched his head around until he could see the pool. He groaned.

Bernard turned to look. 'Christ no,' he whispered.

Squatting by the pool was a lone figure dressed in filthy garments. Even from this distance they could see that he was tall and well-built.

The man noticed they were awake and turned his head away. For a few moments he seemed to hesitate as if he were pondering some course of action.

He reached inside his robe and pulled out a water-bottle, plunging it into the pool. He watched it for a while and then raised the bottle and drank deeply from it.

He glanced over at them and filled the bottle once again.

The man's garments were grey with dust and dirt. But it was clear that they had once been white. Despite the intense heat his face was covered by a deep hood.

He held the water bottle in one hand, a long staff in the other. On the sand beside him was a bell.

The man climbed to his feet and walked towards them, the water-bottle held outstretched in his hand.

'Get away,' John cried.

The man stopped. His head turned to one side although his face could not be seen beneath the hood.

'Don't you want water?' he asked, softly.

'Not from you,' John said.

'As you wish.'

He turned towards Bernard. 'What about you?'

'I want water.' Bernard paused, unable to complete his words. But he shook his head violently.

The man laughed but the laugh was dry and had no sound of humour.

'But like your friend you do not want water from a leper?'

Bernard did not answer.

'It is a fine riddle,' the leper continued. 'If you do not drink you will die. The only person who can give you water is a leper. So what do you choose? Certain death? Or the possibility of death?'

Bernard did not answer for a while. Then he said, 'Can you cut our bonds?'

The leper produced a knife. 'I can indeed. But do you trust me not to touch you as I cut? You must realise that I have two weapons, my knife and my flesh. You seem happier to risk the blade than my fingers.'

'For Christ sake, cut my bonds,' cried Bernard.

The leper approached swiftly, giving no chance for Bernard to change his mind. As the leper sawed at the bonds, Bernard turned his face away, dreading to catch sight of the man's fingers close to his wrist. He found that he was holding his breath, his senses focusing on the possibility of a touch, however slight.

Finally, he felt the bonds loosen. The leper stood up and watched as Bernard shook free the last of the cord.

'Thank you, friend,' he said.

The leper bowed then turned towards John. 'And you?'

John's mind raced. He wanted to say no, to let Bernard cut them. But he knew that the Templars had taken Bernard's knife and that he could only cut John's bonds by using the leper's knife. That would almost certainly condemn him to the disease.

Could he do that? His heart hammered as he considered. No. His pride would not let him stoop so low. Nor would his friendship for Bernard.

He lay on his side, holding his hands out towards the leper. 'Be careful,' he said. 'Please.'

John had never put his trust in another as much as he did at that moment. This man was a stranger but he truly held John's life in his hands. As John felt the slow sawing of the blade he saw in his mind's eye its every slice, felt its very cutting of the fibres. It was as if his own life was being unpicked by the leper. He was being laid bare, all links with people and with the past being slowly but surely removed. He felt utterly alone. Yet at the same time he felt utterly connected. To a leper.

The bonds were cut.

John shook his wrists free and then rubbed them to restore the circulation. He got to his feet and turned to the leper. He took a step forward. And embraced him.

The leper recoiled, tightened into himself. Then, as John continued to hold him, he began to relax. 'Thank you,' he whispered.

John released his hold and turned to see Bernard, immobile with astonishment.

'I had to,' John said simply.

Bernard shook his head.

'You need not drink from my bottle,' said the leper.

Bernard and John staggered off towards the pool. They fell by the side of it, buried their heads in its waters and gulped deeply until they could not manage another drop.

Sated, they sat up and looked around. The leper was sitting a few yards away watching them. He sipped at his own water bottle and chewed on a hunk of bread.

'I would offer you food,' he said, 'but I have touched it.'

John and Bernard shook their heads.

'I understand,' said the leper.

Night began to fall. The leper rose and filled his bottle from the pool then returned to where he had sat before.

'Why were you bound?' he asked.

'Templars did it,' Bernard answered.

The leper gave a bitter laugh. 'That may well be explanation enough. Or is there more?'

'They took a rather strong dislike to us,' John said with a shake of his head.

'For what reason?'

'We were made knights by Balian of Ibelin,' Bernard said. 'We are commoners yet he knighted us to help defend Jerusalem.'

'And the Templars despised us for it,' said John. 'They attacked us, bound us and stole everything we have.'

The leper shook his head. 'So, you are outcasts. Like me.'

John stared at him, shocked by his words.

'Isn't everyone an outcast in Jerusalem?' Bernard said. 'Now at least. And perhaps always.'

The leper pondered this and nodded.

The leper turned towards John. 'Tell me friend, why did you embrace me?'

John shook his head. 'I don't know. I didn't mean to. I just did it. And a moment before I had loathed the thought of your slightest touch.'

The three men fell silent.

A little later the leper glanced up at the sky. Stars began to kindle in the sky, icy cold and beautiful. The leper removed his hood. He sighed with pleasure.

John and Bernard peered at him but his features were indistinguishable in the dark.

'I am called Matthew,' he said.

Bernard bent his head towards the leper. 'My name is Bernard. And this is my friend John.'

'You are a stranger, John, by the sound of your speech.'

'Yes. I am a pilgrim. From England.'

'You have travelled far, then.'

'Very far. And you? Are you from Jerusalem?'

'From Hebron. I was a soldier in King Baldwin's army. I am also called Mule.'

Bernard gasped. 'Mule?'

The leper nodded.

There was a long silence. Finally Bernard spoke once more.

'Yours is a sad story, Matthew,' he said.

John turned towards Bernard, his brows furrowed in question.

'It is better if Matthew tells you,' he said.

Matthew sighed and made himself more comfortable.

'It is a simple story,' he said. 'And can be told in moments or in a lifetime.'

'We have all night,' John said.

'Then let me tell you about King Baldwin. He was a young man, a man of great wisdom and promise. When he was still heir to the throne it was discovered that he was a leper. Yet this did not daunt him. He insisted on ruling the kingdom and the nobles. There came a time when he could no longer ride a horse. This was not a problem for he could always be carried in a litter.

'But one day, distrustful of his brother-in-law, Guy of Lusignan,

Baldwin decided that he would have to lead the army into battle. The ground was too rough for a litter. The king tried to mount his horse but it would not tolerate him and shied away.

One of the nobles dragged me from the ranks. "Carry the king upon your back," he said.

I had no choice.

'From that day on I was outcast. Except when I was needed to bear the king upon my back. This is why I am a leper. This is why I am called Mule.'

John and Bernard stared at him in silence. They could not find words to say for a long while.

'We shall call you Matthew,' John said at last. 'Always.'

The next morning John woke just as the sun was touching the horizon. He went to the pool and scooped some water into his mouth. It tasted sweet and he drank his fill. He sat back on his haunches. Bernard stirred and sat up. He wandered a little way off in order to relieve himself.

John stared at Matthew who was still fast asleep, his head cradled in his arms. John took a deep breath and tip-toed over to him.

He squatted down beside him and gently pulled back the hood.

He expected to see a face horribly ravaged, disfigured to a grotesque mask, something barely recognisable as human.

What he saw astonished him.

He gestured Bernard over, putting his fingers to his lips to signify silence. Bernard joined him.

'Christ,' he said.

John nodded. 'My thoughts, exactly.'

Although they kept their voices quiet, it was enough to disturb Matthew. His eyes fluttered open, shut and open once again.

'No,' he cried, pulling his hood down to cover his face. 'Do not taint your eyes with me.'

John and Bernard exchanged glances. Matthew had curled himself into a ball, his head close to his knees. He was a picture of shame.

For long moment the two friends did not speak. Then John crouched down beside Matthew. 'My friend,' he said. 'You are not a leper.'

Matthew stared at them numbly, not understanding their words, suspecting some trick.

'I am a leper. People could see it in my face. They shunned me, fled me, cast me out into the hills. Damn it man, I could feel the disfigurement with my own hands.'

Bernard raised his hand. 'Tell me Matthew, did you have smallpox in your youth?'

Matthew shook his head.

'I've never had smallpox.'

'Well judging by the pits and hollows on your face, you must have had it very bad at the time you were carrying King Baldwin.'

'Smallpox?'

'Yes. And people assumed it was leprosy and cast you out.'

Matthew touched his face, exploring his scarred face with his finger-tips. 'Smallpox?' he said.

Bernard nodded.

'Smallpox.'

Matthew leapt into the air and began to run up and down, twenty yards this way, twenty yards that, making a zigzag around them. Every time he changed course he would give a leap in the air, crying out with joy.

Eventually he slowed and paced back to John and Bernard.

'You are certain?' he said. 'You are certain it is not leprosy?'

'Certain,' Bernard said.

'I wish I could find a lady's mirror,' Matthew said. 'Then I could see with my own eyes.'

'It's not a pretty sight,' Bernard said with a grin, 'so be warned.'

'That's true,' said John. 'By the look of those scars you had the smallpox very bad. Your face is blemished right enough. But not by leprosy.'

Matthew came close and looked into their eyes. 'You have freed me, my friends. I have carried this burden for almost three years. Now I am free.'

He gazed down at his hands, then up to John and Bernard in silent plea. They understood. They reached out and took held his hands tight.

Matthew wept.

'I am not a leper,' he said at last. 'I am not a leper.'

Bernard released Matthew's hand and pointed to the hills to the east.

'No. you're not,' he said. 'But it would be good if they were to believe that all three of us have the disease.'

John and Matthew turned towards where he was pointing.

A hundred Saracen horsemen were thundering towards them.

CHAPTER 14
ENDLESS MILES
The Road to Damascus

Agnes awoke. She shook her head. She was still in the column of captives, still walking, even in her sleep. She turned, horrified, wondering what had happened to Eleanor. A man smiled at her. He had the child cradled in his arms. Claude-Yusuf and Gerard were watching him closely, making sure that he did not run away with her.

Agnes held out her hands. 'Thank you,' she said. Her tone softened. 'Did I drop her?'

He shook his head.

'How long was I asleep?'

'Moments. Enough for you to stumble and for me to take her. But not enough for you to fall.'

He passed Eleanor back to her. 'My name is Peter. I am a winemaker from Tours.'

'You were unwise to leave your home, Peter.'

He nodded. 'My mother warned me that no good would come of it. I should have listened. She is always right.'

Agnes looked swiftly at Peter. He was short and rather stout. His hair was receding although he seemed little older than she was. He had a round face that was meant to be jolly but now seemed burdened with sorrow.

Peter stayed with Agnes for the rest of the day and when they stopped for the night, rolled himself in a cloak and slept at her feet. She tried to stay awake but her exhaustion flung her into a deep sleep.

She awoke next day stiff and anxious. She had been troubled by dark dreams although she could not remember them. She glanced at Peter. He was still rolled tight in his cloak and she sighed in relief. She wanted him close but not too close.

They continued on the long march north. Peter stayed close to her and although she remained wary she got used to his presence. He was kind to them all, taking turns to carry Eleanor and occasionally allowing Gerard to pretend he was a Templar riding on his back. Every so often Peter would neigh and trot up and down the line which made Gerard laugh and all those nearby smile.

Claude-Yusuf refused to be carried in this way.

During the march the Saracen guards were watchful but courteous. A few offered their mounts to people who were struggling but the officers saw this and forbade any more such kindnesses. A few of the captives died on the march but because the guards did not force the pace most survived.

The biggest anxiety for Agnes came from a man called Gaspard Allanche. He had been a customer at the inn for many years and she had always disliked him. His eyes had always followed her, whatever job she had been doing, and it was the same now that they were captives. Wherever she went he seemed to be there before her. He never spoke to her but contented himself with lewd staring and a knowing smile.

At first she put this down to her imagination but Peter noticed as well and took the opportunity to say it.

'Keep clear of him, Agnes,' he said. 'He has evil intent towards you.'

'I know that,' she said. 'But thank you for pointing it out.'

He looked as if he were about to say more but he merely shook his head and continued walking.

The sun was unseasonably hot for the time of year and as they walked further into the desert so the heat seemed to become fiercer and unrelenting. Yet she found that as she walked a new resolve began to settle upon her. I will survive, she decided. I will survive and keep my children safe and one day I will escape and find Bernard.

She did not allow herself to dwell on the thought of that glad reunion. She knew that to do so would weaken her strength of will.

In the middle of the night she awoke to find a heavy weight bearing down upon her.

'Make a noise and I'll slit your throat,' said a hoarse voice in her ear.

She knew at once that it was Gaspard Allenche. His words came out staccato, his voice thick with emotion.

She tried to push him away but he was too strong for her.

'Your throat and your children's,' he said. 'And I'll have you whether you fight or no.'

He was fumbling at her skirt, dragging it above her waist. His threat kept her quiet but still she struggled, pushing and kicking in silent fury, desperate to escape from beneath him. She glanced once at Peter and saw in the faint light from the nearby fire that he had been knocked unconscious, with blood seeping from a wound in his head.

'Come on you little whore,' Allenche said. 'You know you want it. You've always wanted it and always wanted me.'

He leaned his face closer which was his big mistake. She bit hard upon his chin and he cried out. In moments a furious figure leapt upon his back, pummelling him between the shoulder blades.

'Leave my mother alone,' Gerard cried, kicking and punching.

Allenche reached behind his back and dragged Gerard off, flinging him savagely to the ground. He was up again in an instant, all the breath knocked out of his body but determined nonetheless.

Allenche punched him in the face sending him reeling but he staggered up once more and groped like a blind man back towards the fight.

'Don't touch him,' hissed Agnes.

'You know what will stop me,' Allenche leered.

He had no time to say more.

Claude-Yusuf sprang into sight, wielding a brand from the fire. Allanche saw it but he saw it too late. Before he could move, Claude-Yusuf jabbed the brand into his face, gouging it into his eye.

Allenche shrieked in agony, waking even the most exhausted sleepers nearby.

Two Saracen guards raced over, snatching the brand from Claude-Yusuf just as he was about to push it against Allenche's throat.

An officer hurried after them and quickly sized up the situation.

'What's happening here?' he asked the guard.

'I can tell you,' gasped Agnes in fluent Arabic.

She took moments to tell the officer what had happened, pointing out where Peter and Gerard were groggily getting to their feet and showing where Allenche had uncovered himself for the act of rape.

It took even less time for the officer to make his decision. He summoned a doctor who quickly examined Gerard and Peter to make sure they were not badly harmed. Then, at a further command from the officer, he bent towards Allenche and deftly castrated him.

The man's screams echoed around the camp. One of the guards cauterised the wound and Allenche fell to the ground, writing in agony.

'No women are to be molested,' cried the officer. 'That is the command of Sultan Saladin. Any who disobey will suffer the same fate as this man. And more. I will make them eat their own manhoods.'

He gazed at Agnes, seeing her beauty in the light of the torches. He strode off but then stopped and turned to look at Claude-Yusuf with a thoughtful air. He smiled at the boy and nodded his head as if in recognition of his actions.

Agnes gathered the two sobbing boys to her, pressing them to her with all her strength.

'Brave boys,' she cried. 'Brave, brave boys.'

CHAPTER 15
A NEW LORD FOR SIMON
On the Road to Tyre

Night fell. Simon sat apart from others. The night brought welcome relief from the eyes. It brought the whispers even louder. He craned his head to try to catch the words that were spoken about him. He guessed they were hateful; some would no doubt be threats. He felt for his dagger. He had to be ready for any attack.

Out of the corner of his eye he saw a figure approach. He slid his dagger from its sheath and placed it on his thigh.

'There is no need for alarm, master Knight,' the figure said.

'What do you want with me?' Simon asked. 'Who are you?'

'A friend. Or at least I hope we shall be friends.'

Simon nodded and the figure came close. A second figure darted behind and placed a stool on the ground before departing.

'I saw you in the battle,' the man said, making himself comfortable on the stool. 'You were brave; courageous in the defence of Christ and His Church.'

'And you?'

'I fought in many ways.' He twitched aside his cloak and revealed a heavy mace. 'I am not allowed to shed blood, even the blood of an infidel. But I can crush skulls.' He drew the cloak back. 'Most of my weapons, however, involve prayer.'

Simon shook his head, not understanding.

Eraclius sniffed, angered that the man had not recognised him.

'I am Patriarch Eraclius,' he said softly.

'I remember seeing you,' Simon said. 'When Balian came to the city and also at the negotiations with the Saracens.' He snorted. 'You left behind many of your flock.'

'The negotiations were complex,' Eraclius said. His blood was up at the impudence of Simon's words but he mastered it. 'I bought many souls with my own money and pleaded with the Sultan to release others. Which he did.'

'But not all?'

'Not all.'

Eraclius fell silent. He wondered if he should tell this stranger that he and Balian had offered themselves in ransom for the whole population. But something warned him not to allow such a confidence to this man. To do so would be a mistake; some time in the distant future he might have cause to regret it.

'What do you want with me?' Simon asked.

'Ah,' said Eraclius. 'So you wonder, after all. Tell me your name, my son.'

'Simon Ferrier.'

'Do you leave loved ones behind in the city?'

Simon looked away. Faces flitted through his mind, voices and deeds. He saw two bright eyes begin to fade and deaden in front of him.

'No,' he said. 'No loved ones. Nobody I care for.'

The Patriarch nodded. 'And do you have a lord?'

'Does Balian count?'

Eraclius shrugged. 'It could be argued that you are his man. But he knighted you in defence of the Holy City. It could, therefore, equally be argued that you are mine.'

Simon closed his eyes wearily. He felt like a well-gnawed

bone being fought over by hounds.

'So who decides?'

'In such confused cases it is always God who decides. And He will speak through a humble heart as much as through a noble one.'

'My heart is not noble, my lord. That I can tell you.'

'How so?'

'I did deeds, deeds which I will not speak of.'

Eraclius paused, considering. 'Cruelty against the infidel are as gifts to Christ, my son. And deeds against fellow Christians can be confessed and absolved.'

A moan of pain rose in Simon's throat.

Eraclius held out his hand. 'Do as your heart tells you, Simon. Listen to God speaking to you.'

Eraclius watched him narrowly and pressed home his attack.

'The Holy Church has lost many of its former protectors. It has need of new men now. Men of valour. Men who will do what they are commanded, knowing that only by obedience will they gain eternal bliss.'

The two men fell silent. The only noises were the murmur of the exhausted people, the call of cicadas and the whispering in Simon's head.

'You must not imagine that you will be welcomed by the other knights,' continued Eraclius. 'This kingdom is holiness itself in design but those entrusted with its sanctity are only human. You would not dream of aping your betters at home. Do not make the mistake of doing so here. You will suffer for it.

'Your best hope is to embrace Christ and His Holy Church. I am the representative of both. I need knights to protect me and mine. You, I believe, are the only one available.'

It was a bitter bargain. Yet Simon took the Patriarch's hand

and kissed it.

The next day Simon rode beside Eraclius and his family. He rode a donkey, it was true, but it was a mount nonetheless. On his belt hung a sword. Round his neck a little silver cross.

CHAPTER 16
CAPTIVE ONCE MORE
Beit Lahia

The Saracen horsemen skidded to a halt, causing a choking cloud of dust to rise up above them. John, Bernard and Matthew shrank together, trying hard to master their terror.

One of the horsemen pushed his horse closer and stared down at them.

'Are you a leper?' he asked.

Matthew did not answer for a moment and then nodded. Fear of the disease might prove their best protection from the Saracens.

'And you two?' said the man. 'Are you lepers also?'

'We have spent time with the leper, Excellency,' Bernard answered. 'I assume we have got the disease.'

'Do not assume anything,' the Saracen said. 'We need a man of medicine to tell us truth.'

He turned in his saddle, searching the faces of his followers until he found the one he wanted.

'Issam,' he called.

A man pushed his way towards them.

'Yes, Lord Khalid?'

'Tell me if this man is a leper?'

Issam climbed down from his horse and peered into Matthew's face. He gestured to him to show his hands and then the rest of his arms and his chest and feet.

The Saracen examined everything with great care, even sniffing at Matthew's face.

He stood back, thought for a few moments and returned to the Saracen leader.

'This man had smallpox but nothing worse,' Issam said. 'He is not a leper.'

Khalid nodded, relief clear in his face.

He turned to examine Matthew for a moment before beckoning him closer.

'Christian, why do you dress as a leper?'

Matthew swallowed, wondering what to say. He decided that the truth would be his best choice.

'Because I thought I was a leper, Excellency.'

Khalid frowned. 'But what made you think you were a leper?'

'Because I used to carry King Baldwin of Jerusalem on my back. Then I got boils upon my face and my people cast me out into the wilderness.'

Khalid leaned forward with surprise.

'Then you are the man they call Mule?' he asked.

Matthew nodded.

Khalid stared at Matthew for a while longer before turning towards Issam.

'You are certain he is not a leper?'

'Certain, Excellency.'

Khalid dismounted and strode close towards Matthew.

'We have heard of you, Mule. You are a good man, a courageous man.'

He put his hand on Matthew's shoulder and turned to his troops to make sure all had seen him do it.

'This is the Mule, the man of great courage who bore the Leper

King upon his back.'

A murmur broke from the warriors, part alarm, part curiosity, part respect.

'His people thought he had also become a leper,' Khalid said, 'so they threw him into the desert.'

The warriors gave a low hiss at this news.

'But he is not a leper. He is clean and whole.'

The warriors nodded, wondering why he was telling them this.

'Get some horses for these men,' he cried. 'They are coming with us.'

'We cannot,' said Bernard. 'We are going to Cairo to seek the captives from Jerusalem. My family is amongst them.'

'I have just come from Cairo,' Khalid answered. 'We saw no sign of any captives on the road.'

'But they must be.'

'Why must they? The slavers would have taken them to Damascus or to Baghdad.'

'But a man in Jerusalem said he heard they were to be taken to Cairo.'

'He was wrong. The slave market at Cairo was flooded with the survivors from the battle of Hattin. I doubt Sultan Saladin would have allowed any more captives to go there. Your family have probably been taken to Damascus.'

Bernard looked crestfallen at the news.

Khalid turned back to Matthew.

'I am certain,' he said, 'that my lord, al-Adil would wish to see you. He is a great respecter of courageous men.'

'Al-Adil?' John asked Bernard.

'Yes,' he answered with a bitter tone. 'Saladin's brother. We're being taken back to where we started.

CHAPTER 17
THE SLAVE AUCTION
Damascus

Ten days after setting out they reached Damascus. It was a large city, larger than any Agnes had ever seen before. As they trudged through the streets she marvelled at the fine buildings and the signs of wealth. People were well-fed and well-dressed. The shops were crammed with goods. Most entrancing of all were the stalls piled with meat, fish, fruit, vegetables and bread of every shape and size. The smell tormented her and made her realise that she was famished.

The captives were herded into a central park where tents had been erected for them. They were fed with bread and fresh fruit and given water to drink and wash themselves. Fires were banked up against the chill of the night air.

'Is this where we're going to live?' Claude-Yusuf asked Agnes.

'I don't know, dear,' she answered. She forced a smile. 'The people seem kind. They're looking after us.'

'But they are infidels,' Gerard said. 'And where are father and John and Simon?'

'They stayed in Jerusalem. They stayed with Lord Balian.'

'Will they come and rescue us?'

'All in good time, darling. All in good time.'

The next day the captives were allowed to sleep until mid-morning. They were given food and then led along a wide street to a huge market next to a mosque. The market was crowded with people and at the far end, in front of the mosque, a large platform had been raised.

Agnes stood and watched what was happening. A dozen captives would be led onto the platform, men, women and children. Then the auctioneer rang a bell, a forest of hands rose from the crowd and a clamour rang across the square.

'What's happening?' she asked.

'A slave auction,' Peter answered. 'We are to be sold as slaves.'

There were so many captives that the authorities had decided that the slaves were to be sold in lots of a dozen. As the line of captives moved towards the platform, Agnes counted them time and again, time and again, trying to work out where the guards would make the split between each group.

As they got closer she saw to her horror that there were ten people in front of her making her eleventh and one of the children the twelfth. This meant she was certain to be separated from two of the children.

She tugged at the woman in front of her. 'Please,' she said, 'please swap places with me. I am the eleventh in line but I have three children with me. Would you and a friend please take my place so that my children can be sold with me?'

The woman listened to her sorrowfully but shook her head. 'This is my family,' she said, indicating her children. 'If I take your place then I will be separated from them.'

'What about further up?' Agnes asked. 'Would two people from there swap?'

'Another family,' said the woman, shaking her head.

Agnes turned and gazed at the captives behind her. 'Will two of you swap with me and one of my children?' she asked. 'Otherwise we will be separated.'

The captives eyed her suspiciously, not realising the dilemma she had spotted. They shook their heads. She tried to push past but they forced her back.

'I will swap with you,' called Peter.

'But that will mean I will have to leave one of the children,' she said. 'I cannot do that.'

Peter thought rapidly. 'You will have to choose between the boys. Come here with Eleanor and one of the boys. I will take your place and I promise I will look after the boy you have to leave there.'

Agnes' hand went to her mouth. She looked from Gerard to Claude-Yusuf. She knew she would have to sacrifice one. For the moment she could not bring herself to do it.

The decision was taken out of her hands.

At that moment the guards hurried up and counted the dozen lot that she was in. Peter pushed forward towards her and tried to drag her back but the guards misinterpreted his action and beat him away with clubs.

Agnes screamed as she was dragged off with Eleanor, leaving Gerard and Claude-Yusuf behind.

She pleaded and cursed all the way to the platform until finally one of the guards got tired of it and placed his knife across her throat. She closed her eyes in panic and was dragged away.

Agnes stood on the platform and watched Gerard and Claude-Yusuf. They were screaming with terror and tried to escape the clutches of the guards and run to her. A huge guard pulled out a club and advanced towards them but Peter, his face bleeding, managed to grab hold of them and keep them safe.

Agnes did not see the frantic bidding for her lot. All she could do was keep hold of Eleanor and gaze with frantic eyes upon the faces of the boys.

At that point the clamour of the bidding began to quieten. The crowd lost their frenzy and rippled slowly into two halves, allowing a path to be created down the centre.

Walking down this path towards the platform were a dozen armoured men. At their head was an immensely fat man dressed in the finest of clothes.

They halted in front of the platform and the fat man made careful scrutiny of the captives. He took his time, and as this time passed the crowd became not quiet but silent. Finally, he appeared satisfied and nodded to himself as if well content.

He gave a quick flick of his fingers and Agnes was dragged towards him. He gave a sharp nod and the guard pulled her shirt open, revealing her breasts. Again the man gestured and she was turned round by the guard, very slowly, so that the fat man could get a good look at her.

He made another gesture and the guard pulled up her skirt to display her rear.

By the time she had been spun back to the front he was stroking his beard thoughtfully.

'I take her,' he said.

The auctioneer immediately pulled Agnes towards the steps at the side of the platform.

'Excellency,' she cried to the fat man. 'I have a child, a baby. Please let me keep her.'

The fat man considered her for a while. His eyes looked cold and calculating. Then he nodded and Eleanor was tossed off the platform and caught by one of his bodyguards.

'And two boys,' said Agnes, bowing to the fat man. 'I have

two boys.'

'The Caliph has no need of boys,' said the man. 'He only desires the choicest of women.'

CHAPTER 18
HOW MANY LEAGUES?
The Road to Tyre

Simon Ferrier grew ever more useful to Patriarch Eraclius during the march to the coast. The priests were not used to hard marching and complained and moaned all of the day. Most had little love for Eraclius and considered him ill-bred and worse-educated. Simon took them in hand and made them march almost like soldiers, keeping strict silence whenever the Patriarch was close by.

A few days into the march Simon had an idea which he took to the Patriarch.

'I cannot easily keep an eye on all of the priests,' he said.

Eraclius frowned at him. 'Do you think they need to have an eye kept upon them?'

'There is a great deal of treasure here. It would be a shame if even a tiny portion of it was stolen.'

'By priests?'

Simon shrugged. 'Possibly. Or, if the priests neglect to keep both eyes upon their packs, by the refugees.'

Eraclius bit his lip. 'So. Do you have an answer to this problem?'

'I do, my lord. Some of the older boys are getting restless on the march. I could make them grooms and they could guard the treasure.'

Eraclius was amused by this idea.

He saw at once that Simon would waste no time in shaping them into his own personal guard.

He chuckled to himself. It matters not at the moment. What if he creates a private army for his own ends? It will prove a better one than any he might build for me. I can make use of him and his grooms while we're on the road. It may be different when we reach Tyre.

He smiled upon Simon.

'It is a good idea, Simon Ferrier. Choose the strongest and cleverest of the boys and make them into grooms. We may have need of them before we reach Tyre.'

Tyre was the only city in the Kingdom of Jerusalem still left in Frankish hands. Saladin had laid siege to it earlier in the year but after the Battle of Hattin he could not resist marching upon Jerusalem. Tyre had been given a reprieve but only a temporary one.

Balian knew it was imperative the refugees make the speediest progress they could upon the road. Rumour had reached him that it that it would be a mere few days before Saladin marched from Jerusalem to renew his attack upon the city. He had to reach the safety of its walls beforehand.

'How far is it to Tyre, my lord?' Simon asked. 'Will we reach it before Saladin?'

Eraclius shrugged and turned to his Deacon. 'Do you know, Walter?'

'I have heard it is forty leagues from Jerusalem to Tyre my lord. One hundred and twenty miles.'

'I know what a league is,' the Patriarch snapped. His eyes narrowed. 'Do not take me for a fool.'

Walter bowed but Simon thought that he was not able to hide his lack of respect.

'So we are only about half way,' Simon said. 'Another five or six days.'

'At the rate we are going, yes,' Eraclius said. 'If the route were safe I would press on ahead at a trot.'

'But it is not safe.'

'Not safe enough.'

Eraclius had wrestled with whether to try to persuade Balian to escort him swiftly to the port. But even if he did so he would have to leave all the church treasure with the main column. He had no relish for this. If would be a tempting target for pillage by the refugees.

And if Saladin did march upon Tyre the treasure would fall into his hands. He doubted that the Sultan would be so indulgent to the church a second time.

In the end he decided it was better to bide his time and stay with the column where he could best look after his interests. He also wished to secure his position in Tyre as swiftly as possible and fretted how he might do both of these things.

He kept a careful watch upon Simon. If he thought he could fully trust the young Englishman he might leave him behind to guard the treasure while he pushed on towards Tyre. He would be forced to do so if Saladin got close.

CHAPTER 19
SERVANTS OF THE SARACEN
Jerusalem

The Saracens took the road back to Jerusalem. Bernard was in the blackest of moods, distraught that he was being taken back where they had started and, therefore, delayed in the hunt for his family.

They reached the city just after noon and were taken straight away to see al-Adil.

They waited outside his tent, trying hard to ignore the curious stares of the Saracens who passed by. Everyone kept a good distance from them. Most looked upon Matthew with disgust, a few with pity. He did not seem to mind. He did not seem to mind anything. I'm not a leper, he thought over and over to himself. I'm free.

The flap of the tent was pulled open and al-Adil appeared, followed by Khalid and Issam.

'You are sure he is not a leper?' al-Adil asked.

'On my life,' said Issam.

'If you are wrong, it will be,' said al-Adil. 'I shall have you tied in a sack with him.'

Al-Adil turned his gaze upon Matthew, scrutinising him in silence. Matthew shook in terror, his former jubilation extinguished by the Saracen's deadly manner.

'So,' al-Adil said finally. 'You are the Mule? You are the man who carried King Baldwin into battle?'

'I am Excellency.'

'Tell me if you will, what were your thoughts when you did this?'

Matthew paused, wondering what the best answer would be.

'The truth, Mule,' al-Adil said. 'Tell me the truth.'

Matthew took a deep breath. 'At first, Excellency, I was terrified. Terrified of catching the disease. Then I grew resentful of the king. Finally I grew to be resentful of the nobles who had made me bear this burden. I no longer resented the king. In fact, I became proud that I was the one who carried him.'

'Proud?' al-Adil tapped a finger upon his lips. 'So, you demanded the honour of your peers?'

Matthew thought carefully and nodded. 'Yes, I suppose I did although I would not have dared ask for it. I certainly felt proud for myself. But I also began to expect the honour of my peers and of the nobles.'

'Did you get it?'

Matthew shook his head. 'I was reviled, shunned, condemned. When the king died I was given leper's weeds and thrown out into the wilderness.'

'Men with cowardly hearts cannot abide the truly courageous, friend Mule,' al-Adil said.

'His name is Matthew,' John said.

Al-Adil turned towards him and nodded his head, very slightly. 'I am corrected.'

He turned back towards Matthew. 'You are welcome in my camp, Matthew,' he said. 'For as long as you choose.'

Matthew bowed, startled and confused.

Al-Adil turned back towards John. 'And who are you that is

fool-hardy enough to correct the brother of Saladin?'

'My name is Sir John Ferrier.'

'Sir John?' Al-Adil gave a condescending smile.

'Yes. I was knighted by Balian of Ibelin at the siege of Jerusalem. And so was my friend, Bernard.' He paused. 'You gave us our freedom, Excellency by buying us at the end of the siege.'

Al-Adil smiled. 'So I did. And now Khalid has made you captive once again.'

He fell silent and stared at the sky, thoughtfully.

He sighed and unclipped a purse from his belt. 'How many times will I be forced to buy you?' he said, shaking his head as if weary. He counted twenty dinars into Khalid's hands.

'There,' he said with a smile, 'you are my men again.' He placed his hands upon their shoulders. 'But this time I think I shall keep you lest you get yourselves captured again and cost me yet more.'

Bernard and John gazed at him in consternation.

'Excellency?' said Khalid.

Al-Adil turned towards him.

'The leper?'

'Is there no end to these depredations?' Al-Adil cried. He counted out five more dinars. 'There you are. Five dinars only. He is not a knight. Be grateful that I have given you so much for him.'

Khalid grinned and bowed, gesturing Matthew to join them.

They ate the noon day meal in the tent of al-Adil. It was sparsely furnished, for while on campaign with his brother al-Adil thought it wisest to emulate Saladin's lack of ostentation. The meal, on the other hand, was not sparse. Neither Bernard nor John had seen such plenty. Matthew was so overawed that for a time he could not even bring himself to eat.

Al-Adil and Khalid joined them at the meal, together with several senior officials and officers. They merely watched the Christians; only al-Adil and Khalid spoke with them.

'Tell me where you were going when Khalid found you?' al-Adil asked. 'Some of your friends chose to stay here, in Jerusalem.'

'You gave us our freedom, Excellency,' said Bernard. 'I followed the train of captives because my wife and family are amongst them.'

'Did you find them?'

'No. At the pool where Lord Khalid found us we were on our way south to Cairo. We had heard from someone that the captives had been taken that way although we had no way of telling whether this was the truth or not.'

Al-Adil nodded before leaning towards him. 'You left Jerusalem two nights ago. The pool is how far?'

'Sixty miles, Excellency,' Khalid answered.

'Only sixty miles. Then why were you still at the pool? And what happened to the weapons that I gave you and the fine horses?'

Bernard licked his lips, uncertain how to answer. Matthew had no such compunction. 'Bernard and John had been captured by Templars, Excellency. They beat them and stole everything they had including your gifts. Then they trussed them up like capons for the market.'

Al-Adil and Khalid exchanged glances. Khalid translated his words into Arabic for the benefit of the officers. They looked horrified.

'Why are you so surprised?' al-Adil said. 'The Templars are like mad dogs. We fight to expel them from our lands.'

'We fight to expel all Christians,' said an old officer, speaking in passable French for the westerners' benefit.

Al-Adil shook his head. 'No. Some Christians were here before God gave the land to us. We let them abide in peace. Our war is with the sons of wolves who joined the crusade and stole our land.'

'Especially the knights of the Temple and the Hospital,' said Khalid.

'Especially them.' He turned towards Bernard. 'Would you recognise these Templar scum again?'

Bernard nodded.

'Then,' al-Adil said, 'when we capture them I shall give them to you. They shall be your slaves.'

'We cannot keep fellow Christians as slaves,' John said.

Al-Adil shrugged. 'Then kill them. I care not.'

Bernard and John bent to their meal. John could see Bernard was troubled and feared his anguish at being kept from pursuit of his family might lead him to do something dangerous. Al-Adil was clearly a man who dealt death as easily as he dealt life.

Yet the men around him looked totally at ease. John struggled with this. He had been told that all Saracens were devils and Saladin and his kin the greatest devils of all. Yet here I am, sitting with them. They enjoy their meal like Christians. They are not terrified of al-Adil, nor do they want to slay us. How can this be?

His thoughts were interrupted by the entrance of three soldiers bearing scimitars and shields. They salaamed and al-Adil pointed out the Christians to them. They placed the weapons at their feet.

'What are these, Lord al-Adil?' John asked.

'They are your weapons,' he answered. He drew a scimitar from its sheath. 'They are fine, indeed. The scimitars are from Toledo, the shields from Samarkand.'

'Why do you honour us in this manner, lord?' he asked.

'I told you. I bought you from my brother for ten dinars each and then, within days of giving you freedom, I find I have to pay another ten dinars for you again. Enough is enough. You will remain my men from now on. And as such you will wield Muslim weapons not Frankish ones.'

Bernard wiped his face and bowed low to the ground. 'I am honoured, Excellency. But I beg to remind you that I was searching for my wife and family.'

'What of it? You can find a new wife, a Muslim wife and beget more children.'

'I love my wife, lord.'

Al-Adil sighed. 'I am sure you do. But you do not know where they have been taken. And if you were to find them, what would you do? Have you money to buy them back from their owners? Would you seek to rescue them from some mighty emir?'

He shook his head. 'Forget them, my friend. Get yourself a new wife, a Muslim wife, and breed fine Muslim sons who will make you proud.'

CHAPTER 20
SETTING OUT FOR BAGHDAD
Damascus

'Please take my two boys,' Agnes cried.

The fat man looked at her and said something to one of his soldiers. The whole troop laughed. The fat man looked pleased with his own jest.

When the laughter had ended he turned to her, pouted, and shook his head. 'I've told you already,' he said. 'The Caliph has no use for boys.'

'I'll do anything if you buy them,' she said. 'Anything.'

The fat man gazed at her, his eyes wondering.

She had learnt this lesson in her last days in Jerusalem. It was the most potent tool she had.

She straightened up and tilted her head to one side, looking up at the fat man, glancing shyly away and turning her gaze back once again to hold his eyes with hers.

The fat man licked his lips. The soldiers laughed.

He turned to them in fury and beat his hand against his thigh, making a soft, plopping noise. It was as effective as the crack of a whip. The soldiers fell silent and cast their eyes to the ground.

Agnes placed her hand upon her hip. 'Two boys,' she said. 'That's not asking for much. And I will do anything you need. Anything you desire, anything.'

She gave him a long look which she forced herself to become brazen.

The fat man stared at her for a moment longer, stripping her naked in his mind's eye.

'I will hold you to this,' he said at last. 'Point out the boys.'

Agnes searched in the crowd for Gerard and Claude-Yusuf. They were nowhere to be seen. Then she heard Gerard call to her. He was already on the platform and people were making their bids.

'They are on the platform, Excellency,' she cried. 'Please don't let them be bought by anyone else. Please buy them for the Caliph.'

The fat man nodded and one of the soldiers hurried off the auctioneer. He was angry at the interruption but when he saw four more soldiers hurrying towards him he acquiesced. He threw the boys off the platform and they were caught by the soldiers.

'The Caliph prefers virgins,' the fat man said to Agnes. 'But he is flexible when there is a very beautiful woman such as you.' He reached out and stroked her cheek.

'Although he will not thank me if I bring him goods more soiled than when I bought them. Sometimes, he gets bored with his women and passes them on to his vizier or even to Habib, his factotum.'

He bowed slightly. 'It is then that I will hold you to the promise that you have made.'

Gerard and Claude-Yusuf hurried over to Agnes. She kissed and hugged them, trying in vain to stem their tears. She turned and raised her hand to Peter who was watching them with a curious look upon his face.

'Come,' said the fat man. He turned and led them through the crowd.

For a fat man he could walk remarkably quickly. Within

minutes they had left the hubbub of the square behind them and were walking along a shady road with large houses on either side. Ten minutes later they turned left into a small square fringed by palm trees. In the centre of this were two camels with howdahs upon their backs. A lean man was sitting on a stool beside them, swatting flies from his face with a whisk.

'Habib,' he cried. 'You were quicker than I expected.'

'I know the Caliph's appetites, Dawud,' he said. 'I did not need to spend much time searching.'

'Why this one?'

Habib turned and stared at her.

'She is ordinary, a woman you might glimpse shopping in a souk, yet she is beautiful. She has the freshness of youth but I can sense experience in her glance. She is no stranger to a bed and I imagine she will be generous with herself once she learns to trust.'

'All this from just looking at her?'

'I have selected two hundred women for the Caliph's harem. Do you think I would still have this head upon these shoulders if I didn't know who best to choose?'

'And people think you are a eunuch.'

'It suits me for them to think so. Women feel safe around me.'

Dawud grinned. 'I think that you choose not merely to suit the Caliph's appetites. You are considering who he may cast off and toss in your direction.'

Agnes took a step towards them. 'I can speak Arabic,' she said.

The two men looked nonplussed.

'I understand every word you have said about me.' She glanced back. 'And so can the boys, the big one especially.'

Habib bowed. 'I apologise for my friend's comments.'

Dawud smiled. 'And I apologise for Habib's. Tell me, how do

you know our tongue?'

'If you are married to an inn-keeper you have to know many languages.'

'The language of love best of all, I trust,' Habib said.

Agnes glared at him.

Dawud got up and walked across to the two boys. 'And how does this fellow know Arabic.'

'My mother was a Saracen,' Claude-Yusuf said. 'She converted to the true faith when she married my father.'

'A half-breed,' Dawud said with a look of distaste. 'They will pollute the whole world.'

'That is nonsense,' Habib said. 'You cannot judge a person by his parents. Only by his deeds. Perhaps this one can be won back to the faith.'

Dawud stretched. 'Enough of talk. It is five hundred miles to Baghdad. We should start now.'

'Have you eaten?' Habib asked Agnes.

'A little. This morning. The children will be hungry.'

'Have they ridden on a camel before?'

'No.'

'Then I think it best if they do not eat until we halt for the night.'

He helped Agnes and the children into one of the howdahs before clambering in himself. Dawud got into the other one and the drivers urged the camels to their feet.

Agnes thought she was going to be thrown out of the howdah and gripped Eleanor tight. The camel started off. Eleanor began to cry at the swaying but the boys grinned with excitement.

'You like this?' Habib asked.

'It's wonderful,' Gerard said. 'Better than a horse.'

'Much better. Horses may be pretty and camels ugly but a camel is ten times the beast. He is strong and hardy and wise. He will go where no horse dare.'

'Can we see out?' Gerard asked.

Habib nodded and pulled back the curtains on the howdah. Eleanor howled still louder but the boys peered out with joy.

CHAPTER 21
THE REFUGEES REACH TYRE
The Gates of Tyre

Balian pulled his horse to a halt and pointed to the western horizon. Just visible in the distant haze were the towers of the city of Tyre.

Simon slouched in his saddle, hardly daring to believe that they had reached safety.

The Christians raised their voices in a prayer of thanks.

Eraclius did not join them in this; his mind was solely on how to safeguard the treasure of the Church.

In the course of the march the donkeys bearing the treasure had become less ordered and now straggled hundreds of yards up and down the line. Eraclius ordered Simon to herd them together and move them out to the side of the column.

On the march the people had been concerned solely with their survival. Now that they were within sight of safety they would begin to realise that they had lost their former wealth. The treasure of the Church might prove too tempting a target, an easy way to recoup what they had lost. If the donkeys were grouped together Simon's guard would have a better chance of preventing pilfering.

It was a long and difficult job but eventually Simon and his men had manoeuvred the donkeys into a more ordered group.

'You did well, Simon,' Eraclius said. 'A man who can herd donkeys led by priests will surely command armies with ease.'

Simon stared at him, uncertain whether he was mocking him or perhaps prophesying his future.

The sun passed noon but none of the refugees felt inclined to stop for rest or food. The front of the column was now only three miles from the walls and the far-sighted claimed they could see Christian flags upon the battlements.

No order was given but everyone began to pick up speed, finding from somewhere the energy to force their legs faster.

Simon stared at Eraclius who was riding at the front of the churchmen with his concubine Pasque de Riveri and their daughter. The Patriarch kicked at his horse, keen to reach the city as soon as possible.

What are his plans, Simon wondered. He knew he had been useful to Eraclius on the march but would he continue to be so in Tyre? The Patriarch would be able to call on scores of servants and he could be easily dismissed.

He gnawed upon his bottom lip, plotting how best to make himself indispensable to his master.

Out of the corner of his eye he saw that the Saracen horsemen who had guarded them steadfastly all the way were silently peeling away from the column. A number of them glanced to the south, far beyond the rear of the column and one man pointed something out to his comrade. A knot of fear curled inside Simon's stomach.

He turned in his saddle and peered through the dust of the column to the hills to the south.

A Saracen army was pouring down to the plains from the hills beyond. The sun glinted upon their spears.

Simon turned his donkey and kicked it savagely, racing past the churchmen until he reached Eraclius.

'My lord,' he said. 'It's Saladin. His army is a few miles behind us.'

Eraclius turned and gazed at the Saracen army for the briefest moment. Then he cried out to Simon to come with him, whipped up his horse and galloped to the front of the column to find Balian.

Balian and Jerome were already cantering back down the column. They too had seen the Saracen army and wanted to get a better view of it.

Eraclius skidded to a halt beside them.

'What will we do?' he asked. 'We cannot fight.'

'No,' said Balian. 'And we will not get the whole of the column into Tyre until sundown at the earliest. Three hours or more. Saladin could be upon us in two.'

'Then what will we do?'

Balian turned and glanced towards the west. Far off he thought he could glimpse soldiers upon the battlements of the city but he realised that this might only be his fancy.

'Can you negotiate with Saladin?' Eraclius asked.

Balian gave an empty laugh. 'I think I have exhausted all my stock with the Sultan. No, I think we had better put more faith in our legs than in our tongues at this point.'

Eraclius wiped his mouth quickly. 'Our wives and children? The treasures of the church?'

Balian stared at him for a long while in silence. 'I will not stop you seeking to protect those things if that is your wish, Patriarch.' His voice was cold.

'It is my wish.'

'And for yourself?' Balian continued. 'I presume you will do as I intend to. You will stay with your flock and succour them in their time of need.'

Eraclius looked from Balian to Jerome and back again. He licked his lips, gazed back at the advancing Saracens and returned his gaze to Balian. 'Of course, Lord Balian. Of course.'

He gestured to Simon and they rode back to the treasure.

'Do you really mean to stay?' Simon asked.

'For as long as possible,' he answered. He grasped Simon by the arm. 'Whatever my enemies may say of me they will not say I am a coward.'

As they hurried back along the line it became clear that the people at the back had now seen the Saracens. A dismal wailing began to break from the crowd. They had thought themselves safe, thought they had been delivered out of hell. Now they realised their long march had been for nothing. Yet despite their anguish, they forced their legs to quicken and their walk became a stumbling run.

'They will not be able to keep up this pace,' Eraclius said. He watched in horror as they sped past, a frightened, stumbling rabble.

He held his hands up high above his head.

'People of Jerusalem,' he cried, 'listen to me now.'

It took a while and many such cries but eventually the column slowed slightly and heads turned towards him.

'Have faith in the Lord God and his Son Jesus Christ,' he cried. 'You will be saved, you will reach Tyre before the infidels. But you will only do so if you remain disciplined. Do not become a mindless rabble. Do not run, do not push your fellow man. Walk quickly, walk more quickly than you have ever walked before. But do not run.'

Ten miles to the south, Saladin and al-Adil stood in their stirrups and saw their prey defenceless before their gaze.

CHAPTER 22
HARD DECISIONS
South of Tyre

Al-Adil ordered Khalid to lead his personal retinue closer in case he had swift need of them.

The rest of the vast army did not move.

'What will you do, brother?' al-Adil asked.

Saladin did not answer for a while.

His scouts had only just told him the refugees were close to the city. He had assumed that the gates would be open to receive them. His plan had been to swoop down when almost all had entered the city, leaving only fifty or so still streaming in. The defenders would be sure to leave the gates open for them.

That would be the moment for him to launch his attack.

Too many refugees would impede his horsemen; fifty or so would not.

If he timed it correctly his warriors would be able to secure the gates before the defenders could close them.

But the column of refugees had inexplicably slowed down.

Saladin shook his head in confusion.

They were still a mile from the walls. If the defenders of the city lifted their gaze from the refugees they would see his army. They might well decide not to open the gates at all.

'Curse these Franks,' he said. 'Why have they slowed?'

'I know not,' al-Adil said. 'But it makes our plan difficult.'

Saladin turned to two young men who sat on black stallions beside him.

'My sons,' he said. 'You see now, no matter how carefully a Sultan may plan, it is Allah who makes the final decisions.

'Instead of being a terrified mob, which would serve my purpose best, the Frankish refugees have become a disciplined body and stand between me and my goal. What would you advise?'

The eldest boy, al-Adfal, spoke first.

He pointed at the isthmus which led to the city. On either side of the battlements were marshy strands leading a sandy beach.

'I think you should send a couple of companies of horsemen to either side of the city, close to the shore,' he said.

'They can conceal themselves in the bullrushes. Even if they are seen from the city, the Franks will think them too far away to intervene. They will open the city for the refugees. As soon as they do our warriors can race for the gates and fight their way in.'

'It is an idea full of possibilities,' Saladin said.

He turned to his younger son.

'What do you say, Uthman?'

The younger son studied the field a moment longer.

'I think we should attack the refugees and slaughter them all,' he said.

'No,' said al-Adfal. 'To kill them would serve no purpose.'

'It would,' Uthman said. 'We would win the treasure from their churches and the Templars. And if the Franks inside Tyre see their people being killed they will surely open their gates.'

'Another idea full of possibilities,' said their father.

He turned to al-Adil. 'What do you say, brother?'

He shrugged. 'I think we should wait,' he answered. 'I do not think the commander of Tyre will open his gates once he has seen us. I believe he will wait until dark. Let us be patient and also wait until dark. Under cover of night we can move closer to the city and, when the gates open to allow in the refugees, we can attack according to our original plan.'

Saladin said nothing for long minutes. He had asked his sons' advice because he wanted to get them to think strategically. He also wanted to test them, to know who would be best suited to rule after his death. But now he regretted doing so. Both of their plans had some merit but both had serious flaws. He would have to try to reconcile the contrary views without either of his sons feeling they had lost face.

He sighed. Perhaps I'm foolish to believe they would think like al-Adil and me, he thought. We have years of experience; they have the hot blood of youth. Besides, they want to prove themselves, to me, to their uncle and to my warriors.

He sighed once again, still louder.

'Both of you have given me good advice,' he said at last. 'al-Adfal, I like the idea of the flanking movement and will adopt that. I like the idea of taking the treasure, Uthman and I will order this; although I have no wish to waste effort in killing old men and women.

'So, my sons, we will use both of your plans. But, as your uncle points out, the time to do it is when darkness falls. We must be patient.'

He spoke quickly to his captains and they went amongst the troops, telling them to rest and eat.

John, Bernard and Matthew watched proceedings with relief.

'I thought they meant to butcher the column,' John said.

Bernard shook his head. 'That is not the way of Saladin. He is said to be cruel when he deems it necessary but he prefers to show mercy if he can. I guess he must be thinking about the after-life.'

'Surely he will be better welcomed in their paradise if he slays Christians,' Matthew said.

'Not needlessly,' said a voice from behind them. They turned to see Khalid. He sat beside them. 'You Christians judge everyone by your own behaviour. If we were like you we would have slain everyone in Jerusalem when we took it. The streets would have run with blood as they did when the Christians captured it from us. Your forebears slaughtered without pity. Yet Sultan Saladin let your people go.'

'Not all of them,' Bernard said.

Khalid raised an eyebrow in question.

'My wife, my two children and my nephew were taken into captivity. No mercy was shown to them.'

'Yet you are free.'

John nodded. 'As you said, al-Adil is a man who admires courage. He freed the commoner knights.'

'And now you are his men.'

'Now we are his men.' John paused. 'Excellency, I would ask you about this. I accept that we owe duty to al-Adil. But does he expect us to fight against Christians? It would be wrong for us to do so.'

Khalid smiled. 'Wrong? But you Christians fight amongst yourselves all the time. Here in the Holy Land and, so I hear, in your homelands as well.'

'But we do not fight with Saracens against our brothers.'

'Do you not? That is certainly not the situation here in this past hundred years. Your Frankish barons have ever been ready to ally with us if it gave them advantage in a conflict with one of their fellow Christians.

'And have you never heard of the wars in Spain? Have you never heard of el-Cid? He will fight against men of any faith, just as it suits him.' He chuckled. 'El-Cid is a hero. But he is a hero both for the Christians and for the Muslims.'

'I am no hero, John said.

'Not yet,' Khalid said. 'But who knows what Allah plans for you?'

CHAPTER 23
THE GATES ARE SHUT
Tyre

Simon glanced back to the south, dreading to see the Saracen horsemen galloping towards them. To his astonishment, they had not moved. He called to Eraclius and Balian.

'God be praised,' Eraclius said. 'God has smitten the infidel, robbed him of all movement.'

'I think it more likely that Saladin has decided to halt his army,' said Balian.

'For what reason?' Eraclius asked.

'I don't know. But it will not be for our benefit.' Balian glanced at the column of refugees and beyond towards the walls of Tyre.

'I don't think he's given the slightest thought to the refugees. He is intent on taking the city.'

'But why is he waiting?'

'I suspect he is waiting until everyone has entered the city. No commander wants to fight a battle with a mob of people in the middle of the battlefield.'

'Then we should hurry.' Eraclius turned to Simon who pretended that he had not been listening. 'Simon, get the priests to the front of the column and be quick about it.'

As Simon turned, Balian held out a hand to halt him. 'I know you from somewhere.'

'Yes, my lord. I am Simon Ferrier, one of the commoners you

knighted at the siege.'

Balian nodded. 'Ah, yes. One of the two Englishmen.' He glanced around. 'Is your cousin here?'

'No my lord. He is with the captives.'

'He could not raise a ransom?'

'No, my lord.'

Balian held him in his gaze. 'Yet you were able to do so?'

'Yes, my lord. We had enough money for one but not for both. He begged me to go. I did so but only because I know I will be able to raise money for his ransom from his brother, Alan. They are estranged and John will not plead for aid from him. Alan is a captain in Prince Richard's army. He will accede to my request, I am certain.'

'You have thought it through well, Simon,' Balian said in a quiet voice.

'Yes, my lord.'

Balian nodded, slowly. Simon felt a churning in his stomach and was glad when Balian turned away.

He spent a frantic time trying to organise the priests and donkeys. Finally he managed it. He dismounted from his donkey and led the line of priests at a run towards the city, overtaking the exhausted refugees. His grooms ran beside him, whipping at the donkeys, cursing at the priests.

Finally, in a state of collapse, they reached the gate of Tyre.

It was shut against them.

'What is happening?' cried Eraclius as he hurried up with Balian. 'Why haven't you gone into the city?'

Simon swallowed hard. 'The gate is shut, my lord.'

Eraclius pulled his horse to a halt.

'Shut?'

'Yes my lord.'

Balian rode to the gate and pushed at it. It did not move. He hammered upon it with the pommel of his sword. No one answered.

'My lord,' said Jerome, pointing upwards.

Balian urged his horse towards Jerome and looked up to where he was pointing.

High above their heads a burly man leaned over the battlements and scrutinised them.

Balian stared at him for some moments, then raised his hand in greeting.

'My name is Balian, Lord of Ibelin,' he said. 'These people are refugees from Jerusalem. We seek shelter from the infidel.'

'So you're Balian,' the man said. 'The man who surrendered the Holy City to the filth of Satan. I wondered what you would be like.'

Eraclius exchanged a quick glance of disquiet with Jerome.

'Who am I addressing?' Balian called.

The man wiped his fingers across his nose. 'I am the commander of Tyre.'

'The last I heard, Reynaud of Sidon commanded here.'

'He has left to secure his castle at Beaufort.'

Balian frowned at this. He was a friend of Reynaud and knew he would not have left without good cause.

He stared at the man on the battlements. 'So who are you?' he asked.

'I am Conrad, son of William, the Marquis of Montferrat.'

Balian relaxed visibly. 'I know your father well, and your late brother. Tyre is in good hands.'

Conrad nodded.

Nobody said anything for a few moments more.

'Lord Conrad,' said Balian at last. 'Will you open the gates?'

'No.'

Eraclius' mouth opened wide in astonishment but for a moment no words came. 'What do you mean? There is a Saracen army not five miles away. You must let us in.'

'Must I?' Conrad answered. 'Who says I must. My concern is the defence of this city. We cannot accommodate or feed a horde of newcomers. Besides, if I open the gates the Saracens will try to enter the city.'

'But they are miles away, man.'

'Most of them, yes. But they have placed a force of horsemen to the north. A fisherman saw them from his boat. There may be others who are also hidden from us.'

The refugees outside the wall turned to the north, dreading to see Saracens hurtling towards them. All remained quiet.

'Then all the more reason for you to let us enter,' cried Balian.

'I will not. I will take you and your knights and men-at-arms but that is all.'

Simon's heart beat fast at Conrad's words.

'You would leave these people to the Saracens?' Balian said.

Conrad leant down towards him and shook his head. 'I do not do this gladly. But my concern is to keep the city safe. I have already sent a ship to the Pope telling him of the loss of the army at Hattin and the surrender of Jerusalem. Avenging armies from the west need the port of Tyre to remain in Christian hands.'

'But how will a few refugees jeopardise that?' cried Eraclius.

'I have told you,' said Conrad. 'Fighting men only. I will open the gates to none other.'

Balian gestured to Eraclius and Jerome and they rode a little way into the distance. Simon hesitated for a moment then hurried after them and placed himself next to the Patriarch.

'What shall we do?' Balian asked.

'We must get into the city,' said Eraclius.

'It is barred against us,' Balian said. 'I do not think this Conrad is a man likely to change his mind.'

'Then we are at the mercy of Saladin,' said Jerome.

'Not all of us,' said Balian. 'He has offered sanctuary to fighting men. Perhaps it would be best if they joined him to give him aid in the days ahead.'

'But that would be to desert the people,' cried Eraclius.

'I know,' Balian said. 'But it might be best for the kingdom in the long term. At any rate, we should let those who have been offered sanctuary the opportunity to take it.'

Eraclius stared at Balian. A look of contempt transformed his face. But before he could speak Balian placed his hand upon his shoulder.

'I will not go,' he said. 'I have decided to stay with the refugees.' He turned towards Jerome.

'I am your servant, lord,' Jerome said. 'Where you go, I go.'

'Can't the rest of the fighting men stay?' asked Eraclius.

'There are few of them with us,' Balian said. 'And of knights only Jerome and Simon here. I think those who can bear arms would be of more use in the city.'

'And if there are no soldiers amongst the refugees,' Jerome said, 'then perhaps Saladin may be more inclined to show mercy.'

Eraclius nodded, seeing the sense of this.

'But where will we go?' Simon asked.

'North,' said Balian. 'To Tripoli. And if that is already taken by the Saracens then on to Antioch.'

Eraclius sighed. 'What about the treasures of the church?'

'You must do with that as you see fit. If you send it into Tyre Conrad will make use of it to pay his men and to buy food.'

Eraclius thought for a moment. He shook his head. 'It is too precious for that. Too holy.'

'As you wish. But you should realise that the weight of it will slow us down.'

'It is my holy duty, Lord Balian.'

'As you say.'

Balian made his way back to the gate. He called up to Conrad and told him that he agreed with the plan. Then, summoning the others, he headed towards the huddle of refugees.

The light began to fail. As Balian approached them the refugees gathered up their possessions, ready to make their way to the city.

Balian raised his arm above his head.

'The commander of the city cannot take us,' he cried.

There was immediate consternation. People shouted aloud, some wept, others cursed. Heads began to turn towards the Saracen army.

Balian held his hand up. 'Conrad of Montferrat will allow only fighting men to enter the city. I know that this is dreadful news for the rest of us. But there is insufficient food in the city for all.'

Eraclius nodded. 'Besides, my people, you must realise that within hours, the infidel will launch an assault upon the city. You have survived one siege. Do not be eager to enter into a second.'

'But what will we do?' cried a woman. 'What will we do?'

'We will trust in God,' said Eraclius.

'And I will lead you north to safety,' said Balian. 'Let those fighting men who wish to go to Tyre leave now. Conrad will open a postern gate for you.

'The rest of you, gather your children and your possessions.

Outcasts

The Patriarch and I will lead you to safety.'

At that point there came a shriek from the very rear of the refugees. The Saracen army was marching towards them.

CHAPTER 24
KING GUY'S CONTEMPT
The Saracen camp near Tyre

A Saracen soldier hurried over to Saladin. 'Our spies within the city have sent us a message,' he said. He handed him a parchment.

Saladin read it and passed it to his brother. 'Bring me King Guy,' he told a soldier.

Khalid watched these proceedings with interest.

'Something is happening,' he said. 'Come with me, my friends.'

John, Bernard and Matthew followed Khalid towards where the Sultan and his brother stood deep in conversation.

A few minutes later two soldiers returned with a man dressed in costly garments.

He was tall and slim, with thick, flowing hair and, despite the months of captivity, neat trimmed beard. His face was set and cold. His lips were thin and bloodless.

John stared at him in surprise.

'That looks like the king.' he said, tugging on Bernard's sleeve. 'But I thought that all the nobles were killed at the battle.'

'That's him,' said Bernard in a weary voice. 'That is Guy, King of Jerusalem. He was one of a handful to survive the battle. I doubt my wife's brother was so lucky.'

Matthew scowled at the king as he strode past them without a glance.

Saladin beckoned King Guy towards him and pointed out the mass of refugees crowding in front of the locked gate of the city.

'The commander of the city has allowed only fighting men into the city,' Saladin said. 'He has refused the rest of the people entry.'

Guy did not reply.

Saladin's eyes narrowed. 'What would you have me do?'

'I care not,' Guy answered.

Saladin and al-Adil exchanged looks.

'But you are their king,' al-Adil said.

'They are only peasants,' Guy said. 'I do not concern myself with the likes of them.'

'They are not peasants,' John said. 'These are people with enough wealth to buy their freedom. The peasants have been taken as slaves.'

Guy turned towards him. His lips closed tight and his eyes narrowed.

'Who are you?' he asked.

'Sir John Ferrier,' John answered.

Guy looked John up and down, very deliberately. He turned away as he spoke, 'Let Saladin take those people as slaves, also.'

Saladin took a step towards Guy. 'But you are their king,' he said. 'You are their protector.'

'I have no army with which to protect them,' Guy answered. 'So you must do with them as you wish.'

Saladin and al-Adil walked away a pace and conferred. At length they returned.

'We have no more need of slaves,' said Saladin.

Al-Adil nodded. 'The slavers will not thank us for flooding the market still more.'

Guy shrugged with indifference.

'Because of this,' said Saladin, 'we shall let the refugees go north and seek sanctuary in the empire.'

'As you wish.' Guy crossed his arms and said nothing further.

The brothers watched him for a moment longer, their faces showing incredulity at his lack of concern. Eventually al-Adil touched his brother on the arm and the brothers walked away.

They spoke together for a moment and then Saladin summoned his captains and gave swift orders.

Within minutes the Saracen army began to march towards the city.

Guy turned and stared at the three friends.

'You say you are knights. How is that possible? Your speech and your bearing are uncouth. Why do you ape your betters in this way?'

'We do not ape our betters,' John said. 'We are knights.'

'You are an Englishman by the sound of your speech.'

John nodded.

'I cannot think my kinsman King Henry would knight such as you.'

'He didn't,' John said. 'My friend Bernard and I were knighted by Balian of Ibelin at the siege of the Holy City.'

King Guy laughed.

'So that explains it. Two apes knighted by another ape.'

He leaned closer, his face hardening.

'Let me remind you, peasants. I am King of Jerusalem, not Balian of Ibelin.'

'But he knighted us, nonetheless.'

Guy scowled.

'He did. What bad fortune I cannot undo it.'

He gave a cold smile. 'But do not think his knighting of you will count for anything. Do not think it makes you the equal of your betters.'

He strode away.

'He's the king?' John said.

'Yes,' Bernard answered. 'But only because Queen Sibilla lusted after him. He's a man of little worth.'

'Which is probably why he treats you in the same way,' said Khalid as he walked towards them.

He clapped John on the shoulder. 'Don't look so despondent. You do not need to have any dealings with such men as Guy of Lusignan. You are in the retinue of al-Adil now.'

'Yes,' John answered. 'And we're about to ride down Christian refugees.'

'Then let us hope that the fools flee while they still have a chance,' said Khalid.

'Why do you care about the refugees?' Matthew asked.

'I don't particularly,' Khalid answered. 'I just don't want them to get in the way of our troops.

A trumpet sounded and the army rose to its feet.

'The signal to attack,' said Khalid.

'But I thought we were going to attack at nightfall,' Bernard said.

'We were. But the refugees are leaving.'

'Leaving?'

'Yes.' Khalid shook his head. 'Christians are strange. Your people are in the greatest of need but the commander of the city has refused them entry.'

'I still don't understand why,' Bernard said.

Khalid shrugged.

'I suspect he is ruled by his head and not his heart. He fears to take in those too frail to defend the city.'

'This is no Holy Land,' John said, bitterly.

'Not while it remains in Crusader hands,' said Khalid. 'But it will be. With the help of Saladin.'

'And the ordinary people are left to pay the bill,' Matthew said.

Khalid laughed. 'Is it not always so, in whatever empire?

He clapped his hands and some grooms led four horses towards them. 'Mount up Sir Knights. May Allah keep you safe.'

CHAPTER 25
THE MORNING STAR
On the Road to Baghdad

Habib stifled a yawn. It had been a long night, with the boys chattering and the little girl grizzling. And then there had been the woman, Agnes, to distract him. He pulled back the curtain of the howdah and peered out

The moon was full and close to it shone the morning star, bright and glittering. They were the only signs of night still visible. He loved the morning star and thought its beauty the greatest in the heavens.

He relieved himself in his night-jar, pushed the stopper firm in its neck and readjusted himself.

He glanced across at the young woman sleeping opposite him. The moonlight shone upon her face and he examined it. She was in truth a real beauty. Every feature seemed to fit exactly right, neither too large nor too small. If an angel were to fall to earth she would look like this woman.

Best of all, she did not realise her own beauty. How could she for she would never have seen her own face as clearly as he could. And even if she did he guessed that there she possessed an innocence, a simple charm which would not countenance the thought that she was anything more than slightly pretty.

He licked his lips at the thought. Such innocence added a thousand times to her desirability. He was sure that his master would think the same.

He grew miserable for a moment, thinking of how the Caliph would be able to bed her whenever he wanted. A little fantasy developed in his mind of how one day the beautiful Christian would grow frightened of the Caliph and come to him, Habib the fat, and throw herself upon him for comfort. He would be like a father to her, like a brother. He would sooth and comfort her, whispering soft words in her ear, stroking her hair and her face. And then, when she was calm and beguiled, he would entice her to his bed and act like a beast upon her.

Lost in these dreams he did not realise that she was watching him watch her. He blinked quickly, wondering how long she had been watching and if she could divine any inkling of his thoughts.

'You've been watching me,' she said.

He smiled. 'You are a beautiful woman,' he said. 'In the sky shines the morning star and she too is beautiful. I delight to look upon her crystal gleam as I delight to look upon you. An old man should be allowed his pleasures.'

She looked at him dubiously.

'Where are you taking us? Really?'

'I told you, to Baghdad.'

She frowned. 'What for?'

'I told you in Damascus. I have bought you for the Caliph?'

'I don't believe you.'

He shrugged. 'That is your privilege.'

She pulled back the curtain of the howdah. 'It is morning,' she said. 'Did we journey through the night?'

'We did. These lands are on the border of my master's and those of Saladin. They are infested with robbers who have no respect for Caliph, Sultan or for private property. It is best to hurry through such lands.'

She gave him a thoughtful look. 'Are you telling me that they would attack a servant of the Caliph?'

Habib rubbed his nose. 'Enough of your impertinence. Thieves are thieves everywhere and some show as little deference to their betters as you do.'

She smiled to herself and closed her eyes.

She is a clever one, Habib thought as he stared at her.

He licked his lips, congratulating himself once again upon his choice.

He made his living by his sound judgement in choosing women to allure and satisfy his master. But more than this, he used the women he bought as pieces in the deadly games played by the Caliph's servants within the Palace.

When he brought a new woman of consummate beauty, one who gave his master an abundance of pleasure, his own power and influence within the Palace would grow. A woman who bored the Caliph or fell out of favour would cause his power to diminish.

More than that, the women knew that he was a power himself within the Palace and would tell him gossip and secrets if he would only bend his lips to the Caliph to remind him of their particular charms. The Caliph could not be expected to remember the two hundred women in his harem. He relied upon Habib to give him this information. And so Habib would advance his own favourites and put aside those who would not ally themselves with him.

For thirty years he had played this role with the present Caliph and with his father before him. He had walked the traps and snares of the harem and the Palace like no one else before him and had always chosen women who would serve his purpose as well as pleasing the Caliph.

His mood of self-congratulation soured at that point. He had failed with one, of course, and now she was proving irksome, even dangerous to him.

'What is Baghdad?' asked a voice close to his ear.

It was the older of the two boys, the half-breed.

'Have you been listening to my talk with your aunt?'

'I did not know it was a secret.'

Habib rubbed his hand upon the boy's head. 'It wasn't. No need to worry.'

He returned his thoughts to the harem and the Palace.

'What is Baghdad?' the boy asked again.

Habib clipped him around the ear.

'Are you so ignorant that you do not know about Baghdad?' he said.

'Is it a man or a country or a castle or a town?'

Habib raised his eyes to heaven. 'Infidels,' he murmured. 'No better than the beasts in the field.'

He turned towards Claude-Yusuf. 'What is the centre of your body?' he asked.

'My belly.'

'Idiot.' He thumped the boy in the chest. 'It is here, your heart.'

Claude-Yusuf rubbed his chest.

'Well,' continued Habib, 'Baghdad is the heart of the entire world. It is the capital of the Muslim Empire, the source of all learning and civilisation, the fountain of wealth and glory and pleasure.'

'Then how come I've never heard of it?'

'Because you're a pig. An ignorant, Christian pig. A Frank who should not be allowed to set foot in the Holy Places of my people.'

'If that's the case then why are you taking me to Baghdad?'

Outcasts

Habib turned towards Claude-Yusuf. He was about to answer but found himself smiling instead. He tapped the boy on the head. 'You have a brain in there, half-breed. That must come from your mother.'

He stroked his beard. 'I am taking you to Baghdad because you are a slave. You are as much the possession of my master as is his ox or his pet monkey. More, in fact, for his monkey gives him pleasure. You, however, will sicken him.'

Claude-Yusuf did not answer for a moment.

'How long will it take us to get to Baghdad?' he asked.

'Three weeks.'

'Plenty of time for me to escape then,' he said. 'Or for my father to come to rescue us. Or Uncle Bernard and Sir John and Sir Simon.'

'But look,' Habib said, drawing back the curtain. 'We are in the middle of the desert. How on earth will your family be able to find us?'

They halted at midday and the guards lit a fire and prepared a meal.

Dawud stared moodily at the little family. 'I hope you're right about the woman,' he said. 'She looks too old to me.'

'Nonsense,' Habib answered. 'Am not I the consummate judge of my master's lusts? He is getting tired of fresh meat. He will relish this little bundle. All big eyes and hammering heart but with a tongue which will dance round his mouth like a cobra. Look at her thighs man; imagine them crushing him as she screams with pleasure. Imagine his pleasure. And how grateful he will be to the two servants who brought him this choicest of dishes.'

'And the favourite? How will she view it?'

Habib's face clouded over.

At that moment, Eleanor, playing with her brother, fell and twisted her ankle.

She screamed with pain and distress. Agnes was sitting by the fire, chewing on some bread but she rose immediately and hurried over.

She was not as quick as Dawud, however. He took two steps towards the little girl and picked her up. This only made her scream still louder and hit him on the shoulder.

In a moment Gerard had sprung at Dawud and began to kick at his shins.

Startled by this attack, he flung out his hand and slapped the boy around the head, knocking him to the ground. Eleanor screamed still more loudly at this and Dawud clapped his hand upon her mouth to quieten her.

Agnes reached him within seconds, beating on his chest and grabbing her daughter from him.

Habib looked on with astonishment and then roared with laughter.

Dawud was furious. He shook his fist in Agnes' face, cursing her. She leaned back in fright then stepped forward in fury, shoving him away with her free hand.

'I meant no harm,' Dawud cried. 'You're lucky I don't slit the child's throat.'

Agnes froze. She darted a glance at Habib who merely shrugged.

'If you do that I shall tell the Caliph,' Claude-Yusuf said.

Dawud turned to him in amazement. 'What did you say?'

'I shall tell the Caliph. I shall tell him that you slit the throat of one of his slaves. Eleanor is not your property, she belongs to him. He will be most angry at you.'

Dawud shook his head in disbelief. Habib laughed once more and clapped his hands with pleasure at the boy's response.

Dawud frowned and walked towards Habib, his face confused. 'I only meant to comfort the child,' he whispered.

'I'm sure you did, old friend, but these Franks are foolish and quick to take offence.'

'The boy is clever, though,' Dawud said. 'Did you see how he threatened me?'

He stroked his beard. 'I did. I was impressed, most impressed.

'And I also saw how the young vixen was very quick to fight for her child. I believe I may have chosen a woman who will not only please the Caliph but may well put a certain someone's nose out of joint.'

Dawud shook his head. 'Be careful, Habib. Be very careful.'

CHAPTER 26
CONRAD OF MONTFERRAT
Tyre

John, Bernard and Matthew climbed into their saddles.

'I will not kill a Christian,' John said.

'I don't think they expect you to,' Bernard said.

'Whether they expect it or not I will not kill a Christian.'

Khalid frowned at John.

'Bernard is correct,' he said in a weary tone. 'Al-Adil expects a show from you, to prove to the troops that he can win the hearts of all, even Franks. All he asks is that you gallop with me and look blood-thirsty. He does not expect you to kill any of your people.'

'I might, though,' Matthew said half to himself. 'If I see any of the bastards who stoned me from the city.'

Khalid laughed.

'The leper has good reason for such venom,' I think.

'He is not a leper,' John said. 'He is my friend.'

'And I am yours,' Khalid replied. He leaned forward and tapped John upon the knee. 'But do not presume upon it.'

He raised his hand to lead them towards the plain. They trotted past the marching infantrymen and took their place towards the front of the cavalry.

Khalid turned and smiled at them.

'Come my friends, stay close to me. I will keep you safe, God willing.'

The horsemen began an ordered advance across the plain. When they were a couple of furlongs from the walls, Saladin raised his hand and they halted.

John looked and saw that most of the refugees were hurrying north, away from the city. Two score or more remained, all young men. A postern opened in the walls and a party of soldiers marched out to guard the door while the young men made haste into the city.

They barely made it.

The Saracen horsemen who had been hiding on either side of the city now raced down upon the postern. The soldiers from the city saw them and broke, every man for himself, pushing and panicking, clogging up the door.

A huge cheer rose from the Saracen army. They whistled and called, urging their comrades to greater speed, as if they were watching a race.

At the gate a large man forced himself to the front of the mob. He beat the panicking soldiers with his sword until he had established better order. They appeared more scared of him than of the Saracens so they quietened and filed through the postern.

The last man to enter the city was the large man who had restored order. Just as the gate was closing he turned and spat towards the Saracen horsemen in a gesture of defiance.

'If that is the commander,' Khalid said, 'we will have a battle on our hands.'

Saladin clearly thought the same. He scowled.

The race for the postern had been lost.

Saladin clicked his fingers and sent a herald a hundred yards forward. The herald waited until a group of figures appeared upon the battlement.

'I desire to speak with the commander of the city,' the herald cried. His voice was clear and melodious and carried across the city and the whole of the Saracen army.

'I am the commander of the city,' called one of the figures. It was the large man who had marshalled the panicking troops at the postern.

'My name is Conrad, son of William of Montferrat,' he continued. 'I lead the defence on behalf of the people and commune of Tyre.'

John saw Saladin and al-Adil exchange looks.

'Do you know him?' John asked Khalid.

Khalid shook his head. 'He is new come to these lands. His brother, William Longsword, was married to Queen Sibilla but died ten years since.'

'Their father, the Marquis, lives still,' said Bernard. 'He has eaten in my inn. He has a big laugh and an even bigger appetite.'

'He is not laughing now,' said Khalid. 'He was captured at Hattin and is forced to spend his time in the company of King Guy who he loathes. I have seen him. His face is growing bleaker by the day.'

The herald had turned towards Saladin. He gestured him to continue.

'My master,' he called, 'Righteous of the Faith, Sword of God, Lord of the Hosts of Islam, the Sultan Saladin, acknowledges you.'

Conrad did not deign to reply.

'The Sultan has marched his army to this city,' continued the herald. 'This is the army which has destroyed the forces of the Franks, which has vanquished the Orders of the Temple and the Hospital of St John and thrown down their fortifications. This is the army which has conquered the Holy City of Jerusalem.'

At these words the Saracen army growled with pleasure as if it was a hound being stroked.

'Captive at our camp,' the herald continued, 'are the great lords and captains of the Franks. Languishing there are King Guy, his brother Almaric, Gerard de Ridefort, Grand-Master of the Temple, Humphrey of Toron and Marquis William of Montferrat.'

He paused at this name and Saladin and al-Adil shot quick glances up to the battlements to check Conrad's reaction.

He gave away nothing.

'There are other great lords, too numerous to mention,' said the herald. 'One who is not with them is Reynald of Châtillon. He died under the sword of Sultan Saladin in payment for his wickedness.'

'Enough of this,' Conrad cried. 'Enough of your words. What do you want?'

'The Sultan wants Tyre,' the herald replied simply.

'He cannot have it.'

The herald shook his head, as if in sorrow. 'If you surrender the city, the merciful Lord Saladin will allow all of your people to go free for a ransom of five dinars a person. All weapons are to be given up and all of your soldiers are to leave the city.'

'And if we don't surrender?'

The herald paused. 'Then the city will be destroyed brick by brick, your soldiers slain and your women and children sold in the slave markets of Africa. You, however, Conrad of Montferrat, will be crucified, like your prophet.'

A stunned silence fell upon the city.

'You have an hour to decide,' said the herald.

CHAPTER 27
ROBBED AND REFUSED
Tyre, Niphin and Tripoli

The refugees collected their possessions and headed north along the coast. They wept as they trudged, bitter at their betrayal.

'We must hurry them,' Balian said. 'Saladin will not hold off for much longer.'

'Night is coming,' Jerome said. 'They may stray in the dark.'

'That's true.' Balian smiled at his comrade. 'Will you light the way, old friend?'

Jerome and Simon lit torches and rode alongside the surging mob. As the light began to fail the people moved ever more slowly.

Jerome and Simon exchanged worried glances.

'I could use my guards,' Simon said.

He realised it was not for him to suggest this and quickly rectified his blunder. 'If my lord, Eraclius agrees, of course.'

'Anything to get out of the way of a battle,' Eraclius cried. 'Give torches to your guards. I will take a torch and lead the way.'

'And I will be the rearguard' said Balian.

Half a mile into their march Simon heard screams of terror from up ahead. He drew his sword and whipped his donkey forward. A furlong ahead he saw the refugees frozen with terror. A long line of Saracen horsemen were racing out of the sea-mists towards them.

Simon quailed, his stomach cold and hard as a stone. Then he mastered himself and rode in front of the people, brandishing his sword at the Saracens.

'Salaam, hero,' their commander said, waving his hand extravagantly. His men laughed and they swept past, ignoring the refugees, hurrying towards the city.

'That was courageous,' said a voice from behind him. It was Jerome. He rode past Simon and raised his sword in salute to him.

The refugees stumbled on for a few hours longer until their strength began to fail. Balian called a halt. The refugees slumped to the ground. Despite their fear they slept until dawn.

When they awoke they could hear the clamour of battle from far behind. The Saracens had attacked Tyre but it was clear from the noise that they had not yet taken it. Balian allowed a short time for the refugees to eat and drink and then led them onwards to the north.

The pattern of this day was repeated for the following six. It began to seem like they would remain on this road for all eternity.

But on the sixth day they halted twelve miles south of the city of Tripoli to rest and take their noon meal

Huddled against the coast to their left was a small town surrounded with low mud-brick walls. Beyond this, hard against the sea, Simon saw a peninsula behind a deep moat. High battlements rose above the moat and beyond this he could see the towers of a castle.

He watched as the draw-bridge was lowered and the portcullis raised. A party of horsemen in chain-mail trotted over the bridge and headed towards them.

'The Count of Tripoli must have heard of our progress,' Eraclius said. 'No doubt these men have been sent to escort us to his city.'

'No doubt,' Balian said.

The horsemen began to pick up speed. Soon they were at full gallop. As they closed upon the refugees the horsemen swept out their swords and bellowed terrible war-cries.

Simon instinctively drew out his sword but Balian grabbed his hand to stay him. In moments the horsemen had reached them.

A few of the refugees tried to flee and a dozen were hacked down.

The leader of the horsemen drew rein in front of the refugees and looked them up and down.

'Who leads you?' he cried, brandishing his sword above his head. 'Speak and I may save your miserable skins.'

Balian urged his horse towards the horseman.

He pulled off his helmet and stared at Balian.

He was a man in his forties, and his face was like a skull, his yellowing skin stretched taut over his bones. His eyes were those of a feral cat.

'Who are you?' thundered Balian. 'Who dares to attack and slay poor Christians?'

'I am the Baron Raymond of Niphin,' the man answered. His voice was low and full of menace. 'You travel across my lands without permission. There is a price for such an act.'

'What price?' said Balian. 'Death?'

The Baron shrugged and indicated the corpses on the ground.

'For these, obviously. For the rest, let us see how things transpire.'

His eyes strayed to the packs upon the priests' donkeys.

Balian struggled to master his rage.

'I am Balian, Lord of Ibelin,' he said. 'I am good friend to your lord, Raymond, Count of Tripoli.'

'Not any more, you aren't. He's dead.'

'Dead?' Balian looked at Jerome.

'And not in battle either, as a Count should.' The Baron laughed. 'He died of a cough.'

Balian's bowed his head, shaken by this news.

'So who rules in Tripoli now?' Jerome asked.

'The old man's godson, Raymond of Antioch; the milk-sop.'

Balian could not hide a groan.

'It is to Tripoli that we are headed,' Eraclius said. 'I presume that the new Count has asked you to lead us there.'

'I don't care what the Count wants,' the Baron answered. 'He's a craven wet-the-bed. I do not consider him my lord.'

He placed his sword against Eraclius' throat.

'But I do care for something. Your money.'

Eraclius shook his head. 'The money belongs to the church, to our Saviour.'

'Not any more, friend,' said the Baron. 'It belongs to me.'

The Baron turned to his men, pointing out the baggage which contained the wealth of the Holy Sepulchre and more. They climbed off their horses, grinning at the prospect of such wealth.

Simon turned towards Eraclius, waiting for his instructions.

Eraclius' mind worked fast. He pulled a bottle of wine from his saddle-bag and sipped at it. When he had drunk his fill he passed it to Jerome who took it with surprise.

Eraclius chuckled slightly to himself.

'What are you laughing at?' Baron Raymond demanded.

'Nothing,' Eraclius answered. 'Nothing at all.'

The Baron pushed his horse closer to the Patriarch. 'I demand you tell me what you are laughing at.'

Eraclius shook his head. 'My son, you really do not wish to know.'

The Baron drew a knife and brandished it in front of Eraclius.

'I really do.'

Eraclius stared at the knife and nodded. 'I laugh because what you do is futile,' he said quietly.

'Futile?'

'Yes. The first kings of Jerusalem, Godfrey and Baldwin, laid dreadful curses upon this treasure. Any man who stole it would be struck with leprosy in this life and face eternal damnation in the next.'

The Baron turned and stared at the treasure.

'Why else is it still with me?' Eraclius continued, softly. 'Why else would Saladin not have stolen it for himself?'

The Baron urged his horse away from Eraclius who now gazed upon him with a faint look of pity.

'What about the other stuff?' the Baron cried. 'That can't be cursed?'

'Not by the Kings of Jerusalem,' said Eraclius. 'But if you take it you shall surely taste the torments of hell.'

He stared at Eraclius, considering his words. The features on his face grew rigid, making his face look even more like a skull.

He turned to his followers. 'Leave the priests' bags. They're cursed. Take everything from the rest.'

His soldiers went about the refugees, forcing them to give up all their precious, hoarded treasures. After an hour they had only worked their way down half the line.

Baron Raymond lost patience. He called to his men and they plunged into the crowd. They returned, each carrying three or four screaming children.

'These little ones die,' the Baron called. 'Unless you all bring your riches and place them here, at my feet.'

Silence descended upon the crowd. For a moment nobody moved. Then a young woman stepped forward and dropped a handful of coins and a brooch at the Baron's feet.

'Is one of these whelps yours?' the Baron asked, indicating the children.

The woman shook her head. 'My child died on the march,' she said, 'and my husband in the siege.'

She returned to the line.

An old man stepped forward and emptied a purse of gold and silver on the coins. He stared at the Baron and shook his head before returning to his place.

Eraclius' wife climbed from her horse and placed a small chest beside the woman's coins. She removed her rings and necklace and dropped them there.

Slowly, without a sound, the rest of the refugees followed suit.

They reached the city of Tripoli as the evening came and with it a fierce wind from off the sea.

Balian, Eraclius, Jerome and Simon approached the gate. Eraclius muttered a prayer.

Balian lent upon the wall. The journey had been far worse than he had feared.

Jerome hammered upon the gate.

A light was uncovered in one of the towers on either side.

'What do you want?' came a nervous cry.

'We are refugees from Jerusalem,' Balian cried. 'I am Balian of Ibelin and the Patriarch of Jerusalem rides with me.'

'Wait there.'

The men exchanged looks. Sanctuary at last.

'We should get the old and frail in first,' Balian told Eraclius.

'What about the church's treasure? It is at risk out here.'

'The old and frail first,' repeated Balian. 'If necessary we can ask Count Raymond to send men to guard the treasure.'

'I'd rather we don't alert anyone to it.'

'As you wish. But, Eraclius, your hoard will stay here until the vulnerable are safe inside.' He glanced at the sky. 'I think a storm may be coming.'

They heard the sharp sound of a grate in a postern door being opened.

'Is that you, Balian?' A young man, not even in his twenties, peered out of the door.

Balian nodded. 'It's good to see you, Raymond. I hear that you are now Count of Tripoli.'

'Yes. And what a terrible time to have this thrust upon me.' He paused. 'You have the Patriarch with you?'

'Yes. And hundreds upon hundreds of refugees.'

'You are welcome, Balian, and any knights among you. But I can't let in anybody else.'

'What?'

'I can't. Saladin is a friend of Tripoli and to my father in Antioch. If he hears that I am giving sanctuary to so many he may cease to be a friend.'

'He won't be a friend for much longer,' Balian said. 'Saladin is bent on destroying every Crusader state.'

Raymond groaned. 'I know. What are we to do?'

'One thing we can do is to stand together. If we are disunited then Saladin's victory will come swiftly. If he hears that you have refused us help he will laugh with joy. We are only strong if we support each other.'

'But what offer of support do you bring? Old men, old women, sick children.'

'Yes, and Christians every one,' cried Eraclius.

'You are welcome, Your Worship,' Raymond said quickly. 'You may stay.'

'I'm not sure I want to,' cried Eraclius. 'Show mercy damn it or I shall beg God to show no mercy to you.'

Raymond whimpered.

'We cannot take them, my lord,' said a voice behind Raymond. 'You must deny them.'

'I would give you sanctuary,' Raymond whispered. 'But my captains tell me not to.'

'But you are the Count,' said Balian.

'But I'm from Antioch. The people of Tripoli have accepted me but they are doubtful. I cannot go against them.

'Lick-spittle,' cried Eraclius. He raised his hand above his head and muttered a curse upon Raymond. 'You will not remain Count of Tripoli for long,' he told him.

Raymond's hand went to his mouth.

'These people need shelter,' said Balian. 'A storm is threatening.'

'I will give you food,' Raymond said. 'That's as much as I can do.'

Eraclius and Balian looked at each other in astonishment.

'Then do that at the very least,' Balian cried.

Raymond nodded and disappeared from view.

'What a tragedy Raymond has died,' Balian said. 'My old friend would not have treated us as his godson has done.'

'Count Raymond was always too fond of the Saracen,' Eraclius said. 'But you are right in this respect. He would not have seen the people suffer at his gates in this manner.'

Balian turned and looked at the refugees.

'Shall I tell them?'

'No, my friend,' Eraclius said. 'We need you to lead us on to safety. We shall have to go to Antioch, or even beyond, to the Empire. The people need to keep their faith in you. The bad news will come better from an old, tired priest.'

He walked away into the darkness.

A few minutes later a loud, keening wail of despair rose from the refugees and echoed against the walls.

CHAPTER 28
THE PALACE OF THE CALIPH
Baghdad

Agnes awoke from a drowsy slumber. On the couch opposite the children were twitching in their sleep.

She groaned. She had tried to keep a check on the long days of this ceaseless journey but was no longer sure how long it had been. She realised that she had not seen her husband for weeks and weeks but could not be more certain than that.

Habib snored beside her, his head lolling against her neck. She reached out and pushed his head away gently. She did not want to wake him. His endless talk was beginning to drive her to despair.

She pulled open the curtain.

It was dawn. The sky to the east was a pale grey. A faint smudge of red lay upon the horizon like blood upon a wound. As she watched, it seemed to bubble, a flaccid shape that only gradually resolved itself into the morning sun. The sky turned from grey to an ever-deepening blue. Above the sun a tide of red surged up, painting the blue a delicate shade which made her heart lighten.

The sun heaved itself clear of the horizon. A light flashed on the land in front of her. She turned to look at it and gasped.

Spread before her was a vast city, white and golden, thronged with domes of every colour, pierced by towers and minarets.

Baghdad. The capital of the Muslim world.

Habib stirred, gave a huge yawn and even huger belch. He

saw Agnes looking through the curtain and poked his head out beside her.

'Baghdad,' he cried. 'Now you will see the wonders of a great city.'

'Are we here?' Eleanor asked, as she had every morning of the trek.

'We are, darling,' Agnes said.

'Will we have to stay on this camel?' Eleanor asked.

Agnes turned to Habib. 'Can we walk from here?'

'Of course. There is no better way to enter the city.'

He shouted to the driver. The camel halted and, with great groans, lowered itself to the ground. The driver opened the curtain and helped Agnes and Eleanor down. Gerard and Claude-Yusuf leapt down beside them.

'Brave boys,' Habib said. 'Such brave boys.'

Claude-Yusuf looked at him with distaste.

The camel behind also stopped. Dawud climbed down, munching on a piece of bread.

'At last,' he said. 'My backside is as rough as a date palm.'

'It matches your face then,' Habib said.

Dawud ignored him, staring at the beautiful spectacle before them.

'Have you ever seen anything like this, boys?' he asked.

'Never,' Claude-Yusuf said. 'I thought that Jerusalem was the biggest city in the world.'

Dawud chuckled. 'Jerusalem is dwarfed by the Round City.'

'Why's it called that?' Gerard asked.

'Because it is built as a huge circle with the Mosque in the centre.'

'Next to the palace,' Habib said.

'A palace,' said Claude-Yusuf. 'Does a king live there?'

'A king and more than a king. The palace belongs to the Caliph who is master of the entire Muslim world.'

'Is he more important than Saladin?' Gerard asked.

Habib paused. Why did children ask such difficult questions?

'He is in the eyes of God and in the hearts of the people,' Habib said. 'He has fewer soldiers than Saladin; at the moment.'

Gerard and Claude-Yusuf lost interest at this news. They knew full well that a prince with few soldiers was not as powerful as a prince with many.

They strolled through streets which were beginning to fill with people. Most were too engrossed in their own business to pay any attention to them but those who had time to spare watched the westerners with idle curiosity.

Agnes, on the other hand, stared back at them with fascination. In Jerusalem she had been used to seeing a variety of people, all hailing from different places. Yet even this had not prepared her for the universe that was Baghdad.

Most faces were similar to the Muslims of her own country. In addition, there were traders from Africa, merchants from India, Northmen from Scandinavia, Bedouin from the deserts and, fascinating to behold, people with narrow eyes and yellow skin from the unimaginable steppes to the east.

Claude-Yusuf and Gerard turned and stared with every step they took, astonished at the faces, exhilarated by the voices.

'This is a wonderful place, mama,' Gerard called. 'I like it here.'

'He feels the blessings of Allah,' Habib said with a smile.

'Look at all the food,' Eleanor said. 'It's so pretty.'

They had reached a huge bazaar, its stalls packed with the

produce of the world. The colours were as bright as flowers, the scent a rich melange which sent their heads spinning. A few alleyways stank of rotting meat and vegetables but most were clean and fresh with a great many edged with narrow channels filled with running water.

At length the streets became wider and less crowded. Date palms and lemon trees grew at intervals and the buildings were larger and more grand. They left behind houses and shops and walked past mansions, public buildings and opulent gardens.

Finally, they approached a vast open space with a beautiful mosque on one side and, on the other, a large complex made of sand coloured brick decorated with friezes and elaborate facades. High above their heads was a huge emerald dome which looked too weighty for the walls to hold.

A large paved courtyard contained bowers of roses, a string of fountains and well-cut lawns. Peacocks strutted and beautiful women strolled.

'What is this place?' Agnes asked.

'It is the palace of the Caliph, al-Nasir,' said Habib.

'The palace?' Agnes said. 'Why have we come to the palace?'

Habib frowned. 'You do not think I have brought you across the desert to be a common-place servant? You, my dear, are going to join the harem of the Caliph.'

Agnes' hand went to her mouth. 'You cannot be serious. I thought you were jesting.'

'Such delightful innocence,' Habib said, reaching out for her hand and stroking it gently.

'The Caliph has many women and many wives,' he continued. 'One of my tasks is to find him women of beauty and wit who will entertain and enthral him.'

She blinked. 'Then why on earth did you choose me?'

Habib chuckled. 'Because you are the sort of woman who asks me such a question. Because you are the sort of woman who is not aware of her quality. The Caliph has vain and foolish beauties a-plenty. He is getting tired of them. I know what he likes and what he needs. Someone like you.'

He held her by the arm and gently stroked her cheek. 'You are beautiful, Agnes, but you do not realise it. I imagine that you were a pretty enough young girl but you are one of those lucky females who gain beauty as they grow more mature. Like a promising, tight little rose-bud opens up and becomes a rose of surpassing beauty. Many petals, many layers, every one soft and gorgeous. Yet guarded by thorns which deal out exquisite pain to those who make a grab at them.' He chuckled.

'But I'm married.'

Habib laughed. 'Even a Caliph can't have everything. Still, you won't need to be broken in.'

Agnes turned away, shame reddening her cheeks.

Gerard saw and hurried to her side.

'What about my children?' Agnes asked.

'That is not for me to decide,' said Habib. 'They may go as house slaves or work the fields. The older one is clever. The Caliph may want him for a eunuch.'

'No.' Agnes turned, horrified that Claude-Yusuf may have heard. If he did, he gave no indication of it.

Habib shrugged. 'It was you who asked me to bring them.'

'Don't let this old fool alarm you,' said Dawud. 'He talks of eunuchs only because people mistake him for one.' He squeezed his friend's cheek. 'But his old friends know that he is quite the contrary, quite the old goat in fact.'

'Are you going to promise that he will not be made a eunuch?' Habib said.

'Of course not. But whatever happens to the boys will not be worse than being left in Damascus for some filthy Turk to buy them.'

Habib grinned and turned to Agnes.

'Dawud was a slave of the Turks as a child,' he explained.

'Do Muslims make slaves of Muslims?' Claude-Yusuf asked.

'The Caliph does,' said Dawud. 'If his servants become too arrogant and too fat.'

'Ignore whatever Dawud has to say,' he said. 'He was born a Greek,' he said.

'A Greek?' said Claude-Yusuf. 'Like Alexius?'

'Who is Alexius?' Habib frowned irritably.

'He is our friend. He is descended from an Emperor.'

'I care not for the Greeks nor for Emperors.' He leaned closer.

'Dawud was stolen as a child by the Turks. He hates the Turks with a consuming fury.'

'I thought every Muslim was a brother,' Claude-Yusuf said.

The two men laughed.

'Why do you Christians always think this?' Habib asked. 'After all your own faith is split between Franks and Greeks, Syrians and Copts.'

'It is the same in Islam,' said Dawud. 'The Sunnis hate the Shia, the Shia hate them back, the Arabs hate the Persians, the Egyptians hate the Arabs, the Arabs hate the Turks and everyone hates the Kurds. Especially everyone hates Saladin.'

'I thought Saladin was the King of the Muslims,' Claude-Yusuf said.

'He is Lord of Egypt and Syria,' said Dawud. 'And he

is a Kurd.'

'If anyone can be said to be King of the Muslims,' said Habib with pride, 'it is the Caliph al-Nasir.'

'But you said he has less soldiers than Saladin.'

'I did,' cried Habib. He bent down close towards him. 'But each one of them has a sword sharp enough to slit your throat. So be careful that you do not criticise the Caliph in their hearing.'

'You're frightening the boy,' cried Agnes.

Dawud held his hand up to her. 'He did it for the boy's sake. Saladin may be feared here but he is not loved.'

'This is a new world,' Habib added. 'You had better get used to it.'

He said a word to the door-keeper and they were allowed into the palace.

'A woman for the harem,' Habib told an attendant. 'Take the girl with her. I will look after the boys.'

CHAPTER 29
THE SARACEN ATTACK
Tyre

John glanced at Bernard and Matthew. 'Do you think the hour is up yet?'

Bernard nodded. 'Yes, or very close.'

At that moment, the herald rode out in front of Saladin's army and cried out loudly, 'Conrad of Montferrat. My master, Saladin the Merciful, gave you an hour to make up your minds. Surrender the city of Tyre now. Otherwise all of your people will be slain or sold as slaves and the city torn down. You will be crucified and your body left as food for crows and as warning to all who defy the will of Saladin.'

From the battlements Conrad stared at him, unmoved by his words.

'Tell Saladin that I will never surrender,' he cried. 'If he wants Tyre he must fight me for it.'

The herald nodded and trotted back to the Saracen lines. This was the signal.

At once there sounded a mighty blaring of trumpets and a thunderous beating of drums. The Saracen horsemen fanned out along the walls, racing fast, pouring arrow after arrow over the battlements.

The infantry marched stolidly down towards the walls. In between their massed companies moved catapults and mangonels beyond count.

'This looks more terrible than the battle for Jerusalem,' said Bernard.

'It is because Saladin wants this port in Muslim hands,' said Khalid. 'And he does not like being defied by an arrogant Italian like Conrad.'

John and his friends were astonished by the speed with which Saladin unleashed his fury upon the walls. Within minutes of the herald's return, the city was being bombarded. Boulders smashed against the walls and catapult shafts as thick as a man's arm rained into the city.

The defenders on the battlements were hard-pressed to respond in any way. The hail of arrows from the horsemen was keeping the more sensible soldiers cowering behind cover of the walls. The fool-hardy were picked off as they stood.

'The arrows won't prove fatal from this distance,' Khalid said. 'But they inflict wounds and keeps the Franks occupied while we make our move.'

Scores of infantrymen now raced up to the bottom of the walls with huge scaling ladders. Some were hoisted up by men wielding large poles. These poles had two timbers shaped like a claw at the top which held the rungs of the ladders securely. As the men pushed at the poles the ladders began to inch their way upwards towards the walls.

To hasten the attack Saladin had ordered that thick ropes be tied to the bottom rungs of a dozen of the ladders. Once this was done the Saracens attached the other ends of the ropes to sturdy arrows already in place on the catapults.

The catapults were released. As the arrows sailed over the walls the ropes dragged the rear of the ladders up behind them. The ladders crashed against the walls and, before the defenders could reach them, dozens of Saracens were clambering up to the attack.

The defenders tried to push the ladders back but the storm of arrows meant that too few men were willing to risk their lives to lend a hand. Five or six ladders were toppled back, sending the Saracens hurtling to the plain below. The rest were unmoved and within moments Muslim soldiers were on the walls, fighting ferociously with the defenders.

'So soon,' said Bernard in disbelief. 'The city will be taken in minutes.'

A moment later a trumpet sounded from within the city. The huge gates were thrown open and a hundred armoured horsemen careered out, followed by a hundred footmen.

The knights crashed into the Saracen horsemen, catching them unawares and sending them reeling back. At the same time the foot-soldiers attacked the Saracens around the siege ladders, hacking into them. The Franks swiftly tied ropes to the bottoms of the ladders and threw them to the knights who attached them to their saddles and galloped away from the wall. It was enough to destabilise the ladders. They began to totter.

Up on the walls the defenders began to push on the tops of the ladders. The Saracens upon the ladders fought back in frenzy but it was too late. One after the other the siege ladders were pushed back from the walls and toppled to earth, injuring scores of Saracens as they did so.

The Frankish infantrymen fled back to the gate and held the Saracens at bay until the knights had thundered back and into the city. The gate was slammed shut with a clang.

'Don't show your pleasure,' Bernard hissed at John and Matthew. 'If we look pleased we may have our throats slit.'

'Wise words,' said Khalid. 'Remember who your lord is now and act accordingly.'

'But you have been thrown back so quickly,' John said.

Khalid gave him a pitying look. 'Please, John. This is merely the first move. We have tested their defences and now know their mettle. But it is only a question of time. Be patient.'

Yet as Khalid walked away Bernard thought that the concern showed upon his face.

Night fell and the three friends laid their blankets close to Khalid. They were in a den of lions and he was the only friendly one.

Towards the end of the night John was disturbed by a strange dream.

He was a little boy visiting his uncle's farm in the country. A huge herd of cows plodded towards him. At first he thought they were friendly and waited until they got close so he could pat their leathery backs. Then he saw that they were not cows but bulls and there was hatred in their eyes. Terrified, he fled the herd and took refuge in a forest. For a moment he felt safe. But then he saw a huge tree wrench itself out of the ground and stagger towards him on legs made of roots. Every other tree did the same; and their branches were like arms reaching out to clutch him.

He woke and heard the reassuring snore of Bernard beside him. He smiled at the nightmare and drifted back to sleep.

The sun rose. John stretched and looked around. The Saracen army was stirring. Men had laid out their prayer mats while the servants banked up the fires for the morning meal.

John turned his gaze towards the city and blinked in astonishment.

A dozen huge siege towers had been placed in position a mere ten yards from the walls.

'How on earth?' he began.

'The Saracens dragged them here,' said Matthew. 'I've just been talking with Khalid. The towers come from Jerusalem. As soon as the city was taken they were dismantled and brought by cart to the coast. They were kept beyond that forest yonder and were rebuilt yesterday. The Saracens dragged them here overnight.'

John shook his head in wonder. 'There's not much hope for Tyre now,' he said.

'Unless there's a miracle.'

They had forgotten about Conrad, however. He had been alerted to the approach of the towers during the night and had already made his preparations.

Saladin began his attack as soon as his men had prayed and eaten. Tall infantrymen hoisted their shields above the heads of gangs of sappers who strained to push the towers the last remaining yards towards the battlements.

The defenders in the city poured arrow after arrow upon the sappers but Saladin had placed his own archers to the rear of the towers and they sent up a cloud of shafts to daunt the defenders.

Step by excruciating step the towers inched closer.

Eventually they were only a yard or two from the battlements. At the top of each tower a draw-bridge crashed down and Saracen warriors stormed across to the walls.

If the Saracens saw the long tubes pointing towards them they had no time to do anything about it.

From the mouth of the tubes belched a deep red flame. It caught upon the foremost Saracens and the flames leapt up their bodies. Their screams were terrible to hear.

'Greek Fire,' muttered Khalid. He stared up at the walls as the tubes vented once again.

More Saracens were stricken and the flames went further still, back to the towers themselves. The timbers had been well wetted to protect them from ordinary fire but this was no proof against the strange terror. The Greek Fire appeared to stick against the wet timbers, to pause for a moment as if panting for breath, then leapt up in renewed fury. Soon the towers were blazing at the top as if they were the candles of giants.

A trumpet call sounded from the Saracen lines. The sappers turned and frantically began to push the towers back from the danger. They managed to move them but it was too late.

By the time they had moved beyond the reach of the fire the upper stories of the towers were engulfed. Blazing timbers crashed amongst the Saracens. The flames seized on their flesh and could not be quenched. They leapt away in agony, spreading the dreadful menace amongst their comrades like a plague.

The rest of the army stared aghast as their own friends charged towards them, carrying flame and destruction with every step.

'Shoot them,' cried al-Adil. 'Shoot the men on fire.'

For a brief moment the archers did not move, horrified at the thought of killing their own people.

'Do it,' cried Saladin, beside his brother. 'Shoot the men on fire. They will bless you for doing so.'

The archers shook free of their trauma and aimed arrow after arrow at the stricken men. One after the other the burning men fell to this onslaught. Their comrades watched in horror as they were consumed.

John turned to look at Saladin. The Sultan's face was a mixture of horror and rage. The sight of it chilled John's blood; a terrible naked fear seized him.

CHAPTER 30
MEETINGS IN THE HAREM
Baghdad

Agnes picked up Eleanor and hurried after the silent attendant. He led them through corridor after corridor, so many that, within minutes, she had completely lost all sense of direction.

Finally, they reached a large white door inlaid with sheets of beaten gold. The attendant knocked quietly upon the door. After a moment a tiny panel slid open and two eyes peered out.

'A Frankish woman for the harem,' said the attendant. 'Habib and Dawud brought her.'

The door slid back.

'Wait here,' the attendant said before hurrying back the way he had come.

'Where are we, Mama?' Eleanor asked.

'We are at our new house,' Agnes answered, fighting back the tears that threatened to spill out.

'Is Daddy here?'

'Not yet, darling, not yet. But he will be. Someday soon.'

Eleanor fell quiet, apart from the occasional sniff.

The door slid open to reveal a large man who regarded them silently. He was tall and very overweight but unlike Habib he wore this well. He looked almost as much muscle as fat. His massive head was bald of all hair, including eye-brows.

'Come this way,' he said in a voice like that of a child.

A eunuch, Agnes realised. She shuddered, remembering Habib's threat regarding Claude-Yusuf.

She followed the eunuch into the harem. This was one of the two hearts of the Palace. The other was the Caliph's Council Hall, surrounded by offices, busy with functionaries, where he made policy, ruled his lands and dispensed justice and religious edicts.

The Caliph thought of the Council Hall as his public heart. His private one he reserved for the harem.

Here, in the very centre of the palace, were his private quarters, his dining rooms, bath-house and lounges, his bedroom, his prayer-room and his courtyard gardens. Here, also, were his eighty women. A few were his wives but the majority were concubines, placed there for his amusement only.

Some amused the Caliph insufficiently and he never took them to his bed again. They passed the years waiting for the summons. When it finally became certain that the summons would never arrive they were passed on to the Caliph's favourites or gradually took on more and more menial duties. Many of them became indistinguishable from the female servants who serviced the harem and lived out the rest of their days in this role.

Those concubines who amused the Caliph greatly, or those who bore him a male child, attained a status close to that of his wives. It was, however, a fragile status. Should she cease to amuse, or should the child not survive, it would be better for her to throw herself upon the mercy of the desert jackals.

To prosper in the harem a woman had to have beauty, adroit erotic skills, the political instincts of a vizier and the nerve of a tiger.

Or she had to be like Johara.

The eunuch pointed towards a room and told Agnes to wait

there. It was a small room containing a divan and two large cushions upon the floor. A window looked out upon a courtyard garden. A small fountain cascaded into a pool containing water lilies which were just opening to the sun.

'That's a pretty garden, Mama,' Eleanor said.

Agnes nodded. Tears filled her eyes. It was about the size of her courtyard in Jerusalem.

She felt a presence in the room and turned. A woman was standing in the doorway, gazing thoughtfully upon her.

'I didn't hear you,' Agnes said in Arabic.

The woman shook her head. 'No matter.'

She was fifteen or more years older than Agnes. She was short and round, the sort of woman who seemed designed to take children into her arms and hug them. Yet, as Agnes looked at her she realised that the woman must have been strikingly beautiful in her youth. Most of that beauty had dwindled with the years but there was still a radiance about her which those who troubled to look would find. Her eyes were like those of a wounded deer, melancholy and sad yet still trusting and hopeful.

'You are called Agnes,' the woman said.

Agnes nodded.

'I am Johara.' She held out her hands towards Eleanor who ran to them as if drawn by magic. 'And what is this little one called?'

'I'm Eleanor,' she answered before her mother had time to speak.

Johara chuckled. 'A pretty name for a pretty girl.' Her fingers played with the child's hair for a moment.

'Habib told me that you have two boys as well.'

'Gerard is my child,' Agnes said. 'Claude-Yusuf is my brother's son. He is an orphan and we care for him.'

'There are too many orphans in this world, don't you think?'

Agnes nodded, warily.

Johara smiled and came towards Agnes. She stared at her face, as if she was looking for something familiar in it or, perhaps, seeking for a blemish. She smiled, like she was satisfied at last.

'You will please the Caliph,' she said. 'At least for a time.' She smiled once again but this time there was a wintry look to it.

'What about the boys?' Agnes asked. 'What's happening to them?'

Johara patted her on the arm. 'Do not fret yourself. Habib will look after them. He will keep them with him for a week or so and work out the best position for them within the palace.'

'Will I see them again?'

Johara shrugged. 'Possibly. But do not build up your hopes.'

Agnes closed her eyes and felt the tears squeeze through the lids.

'Do not worry. At worst they will become servants and what better service can there be than that of this Palace. And they may become more. Some of the most loyal of the Caliph's servants are infidels, like you.'

Agnes braced herself. 'I saw a eunuch here. Habib said that Claude-Yusuf was a clever boy and that he might suffer…'

Johara stopped her lips. 'If that is the will of Allah, so be it.' she said. 'But Habib was being provocative for some reason known only to himself. It is not the clever boys who are taken for eunuchs but the strong and handsome ones. If the lad is clever then he may do well and still keep his manhood.'

'What's a eunuch, Mama?' Eleanor asked.

'Just a name for a servant of the Caliph,' Johara answered quickly.

Eleanor reached out for Agnes' hand and stared up at Johara, uncertain of this woman who answered for her mother.

'You mention the Caliph,' said Agnes. 'Who is he? What is he?'

Johara sighed. 'I can see that you will need much schooling,' she said. 'Come, this is best done over food.'

She led the way down a long corridor. Doors were placed at intervals of twenty feet or so and all were shut.

Finally, they turned a corner and Johara opened a door, beckoning them to follow.

Agnes gasped. They were in a large room, perhaps twenty feet by twenty. It was as if they were walking in early morning mist.

Veils and swathes of silk and muslin hung from the ceiling, fluttering in the breeze from open windows. To one side of the room was a large bed, heaped up with cushions as plump as Johara, each decorated with bright colours and lavish designs. Lamps smouldered beside it, giving off not light but the heady scent of spices.

Beside the window were a small table and four chairs. The table was overflowing with food. There was a platter of fruit: apricots, figs, plums, dates and grapes. There were soft breads, some plain, some sprinkled with seeds and herbs. A dish in the centre was crammed with grilled meat, one next to it stacked with fish of every shape and size. On the far side of the table were platefuls and platefuls of cakes.

'Is that for us?' Eleanor asked, open-mouthed.

'It is, child,' Johara said.

Eleanor ran to the table and filled her plate to overflowing with a selection of food.

Agnes wished that she was a child and could fill her plate in the same way. Despite her hunger she did not want to look greedy so she selected carefully.

Johara had no such compunction. She filled one plate with meat, fish and bread and a second with fruit and cakes.

'You asked me about the Caliph?' Johara said. 'What do you know of him?'

Agnes shook her head. 'I don't know anything. The first I had even heard of him was when Habib told me that I had been bought for his harem.'

Johara picked up a piece of chicken and bit on it.

'Do you know about any of the great men of Islam?' she asked.

'Only Sultan Saladin.'

Johara smiled. 'That upstart.' She wiped her mouth with a silk handkerchief. 'Saladin is a Kurdish mercenary, a nobody who just happens to be a very good warrior. He has a brother, al-Adil, who is more of a concern to the wise men of Baghdad.' She plucked the bone from a small fish and swallowed the flesh whole.

'The Caliph is different all together.' She sighed. 'Caliph al-Nasir is the descendent of the Prophet's uncle. He is the head of the whole Islamic world. All emirs and sultans are subservient to him.'

Agnes said nothing but wondered why, if this was the case, she had never heard of him.

'What manner of man is he?' she asked.

Johara sighed. 'He is a wise man, a kind man. He is young, only thirty years of age, but he has the wisdom of an older man.'

She turned towards Agnes and gave a wistful smile. 'His wisdom can be understood when I tell you that twelve years ago, while still a very young man, he decided to give his heart to an older woman who would help him learn the mysteries of life and of love.' She fell silent.

Agnes glanced at her. She could not prevent a smile from growing upon her face, a smile of amusement and of sympathy.

'The older woman was you?' she asked.

Johara nodded. 'And he regards me still with special favour,' she said quietly. 'I have not, however, been his favourite for many years.'

'So who is his favourite now?'

'A Frankish woman, Beatrice. She was stolen from her parents by one of the Frankish barons and sold to the Caliph when she was only six years of age. She is twenty three now and she rules us all.'

Agnes watched as Johara stabbed a piece of meat and tore it into tiny shreds before scooping it into her mouth. Her thoughts looked as if they were focused on something or someone far away.

'And what is Beatrice like?' Agnes asked.

Johara blinked. 'I cannot say,' she answered. 'She is Caliph al-Nasir's favourite. Let that be sufficient for you.'

At that moment there sounded a short knock upon the door and it opened immediately.

A young woman entered and hurried over towards them. She looked startled to see Agnes and Eleanor and turned towards Johara with a questioning look.

Agnes took the opportunity to examine her. She was young, not yet twenty years old by the look of her fresh complexion and clear eyes. She moved like a young antelope, quick and supple yet with a timid way of holding herself. She was the most beautiful woman Agnes had ever seen. Her breath caught and she felt her heart quicken. Out of the corner of her eye she saw Eleanor glance up at her as if perplexed.

'Who is this, Johara?' the young woman asked. Her voice was quiet yet it rippled like a young stream.

'This is Agnes. Habib bought her in Damascus. She is a Frank from Jerusalem.'

'A Frank?' There was a touch of alarm in her voice.

'Don't worry,' Johara said. 'I do not think you need fear this one.'

Silence fell. After a few moments Agnes realised that she was still staring at the young woman. She found herself blushing.

'I'm sorry,' she said. 'I don't mean to seem rude.'

'You're not rude,' said Johara. She reached out and touched her hand. 'Everything is so new to you.'

The young woman sat upon the divan and smiled at Agnes.

'This is Lalina,' Johara said. 'She is almost as new here as you. She has been with us for only a few months.'

'I am from the lands near the Dark Sea,' Lalina said. 'I was caught by Turks in the summer and brought to Baghdad as a slave.'

'Fortunately for Lalina,' Johara said, 'Habib happened to be at the market when he saw her. He was not on an errand to buy slaves but he took the chance and bought her for the Caliph. It was a risk for him.'

'Luckily, the Caliph seemed to like me,' Lalina added.

Johara laughed. 'How could he not? You are like a goddess of the Greeks.'

Lalina blushed and bent her head. She could not, however, prevent a giggle of pleasure from bubbling to the surface.

Agnes saw that, as she gazed upon Lalina, Johara's look of fondness became clouded with a hint of concern. She reached out and brushed the young girl's hair very gently.

'But always remember child,' she murmured, 'that you are mortal.'

At that moment there came a loud rapping on the door.

'Enter,' Johara called.

An elderly eunuch came into the room and bowed. 'The Lady Beatrice desires to see the new concubine,' he said.

Lalina's hand went to her mouth and she looked towards Agnes with alarm.

'I'll go with you,' Johara said, quickly.

'And me,' said Lalina.

Johara stared at her for a moment, pondering whether this was a good idea or not. Then she nodded.

She turned towards the eunuch. 'Look after the child please, Basil,' she ordered.

She led Agnes and Lalina out of the room. The last thing that Agnes heard was Eleanor wailing for her.

They hurried down the corridors and finally reached a room with two guards standing outside. They were expected and one of the guards silently opened the door and gestured for them to enter.

This room was twice the size of Johara's and even more opulent. Where the dominant feature of the older woman's room was silks and fabrics, in this room it was gold and precious stones. Coming from a family of inn-keepers, Agnes knew the value of such things. She only had to glance around to see that in this one chamber there was more wealth than she had seen in a life-time.

A divan lay on the far side of the room, close to the cool airs wafting from off a large terrace. Lying on this divan was a woman with gold and silver glittering in her long dark hair.

Johara led Agnes and Lalina towards the divan and gave a little bow, which the others emulated.

The woman on the divan slowly turned her face towards them and stared at them in silence.

Agnes almost staggered back. Wave upon wave of rage

seemed to beat down upon her. Is she a basilisk she wondered for one terrified moment?

Agnes forced herself to look at the woman. She was beautiful, that could not be denied. Her face looked almost perfect, with high cheek-bones, fine nose and well-shaped chin. Yet, despite this, there was something mask-like about her, as if she had decided to freeze her own face into one rigid posture for all time.

But it was her eyes which were terrifying. They were so green they looked like gems. It was a beautiful colour and it would have made her eyes look beautiful save for one thing. Her gaze was dead and pitiless.

She looked Agnes up and down and then her eyes turned to take in Johara and Lalina in one swift, dismissive glance.

'So,' she said. 'The new toy has already been sniffed out by the old carcass and the pretty doll.'

She sat up and held them in her gaze. Her mouth moved into a smile but it was as bleak as frost. 'Remember this always, ladies,' she said. 'You are nothing but toys and dolls. Or old bloated carcasses. But I am Beatrice.'

She looked away as if she was becoming bored by their continued presence.

When she spoke again it was in a voice little more than a whisper.

'I hold your lives, and your deaths, in my hands.'

Agnes stared at Beatrice. She had never felt such fear in her life.

The Caliph's favourite plucked up a fig and split it open. Her movements were delicate, the delicacy of a cat disembowelling a mouse. Not a sound disturbed the silence of her movements.

Agnes moved her eyes to look at the others. Lalina was snared just as much as Agnes. As Beatrice tore open the fig she watched with something akin to fascination.

Johara, on the other hand, stared at Beatrice with a cold, impassive face. Beneath the surface there was nothing but contempt and scorn but she buried it so well that no one could have accused her of it.

Beatrice finished opening the fig. She held it close to her eyes and examined it closely, turning it this way and that with her immaculate hands.

Then she flung it on the floor.

'The Caliph may take his pleasure with you, inn-keeper,' Beatrice murmured, her eyes fixed in the middle distance. 'Then again, he may not. But even if he does, he will tire of you. Perhaps immediately.'

She yawned and leaned back in the chair.

'And then he will summon me to his bed once again.'

Her mouth took on a smile as cold as midnight.

Agnes stared wide-eyed at her.

'And he will never,' Beatrice continued, 'never, take back in his bed a trollop as fat as a cow.'

Now she turned and looked towards them. 'I mean you, Johara,' she said.

'I know you do,' Johara answered. 'I know you do.'

Beatrice clapped her hands. 'Leave me,' she said. 'All of you. Your grossness troubles my sight, it upsets me.'

They rose, and taking their cue from Johara, bowed to Beatrice and made a swift exit.

They walked back to Johara's room in silence.

Johara slammed the door behind her and paced up and down in fury. 'I will have my revenge,' she said. 'I will have my revenge.'

'Don't say that,' whispered Lalina. 'Don't say that. She frightens me.'

Johara stopped pacing and held out her arms. The young girl flew into them and allowed herself to be held tight.

'There is no need for fear,' Johara said. 'Beatrice may be the favourite now. But a young ram never forgets his first ewe.'

There were tears in her eyes. She knew that the Caliph's fondness for her was the only thing keeping her safe. She also knew that as the years passed by this fondness, this shred of power and this safety were being slowly but surely eroded.

She blinked the tears from her eyes and gently moved Lalina from the hug. She forced a sunny smile upon her face. It fooled Lalina but it did not fool Agnes.

CHAPTER 31
SANCTUARY AT LAST
Antioch

The refugees approached the city of Antioch. They had been journeying for two weeks since being refused entry to Tripoli and most had given up hope of any succour.

There were far fewer refugees than the numbers who had fled Jerusalem. Two months of marching with dwindling food and growing despair had taken its toll on the weakest. It was now close to the end of November and as the nights grew cold Balian feared that many more might succumb.

He tried hard not to show his fears but those like Simon who were in daily contact with him saw and took note. It was only the old lord's determination which was keeping the people on the march and if that were to fail then all might be lost.

Simon pondered this as he gazed upon the refugees.

He could see the hope in their faces as they got their first glimpse of the city. Hope mingled with the fear that they would be turned away from here as they had been from Tyre and Tripoli.

Antioch lay on the river Orontes, in the centre of rich agricultural land. To the west was a huge, brooding mountain chain, to the south-east, at the edge of the city, the mountain of Silpius.

The city looked like a paradise ringed by the outliers of hell.

Simon gazed at the ramparts of the city in awe.

They were immense. They circled the city for sixteen miles and even forced their way up the steep slopes of the mountain. Imposing towers reared above the walls with only a distance of eighty paces between each one. The citizens of Antioch claimed there was one tower for each day of the year.

The walls gave an impression of power and resolve. The citadel crowned the top of the mountain and was considered unconquerable. Upon its heights the huge flags whipped ceaselessly in the fierce winds.

Gregory, one of the grooms who made up Simon's guard, whistled aloud. 'We should be safe here, my lord,' he said.

Simon stared at him. The young man had begun to address him as lord three weeks before at Tyre when he had leapt to defend the refugees against Saladin's horsemen.

Simon had given up trying to reprimand him. In fact he liked being called lord. Continual usage of the term appeared to give it substance. A number of the younger refugees had also begun to refer to him as such, though most of their elders still looked upon him warily, as a parvenu.

'It's bigger than Tripoli or Tyre,' Gregory said, 'and stronger. We'll be much safer here.'

'If they allow us entry,' Simon said. 'It's said that the Prince of Antioch has no liking for the Patriarch.'

'Perhaps we should desert him then, lord.'

'Perhaps,' Simon murmured without thinking.

When the first of the refugees got close to the city the huge gates were slammed shut. Simon's heart fell. Where on earth will we find sanctuary, he wondered.

Three horsemen galloped up from the rear of the column, Eraclius, Balian and Jerome. They reined in when they reached Simon.

'Have they just shut the gates?' Eraclius demanded.

'They have, my lord,' Simon answered. 'Perhaps they fear our great numbers.'

'Maybe Bohemond has heard that you are with us, Patriarch,' Balian said quietly.

'That quarrel was long ago,' Eraclius snapped back. 'I told Bohemond that he had done wrong in the eyes of the church. That was my duty.'

'But you came between the love of a Prince and his wife,' Balian said.

'I came between a Prince and a witch,' Eraclius answered.

'You think that if you wish,' Balian said. 'I know that many in Antioch share your views. But, I beseech you, be temperate and friendly to Bohemond. And be courteous to Princess Sibyl.'

Eraclius scowled but nodded.

The three men kicked their horses and headed towards the gate. After a few yards, Eraclius turned in his saddle and gestured to Simon and he hurried to join them.

They approached the gates. They waited for a few minutes but the gates remained shut. Simon glanced up at the towers on either side and saw soldiers peering down upon them. He recalled that Raymond, who had refused them entry to Tripoli, was the son of Bohemond. It did not bode well for their reception at Antioch.

'Do you think we have any chance?' he asked Jerome.

The old knight shrugged. 'I have only met Bohemond half a dozen times, so I have little more idea than you. People say it's impossible to second-guess him.'

'He sounds like my father.'

Jerome grinned. 'Then perhaps your experience makes you the

best person to deal with him.'

At that moment a small postern door opened. Simon expected a troop of soldiers to hurry out.

Instead, one man did so, a tall, lean man with a face like a market brawler. He glared at Eraclius and put his hands upon his waist as if determined to bar the refugees entry, on his own if need be.

'I have heard from my s.. s.. son,' he said, 'that you were headed this way.'

'Raymond thought there were too many of us to be taken in at Tripoli,' Eraclius said. 'Antioch is a greater place.'

Bohemond's face worked as he struggled to get out his words. 'So you thought that you would try your luck here instead,' he said. 'You thought that the Prince of Antioch would be s.. s.. susceptible to your pleading?'

Eraclius made to answer but then thought better of it and remained silent.

'We hope that you will offer us sanctuary,' Balian said quietly to Bohemond.

Bohemond turned to him. 'You are welcome, Balian. You know that. We are brothers, you and I. But this...' He waved his hand towards the horde of refugees. 'This rabble of filthy, starving folk. They are not welcome. They must go elsewhere and take their priests with them.'

Balian nodded thoughtfully and dismounted.

Simon was astounded by this. Balian will desert us, he thought. This was his plan all along.

Bohemond opened his arms to Balian. 'My friend,' he said. 'I welcome you with glad heart.'

Bohemond and Balian placed their hands upon the other's

shoulders and stared into each other's eyes.

Simon glanced at Eraclius to see his reaction. The Patriarch's face gave nothing away.

'My heart is also glad,' Balian said at last. 'Glad that I have reached your fair city and glad that I can talk once more with you.'

He glanced up at the walls which snaked their way further than the eye could see.

'This is a goodly city, Bohemond, I have often dreamed of it as I marched the long days to get here.'

He removed his hands from Bohemond's shoulders and shook his head. 'But I cannot stay.'

Bohemond straightened and struggled to frame a reply.

Balian raised a hand to silence him. 'I cannot stay,' he said, 'because I made a vow to God to lead these poor folk to sanctuary.'

He paused. 'I also promised Saladin that, if he gave the people their freedom, I would not desert them. And a vow to Saladin stands next to one made to God. I dare not anger either of them.'

Bohemond looked thunder-struck. A vow to God weighed little with him. Yet one to Saladin was a different matter all together.

'You honestly s…say,' he stammered, 'that you will not enter the city unless I allow this litter of people to enter also?'

'I do. I am sorry, Bohemond. But I do.'

Bohemond sighed and clapped his hand upon Balian's shoulder. It was clear to everyone that he was thinking fast. His face grew ever more troubled as he looked from Balian to the refugees and back to the walls of his city. It was as if he were engaged in some arcane calculation which was growing in complexity yet seemed to promise no solution.

He sighed, looked sorrowfully at the refugees and slowly shook his head.

'A word from Balian outweighs all deep and weary deliberations,' he said at last. 'I will tell my nobles that I have reconsidered the matter. You shall be given sanctuary in Antioch.'

The nearest of the refugees heard Bohemond's words. A cheer of exultation and relief began, a cheer which surged from the nearest to the furthest in the column. It was so loud it echoed against the walls.

Bohemond shook his head as if perplexed.

He leaned close to Balian and whispered in his ear. 'I feel disconcertingly noble about doing this.'

Bohemond raised his hands high above his head and the cheers redoubled in volume. A slow smile crossed his face and then he beamed with genuine pleasure.

Eraclius dismounted, followed by Jerome and Simon.

The gate to the city opened slowly. Bohemond took Balian's arm in his and, together, the two old warriors led the people into safety.

CHAPTER 32
AN ARROW TO THE HEART
Tyre

The Saracen army flung itself against the walls of Tyre once more. They had done this every day for three weeks now and every day they had been repulsed.

This day's fighting was more than usually savage. The defenders drenched oil upon their attackers and poured Greek Fire upon them. There was a stiff wind blowing from the sea and the blaze whipped up into a firestorm which engulfed hundreds of Saracen warriors.

Saladin called a halt to the attack. He rode back to his camp and summoned his emirs.

'No smiles,' Khalid warned the friends as he headed towards the council tent. 'No jubilation. The soldiers are wrathful and I will not be here to protect you.'

He considered for a moment longer, then ordered his own guard to keep watch on the Christians.

It was mid-afternoon before anything further happened.

There was a flurry of activity and King Guy and a number of the Frankish nobles were force-marched to Saladin's tent. Some looked terrified. A few, like Guy and the Master of the Templars, looked contemptuous.

A half hour later Khalid hurried from the tent and approached them.

'You are wanted by the Sultan,' he said.

'Us?' said Bernard. 'What for?'

Khalid shrugged. 'The Sultan will tell you.'

An hour later Bernard, John and Matthew rode in full Saracen armour towards the battlements of Tyre. Riding with them were Khalid, the Saracen herald and Conrad's father, William, the aged Marquis of Montferrat.

The Marquis turned towards Bernard. 'I'd rather we were drinking wine in your inn,' he said.

'Me too, my lord,' Bernard answered.

'If this goes well,' William continued, 'we shall return there and have one of Agnes' fine dinners.'

Bernard opened his mouth to tell him that he had lost Agnes but decided now was not the time.

They halted a few paces from the battlements. A long line of defenders stared down upon them and in their midst was Conrad of Montferrat.

The herald scanned the battlements and addressed himself to Conrad.

'The magnificent and ever-merciful Saladin,' he cried, 'has seen fit to send another envoy to talk with you.'

He waved his hand. The old Marquis and the three friends stepped forward.

'See,' continued the herald, 'how this new envoy is escorted by two of the heroes knighted by Balian of Ibelin. Also with him is Matthew the Mule, the man of courage who bore the Leper King into battle upon his own back.'

He paused for effect before continuing.

The defenders craned their necks to catch sight of this man of legend but Conrad did not respond in any way.

'These courageous men,' continued the herald, 'have taken service with the mighty Saladin, swayed by his magnificence, his clemency and his invincibility.'

'Enough of your platitudes,' Conrad cried. 'Say what you must and then leave.'

William of Montferrat turned to look back at the herald who gestured to him sharply.

The old man looked up towards the battlements.

'My son,' he cried. His voice was weak and faltering and he coughed to clear his throat. 'My son. I have been held captive since the Battle of Hattin, near five months ago. In all this time, Sultan Saladin and his people have treated me, and the other lords, with the greatest respect and kindness.

'I come here now, to plead with you to surrender the city to Saladin. His army is mighty, his soldiers courageous and resourceful. Even now, more armies are marching towards you, from Syria and from Egypt.

'Saladin has taken every Christian city he has attacked. Tyre will be no different. You are a man of courage, my son. It is no shame to submit to reality. It is no shame to surrender to such a mighty war-lord as Saladin. No shame to save the people of Tyre from torment, torture and death.'

He fell silent and held his hands up, pleading with his son to heed his words.

For a moment, Conrad did not respond. Then he snatched a cross-bow from one of his soldiers and aimed it at his father.

'If this is all that you have to say to me,' he cried, 'then be gone or I shall kill you. I have no time for traitors who whine and plead to me.'

John turned towards William. All colour drained from the old man's face. His arms slumped to his side. He swayed. Bernard hurried to his side and caught him.

'It's all right, my lord,' he said, 'it's all right.'

'No,' William said. 'No. It is far from right. What do these wars mean if they lead to this?'

Khalid nodded and Bernard led the Marquis away from his son towards safety.

As they trudged past Saladin and al-Adil the two brothers gazed upon the old man with pity.

That night the three friends began a meal of bread, fine cheese and some young goat which they had grilled over their fire.

They thought they had no appetite until they smelled the sizzling meat.

'May I join you?' said a familiar voice.

'Of course, lord,' said Bernard.

Khalid sat beside him and accepted the food which John passed to him.

There was a long silence before Khalid spoke again.

'What do you think about of how Conrad acted towards his father?' he asked.

'I don't know what to think,' said Bernard. 'William is a good man, a decent man. He does not deserve to have an arrow aimed at his heart. Especially not an arrow aimed by his son.'

Khalid nodded. 'It makes me wonder what sort of a man this Conrad is.'

'A fierce opponent,' Matthew said. 'That is certain.'

Khalid nodded and chewed upon a chunk of meat.

'Tell me, my friends,' he said at last. 'Is this normal behaviour for the Franks? Do all sons hate their fathers in this manner? Do they not owe them duty and honour?'

'Most do,' said Bernard. 'I've never known anything like this.'

'But kin can quarrel,' John said quietly.

Khalid turned towards him. 'You have knowledge of this?'

'Yes. With my brother.'

'Brothers are different. Brothers always fight with brothers and sisters with sisters.'

'But most forgive each other,' Bernard said. He gave a questioning look towards John.

'Not my brother and me,' John said. 'I will never forgive him.'

'Why?' asked Khalid. He put down his meat. 'What happened between you?'

'My brother Alan is five years older than me,' John said. 'Ten years ago he joined the retinue of Prince Richard and he started to change. He began to think himself superior, he looked down upon us.'

'That is not so surprising,' said Matthew.

'Perhaps not. But what he did five years ago is very surprising. Our mother was dying. Alan came to see her and it was obvious that she would only last a few days longer.

'Then a message came from the Prince, demanding that Alan join him in France. My brother left within the hour, despite the pleas of all of us to stay. I cursed him as he rode away. I vowed I would never speak with him again.'

The others listened to this in silence.

Khalid placed his hand upon John's shoulder. 'I understand your feelings. Yet I also understand the dilemma faced by your brother. He was torn by two terrible demands, to stay with his mother until she died, and to obey the command of his master, who is a prince.'

'Well, he did choose,' said John. 'And there are consequences to that.'

'For both of you,' said Khalid. 'For your brother and for you.' He fell silent for a moment. 'Do you have any other kin?'

John shook his head.

'What about Simon?' Bernard asked in surprise. 'What about your cousin?'

'He is kin to me no longer,' John said. He got up and strode off into the darkness.

'John is a man who holds a great rage within himself,' said Khalid quietly.

Bernard nodded. 'You are right and I am saddened by it.'

'Don't be. Such a rage can utterly destroy a man or it can transform him into a hero. Only Allah can decide John's path.'

CHAPTER 33
THE SORCEROR PRINCESS
Antioch

Simon had been surprised by the different peoples who lived in Jerusalem but even this had not prepared him for Antioch. As he followed Eraclius up the winding street to the citadel it sounded as if he were traversing the Tower of Babel. He saw a few Franks but not many; far fewer than had lived in Jerusalem. In their place he saw a myriad of people, from where he could not imagine. There were Greeks in plenty, Armenians, Jews, Circassians, and Scandinavians. Most of the population, by their dress appeared to be Muslims.

Yet as he walked Simon realised that this term, sufficient until today, could not describe the people adequately. There were the Saracens he had seen in plenty; short, quick-moving people. There were Arabs from the desert, swishing along in long robes. There were Turks with dark features, Moors of varying shades of black, Persians who looked almost identical to the southern Franks, people from further east with flatter faces and slanting eyes.

'This is the melting pot of the world,' Jerome said. 'People come here from every land, more so than even Constantinople or Baghdad. It is the meeting place of the Christian, the Muslim and the Jew. And other people who worship animals and the ghosts of their fathers and have never even heard of Europe.'

'Bohemond looks to be a Frank.'

'He's a Norman.'

'Like our kings?'

'Not as exalted as that. His great-grandfather was Bohemond I who captured Antioch in the First Crusade. He was the son of Robert Guiscard, a soldier of fortune who conquered half of Italy.

'But in the Holy Land it is deeds as much as blood which give a man his standing.'

Simon smiled. 'Of that, at least, I am glad.'

Jerome paused. 'Remember that I speak of the deeds of the past,' he said. 'It may not be so today.'

The climb to the citadel was arduous but they arrived there at last.

Bohemond led them into a huge hall. Every wall was decorated in dazzling colours which would have looked garish in other chambers. Here, because of the size of the hall, the decoration pleased the eye. Tapestries displaying scenes of hunting and battle hung at intervals along the hall and two fires blazed at either end.

On the narrow side to the east there was a dais of four steps. Upon this were two thrones, each made of ebony and inlaid with precious jewels.

Curled in one of them, regarding the strangers with languid gaze, sat the most beautiful woman Simon had ever seen.

She was about thirty years old but her slim figure gave the impression that she was younger. Her skin was a cool olive colour and her hair was black, hanging in curls upon her forehead and by her cheeks. Her eyes, however, were a piercing blue, as blue as the coldest seas of the north.

Her cheek-bones were high and prominent, giving her the appearance of a cat, but a dangerous one. Curled in her lap was a bear-cub with a jewelled collar.

'You know Princess Cybil,' Bohemond said to Balian.

Cybil uncurled from the throne and came towards them. She walked slowly, as if giving the men a great gift by doing so, allowing them time in plenty to feast their eyes upon her. Again the image of a cat came to Simon, not only dangerous, but powerful and beguiling.

'Welcome, Balian,' she said. 'I am glad that young fool Raymond refused you entry to Tripoli for I so desired to see you again.' She held out her hand for Balian to kiss.

She gave Balian a radiant smile before turning to his companion. 'And welcome to your friend,' she said. 'Jeremy, if my memory serves me well?'

'Jerome, Highness. I am surprised you even remember me, for you have only seen me once.'

'You have a memorable face,' Cybil answered. 'Besides, your courage and your loyalty to Balian are legendary. Once you are seen, you can never be forgotten, at least not by me.'

Simon was amused to see the old knight blush like a youth.

Cybil glanced at Eraclius, held his gaze for a moment and then stepped away and approached Simon.

'And who might you be, who stands in the company of Balian and Jerome?'

For a moment Simon was tongue-tied, not expecting her to address him. 'My name is Simon Ferrier,' he managed at last.

Cybil clapped her hands in delight. 'He is like you, my darling Bohemond. He stammers and cannot find his words.'

'I don't normally do so,' Simon said quickly. Then he repented of it, wondering if this would seem an insult to Bohemond.

Cybil leant close to him and stared into his eyes. 'Do not apologise for any human weakness, young man,' she said. 'Even the noblest have their weaknesses.'

He did not know how to answer so nodded like a country bumpkin.

She smiled. 'So how does Simon Ferrier come to be in the company of Balian?'

'I was in Jerusalem, Highness,' he answered. 'During the siege. There were too few knights to lead the defence so I was knighted by Lord Balian along with thirty others.'

'And are they all as manly as you?'

Simon found himself blushing and lowered his gaze. 'I cannot say, Highness.'

He heard the tinkle of her laugh and felt her step away.

He glanced up to see her staring at Eraclius. Her head was to one side as if she was considering a joint of meat and how best to prepare if for the table.

'Greetings, Princess Cybil,' he said.

Cybil held out her hand. Eraclius bent to kiss it but she removed it just before his lips made contact.

'Whatever am I thinking?' she said. 'Such a high Churchman is accustomed to having rough men bend to kiss his ring. It would be unseemly for such a high priest as you to do likewise.'

'But you are a lady,' Eraclius began.

She held her finger up to silence him.

'I am a Princess,' she said. 'Always remember that.'

She turned and glided back towards the throne. It was as if she had weaved a spell and only at this instant could the men shake free of it.

She rang a bell and a servant stepped forward and bowed. 'Tell the steward to make chambers ready for our guests,' Cybil said. 'And tell the butler to bring food.'

The servant bowed and hurried off.

Eraclius turned towards Bohemond. 'The people,' he began, 'will need feeding also.'

Bohemond sniffed and rubbed his nose vigorously. 'So it begins, as I feared.'

'They have been walking for months,' Balian added. 'They will need food and shelter for a while at least.'

'I shall arrange that.' He gestured to another servant. 'But know that there is a limit to my treasury and to my patience.'

Balian grinned. 'So you say, Bohemond, so you say.'

Bohemond gave him a sour look.

CHAPTER 34
THE CALIPH
The Harem Baghdad

Johara and Lalina took Agnes to the room which had been assigned to her. It was a small room but it was clean and had a window which looked out upon a lawn. The bed was the largest object in the room and was soft and inviting. Besides this there were two chairs and a little table.

To one side of the room was a curtain hanging to the ground. Agnes pulled back the curtain and blinked in astonishment. A small bath stood there, already filled with warm water. Thick towels were heaped upon a stool beside it.

'I ordered the servants to prepare you a bath,' Johara said.

Agnes sighed with pleasure. Tears began to film her eyes.

'I've only been in a bath twice,' she said. 'And I never thought I would have one of my own.'

'Let us take away your old clothes,' Johara said, slipping the sleeve from Agnes' shoulder.

Agnes blushed. 'I can do it myself,' she said. 'I would prefer it.'

'As you wish,' Johara said. 'Lalina will bring you some fresh clothes.'

Agnes waited until Johara had left the chamber before slipping off her clothes. She climbed into the bath and sighed with pleasure. The last time she had been in a bath was when she visited the home of her brother's father-in-law, Yacob. The first time had been the night before her wedding when a wealthy friend of her mother had allowed her the use of her own bath.

This was different. This bath had been provided for her and for her alone.

She lay back in the bath and began to weep. Where is Bernard now, she wondered. The quick heat of guilt swept over her as she thought this. She had been brought to a heaven of earth. What sort of hell was he living through?

The curtain was pulled to one side and Lalina glanced in.

'I have brought you clothes,' she said, holding up a gown of pale green silk.

'It's beautiful,' said Agnes, biting her lip with worry at the thought of wearing such a thing.

'No more than you are,' said Lalina. 'It will suit you well.'

She left the robe on a stool at the foot of the bath.

The water in the bath was beginning to cool now and Agnes washed herself quickly. She climbed out of the bath, towelled herself dry and put on the gown.

Lalina clapped her hands with pleasure when she saw Agnes in the gown. 'It's perfect for you,' she said.

'It feels so strange,' Agnes said. 'It's cool yet warm at the same time.'

'I think it's a magic cloth,' said Lalina. 'I believe it's made by wizards.'

'Nonsense, child,' said Johara as she stepped through the door. She gazed at Agnes and smiled. 'It looks beautiful on you,' she said. 'But it's not magic. It is made of silk, a material that comes from far to the east.'

She approached Agnes and looped a necklace around her neck.

'It's one of my old ones,' she said. 'It was one of my first gifts from the Caliph. He is fond of it so I thought it would be good for you to wear it.'

Agnes felt a chill in her heart and placed her hand upon Johara's.

'Tell me,' she pleaded, 'what is the Caliph like?'

At that moment the door opened and a huge eunuch stepped into the room.

'Ask him yourself,' Johara answered. 'This is your summons.'

Agnes could barely keep up with the swift, long strides of the eunuch. She already felt lost within the palace but now as they hurried through corridors, halls and courtyards beyond imagining she gave up any pretence of trying to keep a grip on its complex vastness.

Her breath became so short that she reached out for the eunuch and begged him to stop. He shook his head but slowed a little.

Finally they arrived at a vast door inlaid with jade and precious jewels. The eunuch pulled upon a silken bell-cord and stepped back.

The door slid open and the eunuch gestured her to enter.

She was surprised at what confronted her. Unlike the rich opulence of the rooms she had been in already, this one was austere. The floor was lined with black and white marble but the only furnishings were a huge desk inlaid with patterned wood and half a dozen chairs and stools.

She looked around. The room was empty. Plucking up courage she walked across to the desk.

Stacked upon it were two neat piles of parchment. She could read a little, enough French and Arabic to make out words necessary to run an inn. She recognised the writing as Arabic, although much neater and more regular than the rough jottings she had ever seen. She glanced around and saw that the chamber was empty. Filled with curiosity, she picked up the parchment. It was light and very white, with a different feel to any parchment she had touched. She tried to read what it said but failed with more than a few familiar words.

Next to the papers were a beautiful glass ink-pot and half a dozen sharp quills. On the chair behind the desk was the sole concession to luxury within the room, a deep cushion, richly embroidered.

She picked it up and examined the fine needlework. It contained hunting scenes and images of horses and strange beasts she did not recognise. She turned the cushion this way and that, fascinated by its beauty.

'You like the cushion?' said a voice from her left.

She dropped the cushion and turned. A man was watching her from a deep alcove, his features lost in shadow.

'You admire its beauty perhaps?' he said. 'And why wouldn't you? You, yourself, are very beautiful.'

The man took a step towards her. He was short yet slim, with rich olive skin and deep, dark brown eyes. He was clean-shaven except for a well-trimmed moustache which drew attention to his round, thick lips. His hands were smooth, as though he had never had to do any rough work, and his nails were like those of a wealthy lady.

He was dressed in a simple tunic of white silk with long, flowing trousers of a delicate green. A large gold chain hung around his neck. On his head he wore a little hat with a brooch made of flashing green gems.

As best she could judge, Agnes thought he was similar in age to her, maybe a few years older but no more.

'Have you got a tongue?' he asked. 'I know you have and I know that you speak Arabic. So speak to me now.'

She did not answer and he stepped closer towards her. 'I am Caliph al-Nasir, supreme head of the Muslim world.'

Agnes felt the blood drain from her face. She shook her head, tried to find words.

'I do not know what to say,' she said. 'I've never met such a great lord as you.'

The Caliph smiled. His whole face lit up with a warmth mixed with a twinkle of mischievousness.

'And I've rarely met such a beauty,' he said. He walked round her, examining her closely in the same manner that she might look at a piece of fruit or meat in the market. He peered at her necklace and gave a little smile.

'Yes,' he said. 'You are unusually beautiful. Especially for a woman of your age.'

He took her hand in his and kissed the tips of her fingers, gently releasing each one as if they were the petals of a flower.

'I'm not beautiful, my lord,' she said.

The Caliph smiled. 'How can you say that?' he murmured. 'I wonder that you dare to contradict the opinion of my trader. Habib is an excellent connoisseur of beautiful women. Better, obviously, than one woman is of herself.'

Agnes bowed her head, at a loss as to how to answer.

'This room is where I work,' he said. 'It is functional, uncluttered. It is, of course, hardly a place for a lady such as you.'

The Caliph held his hand out towards Agnes.

Astonished at this civility, she placed her own hand in his and allowed him to lead her across the room and through a small door.

As soon as she stepped over the threshold she gasped. She had been astonished by the sight of Johara and Beatrice's rooms. Not even these, however, had prepared her for the wonder of the Caliph's quarters.

They were in a large and airy chamber, with many other rooms leading from it. The floor was made of pure white marble. Divans and couches had been placed artfully across the room to make a picture pleasing to the eye, restful to the soul. Wall hangings of silk in a myriad of colours fluttered in the artificial breezes made by a dozen tall men waving palm fronds with a slow and graceful motion.

Tables of every size were dotted about the room. Some bore a figurine of exquisite design, others a decorated bowl or a bottle made of glimmering glass. On a large sideboard to one side of the room were laid out twenty dishes of food, some hot, some cold.

In the centre of the room a small fountain played, its shimmering waters cascading onto little bells which tinkled in an ever-changing melody. This acted as a counter-part to the glistening sound of harps played by musicians who could not be glimpsed.

'This is a fairy-land,' Agnes said.

The Caliph beamed with a sudden, youthful delight.

'It is my life's work to restore the Caliphate to the glory of the earliest years,' he said. 'The days off al-Mansur and Hārūn al-Rashīd. I seek to do this in the larger world and in Baghdad. And I also seek to do it within my own quarters.'

He pulled Agnes' hand to rest against his chest. 'And most of all,' he said, 'I endeavour to restore that glory here, to my heart and to my soul.'

She found herself staring into his eyes. For the first time since Saladin's army arrival at Jerusalem, she no longer felt afraid.

'What will you do with me, lord?' she asked.

Al-Nasir smiled. 'First, I would have you dine with me.' He pointed out the array of food.

'I have just eaten, with Johara.'

'Then you shall watch me dine,' he said.

'And afterwards, Excellency?'

He stroked her hair. 'After I have dined you will learn what it is to be one of my concubines.'

Agnes hid any reaction, closing her eyes so that he could not read them. She bowed to the inevitable and to the Caliph.

'I am honoured, Excellency,' she whispered.

He smiled and signalled for a servant to bring him food.

She watched him as he ate. She was surprised by the thoughtful way he selected from the dishes. She was even more surprised by the neat and fastidious way in which he ate. She had never seen any man eat like this before.

Eventually she spoke once again. 'I have three children in my care, my lord,' she said.

'What of it?'

'My daughter is to stay with me, I am told. But I know nothing of my son and my nephew.'

The Caliph smiled and looked into her eyes. He wrapped a lock of her hair around his fingers and she felt it tighten. 'I trust you don't think you can bargain with me,' he said. He spoke quietly.

Agnes touched him upon the chest. 'Not at all, my lord. It is a mother's lot to feel anxious about her children.'

She felt his fingers relax and her hair loosen in his grip.

His fingers touched her chin and he lifted her face up to stare into his eyes. 'I honour you for your concern,' he said. 'I will make no promises for the moment. I will ponder on it. But I am tired now and would go to my bed.'

He kissed her lightly on her lips. Her heart chilled. She pressed herself to him and kissed him with gentle passion.

CHAPTER 35
THE ENMITY OF KINSMEN
The Saracen Camp near Tyre

Bernard and Matthew sat under a cedar tree and stared at the Saracen camp. The Saracen soldiers had spent another fruitless day hurling themselves against the walls. They raised up ladders which were thrown down. They battered at the gates and boiling oil and fat were flung upon their heads. The death toll was horrific.

The rocks and rubble which the Saracen catapults and mangonels sent flying over the battlements were almost immediately turned against them. The desperate defenders heaved them up, manhandled them to the edge of the battlements and hurled them back down upon the heads of the attackers.

The Saracen sappers watched where the rocks fell and raced out like hares to retrieve them and take them back to the mangonels ready to be hurled aloft once again.

'Will this ever end?' Bernard mumbled.

'It could go on for years,' Matthew answered.

'Years?' Bernard looked astonished. 'Yet it did not take Saladin long to conquer Jerusalem.'

Matthew chewed on a piece of bread. 'That was because the walls were less well-defended,' he said. 'Tyre's defences are being led by a most astonishing man. He seems to have a will of iron and not a trace of human frailty. It is hard to defeat a man such as him.

'And there's another difference. In Tyre there are hundreds of soldiers, most of them mercenaries. You didn't have that luxury in Jerusalem. You may have been made a knight, Bernard, but your soldiers were ordinary people and children.'

'I am an ordinary person,' Bernard answered. 'Or at least I was then. Now I don't know what's happened to me.'

'You've been caught up in something that's bigger than any of us,' Matthew answered.

'I know that,' Bernard answered. 'And it's destroyed my life.'

'You're still alive.'

'Bernard Montjoy is still alive,' he answered, jabbing himself savagely in the chest. 'But my Agnes, my Gerard and my Eleanor have been taken from me. The shell of Bernard Montjoy still lives but what good is a shell without a heart and without the love of a family?'

Matthew bit his lip. It had been years since he had held a woman in his arms but he judged that now was not the time to say this.

'What is the point of it all?' Bernard cried again. 'My people have lived here for almost a hundred years. My friends are not just Franks; they are Greeks, Jews, Armenians, even Muslims. Agnes' brother Robert married a Muslim woman for love.'

He reached over and grabbed Matthew by the arm.

'Tell me what has changed? Tell me what has changed so much that I must no longer see people of a different creed as my kinsmen? When Robert married Farah I found out that the God the Saracens worship is our God, the same God, the very same. Shouldn't that make us brothers?'

'Perhaps it does,' said Matthew. 'Perhaps this very closeness is what makes us fight so fiercely. Look at John and his sudden hatred for his cousin.'

Bernard nodded. 'I know. I am shocked by this.'

Matthew stared up at the sky as if he would find an answer to the puzzle there.

'Do you have any idea of what caused the enmity?'

Bernard shook his head. 'None whatsoever.'

'Then it must be about a woman. Inexplicable hatreds are always about women.'

Bernard nodded in agreement and then stopped. He turned towards Matthew, his face suddenly troubled.

CHAPTER 36
THREE BOYS
Baghdad

Gerard and Claude-Yusuf watched Agnes and Eleanor disappear into the depths of the harem. Gerard tried to fight his tears but failed and was soon wailing and snuffling.

'Where have they taken them?' he repeated over and over. 'Where have they taken them?'

Claude-Yusuf tried to calm Gerard but he was inconsolable. In the end, desperate, he threatened to punch him. It had the desired effect and Gerard fell quiet.

Habib and Dawud exchanged glances.

'See,' Habib said, 'I told you that the older boy was intelligent. A diplomat and a thug. What more could the Caliph ask for?'

Dawud chuckled. 'We'll see. Let's put them to the test.'

So began the worst seven days the boys had ever known. They were not told what had happened to Agnes and Eleanor or what was going to happen to them. The whole point of the ordeal they were about to undergo was to cut them loose from all certainty and security.

Habib and Dawud led them down a corridor which took many turns to right and left. As they walked, Claude-Yusuf noticed that the corridors got narrower, the lights less frequent. They turned one corner and the walls of the corridor were no longer well-finished but showed the rough stone beneath. They tramped down steps and the walls became cold and clammy.

Eventually they came to a door which Habib unlocked with a large key. The door opened to reveal a dark and filthy cell with a cold mud floor and water running down the walls. A tiny opening near the ceiling was the only source of light.

One chipped platter was handed over to Gerard. Upon it was a hunk of hard, black bread. A large pitcher of water was thrust at Claude-Yusuf. Then they were pushed into the cell and the door was closed and locked.

This was too much for either of the boys and they set up a disconsolate howling which went on until their voices cracked.

Nobody responded.

Eventually they stopped and Claude-Yusuf pressed his ear to the door. He could hear nothing. The two cousins looked at each other.

'Are we to stay here forever?' Gerard asked.

Claude-Yusuf tried to force a smile upon his face but failed. 'I don't think so. In any case, your father and John and Simon will come to our rescue.'

'What about your father?' Gerard asked.

Claude-Yusuf did not answer. He had long ago given up all hope of his father returning from battle.

They talked for a while, recalling their adventures in the streets of Jerusalem, trying to ignore the cries of the scurrying rats and the clatter of hungry cock-roaches. Eventually, when they had shared the bread and drunk all the water, they fell into a fitful slumber.

The next morning they awoke to find that the door had been opened.

'What does this mean?' Gerard asked.

Claude-Yusuf pressed his fingers to his lip to signify silence and craned his neck to listen for any sounds. Neither could hear a thing.

'Does it mean they've let us off?' Gerard asked.

'I don't know,' said Claude-Yusuf. 'Perhaps they came to give us food and were killed or ran away.'

He tip-toed to the door and squinted out. He waited for a while, turning his head first one way and then the other. Eventually he shrugged and returned to Gerard.

'I don't understand,' he said.

'But is there anyone there?' Gerard asked.

Claude-Yusuf shook his head. 'Nobody I can see and nobody I can hear.'

'Then let's get out of here.'

Claude-Yusuf stared at his cousin for a moment. He was too young to guess that this might be a trap. But there again, what he suggested might be the most sensible thing to do.

Claude-Yusuf put his hand upon Gerard's shoulder. 'Let's go then. But we must be absolutely silent. And you must promise that you will do exactly what I tell you.'

Gerard nodded, half in eagerness, half in terror.

The two boys crept out of the cell and turned left, which Claude-Yusuf remembered was the way they had been brought. He led the way down a musty smelling passage-way lit by guttering torches and festooned with the webs of innumerable spiders.

Finally, after what felt like an age, they came to a door with a large metal handle.

'I don't think we should go through there,' Gerard said.

'Nor do I,' said Claude-Yusuf. 'But there's nowhere else for us to go.'

He blinked at Gerard, his eyes wide as an owl's in the dim

light. Then he took a deep breath and pushed open the door.

He had expected a noise, an alarm or at least a ghostly creak. Instead the door slid open without a sound.

The two boys peered out and nearly died of fright. Habib and Dawud were sitting on two stools, staring straight at them.

'At last,' Habib said. 'I thought you'd never get here.'

Dawud chuckled to himself and pointed to a table. Two huge plates were piled up with food. There was broiled chicken, skewered lamb, fruit, cakes and sherbet.

Gerard raced over to it and reached out for some cake.

'Wait,' cried Claude-Yusuf. He sounded frightened. 'Don't eat anything. It may be poisoned.'

'But I'm starving,' Gerard said.

'You'll end up dead if it's poisoned.'

Gerard stared at the food doubtfully. 'What shall we do?' he breathed.

Claude-Yusuf glanced at the two adults. They did not move. He stepped up to the table and placed his face close to the food. He sniffed at it carefully, trying to detect any scent that should not be there. Finally he straightened up.

'It smells all right,' he said although his voice sounded full of doubt.

Gerard reached out for the food once again. Claude-Yusuf grabbed his hand and then turned and stared at Habib and Dawud.

'It is rude of us to eat before our elders,' he said in a measured tone.

He picked up a plate and took it over to the two men. 'Please, sirs,' he said quietly. 'Take your pick.'

Habib rubbed his hands together, picked up a chicken leg and began to gnaw on it. Claude-Yusuf chose a piece of bread and passed it to Dawud. 'I'm sure you will enjoy this,' he said.

Dawud smiled and bit upon the bread.

'You pass the first two tests,' Habib said, his mouth spraying meat. 'You left the filthy cell and you found a way of testing the food. Well done.'

'They took a long time to leave the cell,' Dawud said.

'True. But what a clever way of testing the food.' He beamed at the boys. 'Now eat your fill and we will take you to the next test.'

The two boys crammed their mouths with food and stuffed even more into the front of their shirts before following the two men out into the open.

The next tests were more straight-forward although more tiring. They were told to throw stones, rocks and sticks and better the distance each time, they were made to race against each other over a certain distance. They were told to stand on one leg until they fell, made to crouch down upon their haunches until they cried out in pain. They had to carry heavy loads, to walk with shallow dishes filled with water and not allow any drips. They were even told to juggle.

That night they did not return to the cell with the rats but were given food and allowed to sleep in a soft bed in an airy chamber.

The following day they were ordered to recite verses from memory, to tell stories and to sing. Habib was especially pleased when he heard that Gerard could read and write; arts with which his older cousin was unfamiliar.

That evening Habib and Dawud took great pains to make sure that they were comfortable in their rooms. Habib inspected the bedding to make sure that it was fresh. Dawud asked them if the room was cool and airy enough and opened the window still wider, propping it ajar to catch the evening breeze. Habib examined the food with intense scrutiny.

'There are roast meats and a stew of eels,' he said, opening covered dishes for their inspection. 'Bread, cheese, figs, grapes and pomegranate, delicious custards, cakes and sherbet.' He rubbed his own belly appreciatively. 'You will eat well tonight, as token of all that you have accomplished.'

The two men left and the boys dived on the food.

'Does this mean we have passed all the tests?' Gerard asked. 'Is this our reward?'

Claude-Yusuf swallowed what he was eating with difficulty. He did not know how to answer.

'Eat up,' he said eventually. 'Enjoy the feast.'

The two boys set to again but it was not long before Gerard noticed that Claude-Yusuf was eating ever more slowly. He put down his plate with half the food still on it.

Gerard felt the sweet, soft bread cloy in his own mouth. 'Why aren't you eating?' he asked nervously.

Claude-Yusuf's hand squeezed him on the shoulder.

'Because I fear that this food is to make us feel happy,' he said. 'I think that tomorrow will bring far worse tests than any we have had to face so far.'

Gerard dropped the bread on his plate.

'Worse?'

Claude-Yusuf nodded.

The boys sat in silence for a while, contemplating what dreadful things may be in store for them.

They went to bed and fell into a fitful sleep.

Claude-Yusuf woke in the dark hours of night. He felt hungry now and tip-toed over to the table to take some more food.

Every last piece of food and every drop of drink had

been taken.

The next day, the fourth, they were made to run around the courtyard until first Gerard and then Claude-Yusuf dropped with exhaustion.

'That wasn't so bad,' said Claude-Yusuf in an attempt to cheer up Gerard.

In the afternoon they were thrown into a deep pool which Habib said was full of snakes. Neither of the two boys could swim and they screamed in terror. Eventually they had to be rescued by Dawud.

That night they cowered in their room, terrified at what the next day would bring.

'Every day's getting worse,' said Gerard. 'Do they mean to kill us?'

'Of course not,' Claude-Yusuf answered. He turned his face away, not wishing Gerard to see that this was exactly what he was beginning to think as well.

On the fifth day they were made to repeat verses which Habib recited from the Koran and beaten with a stick when they made a mistake.

On the sixth day they were taught to play chess and ordered to play against each other and the adults.

On the seventh day they were hoisted onto ponies. They began to walk and then to trot around a small field. Claude-Yusuf kept falling off but Gerard had as much a way with the pony as he did with any dog and he kept his saddle. Finally, they were given blunt swords and commanded to fight against each other.

A little while after noon Habib and Dawud called the two boys to them and told them to sit at their feet.

'We have put you through the tests required by the Caliph for his servants,' Habib said. 'We do this in order to identify your skills and decide upon the role you are most suited for.'

He turned to Gerard. 'You are to be a huntsman, to work with the hounds and the horses.'

'Thank you,' Gerard said, not believing his good fortune.

'You, Claude-Yusuf, are to be trained as a clerk.'

'But I cannot read or write.'

'You will be taught this. And you will be taught many secrets of law and of diplomacy. If you work hard, who knows, you might even aspire to being Vizier.'

'Before this, however,' said Dawud, 'you will be assigned to a futuwwa.'

The two boys looked blank.

'They are brotherhoods,' he explained. He cast in his mind for something the boys might be familiar with. 'Something like your guilds,' he said.

'Not the guilds,' said Habib. 'The futuwwa are more like your military orders, like the Templars and Hospitallers.'

The boys' faces shone with joy.

'And later,' said Dawud solemnly, 'you will need to decide whether you remain as infidels or embrace the true faith of Islam.'

Gerard was shocked at the suggestion and nearly burst into tears. Claude-Yusuf, however, bit his bottom lip thoughtfully.

'But there is no need to decide this yet,' said Habib. 'You will, of course, be instructed in both Arabic and in Islam.'

'We speak Arabic,' Claude-Yusuf said. 'We had to when we lived in Jerusalem.'

'You speak a mongrel version of it,' said Dawud. 'You will be taught better.'

As he said this, the door to the chamber was flung open and a small boy of about Claude-Yusuf's age hurtled in.

Habib and Dawud immediately threw themselves to the ground.

Claude-Yusuf and Gerard stood open-mouthed with astonishment and turned to look at the boy.

He was smaller than Claude-Yusuf but sturdier, dark haired and with piercing black eyes. He was dressed in a shirt of white silk with billowing white pyjama trousers beneath. Both were embroidered with fine designs in gold and crimson and both were covered with mud.

'Who are you?' the boy demanded.

Claude-Yusuf stepped towards him. 'I am Claude-Yusuf from Jerusalem and this is my cousin Gerard. Who are you?'

'You mustn't ask this?' hissed Habib.

'Be silent,' the boy told him.

He took a pace towards Claude-Yusuf and looked him in the eye. 'I am al-Dahir, son of Caliph al-Nasir,' he said.

He grinned. 'Let's be friends.'

CHAPTER 37
SPYING OUT THE CITY
Antioch

'Shall we be friends?' Eraclius asked.

Simon gave him a wary look.

'But you are my master,' he said. 'I am your servant.'

Eraclius poured two beakers of wine and gave one to Simon. 'That need not stop us being friends,' he said. 'Look at Balian and Jerome. Balian is the master and Jerome the servant yet they are friends nonetheless.'

Simon bowed his head. 'I am honoured, my lord.' Yet, even as he said this he wondered about Eraclius' motives. What possible benefit could there be to the Patriarch to count Simon Ferrier as his friend? What possible blunder would it prove for Simon to count the Patriarch as his?

The words had been spoken, however, the friendship acknowledged. Simon's stomach grew cold at the thought.

Eraclius hid a self-satisfied smirk. He recognised that Simon was the sort of person who would always sell his service to the highest bidder, and so had limits to his trustworthiness. Yet, this sort, once deluded into believing in the friendship of master and servant, invariably found these bonds far more difficult to break.

'Tell me, Simon,' the Patriarch asked. 'What think you of Princess Cybil?'

Simon drew a breath. From the audience of a week before it

was clear that the Princess had no liking for the Patriarch. Eraclius, on the other hand, had been very careful to keep hidden his opinion of Cybil.

Simon realised he would have to be wary in his answer.

'She is very comely,' he said.

'A market urchin could say as much,' Eraclius answered. 'There is no denying her beauty, or her sexual allure. I mean, what do you think of her as a person?'

'She acts like a Princess.'

'Ah, she acts like a Princess. So you also detect the falseness? You detect the mask the temptress wears.'

Simon had meant it as a comment on her regal air but Eraclius assumed that he saw beyond this to some false charade.

Simon took note. He knew the Patriarch's view now and nodded to show he shared them.

Eraclius came close and lowered his voice. 'Sibyl herself is little better than a street walker. And she indulges in the Black Arts.'

'The Black Arts?'

'Sorcery. Magic, curses, spells.' He passed his hand over his head as if in pain. 'Witchcraft, the snares of Satan.'

Simon was shocked. 'Does her husband know it?'

Eraclius laughed. 'Bohemond is the one person who does not. He was bewitched by her. Why else would he have put aside his Byzantine Queen and taken Cybil into his bed?'

Perhaps because she has the face and body of a goddess, Simon thought. 'You are right, my lord,' he said. 'There is no other explanation. Bohemond must have been enslaved by her spells.'

'Do well to remember it, my son.' He thrust a tiny crucifix into Simon's hand. 'Have this about your person whenever you have dealings with her.'

He drained his cup of wine and poured himself another.

'Now,' he said. 'We must think of the future. There is an Archbishop in Antioch, an old fool under the thumb of Bohemond. Naturally, I am his superior. Despite this, he has seen fit, commanded no doubt by the Prince and his witch, to allow me only a small chapel as my church. For now, I shall have to accept this. But an early task must be to secure a more fitting establishment. I want you to scour the city for a suitable church for my worship.'

'I shall go straight away, my lord.'

'Stay a moment.' Eraclius held up his hand. 'Learn this, Simon, from the beginning. I am efficient. I will never give you only one task at a time.'

Eraclius walked over to the window and gazed out at the city below. 'Antioch is like Babylon,' he said. 'It is a stew-pot of races, religions and ideas. While the Prince remains strong the people will obey him. But beneath the surface, just beneath, swills a torrent of wrath and treachery. Most of the population are Muslims, the rest a rag-bag of Syrians, Amenians and Greeks.

'For a Frank to walk alone in the streets is to invite a blade across the throat. Even more so when that Frank is a man of renown such as myself. So I require two further tasks of you. One is to transform your gaggle of grooms into a professional bodyguard for me. The second is to build a network of spies to sniff out the city for danger. And for opportunity.'

He flung a large bag of coins towards Simon. 'That should get you started. Be gone.'

Simon picked up the bag. He had an idea how to train the bodyguard but none whatsoever about how to build up a spy network. He wanted to ask for advice but something told him that to do so would diminish his credit with Eraclius, perhaps fatally.

He bowed and left the chamber, pondering how to start.

An inn, he thought, I'll start in the lowliest inn I can find.

He sought out Gregory, the groom he considered most promising, and most loyal. He found him in the hall, gambling with another man, an ugly, well-built youth with strong arms but little else to recommend him.

'Gregory,' Simon said. 'I want you to come with me into the city. We have work to do.'

Gregory immediately reached for his sword and dagger, actions which commended him still further to Simon.

As they reached the door, Simon paused and glanced back at Gregory's companion, who was trying to work out how much he had just lost.

'You,' he said. 'What is your name?'

'William, my lord.'

'Can you fight?'

William's face gave a grin of empty delight. 'Like a bull-dog, my lord.'

'Then get a blade and come with us.'

The light was failing as the three men headed down to the poorest quarter of the city. On every corner a high bracket held a flaming torch which gave some semblance of light. Standing beneath these were torch-boys who would light their own torch from the flame and lead anyone anywhere for a few coins.

Simon spoke quietly to Gregory and he engaged a small runt of a boy to lead them to an inn. The boy gave a lascivious grin. 'You want fat girls or thin ones? Expensive girls or cheap?'

Gregory turned towards Simon.

'Cheap,' he said. 'The cheaper the better.'

Outcasts

The boy tapped his nose slyly and led them swiftly down a narrow alley which turned crooked ways until it became so narrow a fat man would have been unable to go further.

Finally, when Simon was beginning to fear a trap, the boy halted outside a little drinking house. Angry voices sounded loud from within.

'This inn is called Gates of Heaven,' the boy said. 'But you'll find no angels here.'

He turned to go and then came back a few paces. 'Do not eat any food,' he said. 'And don't drink the white wine.'

He scampered off as if wary of staying here.

Simon gestured to William to lead the way into the inn.

It was a single room about ten feet square. Crammed into it were thirty or so men, all with flagons in their hands. There were no seats. Every customer was either standing or leaning against the noisome walls for support.

A small table stood at the far end. This was laden with bottles of wine and a large cauldron with a fume billowing from it, presumably the food the torch-boy had warned them about.

Lounging on mats to the side of the table were filthy, scrawny women, either very young or very old. At the sight of the newcomers they brushed the traces of food from their clothes and flicked their hair in what they thought was an enticing manner.

Simon felt Gregory turn towards him with a look of astonishment.

'We're here on business,' Simon muttered. 'We don't touch the whores.'

'That is good news,' Gregory said.

William, on the other hand, looked rather less happy.

Simon told Gregory to go to the bar for a jug of red wine. He found a corner of the bar which looked slightly less full of bodies and shouldered his way towards it with William.

They had no sooner perched themselves against a wall when two women slid through the crowd towards them. One looked about sixty years old with breasts hanging low, hooked nose and hairs curling from her chin. The other appeared to be about fourteen or so. Simon peered beneath the grime on her face and saw that she was pretty. He was shocked to see such a girl in such a situation.

'What would you like?' said the old woman. 'Straight sex, mouth, arse or something unusual?'

'Nothing with you,' Simon said.

'In that case, how about my grand-daughter? She'll do anything you please. Beat her if that's your pleasure, flog her even. But don't mark her face. It's bad for business.'

Simon pushed the old woman away. 'You disgust me,' he said.

Gregory arrived with the drinks and the old whore grabbed one of the cups and swallowed it down.

'Thanks very much, my darling,' she said, grinning to reveal blackened teeth. 'But next time buy me the white wine.'

Gregory glanced at Simon but he shook his head to let her be.

The old woman clicked her fingers and the young girl stepped forward.

'What'll it be then, sir?' she said. 'Don't worry. You don't have to say. Have her for all night and you can do what you want with her.'

'Really?' Simon asked.

'A half dinar,' she said, holding out a hand.

Simon nodded. He dropped the coin onto the old woman's palm and it shut like a trap.

'Gabriella, ' she said, 'make good and sure you please the

gentleman. Anything he wants.'

'Yes, Grandma,' the girl said.

She looked at Simon anxiously. 'Where will you take me, sir?'

'I don't know.'

'We could go back of the alley, by the latrine. I'd take you home but my brothers will be deep in drink and they might attack you.'

'How many brothers do you have?'

'Just the six. And four sisters, all young.'

She fell silent, as if realising what she had said. 'They're too young for business,' she said anxiously, pawing at Simon's arm. 'Please, sir, far too young.'

'I've no interest in your sisters, or your brothers. Just you.'

He nodded towards his companions. 'Let's go.'

William led the way out of the den and into the alley.

'Where we going, my lord?' he asked.

'Back to the house,' Simon said. 'And keep your eyes skinned for anybody following us.'

'You're not going to do away with me, are you?' Gabriella asked.

Simon laughed. 'Why would I pay good money if I was going to harm you?'

They had only gone a few steps when a shape stepped out in front of them. Their hands went to their knives.

'It's only Theo,' Gabriella cried.

The torch-boy showed his face. 'I thought you might want a light back home,' he said, holding out his hand.

The small party hurried up the alley and soon arrived at the grand house which had been allocated to Eraclius and his staff.

Simon hesitated. Now that he had brought the girl back here he began to doubt the wisdom of it.

He beckoned his men over. 'I have procured this girl,' he said softly, 'in order to find out information about the city. For no other purpose.'

Gregory and William nodded earnestly. Simon stared at them, certain they did not believe a word of it. 'This goes no further, understand.'

Again, the two men nodded. William tried to hide a smirk but failed.

'Don't be so pathetic,' Simon said. 'You can both go now but remember, not a word.'

Gregory and William nodded and hurried into the house.

Simon turned to the torch-boy. 'You must know a lot of what goes on in the city?'

'What I don't know I can find out,' Theo answered.

'Good. Meet me at the cross-roads tomorrow at noon and we will talk further.'

The boy held out his hand.

Simon shook his head. 'That may feel coin again if you meet me. Not until.'

Theo grinned and hurried off to find more customers.

Simon turned towards Gabriella. 'I meant what I told my men,' he said. 'I need to find out everything I can about the city. You strike me as being someone who could tell me much of what I need to know.'

'Of course, sir,' Gabriella said.

Such falsehoods were often told to her and she always pretended to believe them. Whatever the story she knew she was only wanted for sex.

'Come on then,' Simon said, 'and be sure to be silent.'

Simon led her into the house and up the stairs towards his tiny chamber in the rafters. It was warm and dry but contained nothing more than a bed, a small cupboard, a chamber pot and a basin and ewer. A candle was guttering in its holder and he hurried to light a fresh one before it went out completely. The room was plunged into darkness for a moment while the wick caught and then the flame strengthened and a dim glow lit the room.

He turned to where Gabriella was standing nervously by the door. 'Don't worry, child,' he said.

He picked up the candle and held it to her face in order to examine her. Yes, she was pretty beneath the grime. She looked nervous but attempted a smile. She had an oval face with a little nose and full lips. Her hair was so dirty and matted that he had no idea what colour it might be. She was slightly cross-eyed which gave her a rather vulnerable look. He sniffed. She clearly had little familiarity with water.

'You're very dirty,' he said.

Her eyes blinked and filled with tears. 'Sorry sir, I don't mean to be.'

'Forgive me,' he said. 'It is I who should apologise.'

She looked at him in wonder as he put the candle back on the cupboard and reached for the ewer.

He turned to her and stared at her more closely. It's not just her face, he thought. He found that he was trembling with excitement.

He picked up the basin and placed it on the floor. Then he gave the girl a cloth.

'I want you to wash,' he said. 'Take off your clothes and step into the basin.'

She nodded and stepped into the basin. She reached down and pulled the tunic over her head. He felt his throat tighten.

Slowly he poured water from the ewer over her head and watched it cascade over her shoulders and down her breasts and belly.

'Use the cloth,' he said and was surprised at how thick his voice sounded.

The girl rubbed the cloth gently as the water played over her. The dirt began to wash away although there were streaks of shadow still left upon her skin when Simon had poured the last of the water. It did not matter. She looked beautiful.

Simon gave her a towel and she dabbed herself dry.

He could not take his eyes off of her.

She stepped out of the basin and climbed onto the bed. She went on all fours and peered round to look at him.

'I'd like it this way, please, sir,' she said. 'I'm young and I don't want to be with child.'

Simon nodded, not trusting himself to speak, and climbed onto the bed behind her.

CHAPTER 38
YOUNG MUSLIM LORDS
Baghdad

Claude-Yusuf turned to look at Gerard and then at the Muslim boy who was waiting patiently for his response.

'You are the son of the Caliph?' he asked nervously.

The boy nodded. 'If you doubt me, just look there.'

Claude-Yusuf turned to where Habib and Dawud remained prostrate upon the ground.

'You may rise now,' the boy said.

The two adults struggled to their feet and bowed once more to the boy.

'What is your name, again?' Gerard asked. 'It sounds strange.'

'I am al-Dahir, son of Caliph al-Nasir,' the boy repeated. 'It is only strange to uncivilised ears. What are you called?'

'I am Gerard. My father is Bernard Montjoy of Jerusalem. He owns an inn and is now a knight.'

'A knight?' al-Dahir grinned with delight at this.

'Yes, he was knighted by Lord Balian to fight the infidel Saladin.'

He felt a sharp clip around his head. He turned to see Dawud's eyes blazing at him.

'And what about you?' al-Dahir asked, turning towards the older boy. 'What is your name?'

Claude-Yusuf stared back with a hint of belligerence. 'My

name is Claude-Yusuf Godwin. My father is a soldier of King Guy.'

'Not a knight?'

Claude-Yusuf shook his head.

Al-Dahir folded his arms and considered the cousins closely. 'If your fathers are such warriors,' he said finally, 'how are you prisoners in Baghdad?'

The two young boys gazed at each other, uncertain for a moment how best to answer.

'My father fought at a great battle,' Claude-Yusuf said. 'He fought hand to hand with Saladin himself and was terribly wounded by Saladin's guards. He has been taken to the coast to find healing. He wanted to ride after us but his doctors forbade him and hid his horse.'

Gerard turned to Claude-Yusuf, his brow furrowing.

'Gerard's father,' Claude-Yusuf continued, 'fought at the siege of Jerusalem and has been captured by the Saracens. I expect he is in prison and being tortured as otherwise he would have rescued us.'

Gerard was astonished and horrified at this news. It had obviously been kept from him until now. He began to sob at the thought of his poor father's sufferings.

Al-Dahir pulled a silk handkerchief from his trousers and handed it to Gerard. 'Do not weep,' he said. 'I expect your father will bear his torment bravely. If you like I will get my father to send a message to Saladin to stop the torture.'

'Would Saladin agree?' Gerard asked, his face a mixture of doubt and hope.

'My father is the master of Saladin and his command is law. Saladin would not dare to refuse.'

Claude-Yusuf gave a doubtful look. 'Are you really saying that your father is more powerful than Saladin?'

'Of course. Saladin is always asking him for aid in his wars against the Franks. That's true, isn't it Habib?'

'It is, my lord,' Habib answered. 'He asks and the Caliph refuses.'

Claude-Yusuf scratched his head. 'Why does your father refuse to help?'

Al-Dahir shrugged. 'My father must have his reasons. He is the Caliph.'

'What is a Caliph?' Gerard asked.

Al-Dahir laughed. 'You don't know?'

Gerard shook his head.

Al-Dahir looked at a loss for a moment. He glanced at Dawud. 'You tell him,' he said.

'The Caliph is the leader of the Muslim world,' Dawud answered. 'He is the head of the faith…'

'Apart from the Shia,' said Habib.

'He is the head of even them, although they do not admit it,' said Dawud, sharply. 'The Caliph rules the lands around Baghdad directly and allows emirs like Saladin to rule other lands in his name.'

'Administer other lands,' corrected Habib. 'Not rule, administer.'

'That is what I said.'

'You said rule. The vizier will have your tongue branded for such a statement.'

'Only an idiot like you would think I meant rule,' Dawud said. 'You must learn to sift words, to understand figures of speech.'

'Enough,' said al-Dahir.

The two men fell silent.

'I asked if you wanted to be my friends,' al-Dahir reminded them.

Both boys nodded eagerly.

'Good. It is so. But first I will sponsor you to join my futawwa.'

Gerard clapped his hands with excitement. 'You mean you are a member of one of them?' he cried. 'You are like a Hospitaller.'

Al-Dahir shrugged. 'I don't know what you mean by Hospitaller,' he said.

Now it was the turn of Claude-Yusuf and Gerard to give disparaging looks.

'The Hospitallers are knights of God,' Gerard said. 'And so are the Templars.'

'The futawwa are the champions of God,' al-Dahir said. 'I have never heard of your knights. The champions delight in warfare and hunting as well as the worship of Allah. They sing songs and wrestle.'

'I told you about the fatuwwa,' Dawud said. 'You are honoured if his Excellency will sponsor you to be a fata in the Caliph's fatawwa.'

Habib put his hand fondly upon Claude-Yusuf's head. 'You will be grateful that Dawud and I prepared you so well for this honour,' he said, with a quick glance towards al-Dahir.

'They might not be so grateful,' Dawud muttered. 'Not when they meet Sheik al-Djabbar.'

Al-Dahir dismissed Habib and Dawud and led Claude-Yusuf and Gerard out of the palace to a huge lawn which was fringed by large buildings gleaming in the sun. Half a dozen guards strode after them, at a distance, unnoticed by any of the boys.

'I didn't know that my father was being tortured,' Gerard said to his cousin. 'Why didn't you tell me?'

'Because it's not true,' whispered Claude-Yusuf. 'I didn't want al-Dahir to think our fathers are cowards who wouldn't rescue us. And whatever you do, don't ever say anything different to anyone.' He pinched Gerard's arm and made him yelp.

Al-Dahir paused outside one of the buildings. It was a long, low structure with many doors and a veranda running all of its length. Sitting underneath this was a group of young men who all rose and salaamed to the Caliph's son.

Al-Dahir acknowledged them with a wave of his hand and turned towards the cousins.

'This is the headquarters of futuwwa my father and I belong to,' he said. 'I will take you to the chief of the order, Sheik al-Djabbar.'

He led them into cool and light building. It felt calm and pleasant and the boys immediately felt at ease.

Many chambers led off of the central hall but al-Dahir did not turn into any of these. He led them through an arch which came out into a central courtyard. It was flagged with stone but in the middle was a lawn with a fountain and a pavilion to provide shade.

Two elderly men sat beneath this shade, intent upon a game of chess.

Al-Dahir led the boys across the courtyard to the pavilion. He waited there in silence, unacknowledged by either of the two old men. Claude-Yusuf and Gerard looked at each other, wondering what would happen next.

Finally, one of the old men looked up. Gerard took a step backwards at the sight of him.

He was very old, or so it seemed, and his face was very lined. He had a large nose which thrust out from his face like a raised fist. His lips were thin and clamped tight with a downward droop which made him look resolutely bitter. A large red scar ran from his neck, up his chin and to his left eye.

He stared at them in silence. His gaze was sharp and searching and cold.

'Greetings, my Prince,' the old man said at last, ducking his head slightly. 'To what do I owe the pleasure?'

'Sheik al-Djabbar,' answered al-Dahir. 'These are my friends, Claude-Yusuf and Gerard. Their fathers are knights of the Frankish emirates to the west. I desire that they join our futuwwa, if you are willing.'

The sheik sniffed. It was a loud, wet, gurgling sniff which seemed to hang in the air, almost as if it were listening to the conversation and had a view upon it.

He turned to look at the boys. 'Why would I want such puny weaklings to join the order?' he asked.

'Because they are my friends.'

'Is that a good enough reason?' he asked.

'That depends on who is making the request,' said the other man in a voice which squawked like that of a bird, something he seemed, in fact to resemble. 'If it was a beggar on the street then it is no reason whatsoever. If it is a prince then it requires no reason; it is reason enough.'

'Silence,' the sheik said. 'When I desire comments from a fool with a washer-woman's brain I will ask you.'

His hand lashed out like a snake's and Claude-Yusuf and Gerard felt the stinging cut of a thin cane across their cheeks.

'Don't touch,' the old sheik commanded in a chill voice.

They dropped their hands instantly. The pain on their cheeks, though intense, was not as forceful as the old man's cry.

He turned his snarling eyes upon them once again.

'Do you want to join the order?' he asked.

Claude-Yusuf nodded eagerly. Gerard was not sure and bobbed his head once, miserably.

The old man chuckled. 'Let me make a prophecy,' he said. 'Even if you do want to join the order I doubt you want to join it enough. And if I allow you to join you will, by the time I have finished with you, crawl on your knees from here to the Hindu Kush to be allowed your freedom from it.'

A little tinkling noise followed fast upon his words. Gerard was wetting himself.

The two old men cackled with pleasure at the sight.

The sheik picked up two dates from a plate beside the chessboard and gave one to each of the cousins.

Gerard immediately popped the fruit into his mouth and received another slash of the cane in rebuke.

'I did not command you to eat,' said Sheik al-Djabbar. 'Spit it out onto your hand.'

The second old man giggled. 'I remember this now, Excellency,' he said. 'A very good choice.'

The sheik turned to him and gave a thin smile.

His friend returned it, nodding like a bird pecking at crumbs.

'How long do you think you can hold this little date in your hand?' the sheik asked the boys.

Neither of them dared to answer so he beat the cane upon the table.

'For as long as I'm asked to,' answered Claude-Yusuf, trying to fight back the tears.

'And how long might that be? One hour, two, three? It is such a little thing, a date; so dainty, so light in weight.'

'I could hold it for three hours, I'm certain,' said Claude-Yusuf.

'He is certain, Excellency,' cried the other man. 'The little infidel is certain.'

The sheik ignored him. He leant forward and his voice was low as a sigh.

'Such a little thing, a date.' He glanced up at the sun which was just beginning to fall towards the west. 'Do you believe you can hold it until sunset?'

'Of course.'

The sheik nodded. 'Then we shall see.'

He gestured quickly and both boys held the fruit out on the palm of their hand.

This is not much of a test, Claude-Yusuf thought.

Out of the corner of his eye he caught a glimpse of the Caliph's son. His face wore a look of concern.

Minutes went by. Both boys felt their arms begin to shiver and then to shake. Every time their arms began to droop the sharp crack of the sheik's cane upon the table made them straighten them immediately.

The two old men returned to their chess.

A light meal was brought out to them which they picked at in the interlude between their play.

And still the boys held out their hands.

After an hour the dates began to feel like heavy stones. Gerard could stand no more. He started to cry and dropped the date on the ground, collapsing upon the ground beside it.

The old sheik stared at him. But he did not lash out as Claude-Yusuf assumed he would.

Al-Dahir rushed over to Gerard, helped him up and told one of the guards to carry him into the shade.

A second hour went by.

Outcasts

Still Claude-Yusuf stood in the full glare of the sun, his arm outstretched although he thought it would be wrenched from its socket by the weight of the date. It felt like a boulder.

The two old men finished their game of chess and began to talk. Yet every few minutes they glanced at Claude-Yusuf and their eyes were sharp.

Once, al-Dahir bent and whispered something in the sheik's ear. But the old man shook his head sternly and al-Dahir stepped back, wringing his hands in anguish.

A third hour went by and the sun began to colour the western sky with a pale pink. Still Claude-Yusuf stood although he thought that he would probably die this day.

Eventually the sun kissed the horizon and the voices of the muezzins sang out across the city.

Claude-Yusuf groaned and slumped to the ground.

'Is the infidel dead?' squawked the sheik's friend.

Al-Djabbar cursed him under his breath. He crouched to the ground and listened for the young boy's breath.

CHAPTER 39
DEATH THROES
Tyre

Saladin surveyed the battlements of Tyre. They had been battered by his siege engines but still they stood, as strong and solid as ever.

The flags of the Franks fluttered defiantly in the morning breeze. Foremost among them was the standard of Conrad of Montferrat, his foe.

He glanced at his own army. His men had risen from prayer and were beginning to prepare the morning meal. They had been in the field for six months now. For the first four months they had known only victories, victories so astonishing they seemed little short of miracles.

For the last two months, however, this had changed utterly. Since arriving at Tyre they had known only stalemate.

They had battled valiantly against the Franks but to no avail. Determined assaults had been thrown back by determined defence. Little skirmishes had been won and lost, brave men killed and wounded by the score. Yet still there was stalemate.

The two armies were like fighting dogs, each gripping the other by the throat, fearing to let go of the other, unable to give the killing bite.

Saladin's officers had warned of a subtle change in the men, a dulling of fervour, a hint of doubt. All was as insubstantial as faint shreds of cloud upon the horizon. Yet it was potent nonetheless.

Saladin observed these doubts with growing anxiety. They could destroy an army more swiftly than the plague.

'How goes it, brother?' called a familiar voice.

Saladin turned and saw al-Adil strolling towards him.

'No better for me staring at Conrad's standard,' Saladin answered, 'but much improved by you joining me.'

Al-Adil stood with hands upon his waist and gazed upon the city.

'Another night without a breach miraculously appearing in the walls.' He shrugged. 'So we will have to rely upon our soldiers once again.'

Saladin gave a faint smile but then grew serious once again.

'God performs his miracles through men such as these,' he said. 'But should God desert us then no amount of determination or courage or cunning will avail.'

'There is no sign that God has deserted us, brother, so raise your spirits. It is merely that, to keep you on your mettle, God has chosen an adversary worthy of you.'

Saladin smiled. 'Thank you, brother. Whenever I feel lost, you are ever my guide.'

'And you are the Sultan and have a foe to defeat.'

Arm in arm the two brothers returned to the camp.

So, with their back to the city, they alone could not see what was happening beyond the city.

'Christ and all his angels,' Matthew cried, pointing out to sea.

John and Bernard turned and stared. A hundred and more galleys were speeding towards the city from the south.

Ten yards away Khalid and his guards climbed to their feet.

'Allah be praised,' Khalid called. 'The Egyptians have arrived.'

The cry was taken up throughout the army.

Saladin and al-Adil were close to the camp now and at the sound they turned and saw the ships. They stared for a moment and then raced into the camp, calling to their officers to join them in Saladin's tent.

'Come with me Bernard,' Khalid called. 'When Conrad capitulates we may have need of you as interpreter.'

Bernard hurried after Khalid, still chewing on a mouthful of bread.

Saladin's tent was filling up with officers as they arrived. Just as they were about to enter they heard a shout and stared once more out to sea.

Issuing forth from the city were scores of Frankish ships. Conrad had decided to counter-attack the Egyptian fleet.

Within minutes the two navies had closed upon one another. Even from this distance they could see the shoals of arrows swarming through the sky between the ships. Then, from the bows of the Frankish ships long tubes belched out Greek Fire.

Wherever they struck there was chaos. The fire caught even upon wet timbers and leapt from there up the hull and onto masts and sails.

The Egyptian sailors tried to beat out the flames but if the fire touched their clothes it clung to them, devouring their flesh and turning them into human torches.

'The devils have Greek Fire upon their ships,' Khalid cried.

'But we have more ships,' cried another.

It was true. The Egyptians had far more ships. Yet, already the toll taken by the Greek Fire was eroding this advantage. Nevertheless, the superior numbers of the Egyptian fleet began to force the Franks back to port.

Outcasts

The exultant cries of the Saracen army became a thunderous barrage of noise. Yet in moments their attention switched from the sea-battle to the walls of Tyre.

The battle of the two fleets had excited the soldiers of Tyre just as much as the Saracens. They deserted their posts and ran towards the western wall to get a better sight of the battle. Not even the curses and blows of their officers could stop the stampede.

In moments, the whole of the landward battlements were empty of defenders.

In a moment, all thoughts of plans and strategy were abandoned.

Saladin and al-Adil exchanged one silent look and nodded to each other.

'To horse,' Saladin cried, 'to horse.'

In seconds the officers had turned and raced to their men. Khalid pushed his way back towards his own troops, Bernard hurrying to keep up.

Saladin had ridden out in front of the army and now his magnificent Arab stallion reared up, its forelegs clawing the air.

'Forget the ships,' Saladin cried. 'Attack the city.'

With a roar of fury the army launched itself upon Tyre. Two months of death, disillusion and despair gave renewed strength to the men. The horsemen reached the city walls within a minute and the infantry soon after.

They were completely unopposed.

Hardly believing their luck, the Saracen soldiers hoisted dozens of siege ladders against the walls. They began the long climb up to the undefended battlements.

Two dozen sappers raced towards the main gate with a battering ram and began to hammer upon it, unimpeded by oil or arrows from above. Slowly but surely the timbers began to shatter. Saladin and al-Adil summoned troops of horsemen to the gate, waiting for its overthrow.

The horsemen arrived in a melee and, in the moments before their captains were able to restore order, the gate was flung open from within. A trumpet blared and hundreds of heavily armoured knights plunged into the Saracens. Conrad had timed the attack to perfection.

The Saracen horsemen were still in a disordered state, the nearest ones skittish, most still galloping in from the plain. The Frankish knights were like a hammer blow. They cleaved through the foremost horsemen and, as they rode onward, opened up their charge so that they cut an ever-widening swathe of their enemies.

The lightly armed Saracens were no match for their heavily armoured foes. Their normal tactic was to shoot their bows from the saddle and then retreat. So sudden and unexpected was the assault, so close quarter the attack that they had no defence. Within moments, heedless of the cries of their captains, they broke and fled, trampling their foot-soldiers in their flight.

Seeing this, Conrad took a gigantic gamble.

He ordered his soldiers to leave the battlements in the possession of the Saracens and race down to the gate. Within minutes every soldier of Tyre poured out of the gate in the wake of their triumphant knights.

The slaughter of the fleeing Saracens was terrible.

Saladin tried to rally his men. By this time the foremost of Conrad's knights were closing on him. Three of them raced towards him.

Saladin parried the sword stroke of one and plunged his scimitar into a second. The third swept his sword down, missing Saladin's head by inches, but hacking open his stallion's neck. The horse fell and Saladin with it.

Al-Adil plunged back into the chaos and fended off the attacks upon his brother while a fresh horse was brought to him.

By this time the Saracen army was routed. The men of Tyre raced after them, slashing and hewing at every man.

Saladin flung his troops back into battle to secure the area of the siege-engines. Within minutes he realised that no hope remained and ordered their destruction.

Al-Adil led a hundred horsemen back to the attack to give time for the sappers to set fire to the towers and catapults. Khalid and his company joined him.

Seeing this, and having no other friends in the whole of the Muslim host, John, Bernard and Matthew cantered after him. Khalid grinned with delight when he saw this.

'I'll make believers of you yet,' he cried.

'Maybe,' yelled Matthew. 'If I come through alive.'

The hundred Saracen horsemen galloped towards the vanguard of the knights, now far ahead of their infantry.

The knights' thunderous charge had taken its toll of their horses and now, no matter how much they kicked and whipped, they could not get their steeds to manage more than a ragged canter.

The Arab horses, bearing far less weight, swept round them, darting in and out, tormenting men and horses with swift arrows.

Al-Adil led his men behind the knights and turned to circle them. As he raced towards them his horse fell and he was thrown to the ground.

Conrad saw this and swiftly turned to the attack. He hammered his horse towards al-Adil, yelling at the top of his voice for his men to follow.

Al-Adil regained his feet. He caught his horse by the reins and tried to quieten her. He glanced down. Her leg was broken. He patted her head and plunged his knife into her neck, lowering her gently to the ground by her reins.

He turned and looked up. Conrad was twenty yards away and rapidly closing on him.

Knowing that his time of death had come al-Adil bent his head and began to chant a prayer. Conrad's cry of triumph echoed across the battle-field.

The next moment al-Adil was pulled off his feet and thrown over a saddle.

'Hang on,' John cried, turning his horse savagely.

His horse staggered under the combined weight of the two men but picked up pace.

Bernard and Matthew dashed their mounts towards Conrad, blocking his advance.

He swung his sword at Bernard but missed him by an inch. Bernard and Matthew spurred their horses hard and raced off, chasing after John and al-Adil.

Five minutes later, judging that there was sufficient distance between them and the knights, John trotted to a halt and allowed al-Adil to drop to the ground. He was filthy with dust but unhurt.

'I thank you,' al-Adil said.

Before John could answer he felt his own horse stagger. Two thick arrows had pierced its neck. He slid out of the saddle and saw Bernard and Matthew's horses had also been wounded.

'We'll have to run,' he cried.

The four men leapt towards the Saracen lines.

More arrows darted among them, one slashing the flesh of Bernard's arm although not lodging in it.

A further flight rained down upon them.

Al-Adil cried out and fell.

An arrow had pierced his calf, the point slicing through the flesh. He struggled to rise but fell immediately.

John glanced towards the Saracen lines. They were still three hundred yards distant.

He looked back and saw the Frankish horsemen closing on them.

He turned to his friends, uncertain what to do.

'I'll carry him,' cried Matthew.

Matthew grabbed hold of al-Adil's arms and hauled him onto his own back, dragging his feet off the ground.

'Come on lads,' he yelled. 'The Mule is back.'

He raced off with astonishing speed, almost as if he were not burdened.

Al-Adil bellowed with pain then clamped his mouth shut.

'Keep up,' Matthew cried and John and Bernard leapt after him.

They had almost reached Matthew when the sound of horses grew loud in their ears.

'Go on,' they cried to Matthew, then turned, slashing at the foremost riders with their swords, missing them but making them swerve out of the way.

The horses following also swerved, causing those behind to slow.

'Come on John,' Bernard cried and they raced once more after Matthew and al-Adil.

The Saracen horsemen had grasped the situation and now thundered to the rescue.

Mere yards in front of Matthew their ranks split and they hurtled past leaving a narrow corridor for the friends to run through.

They smashed into the Frankish horsemen sending them reeling.

'Al-Mule, al- Mule, al-Mule,' roared the Saracen warriors as Matthew staggered to a halt and stood gasping, al-Adil still clinging grimly to his back.

A Saracen officer rode towards them and leapt off of his steed, helping al-Adil climb onto it. He pointed out where Saladin stood beneath a cedar tree, watching the destruction of his army.

The Sultan hurried towards them.

'Are you hurt, little brother?' he called.

Al-Adil shook his head. 'I will live. What about you? Are you wounded?'

Saladin turned a stricken face towards him.

'To my soul,' he said. 'This is terrible butchery.'

Within an hour, Saladin's army had fled the field, the only ones remaining those abandoned on the walls of Tyre. They fought for two hours longer until every last one had been slain.

Saladin watched as Conrad of Montferrat led his battered yet triumphant troops back to the city of Tyre.

'Allah has decided,' he murmured. 'I should have taken Tyre before attacking Jerusalem. He must have felt my decision was caused by vanity.'

He turned to where his brother was having his leg bandaged by a doctor.

'I could have conquered Tyre,' the Sultan continued. 'If it had any other commander than Conrad of Montferrat.'

He turned and stared at the walls of the city.

'It is a lesson in humility, little brother. Allah has sent this devil of a Marquis to defeat me.'

'Do not think that, Saladin,' al-Adil said. 'Conrad is a man like any other. He can be defeated like any other.'

'True. But not, I think, by me.'

He turned his back on Tyre and ordered his army to march inland.

Al- Adil turned to Matthew, John and Bernard.

'I am forever in your debt, he said. 'Whatever you desire is yours, my friends.'

CHAPTER 40
GABRIELLA
Antioch

Simon lay in his bed and listened to the sound of Gabriella breathing beside him. He imagined the breath going through her nose, into her chest and then blowing gently back out of her mouth. It was a breath he loved to take into his own lungs. By doing so he felt he could possess her even more, be one with her even more.

He sighed. The girl had bewitched his heart.

It was not merely that she was skilful in bed. That was to be expected from one such as her, a whore born of whores and trained to it from the earliest age. No, it was much more than that.

He felt attached to her in a way which was almost frightening. Whenever he was away from her he grew anxious and fretful. The only thing which brightened his days was when she appeared in the doorway or glanced up at him from staring out of the window or picking at some food.

That glance made him a fool. He felt unmanned and weakened. He would shiver and shake as if he were in the grip of a fever.

I suppose I am, he thought. In a terrible fever. He could not bring himself, dared not bring himself, to give the fever a name.

'Is it day yet?' Gabriella asked him sleepily.

He kissed her on the eyes.

'Not yet,' he said. 'I'll wake you when it is.'

He knew that people laughed at him for consorting with a gutter whore. He knew the whispers behind his back, the contempt with which people held him. He had even caught some of his own men smirking when he appeared before them with Gabriella beside him. Those who smirked soon learnt to control their faces better. The least they could expect for such disloyalty was a punch to the head or even a beating.

The nobles of Antioch were even worse. They played an elaborate charade whenever they saw him, calling him poet and troubadour of love. But they did not wait for him to pass by before showing the real contempt they felt for him.

It was not because he was sleeping with a prostitute. That was common and the men of the city spent so much on the trade they made the flourishing whore market one of the richest and most esteemed in the world.

No, sleeping with a whore was not the problem.

The problem was that he had fallen in love with her.

The only one who did not seem too concerned about this state of affairs was his master, the Patriarch.

But that may have been because he had slightly misunderstood the situation.

'Keep her while she's useful to us,' he said. 'She's giving us good information about what goes on in this charnel house of a city.'

He passed some coins over to Simon. 'Keep little Gabriella sweet,' he said. 'She's fallen in love with you, my boy, and a woman in love is the most pliable of all tools. Keep the delusion going while she remains useful to us.'

Simon nodded but did not answer.

Such words were an agony for him. He had fallen in love;

he had lost his soul and mind to her. What he did not know, and yearned to, was exactly what Gabriella thought about him.

CHAPTER 41
VOICE OF THE EMIRS
The Saracen Camp at Tyre

Saladin looked out to sea. His guards stood at a respectful distance, wondering about his plans.

On the evening of the defeat at Tyre he had pulled his army ten miles south. The whole of the following day he had been too busy to give any thought to anything other than getting the army organised and listening to reports of casualties. He had been most troubled about al-Adil. The doctors eventually announced that his injury was clean and he was soon limping around and making light of it.

This morning, two days after the defeat, Saladin bent his thoughts to other matters.

After a long silence he turned to his companion. 'Have you ever sailed on the sea, Khalid?' he asked.

Khalid shook his head. 'Never, Excellency. My feet are happiest on the earth.'

Saladin smiled. He turned his gaze once more to the sea.

'Out there lies the Kingdom of the Franks,' he said. 'Somewhere out there, across the sea. It is teeming with warriors. When they hear we have taken Jerusalem they will send another Crusade against us.'

'They will regret the decision, lord.'

'Perhaps. But they will be able to land their ships at Tyre

because I have failed to conquer it.'

'I was told that the first army of the Franks did not come by sea but overland, by way of Constantinople.'

'That is true. But if they had a port such as Tyre in their hands they would have sailed straight to it.'

Khalid drew a deep breath. 'If they had been unlucky enough to find Sultan Saladin as an enemy, then no armies, fleets or ports would have sufficed to allow them to have taken Jerusalem.'

Saladin turned to his young captain, considering his words. He smiled and placed his hand upon his shoulder. 'I thank you for these thoughts, Khalid. Perhaps I have allowed myself to be too troubled by this madman Conrad.'

He climbed on his horse and cantered back to the camp.

As soon as he arrived, the good humour that Khalid had instilled in him was dampened by the sight of King Guy and Gerard de Ridefort, Grand Master of the Templars. They lounged beneath a cedar tree and did not trouble to rise as he approached.

'Good morning, Saladin,' Guy called. 'I glimpsed you standing by the shore, staring out to the west. Did you see any ships upon it? Ships from Tyre? Or ships from France?'

'I saw only the waves, breaking upon the shore,' he answered. 'And then, when I arrived at my camp, I saw my captives.'

He rode past without a further look.

'You will see more, this morning, Saladin,' Guy called. 'Your emirs are gathered in front of your tent, demanding your presence.'

Guy watched as Saladin rode towards his tent. A malicious grin played upon his face.

He turned and stared at Khalid and the three men who rode behind him.

'So, Emir Khalid, you are still playing protector to the

vainglorious serfs?'

'Men of courage such as these need no protection,' Khalid answered.

'Men of courage,' said Gerard de Ridefort. His face broke into a grin and he pointed at Matthew. 'This one is not a man.'

He stood up and stared, searching Matthew's features.

'Yes. I remember you,' he said. 'It was I who chose you to haul around that broken-down leper.' He laughed, remembering the incident.

'I recall that as well,' said Guy. 'You chose the biggest, ugliest brute you could find.'

De Ridefort nodded and turned once more to Matthew.

'What did they call you?'

'It was Ox,' Guy said.

'Ox. That was it.' de Ridfort beamed. 'No, my lord. It wasn't Ox. It was Mule. That is what they called him. Mule.'

'Better a mule than a donkey,' Matthew answered. 'Especially one who brays praises of a king who has lost his throne.'

The Grand Master's jaw dropped. He could not believe what he had heard. 'How dare you talk like that to your betters?' he cried.

'If I were talking to my betters I would not speak that way,' Matthew answered. He spurred his horse and rode away.

'That was pithy, Matthew,' said Bernard. 'It was most unwise but it was pithy.'

The King and Grand Master stared at them in fury.

The friends followed Khalid and Saladin. It was as Guy had said. A large crowd of emirs and captains were waiting in front of Saladin's tent. They were silent which was unusual and ominous.

Saladin salaamed to his men and they rose and salaamed back.

'Good morning, my friends,' Saladin said. 'It is always a pleasure to see you.'

The emirs looked uncomfortable, their eyes shifting anxiously from side to side.

Finally, one man stepped forward.

'Salutations, mighty Sultan,' he said.

Saladin opened his arms in mock surprise. 'I think I should be worried when Emir Walid speaks in such civil tones to me.'

The emirs laughed at his joke.

'It is with uneasy heart that I tell what I have to,' Walid answered.

'I know it must be,' Saladin said, giving him a serious look. 'Please sit.'

'You have won many great victories, Excellency,' Walid said. 'You have fought with greater success against the infidels than anyone since the earliest of days. Your warriors, and your captains, have been proud to aid you in your task.'

Saladin nodded. 'Not more proud than I to have led such lions.'

Walid smiled appreciatively. But then his face grew more serious.

'However, Excellency,' he said, 'I have to tell you that many of these lions are tired beyond endurance. They have fought with you for six long months, many miles from their loved ones. They fight, they march but they are exhausted. They long for home. Worse, many are beginning to sicken.'

'Six of my company have died of the flux,' said another of the emirs.

There was a murmur of assent from the rest.

'The days grow short,' Walid continued. 'The worst days of winter will soon be upon us. Our warriors begin to weaken.'

He fell silent.

Saladin looked at al-Adil. His brother's face wore a pained expression and he nodded to confirm what Walid had said.

Saladin turned back to the company.

'It is a foolish general who does not heed the advice of his captains,' he said. 'I sense that you have long troubled over telling me this.'

They nodded.

Saladin gave a long bow. 'I thank you for your wisdom and for your counsel,' he said.

He turned towards Walid. 'Especially, old friend, I thank you for your courtesy. Though why my captains should choose a brigand like you to be their diplomat is beyond me.'

Walid slapped his thigh with pleasure and the rest of the company roared with laughter. The tension relaxed and all turned expectant faces towards Saladin.

'No man,' he continued, 'no matter how strong, no matter how brave, can fight without rest. Look at my little brother here, for example. See how he hobbles.'

'He was so tired he fell off his horse,' cried a voice, causing much merriment.

Saladin joined in the laughter and held his arms out. 'My brother's spirit is willing but his flesh? Maybe his flesh needs some care.

'You are right, my friends. As it is with al-Adil, so it is with your men.'

He paused for several heart-beats. Only when the silence seemed to hang in the air did he speak. His voice was soft.

'Emirs, I will heed your advice.'

The captains cried out with pleasure.

Saladin waited until the noise had quietened and then spoke once more.

'Walid has compared me to the great warriors of the early days of Islam. If you will allow me, then I would emulate them still further. They knew that it is one thing to conquer the lands of the infidel, quite another to hold on to those conquests. They had to give thought to this and so must I.'

He paused and looked around at his captains, weighing up how far he might be able to push them.

'I suggest that I disband half of the army, those who are sick, those who have wives and children, those who are most exhausted.

'The rest, the youngest, the healthiest, the ones who still rage in their hearts when they see the infidel squatting on our lands; these I will keep in arms for a little while longer.'

He fell silent. He sensed his brother scrutinising the men for their reaction so he bowed his head as if awaiting their decision.

The captains began to murmur amongst themselves, considering his proposal and how it might be received by their men. Finally, after long minutes, Walid bent and listened to the front rank of the emirs.

Saladin had remained all of this time without moving, his shoulders bent, his face to the ground, his arms open as if in prayer.

As Walid approached, al-Adil spoke.

'You have decided?'

Saladin straightened.

'Yes, Excellency,' he said. 'Your plan seems good to us. We are happy and our soldiers will be so as well.'

'God is great,' cried the emirs. 'God is great.'

Saladin salaamed and the assembly broke up.

Khalid left the company and hurried over towards the friends.

'You heard?' he asked.

They nodded.

'What does this mean for us?' John asked.

'That is for you to decide. You are al-Adil's men. He said that for saving his life he would reward you in any way you choose. I think the time of choice is now upon you.'

He turned and strode off to tell his men about Saladin's plan.

Matthew turned towards the others.

'What shall we do?' he asked.

'I shall ask for my freedom,' Bernard said. 'I must find Agnes and the children.'

'I will help you in this, my friend,' said John. 'And then I will seek out my cousin and slay him.'

The three men stood in silence. Each seemed to be holding his breath.

Finally, Bernard touched John on the arm.

'Why this sudden hatred for Simon?' he asked. His face was troubled and perplexed.

John rubbed his forehead wearily, as if seeking to soothe away the thoughts which raged inside him.

'I cannot tell you,' he said. 'If I were to, you would understand and support me. It is best you do not know.'

Bernard and Matthew looked at each other. It seemed clear to John that they had talked about this together already, more than once.

'It is a terrible deed to kill a man,' Matthew said at last. 'Still more if he is your kin and once your friend.'

'I know.' John's face grew hard and set.

Matthew placed his hand upon John's shoulder. 'If you want to tell me, I will listen.'

'Like a priest,' John said bitterly, shrugging Matthew's hand away. 'I need no confessor.'

'I did not offer that,' Matthew answered.

John stared at him with cold determination.

'I do not seek your help in this, Matthew,' he said. 'Nor even your approval.'

He half turned away, as if he did not want them to see his face any more.

'I have said what I will do. I will help Bernard find his family and then I will hunt for Simon.'

They fell silent. Across the camp a loud roar of joy rolled like thunder as the men received news of the plan. It echoed against the hills to their rear and then faded.

'We have said what we will do,' Bernard said. 'What about you, Matthew?'

Matthew sniffed. 'If I was alone here then I would consider staying here and fighting with Khalid and al-Adil. But I owe my succour to you two. You offered me friendship when I had received only hatred. I too, will come with you and help you find your loved ones.'

Bernard shook him by the hand.

'I would like to set off straight away,' he said.

'Then let us find al-Adil,' Matthew answered, 'and see if he will stand by his pledge.'

They sought out Khalid first and told him.

He listened carefully to them and shook his head, deep in thought.

'Are you sure about this?' he asked.

'Why wouldn't we be?' Bernard said.

'The world is a huge place, Bernard. Your wife and children

could be anywhere. Damascus, Cairo, Aleppo, Baghdad, Persia, even India or beyond. How do you think you will find them? It will be like searching the desert for a shred of cloth.'

'Nevertheless, I must do it.'

Khalid stared at him for a while as if trying to fathom the strength within the man.

Finally he nodded. 'I understand. And I would do the same if I were in your position.'

He placed his hand upon Bernard's shoulder. 'I will come with you to al-Adil.'

They could see the camp breaking up as they walked towards al-Adil's tent. The men who had been selected to depart were gathering up their possessions and heaping good-natured insults upon their friends who had to stay. There was much laughter and even more haggling over goods. Those who were leaving wanted to travel as lightly as possible; those who were to stay were keen to relieve them of their goods at the cheapest price possible.

They waited outside the tent until a guard opened the flap and beckoned them in.

Al-Adil rose and gestured them to sit on camp stools. A servant brought them each a drink.

'You have come to ask me to fulfil my promise to you?' al-Adil said.

'Yes, my lord,' Bernard answered.

'Speak, then, my friends. If it is within my power then I will accede to your request.'

'We want to be released from your service, lord,' Bernard said. 'My wife and children have been sold as slaves and I wish to find them.'

'It is granted, of course.'

Al-Adil sipped at his drink. 'You know where your family have been taken?'

Bernard shook his head. Al-Adil's eyes widened and he glanced at Khalid.

'I have told Bernard his quest will prove impossible,' Khalid said. 'His family could be anywhere in the Muslim world or even beyond. They may no longer even be together.'

'It is as Khalid says,' al-Adil murmured. 'But I don't suppose that will sway you for one moment.'

'No, my lord.'

Al-Adil smiled and touched his forehead in salute.

'Then go with my blessing and with all the aid I can give to you.'

He clapped his hands and a servant appeared. 'Get me a clerk,' he said.

'And what of you two?' he asked John and Matthew. 'Will you go with your friend?'

'I have sworn to,' said John.

'And I will not forsake him,' said Matthew.

Bernard looked at Matthew and smiled.

'It is good,' said al-Adil. 'A man on a perilous quest has need of staunch friends.'

The flap of the tent opened and an elderly man entered with parchment and ink. Al-Adil gestured to him to sit.

'Khalid,' al-Adil continued, 'I want you and the other emirs to see if any in the army has knowledge of Bernard's family.'

Khalid nodded.

Al-Adil pulled a map onto the carpet in front of them and pointed to it.

'We are here,' he said, pointing to Tyre. 'My guess is they will have been taken to the slave market of either Cairo or Damascus.'

He placed his fingers on these cities, both of them more than twice the distance that Jerusalem was from Tyre.

'Tyre is a hundred and fifty miles from Jerusalem,' he said. 'Damascus is half that distance from her but Cairo is three hundred miles from Tyre. These cities are far distant from each other, and you may well have to journey to both. I will give you good horses, armour, weapons and gold. You will need them.'

'You are truly generous, my lord,' Bernard said.

'I will do more than give you these gifts,' he said. 'I will write a letter, demanding that anyone you meet is to give you all the aid and assistance you desire. I will sign it and get my brother to counter-sign it. This document will be worth more than any gold that I give to you.'

He turned to Khalid. 'I cannot spare you otherwise I would send you with them,' he said. 'Do you know of anyone who would be a good guide for them?'

'I could ask,' Khalid answered. 'I doubt that any would willingly volunteer.'

'Perhaps not,' al-Adil said. 'But ask, nonetheless.'

He dictated a short letter to the clerk.

'I want copies for me,' said al-Adil.

He glanced at Bernard. 'If Khalid cannot find a guide for you where will you go?'

'Perhaps to Tyre, my lord,' he said. 'We might be able to find news of them there.'

Al-Adil frowned. 'You might. Or you might find other things.'

He turned and watched the clerk as he began to make the copies.

'Perhaps your plan is a sensible one,' he said at last. 'However, my heart misgives me. I think that you may not be well received in Tyre. The world has grown savage and many men's hearts are cankered with suspicion and hate. If you go to Tyre go warily, I beg you.'

He rose and salaamed to them. 'I will see the copies are signed by Saladin and send them over to you. Khalid, help them choose three of my best stallions, good armour and give them one thousand dinars each.'

The clerk stopped writing when he heard of this largesse but al-Adil glanced at him and he continued his work.

They rose, salaamed to al-Adil, and left his tent.

'A thousand dinars,' Bernard whispered. 'I cannot believe it. I could not find even ten dinars to buy my freedom. This will last me a lifetime.'

'Why does al-Adil think we're worth that much?' John asked.

'He doesn't,' said Matthew. 'But we saved his life. He knows that he is worth that much.'

Within an hour they had donned their armour, secured their pouches of treasure and were galloping towards the city of Tyre.

CHAPTER 42
SUBTLE FRIENDSHIPS
The Harem in Baghdad

Johara and Lalina walked into Agnes' room as she was finishing her morning meal. They looked worried.

'Is there something wrong?' Agnes asked.

Johara nodded. 'There is rumour in the harem that the Caliph is growing very fond of you,' she said.

Agnes shrugged. 'Why is that a cause for alarm?'

Lalina bit her lip.

Johara took Agnes' hand and sat beside her on the divan.

'You must learn the ways of the harem better, my dear,' she said. 'If you are to prosper here you must learn how to tread its paths and snares for there are plenty.'

Agnes shook her head. 'I don't understand.'

'Tell her,' Lalina said. 'Tell her, Johara.'

Johara poured herself a glass of cordial and plucked up a sweet biscuit, popping it whole into her mouth.

'You must understand,' she began, 'that the whole purpose of the harem is to please one man and one man alone, the Caliph. The function of every woman here, whether wife, courtesan, harlot or slave is to meet his needs and to pleasure him.'

'I know that,' Agnes said. 'I'm not a child.'

'You are if you believe that this is the whole truth,' Johara said sharply.

'Isn't it?'

'No,' said Lalina, kneeling at Agnes' feet and taking her hands. 'Not the whole truth.'

'There is another truth about the harem,' Johara said. 'Although it is here to serve the Caliph it has also come to serve itself. It is a city, Agnes, a city made up of women more dangerous and desperate than the feral cats that slink about the alleys of Baghdad.'

'It's like a bedlam,' said Lalina.

'It's worse,' said Johara. 'A bedlam is made up of people who are truly mad. The harem is made up of people who are maddened and frenzied but as sane as any woman who shops in the market. It is a place of deadly danger, subtle friendships.'

'Dangerous friendships,' said Lalina.

'Deadly friendships,' added Johara.

'But what's all this got to do with me?' Agnes asked.

'You are living in the harem as if unaware of all the perils that lurk around you. Would you walk amongst a pride of lions in such a foolhardy fashion? Would you nod and smile at each of the cats as if they were all of one mind, all equally friendly to you?'

'And none of them hungry,' said Lalina.

'And none of them hungry,' said Johara with a glance at Lalina.

She leaned closer towards Agnes. 'Whispers say the Caliph is very fond of you. Worse than that, they say he is beginning to favour you over other women.'

'But I don't seek for this,' said Agnes. 'I don't work to make this happen.'

'Nevertheless it is happening,' said Johara.

She picked up a bunch of grapes and began to swallow them.

'All of this, however, can be understood by the harem. Sometimes these things just happen. The Caliph gets besotted for a season and the other girls are neglected. That is the way of men, even the most exalted.'

She finished the grapes and reached out for a honey cake.

'What the harem is less understanding of is this. The fact that you have become ever more popular with the Caliph is beginning to unnerve a certain person.'

Lalina's eyes darted around the room as if there were listening figures in every corner. 'Beatrice,' she whispered.

'And if Beatrice gets unnerved, if Beatrice gets unsettled, then the harem begins to pitch and toss like a ship in a tempest. There is no telling how she may react, no telling who will suffer from her in her fury.'

'But that's not my fault,' Agnes cried, holding her hands to her cheeks.

'Of course it's not,' Lalina said, the tears starting in her eyes.

'Of course it's not,' said Johara. 'Every woman in the harem knows it. But that doesn't stop the ship careering out of control. That doesn't make the women in the harem sympathetic or understanding. No, they begin to feel they are in danger. They are too weak and frightened to do anything about Beatrice. So they go after the person they can more safely destroy.'

Agnes felt Lalina squeeze her hands.

'You mean me,' she said. 'I can be safely destroyed.'

'Feral cats,' Johara said. 'Feral cats in terror and enraged.'

CHAPTER 43
KNIGHTLY HONOUR
Tyre

John, Bernard and Matthew pulled their horses to a walk. The imposing walls of Tyre were a little more than a mile away. The standards of the Franks fluttered upon the walls. Overtopping them all was the flag of Conrad of Montferrat, defender of Tyre.

'I've had an unpleasant thought,' John said. 'We look like Saracens. Their bowmen will be taking aim if we get any closer.'

'Damn,' Bernard said. 'We should have brought a flag of truce.'

'We could call to them,' said John.

'Or maybe we should avoid the city completely,' said Matthew. Bernard looked perplexed.

'Remember al-Adil's warning,' Matthew continued. 'He thought we might not be well received in Tyre.'

'Why wouldn't we?' asked John. 'We are Christians and knights.'

'But we have been in the Saracen camp for weeks now,' said Matthew. 'And we wear Saracen armour and bear Saracen gifts. I do not think we will be welcomed with open arms by Conrad.'

'But we need to find news of Agnes,' said John.

'What news will we find there? The Saracens would not have taken the captives near to the only city in Christian hands. They would have gone far to the east and made directly to Damascus.'

Both men turned to Bernard. He stood in an agony of indecision.

Finally he nodded. 'Matthew is right,' he said. 'I don't think we would find out anything about the captives in Tyre. We should make straight for Damascus. But I don't expect any of you to come with me.'

'I will not desert you,' said John.

'Nor me,' said Matthew.

Bernard smiled and pulled on his reins. 'To Damascus then.'

'And if need be,' said John, 'to the ends of the earth.'

They rode for an hour in an easterly direction. The coastal plain soon gave way to higher, broken country. Searching winds blew from the east, sending plumes of dust into the sky. They bowed their heads against the onslaught, watching the feet of their horses as they ploughed their way along. That was their downfall.

They never saw the company of horsemen cantering down the track towards them.

'Halt,' cried a loud voice.

They looked up in consternation. Barely a hundred yards from them were a party of Frankish horsemen with swords drawn.

Two men broke away from the party and came close.

'You must be from Saladin's army,' one of the men said in poor Arabic.

'No we're not,' answered Bernard in the same tongue. He realised his mistake and switched to French. 'We're Christians, Franks from Jerusalem.'

The horseman frowned. 'Then why are you dressed as Saracens?' he asked.

The three friends looked at each other, wondering how to answer.

'We are knights of Jerusalem,' John said, 'the companions of Balian of Ibelin. We were captured at the siege but Saladin's brother freed us and gave us this gear.'

The two men looked doubtful.

'Get off your horses and throw any weapons to the ground,' the leader ordered.

They obeyed instantly.

The man walked up to them and examined them closely. 'You look like Franks to me,' he said. He stared at Matthew. 'But I'm not sure about this one. What have you done with your face?'

'Smallpox,' Matthew answered. 'Plus a hard life. I used to be known as the Mule.'

The man stepped back a pace.

'You carried the Leper-King?'

'I did. But God protected me from the scourge because of my goodness.'

The man looked at him dubiously and then grinned. He held out his hand. 'My name is Laurence Dubois. I'm a captain in the city guard.

'There are few enough women in Tyre so it's good to see that newcomers are so grim of face they will not be competition for me and my lads.'

The other soldiers laughed, although their proximity to Matthew made the laughter have a nervous edge.

'Pick up your gear and follow me,' Laurence said. 'We're taking you to Tyre and to the Marquis.'

Bernard groaned. Another delay and this one might prove a deadly one.

They retraced their tracks until they were close to the city.

The land in front of them was still littered with battle gear and corpses. A start had been made on moving them; in the distance they could see parties of men heaving bodies into a recently dug pit.

'I wonder if the Christian corpses will lie with the Saracens,' John said.

'It will make no difference to them,' Matthew said. 'The surprise will come when they get to heaven and discover that their enemies are already there and waiting for them with a glass of wine.'

John looked shocked. 'Infidels go to hell,' he said.

'And how do you know?' Matthew asked. 'Have you been there? I've heard that the Saracens and the Jews worship the same God as us, so why shouldn't they go to the same heaven.'

John looked at him in amazement.

'I shouldn't talk that way when you reach the city,' said the leader of the horsemen. 'You'll have trouble enough explaining yourselves as it is.'

They did not expect to see the sight that met their eyes. The streets were littered with filth, with dead bodies and wounded men.

'Probably a good job you got the smallpox,' Laurence said to Matthew. 'If we don't get this lot cleared up soon we'll have that and cholera and plague in no time.'

The stench was already beginning to settle upon the streets.

'Where are you taking us?' John asked.

'To the citadel. To see the Marquis.'

They climbed up streets which became ever steeper and ever more narrow. As they climbed, Laurence interrogated them about their doings

Before they even reached the city they had realised that their story was so far-fetched people would doubt every word. In the end they agreed that the best thing would be to speak the truth and hope that this was believed. They could see from Laurence's expression that they were having difficulty convincing him.

Finally, when their breath was labouring, they turned a corner and saw the looming walls of the citadel. Even if Saladin had taken the city he would have had difficulty in conquering this stronghold.

Laurence led the way into the Great Hall. At the far side, a group of men were leaning over a table, intently staring at a parchment upon it.

'Wait here,' he said before hurrying over towards them.

They watched while Laurence talked to one of the men around the table. His head shot up and he examined the newcomers keenly while he listened. Then, with one wave, he beckoned them over.

Conrad of Montferrat was a short, stocky man in his forties. But his age had not weakened him; he looked tough and strong. Strong enough to defeat even the mighty Saladin. His gaze was sharp and his eyes seemed to bore into them.

'Laurence tells me strange tales about you,' he said.

'It's all true, lord,' Bernard said. 'I know your father well and he will vouch for my honesty.'

'That old fool,' Conrad snapped. 'He was ever the dupe of the cunning. Tell your story to me now. And you, Laurence, listen carefully and tell me if their tale differs this time.'

Thank God we agreed to tell the truth, Bernard thought, before launching into their story once again.

When he had finished, Conrad turned to Laurence.

'Well?' he asked. 'Was the story the same?'

'It was, my lord. Except that he did not mention King Guy this time.'

Conrad turned intimidating eyes upon Bernard.

'What about King Guy? And why did you tell Laurence and not me?'

'I can answer that,' John said.

'I'm sure you can,' Conrad answered, 'for you have each learned your parts of the story, no doubt.'

'No,' cried Bernard, silencing John. 'I will speak.' He proceeded to tell Conrad about the hot words between Matthew and the King.

As he did so, Conrad's eyes widened. He roared with laughter when Bernard finished.

He wiped his eyes and turned to Matthew. 'It takes a brave man to beard a King,' he said.

'Not if you don't consider him a King,' Matthew answered.

Conrad's laughter ceased. He stared at Matthew in silence, tugging at his moustache thoughtfully.

'Inn-keeper,' he asked suspiciously, 'why didn't you tell me this story?' Although he addressed Bernard he never took his eyes from Matthew.

Bernard swallowed. 'Because I thought that a great lord such as you would not wish to hear of any disrespect towards the King.'

'I understand,' Conrad said. He started to grin but hid it.

'And you, Mule,' he said to Matthew, 'why do you not consider Guy the King of Jerusalem?'

'Because he rules the kingdom through the marriage-bed,' my lord. 'If he hadn't turned Queen Sibilla's head then he would still be merely the adventurer he was when he arrived from France.'

Conrad pursed his lips and nodded thoughtfully.

There was an immediate lightening of the atmosphere. Bernard began to breathe more easily.

The Marquis crossed his arms and examined them carefully.

'You look strong enough,' he said, quietly. 'And you swear that you are no longer Saladin's brother's men?'

'Quite sure, my lord,' John said. 'If we are anybody's men then we are Balian's.'

Conrad turned towards him. 'Ah yes,' he said. 'That is a strange tale which I would hear.' His eyes narrowed. 'Your accent is also strange.'

'I am from England,' John said.

'Are you, indeed? Do you think that King Henry will honour his pledge and take the cross?'

'He is an old man now. He must be fifty years or more.'

'Then maybe his heir will, Prince Richard?'

The mere mention of Richard's name made John rage inwardly. 'I know nothing of Prince Richard or his intentions, my lord.'

'Yet you know of Balian of Ibelin. Tell me this farrago of a tale concerning knighthoods.'

Conrad was obviously angered by this and John cursed himself for mentioning it again. He took a deep breath. 'There were a handful of knights in Jerusalem when Saladin besieged the city,' he began. 'Balian considered it necessary to make new knights in order to lead the defenders.'

'And you three were amongst the chosen?'

'Bernard and I were knighted, lord. We met Matthew later, after the fall of the city.'

'Yes, the city fell,' Conrad said. There was a new and dangerous edge to his voice. 'So Balian's knights were not successful.'

'There were thirty of us, my lord.'

Conrad stared hard at John, not liking the hint of argument in his manner. He held the young man's eyes until he lowered them and looked away.

He waited for a moment, considering. He reached out and turned John's face to face him.

'What would you do,' he murmured, 'if I say you are a liar concerning this notion of knighthood?'

'I would say that you are wrong.'

Bernard stared at him, horrified at his temerity in saying this to a nobleman.

'We were knighted by Balian,' John continued, 'and if he were here he would confirm what I said.'

Conrad smiled; a cold smile.

'But he's not here, is he? There's no one here to corroborate your story at all.'

He turned to his companions who had been watching the proceedings with fascination.

'Tell me, friends,' he asked blandly. 'What should I do with Franks who pretend to be knights but are really Saracen spies?'

'They pretend to be knights?' asked one.

Conrad nodded.

The nobles crowded closer and scrutinised the three.

'Speak to me,' one of them commanded.

'What do you want us to say, my lord?' Bernard asked.

The noble laughed. 'You need say nothing more,' he answered. 'Your speech tells me your mother was a whore and your father her pimp.'

The others joined in the laughter. They moved still closer and began to push at the three, jabbing them sharply in the chest and stomach.

One spat in Matthew's face. He did not flinch or react in any way.

'See, my lord,' the man said. 'He does not respond. He is used to being spat upon, as all peasants are. He is no knight.'

Conrad held up his hand to stay him. 'Enough, Gilbert. Desist.

I repeat my question. What shall I do with them?'

'Kill them,' said one of the nobles. 'Painfully, so that people can learn the fruit that treachery bears.'

'Set them to work,' said another. 'If they have stomachs enough to sup with the infidel then scraping up corpses should prove no burden.'

'Whatever you do, my lord,' said a third, 'question them about the infidel's plans.'

Conrad turned to the three and smiled. 'See, my friends. Not one of them suggests clemency.'

'But we told the truth,' said John.

Conrad shrugged. 'Do you know what truth is, young man? Here, in Tyre, truth is whatever I choose it to be.'

'God's truth does not change, no matter what a Marquis may say.'

Conrad frowned at this, wondering at the young man's audacity.

The man who had spat in Matthew's face stepped forward and slapped John across the face.

'Don't dare speak to the Marquis like that,' he said.

John shoved him backward, almost pushing him to the floor. He came back in a moment, drawing his sword as he did so.

'Keep your sword in its scabbard, Vallon,' Conrad cried. He turned and regarded John closely.

'You show courage, Englishman,' he said. 'Courage or stupidity. Few men would dare to cross Sir Gilbert Vallon, let alone strike him. I have use for both courage and stupidity. So I shall not kill you. You will help clear up the city before the pestilence bites.'

'He struck me, my lord,' Vallon said. 'I demand he be punished.'

Conrad gazed at the lord.

'It was merely a push, Gilbert. Nothing more.'

'It is not just that,' Vallon continued. 'He claims to be what he is not. A peasant boasting he is a knight. He should be flogged for his presumption.'

The other lords murmured in agreement.

John's anger began to flame. Bernard noticed, alarm flooding his face. He reached out but it was too late, John was beginning to draw his sword.

He had reckoned without Conrad.

John's fingers had barely tightened on the hilt as Conrad chopped him on the wrist and hauled the sword from its scabbard.

'Disarm them all,' he commanded.

His nobles were quick to obey.

The one searching Bernard found the letter of safe passage from al-Adil. He glanced at it quickly, peering at the Arabic script in confusion.

'What is this?' he said. 'This is not French.'

'That is my letter,' John said. 'It is written in English. It's a letter from my brother Alan who is one of Prince Richard of England's comrades. Bernard was keeping it safe for me.' He breathed a silent prayer that nobody there could read English.

The noble made to screw it up but Conrad stopped him.

'Your brother is one of Richard's comrades?' he said.

John nodded.

'Then you may keep it.'

The noble gave the letter back to Bernard.

Gilbert Vallon advanced on John and speedily rummaged through his clothing.

His hand groped something which was not a weapon and he grinned.

'My lord,' he called, pulling out the purse which al-Adil had given.

The other nobles found Bernard and Matthew's purses and held them up.

Conrad nodded towards the table. Vallon led the way and emptied John's purse. The gold coins cascaded across the board. Vallon gasped, his hand twitching over them for a moment as if he were about to snatch some up.

'This is a treasure such as I have rarely seen,' Conrad said softly. 'Where did you get it from?'

None of the three friends answered.

'Did you steal it from Jerusalem?' Conrad asked. 'Did you loot it from the dead and dying?'

'We would never do that,' cried John, his anger still hot.

'Then where did you get it from? It could only have been stolen.' He stepped close to John, his face only inches away, his eyes drilling into him.

'It was a gift,' said Bernard.

Conrad turned, a look of derision on his face. 'A gift? Who would give you such a gift?'

'Al-Adil,' Matthew answered. 'Saladin's brother.'

Conrad turned to him, digesting this fact and pondering what it would mean.

He sat in a chair and gazed up at Matthew. 'Tell me, Mule, why would Saladin's brother give such a kingly reward to three peasants such as you?'

'It was for spying,' Vallon said, 'or worse.'

Conrad did not respond but continued to stare at Matthew. 'You will tell me,' he said. 'You will tell me; either voluntarily or in great pain. Trust me in this.'

'It was not for spying, my lord,' said Bernard. 'It was for saving al-Adil's life.'

Vallon slapped Bernard across the face, sending him crashing to the floor.

'You saved an infidel's life?' he screamed. 'And the life of Saladin's brother at that.'

'It was I who saved him,' said Matthew.

Vallon took a step towards him, face red and swollen. He did not lash out this time. Matthew was far larger and stronger than Bernard.

'Tell me,' Conrad said simply.

'It was on the field of battle,' Matthew said. 'Saladin's brother had been unhorsed and he cried out for help. We were the closest to him. I picked him up on an impulse.'

'If we had not have done it we would have been slain by the Saracens ourselves,' said John.

'Typical of peasants to think about their own skin rather than the greater cause,' Vallon sneered. 'And you dare call yourself knights.'

Conrad leaned back in his seat.

'The story rings true to me,' he said. 'Impulse and fear can make a man act strangely during the heat of battle.'

He picked up a handful of coins.

'And look at the outcome of this act of impulse. Our coffers are replenished. We will be able to buy new weapons with the infidel's gold and repair the city walls.'

The nobles smiled and could not help but cast greedy looks upon the treasure.

'This act of treason merely adds to their crimes,' Vallon said in a soft voice. 'They claim they are knights, they ape their betters, they aid the enemy and they even draw swords against us. I say again, they should be flogged, or worse.'

Once again there were noises of agreement from the others, louder now and more determined than previously.

Conrad looked from the three friends to his nobles and nodded.

'They will learn their lesson immediately,' he said.

The friends were dragged out of the citadel by a dozen grinning guards.

It had started to rain and they slipped on the treacherous steps which led down towards the market square.

They were hauled across the square and tied to three stakes set in the earth. Their shirts were torn from their backs and their hands tied tightly to the stakes.

Word spread like wild-fire that the Marquis had ordered a flogging. Hundreds of people were soon pouring into the square. The siege had been a terrible ordeal and they were delighted to see such a pleasant entertainment was about to take place.

John was surprised to see how quickly men appeared bearing trays with goods to sell. Some bore food, others cups of wine. Two men bore trays of very rotten fruit to throw at the prisoners. But old women snatched up these bargains and carried them home in triumph. The scarcity of food in the city was more powerful than entertainment.

Out of the corner of his eye, John saw Laurence approach. He bore three pieces of wood in his hand, little larger than twigs.

'These are the best I could find,' he said. 'I'm sorry.' He pushed a piece of wood in each of their mouths and told them to bite hard upon them. 'And I'm sorry that this is happening,' he said. 'The Marquis has promised that I shall have you in my service, after this is over.'

He walked away.

John tried to turn his head to see what was happening. At that moment he saw the flicker of something on the edge of sight and then heard a crack like lightning striking a rotten tree.

The crowd grew quiet.

The crack sounded again. John gasped. He wanted to cry out but the breath had been snatched so brutally from his lungs that no sound came. He braced himself for the next lash. The pain slashed into his back-bone, and his heart. It reverberated around his body, jarring and tearing at parts far from where the whip touched. The crowd gave vent to a delighted cry.

Again the whip cracked. Again the crowd yelled. Again the pain swept across every part of his flesh. He cried out this time, a yell which began as a gurgle and became a whimper. Once more he heard the whip's report. This time he could make no noise beyond a gasp.

Water was thrown over him. He shook his head. If he thought this was an end to his suffering, he was mistaken.

He felt the lash countless times more. He felt that the rest of his life would be this torment and nothing more. He moaned at the pain and at his folly. 'I'm sorry,' he tried to say to Bernard and Matthew but his words came thick.

Eventually he could no longer cry out and his body barely responded to the pain. The whipping stopped.

John was untied and thrown into a corner. The burly figure walked up to Bernard and sneered.

'Three lashes only for this one,' Laurence said.

'But that one had a dozen,' said the flogger.

'Three,' repeated Laurence. 'And if you argue, I'll make sure that you'll be on the receiving end.'

The crowd jeered, angered at being thwarted of more. They jeered as they watched Bernard trying to arch his body away from the whip without success.

When they heard that Matthew was to receive only three lashes as well they raged at Laurence. However, they were stunned into silence when they caught sight of Matthew's muscular frame. They were awed even more by the fact that he made no sound and did not flinch. A few cheered him for his courage but most jeered. Disappointed that no more was to come, the crowd drifted away.

John came round towards evening. He was laying face-down on a wooden trestle bed with a thin scatter of straw.

He cried out. His back was on fire. He moved a little and regretted it at once. It felt as though a blacksmith had heated a shirt of mail upon a furnace and placed it tight against his flesh.

'I'm sorry,' he muttered.

'Not as sorry as we are,' Bernard answered. 'Nor as sorry as you'll be when I recover.'

John felt a hand ruffle his hair. 'You'll live,' said Matthew. 'But keep your gob shut in the future.'

'You've some need to talk,' he answered, weakly. 'You argued with King Guy.'

'Yes,' Matthew said. 'But he couldn't do anything about it. Conrad and the nobles could and did.'

'How many lashes did we get?' John asked.

'That's the only good part,' Bernard answered. 'Matthew and I got three each and they were fairly light. You got a dozen and the flogger put his all into it.'

John raised his head and gave a questioning look.

'Because you kept boasting about being a knight,' Matthew explained. 'These so called nobles are all bastards. They hate the infidels but they hate their peasants even more. They weren't going to let someone like you get away with claiming to be a knight.'

'But I am a knight,' said John. 'And so is Bernard. They can't take that away from us.'

'Maybe not,' Matthew said. 'But they can take the flesh from your bones instead.'

A heavy footfall sounded behind John.

'So the baby awakes at last,' sounded a voice.

Laurence squatted down and peered into John's face. 'You're harder than you look,' he said. 'I shall make good use of you when you recover. Because you act as stupid as a donkey I shall set you to pull a corpse wagon.'

'Why should I do that?' began John.

'Shut up,' cried Bernard. 'Don't you ever learn?'

'I couldn't agree with your friend more,' Laurence said. 'Learn some sense from him and you may survive. Conrad is as hard as the devil's hoof but he's fair. If you work well for me you'll be all right.'

'We did not come here to work as serfs,' John said. 'We need to find Bernard's family.'

Laurence shook his head and leaned close towards him. 'Don't go claiming you're on a quest, like some knight of Camelot. For all of your sakes you must drop all pretence that you are a knight.'

'But I am,' John said.

'I didn't hear that,' Laurence said. He slapped John on the back, making him curl up in agony. 'Sorry,' he said lightly. 'I can't think what made me do that.'

He walked over to Bernard.

'What does that young fool mean, you're searching for your family? Are they in Tyre?'

Bernard shook his head. 'I don't know. The Saracens took them as slaves. Saladin's brother thinks they may have gone to the markets of Cairo or Damascus although Emir Khalid had seen no sight of slaves in Cairo.'

Laurence frowned and shook his head gently. 'I'm sorry, friend, but if that's the case then you must say goodbye to them.'

'That's what everyone says.' Bernard's voice was bitter and reproachful.

'Because it is the truth,' Laurence said. 'We Franks may choose to ignore it but our kingdoms are like a sliver of a finger-nail on the edge of the Muslim world. It is countless leagues to Damascus and even more to Baghdad. Beyond that, their realm stretches to the fiery chasm where the sun is born. And to the west their lands march from Egypt to the ocean, to Spain and to France.'

'Does Saladin rule all that?' asked John in amazement.

'Saladin is only one of the rulers of the Muslim world,' Laurence said. 'There are scores more like him, just as powerful, just as war-like.'

'I don't care how wide their lands are,' Bernard said. 'I will search for my family.'

'The searching will prove the easy part,' Laurence said. 'It is the finding that will be impossible.'

'Nevertheless,' Bernard said.

'I wish you good luck in your search,' Laurence said. 'But you need to remember that you are now in Conrad's service. And he will not countenance you leaving.'

CHAPTER 44
FIGHTING OVER SCRAPS
Antioch

Simon snatched a piece of bread from the table and stuffed it into his mouth. He swilled it down with a gulp of wine.

Patriarch Eraclius had summoned him more than an hour before but his servant had neglected to give him the message.

'The next time you fail me,' Simon told the servant, 'I will flog the skin off your back.'

The servant wrung his hands and tried to stop the tears.

Simon strode out, cuffing the boy to the ground as he did so.

Gabriella sat up in bed, hiding her nakedness with a sheet. The servant got to his feet and gave her a lewd grin.

'Ring the bell if you want more than our master can provide,' he said. 'I'll be more prompt to answer a call from you than from Simon, believe me.'

'Get out,' she said, flinging a shoe at him.

The door closed behind him and she stared at it in silence. Her heart was beating fast and she was not sure why. She rested her chin in her hand. So much had happened to her since Simon had taken her from the inn. Too much.

She lay back on the bed, bent her legs high to her chest and sucked on the knuckle of her thumb.

It was a short walk from Simon's lodgings to the grand house which Eraclius had settled into with Pasque de Riveri, the woman who the people of Jerusalem had nick-named Madame la Patriarchesse. She was a wealthy woman from Nablus, a widow, and Simon was wary of her.

Because of this he made a lot of effort to befriend their daughter who was six or seven years of age. Both parents noted this, Eraclius with approval, Pasque de Riveri with contempt.

He pushed open the door and entered the hall. Eraclius was waiting for him, bent over a table and writing carefully.

'Where have you been?' he asked without looking up. 'I summoned you two hours ago.'

'My servant did not tell me,' Simon began to explain.

'Enough of your excuses. No doubt you were riding that little whore of yours and thought that I could wait while you pleasured yourself like a hound.'

Simon did not answer. It was, in truth, partly the reason. The servant had heard the noises of his coupling with Gabriella and decided not to interrupt them. It had gone on for much longer than he had anticipated and other tasks had prevented him from giving the message for a while.

Eraclius threw down his pen. 'I am summoned to a council of the great lords,' he said. 'It will take place at noon. You will come with me. I need one pair of ears who will listen out for my good.' He held Simon's gaze.

'At least I assume you will listen out for my benefit.'

The Patriarch's words alarmed Simon. 'Of course, master. I am your servant.'

'You are. And don't ever forget it.' Eraclius' eyes were cold. 'I built you up, Simon Ferrier, and I can just as easily tear you down.'

Simon licked his lips nervously. 'Would it be helpful to you if I knew the reason for the council?' he asked.

'It may be.' Eraclius gestured Simon to pull up a stool.

'We have had a message from Tyre,' Eraclius continued. 'It appears that Conrad of Montferrat has done the impossible and thrown the Saracens back from the walls. So, the all-conquering Saladin has been defeated by the son of an Italian buffoon. What do you think of that?'

'I think that any defeat for the infidel should be a cause of rejoicing.'

Eraclius turned and gave him a doubtful look.

'Don't be so bloody naive. This is the Holy Land, not England.'

Simon shook his head. 'I don't understand, my lord.'

'You will do. If you survive long enough.' Eraclius sighed. 'You will learn,' he continued, 'that the only way in which we Christians prosper in this country is by making peace with the Saracens.'

Simon was shocked. 'You cannot mean that, my lord.'

'I do indeed. This land has been fought over since the time of Moses. Who can really say has the best claim to it? The Jews, the Syrians, the Greeks, the Saracens?'

'Surely it is us, my lord? We Christians.'

Eraclius laughed. 'Almost everyone in the Holy Land would question that statement. And if Christians do have a place here then it is almost certainly not the Franks.'

'But you are a Frank, my lord.'

'I am. And while I hold office I will do my utmost for my flock and for my faith. I will raise money for the nobles, I will bless them as they go into battle, I will condemn the infidel. Yet, in my heart I know that this path will not allow us to prosper. It will merely allow us to survive. If we are lucky.'

The Patriarch gestured for a cup of wine and Simon hurried to bring it to him. Eraclius took a long sip, his eyes staring over the rim at him all the while.

'Tell me the news,' he commanded softly.

Simon gave a sigh of relief. He was about to prove his usefulness.

'The city is full of the rumour concerning Raymond, the new Count of Tripoli.'

Eraclius glared. He would not easily forgive Raymond's cowardice in refusing the refugees entry to Tripoli.'

'What rumour?'

'He is said to have sent congratulations to Conrad for his defence of Tyre. He has pledged his friendship and promised to support him in his ambitions.'

'Ha, I wonder what Bohemond will say when he hears his milk-sop of a son has made such a pledge.'

Eraclius rubbed his cheek thoughtfully. 'And what do your friends the gutter folk say of Conrad's ambitions?'

'They say he wants to replace Guy as King of Jerusalem.'

Eraclius laughed. 'And you give credence to this?'

Simon nodded. 'I do, my lord. I have often found that the filthiest ear can hear most clearly.'

Eraclius swilled the last of his wine around his mouth. 'You may be right, Simon Ferrier, you may be right.'

He paced about the room. 'Guy is lower-born than Conrad yet he bedded his way to the throne. Perhaps Conrad will try the same tactic.'

'But how, my lord?'

'Princess Sibilla is not the only woman with a claim to the throne,' he said. 'There is another, young Isabella. She is Sibilla's half-sister and some, like Balian, believe she has the better claim to the throne. She is married but to an effeminate, Humphrey of Toron. Perhaps Conrad is casting his eye towards the girl.'

He rose and a servant brought his cloak. Simon gestured to Gregory and William to accompany them to the citadel.

They arrived just before noon. Eraclius loathed being the last to arrive at a meeting, for preference he would arrive first. He scowled at Simon for getting him to the citadel late.

Simon told his men to wait for them in the guardhouse and followed the Patriarch into the Great Hall.

A huge table had been placed in the centre of the hall. At its head sat Bohemond, with two chairs on either side. To his left sat a young man Simon had not seen before. He looked to be sixteen or seventeen years of age. His face was cold and hard. He sat in silence, staring moodily at a knife which he spun upon the table. The chair to Bohemond's right was empty.

Around the table were gathered all of the nobles of Antioch together with other great men who happened to be in the city. Simon recognised a dozen by sight but few by name. Balian was sitting close to Bohemond. Next to him was his friend Jerome who was the only one in the assembly to acknowledge Simon. Eraclius headed towards an empty seat next to the old knight.

Balian's squire, Ernoul lounged at the end of the table and beckoned Simon over. Simon pursed his lips. He enjoyed Ernoul's company but did not trust him. He suspected that these feelings were fully reciprocated.

'You look tired,' Ernoul said with a grin. 'I hear that your girl has killed several of her previous lovers with her insatiable demands.'

'You are only jealous,' Simon said.

'I don't deny it. She has the look of an angel.'

'Thank you,' Simon said.

'And the appetites of a devil,' added Ernoul with a crooked grin.

Simon chose not to rise to the insult. He gestured towards the top of the table.

'Who is the boy sitting next to the Prince?'

'That is Bohemond's second son,' Ernoul answered. 'He is the apple of his father's eye. He is also called Bohemond.'

'He looks troubled.'

'He is. And he means trouble. Steer clear of him, Simon, for your own good.'

'He is only a boy.'

'True. But he has the brain of a Pope and the heart of a Saracen.'

Simon chuckled.

At that moment, Prince Bohemond stood and the other nobles did likewise. The only person who did not rise was young Bohemond. He had to be dragged to his feet by his father.

Simon craned his head to see the person they had risen for. It was Princess Cybil. He was surprised to see her take the vacant seat to the right of her husband.

'A woman at a council meeting?' he whispered to Ernoul.

'I know. Astonishing isn't it? Look how the nobles scowl. They think it's disgusting. Yet she has the intelligence of any half dozen of them combined.'

Simon looked at him in surprise. 'You jest?'

Ernoul shook his head. 'Watch and listen. You will see.'

Simon examined Cybil as she glanced swiftly at the men around the table. He could barely drag his eyes from her. She was beautiful yet there was more to it than this. She had a confidence and a glamour like he had never seen before. She stole the attention of everyone in the hall. The nobles might hate her but they were also enthralled by her.

All except for one.

'Bohemond's son does not like her,' Simon murmured.

'Of course not,' said Ernoul. 'In fact, I'd say he hates her. When he was a small child his father divorced his mother, Orguilleuse d'Harenc. It still rankles with him.'

'Bohemond divorced her because of Sibyl?'

'Oh no. He divorced Orguilleuse for Theodora, the niece of the Byzantine Emperor. It was a marriage of convenience, of course. As soon as the Emperor died Bohemond got rid of Theodora and climbed into Cybil's bed.'

'I can't blame him.'

Ernoul chuckled. 'Me neither. But others did. The Pope excommunicated him and placed the city under an interdict.'

Simon turned towards Ernoul. 'Excommunication?'

'Yes. But it didn't bother Bohemond one jot. He imprisoned the archbishop and looted all the churches.

'A delegation from Jerusalem came to try to make peace. Bohemond laughed in their faces, robbed them of their cash and kicked them out of the city. The delegation was led by your master, Eraclius.'

'So that's why Bohemond and Cybil were cold towards him.'

'That and the fact that Eraclius finds it hard to hide his lust for the Princess.'

Simon grinned. 'He's not the only one.'

Ernoul laughed quietly. 'Content yourself with your little whore, my friend. Princess Cybil is far beyond your sights. Dismiss any thought of her from your mind. At best you would be a morsel to her, a frightened mouse in the jaws of a cat.'

We shall see, Simon thought, remembering his first meeting with her.

Bohemond rapped upon the table and the council commenced.

'I have sum…sum…summoned you here today because of disquieting news,' he said with an effort. His stuttering always grew worse when he had to address a large meeting.

'We have heard that Saladin's brother al-Adil has led a large part of the Saracen army to attack the castle of Kerak. It is completely surrounded.'

'What does that matter to us?' said an elderly noble. 'Kerak is in the deserts of Moab. What importance does it have to Antioch?'

'Humphrey of Toron is said to have fled there,' Balian said. 'He is strengthening its defences.'

'I thought he was still Saladin's captive,' said the old noble.

'He was,' said Bohemond. 'Saladin let him go free to join his wife on condition he take no further part in the war. But Princess Isabella has put fire in his soul and persuaded him to defend Kerak.'

A man laughed quietly. He was as dark as a Saracen, as skinny as a bone and very tall. 'Forgive me for saying so,' he murmured, 'but the thought of Humphrey of Toron defending anything is just laughable.'

'This is no time for jest, Armengol,' said Eraclius. 'You may not be the Grand Master of the Hospitallers but you are the Provisor. You should behave in a more seemly fashion.'

Armengol raised his hand with a flourish. 'In matters of morality,' he said, 'I always defer to the Patriarch of Jerusalem.'

There were loud guffaws from the assembly. Some of the knights even banged on the table to show their appreciation of Armengol's jest.

'Saladin appears to be treating Humphrey with more

seriousness, at any rate,' Balian said, looking around the room as if defying anyone to gainsay him.

'He knows that Kerak is at the cross roads between Damascus, Mecca and Cairo,' he continued. 'Whoever controls Kerak controls the key trade routes in the Holy Land. Saladin also realises the importance of Isabella to all Christians. If he were to capture her then he would have a hostage beyond value.'

'So is this the purpose of the council,' said Armengol, 'to debate the fate of a chit of a girl.' His face showed a mixture of contempt and astonishment.

'This girl is the daughter of King Almaric,' said Balian. 'Many would agree she should be Queen of Jerusalem.'

Bohemond raised his hand for silence. 'Enough of that. We are not here to resurrect past man...man...manoeuvrings. It matters little to Antioch who is King of Jerusalem. What does matter is that al-Adil does not conquer the castle of Kerak or seize the young princess.'

'So what would the Prince of Antioch suggest we do?' asked Armengol in a condescending tone.

Bohemond stared at him. He had no liking for the man but was well aware that he might be confirmed as Grand Master of the Order. He would need to be civil at the very least.

'That is for this council to decide,' he answered. 'My view is that we are too weak to attack al-Adil's force. But we could mount a rescue mission for the Princess.'

'And what about the Lady Humphrey?' said Armengol. There were loud guffaws at his jest, only silenced when Bohemond slammed his fist on the table.

Armengol chuckled aloud before he continued.

'Will you leave him to the Saracens' mercy. Although I

presume he secured his freedom by offering his person to Saladin.'

The nobles drummed upon the table. Armengol said what they all wanted to believe.

'I don't care one way or another for the boy,' said Bohemond. 'But Isabella is fond of him so we shall have to rescue him as well.'

Armengol flung his arm in the air in a gesture of disgust but contented himself with this.

At this point Princess Cybil placed her hands together and leaned forward. The gesture was seen by everyone and the council fell silent.

'I believe it is vital that Isabella is rescued immediately,' she said. 'It is, however, a dangerous mission. I know that the Lord of Antioch, my husband, would wish to lead the attempt and I support him in this.'

She paused and sighed softly. 'However, I am certain that everyone here will do their utmost to dissuade him, preferring him to stay in Antioch and guard it against any potential attack.'

Almost all the nobles raised their voices to prove that she was correct in this assumption. She turned towards her husband with a sorrowful face as if to say that her worst fears had been proved.

Ernoul grinned and bent towards Simon.

'See how she plays the dupes?' he whispered. 'And this is only the beginning. I wonder what her ultimate purpose will prove to be.'

'If you will not allow the Prince to lead the rescue,' she said, 'then who would you suggest?'

She sighed once again, even louder, her bosom rising like the moon above water. 'I really think it should be someone who is high-born.'

Her step-son leapt to her feet. 'I am the highest born in this room.'

He paused and then bowed towards Bohemond. 'Saving my father of course.'

'Of course you are,' said Cybil. 'Now that your brother Raymond is Count of Tripoli.'

The young man gave a look which would have made any one quail but she affected not to have seen it.

'As such,' he said through gritted teeth, 'I plead the right to lead the mission to castle Kerak.'

Bohemond beamed with pride at the courage of his son. Then a flicker of doubt filled his eyes.

'But you are much too young, my dear,' Cybil said quickly before her husband could speak. 'This is a job for a man, not a boy.'

The young man stared at her in fury. 'I am a man. And I am the noblest born here. I claim my right to lead the mission.'

The council rose to their feet in loud support of the young man.

Cybil bowed her head, as if to the inevitable, and turned towards her husband.

'If this is what you want, my son,' he said, 'then so be it. I am proud of you. But the task is a deadly one and no one will blame you if you change your mind.'

'He will not change his mind,' said Cybil. 'Talk of danger will only strengthen his knightly resolve.' She gave the young man a smile so warm that even his hatred of her was momentarily soothed.

She held out her hand to him and he bent and kissed it. For a moment, all seemed well. Then Cybil shook her head and began to mutter aloud. She took a deep breath and addressed the council.

'You have made the right decision in sending my step-son to rescue Princess Isabelle,' she said. 'However, I think that such a young head as his should be supported by wiser, more experienced ones.'

She turned her gaze towards two of the men around the table. 'I would like to suggest that young Bohemond be accompanied by a mighty warrior and a wise and intelligent thinker. I suggest that he be accompanied by Provisor Armengol de Aspa and Patriarch Eraclius.'

Both men blanched at the thought, both men began to wriggle, seeking for a way out.

Eraclius was the more swift to find one.

'I greatly desire to go with young Bohemond,' he said, 'for I seek retribution against the infidel. However, alas, the Holy Father in Rome has commanded me to stay in Antioch and re-build the Church of the Holy Sepulchre here in Antioch.'

'Really?' said Bohemond. 'When did he say that?'

'I received the letter yesterday,' Eraclius answered.

He turned towards Simon. 'You have the letter safe?'

'I do, my lord,' Simon said.

'Shall I ask my servant to run and bring it to the council?' Eraclius continued.

Simon's stomach churned. There was no such letter. Was Eraclius expecting him to forge one and bring it back?

'Why not?' Bohemond said.

'There is no need, surely,' said Balian. 'Even if the Holy Father had not commanded the Patriarch to stay here, I think we can all see the wisdom of it.'

Cybil gave Balian an angry look but he affected not to notice.

'Armengol de Aspa, then?' she said. 'Will the Acting Head of the Hospitallers go with my step-son? I am sure that all of the Barons of the Kingdom would thank him for doing so.'

Armengol licked his lips. He had been trapped and he knew it. Yet his burning desire to become Grand Master overcame his doubts.

'I would be honoured to accompany the Prince's son,' he said.

Cybil sat back, well pleased. She had rid herself of two out of the three people she wanted out of the way. She would have to set another trap for the wily Eraclius.

The nobles strode out and Simon waited with Ernoul until the chamber was empty and they could leave.

'I must attend upon my lord,' Ernoul said. 'Farewell, Simon. I hope you keep safe.'

CHAPTER 45
ILL-BRED KNIGHTS
Tyre

The pain from the whipping began to ease. The following day, although they were still in pain, John, Bernard and Matthew found themselves hard at work under Laurence's direction. Clearing the city of the damage and of the dead was proving a monumental task. The streets near the city walls were littered with boulders from the Saracen siege engines. Elsewhere, the walls and timbers of houses had slid into the streets, making them all but impassable.

However, it was the dead who were proving the worst problem.

The stench from the bodies was overpowering and threatened pestilence. Huge swarms of flies buzzed above every corpse, so dense they looked like the smoke from fires. Cats and dogs feasted upon the remains, fighting for scraps, tearing open the bodies to reach the succulent innards. The animals were beaten off by the disposal crews but they did not slink far, crouching down in the dust to watch for a chance to return to their meal. The disposal crews worked at top speed to try to clear the bodies.

Laurence had assigned John, Bernard and Matthew to work one of the corpse carts. Because of his great strength Matthew was assigned to pull the cart. John and Bernard had the less physical but more grisly task. They had to haul the bodies off of the streets and onto the cart.

Outcasts

Because of the heat and the depredations of the hungry animals, few of the corpses were any longer whole. Often, John and Bernard would grab a corpse by its arms and legs and feel the body untangle from itself, leaving just the limbs in their hands. The stench from the oozing flesh was unbearable. No matter how many herbs they stuffed into their nostrils they could not avoid the gagging reek.

Laurence was sympathetic. He had taken the strangers under his wing and was impressed at how hard they worked despite the pain from the flogging. Despite this friendship, he remained a hard task-master, so determined was he to get the job finished and the city cleansed.

'How long will this go on for?' Bernard asked him on the second day.

'Until the city smells as sweet as a bride's arse,' Laurence answered with a grin.

'You are an expert, I suppose,' said John.

'I am indeed,' Laurence answered. 'I've been wed four times myself and have deflowered a further seven brides on the morning of their nuptials.' He closed his eyes. 'Oh the fragrance as I toyed with them.'

'Why would any decent woman want to sleep with you?' John asked.

'Who said anything about them being decent?' Laurence answered. 'In any case, I am famous for the size and girth of my member.'

'Pity their little arses, then,' said Bernard.

'I agree. But I had to do it that fashion or I'd have been found out by their husbands and my gizzard would have been slit.'

'A pity it wasn't,' John said.

Laurence smiled and then gave him an almighty slap upon his back, exactly where the whip had scarred. 'Don't be like that, John,' he said. 'You should be grateful it's me who is in charge of you.' He sauntered off, whistling out of tune. John doubled up in pain.

In truth they were glad that Laurence was their overseer. He was loud and bluff but he treated the men in his crews fairly, rewarding the hard working with a brief word of thanks, yelling and kicking at the slackers. As a senior member of the city guard he was accustomed to giving orders and his men obeyed him concerning the disposal of bodies in the same way they obeyed his commands in battle.

On the third day the city was finally cleared of corpses and they were relieved of this onerous duty. From this point on they would be able to tackle the litter of war, the Saracen shot and boulders, the fallen masonry and timbers, the dangerous buildings.

A week after they had started on the clearance Conrad ordered that all crews take the following day to rest. Most decided to spend it in the taverns. They had been the first establishments to open for business when the Saracens ended the siege and they did better trade than the food stalls and the churches combined.

As soon as he heard the order, Laurence led his crew into The Saracen's Throat, the largest tavern in the city. 'The drinks for my crew is on Lord Conrad,' he cried, throwing a large bag of coins upon the table.

His men could not believe their ears. They had never known such largesse in their lives.

Matthew's size and strength proved invaluable now. He shouldered his way through the crowd with John and Bernard in his wake.

'Three pints of your best wine,' he yelled at the inn-keeper.

'I prefer ale,' John said. 'English if you have it?'

'I've got ale,' the inn-keeper said. 'Christ knows where it came from but it will give you a head like mill-stones.'

'That will suit him,' said Bernard. 'He needs something powerful to penetrate his skull.'

'Hey,' cried a man from further down the bar. 'Hey, is that Bernard Montjoy?'

Bernard turned and scanned the line of men at the bar. A tall, stocky man was gazing towards him and now raised his hand in greeting.

'Jurgen,' Bernard cried. 'Is it you?'

'As ever was. Wait there.'

In a moment the tall man had joined them, together with his companion, a man as short as Jurgen was tall. As soon as the smaller man saw Bernard he grinned and shook his hand. When they relaxed their grip the man hurriedly counted his fingers.

'Four fingers and a thumb,' he said. 'For once you haven't robbed me.'

'I had no need to rob you Oliver,' Bernard answered. 'You consumed enough wine in my inn to keep me in a life of luxury.'

'That looks to have changed.' The tall man bent and sniffed him. 'You smell like a cesspit.'

'Thank you, Jurgen. You would smell as bad if you had been carrying rotting corpses around all day.'

'So, they've had you slaving as well,' Oliver said. 'Jurgen and I have been dismantling the Saracen siege engines.'

'That sounds like bliss compared to what we did,' said Bernard. 'Here, do you remember John?'

Oliver nodded. 'The young Englishman. You were also

knighted by Balian.'

'I was,' said John. 'I think we ate together once, sheltering behind a wall from Saracen arrows.'

'We did indeed. We ate broiled dog.'

'Trust Oliver to find the delicacy,' Jurgen said. He extended a hand to John. 'You had a brother, or a cousin, if I recall right.'

'A cousin,' John said. He did not wish to continue this line of conversation with the big German. 'I never met you, Jurgen,' he said, 'but I remember you at the siege. You were always in the thick of the battle.'

'Yes, but always trying to get out of it,' said Oliver. 'You only noticed him because he is so big. So did the Saracens. They always made a bee-line for him and he always ran away.'

John smiled. Jurgen was known as one of the most courageous of Jerusalem's defenders.

Bernard indicated Matthew to the newcomers. 'You won't know Matthew. He wasn't at the siege.'

Oliver held out his hand and shook it warmly.

Jurgen stared at Matthew's face and nodded. 'I do know you,' he said. 'You are called the Mule. You used to carry the leper King on your back.'

The men close by heard this. They fell silent and turned to stare at Matthew.

Matthew felt Oliver's hand go dead in his. A moment later he felt the grip tighten. The little man shook it even more vigorously. 'That was years ago, you big dolt,' he said to Jurgen. 'He obviously didn't catch anything.'

Matthew gave a smile of thanks to Oliver. The crowd surrounding relaxed at his words and returned to their wine.

'Why are you in Tyre?' Bernard asked.

'It started on the day that al-Adil freed us,' Oliver said.

'The day after, actually,' said Jurgen.

'The day after then. Nobody knew what to do. It was clear that we could no longer go back to our homes in the city. Those of the knights with relatives in the country headed that way. That left about a dozen or so of us.'

'More than that,' Jurgen said. 'Nearer a score.'

'A dozen. A score. The number's not important. Anyway, about half the group decided to go off to the castle at Kerak. It was said to be impregnable so it seemed a safe place to go.'

'The rest of us did not think so,' Jurgen added.

'No,' Oliver said. 'Too far to the east, too close to the Saracens. A couple of men had families who had bought their freedom so they went in search of the columns led by Balian.'

'Half a dozen of us did not trust the Muslims who were guarding Balian's columns so we headed north instead.'

'We would have been better putting our trust in the infidels,' Oliver said. 'We travelled to Belvoir Castle and sought service there. Our offer was not welcomed; we were called cowards and traitors and thrown into the prison.'

'By Christians?' John asked.

'By Hospitallers,' Jurgen answered. 'I could not believe it of such a holy order.'

The tall man took a deep drink at his wine and banged upon the table for another. The memory of it still shocked him.

'We would have been rotting there still,' continued Oliver, 'if it hadn't been for the Saracens. They arrived soon after we did and besieged the castle. One of the guards took it into his own head to free us to fight.'

'More fool him,' said Jurgen.

'More fool the four of us who agreed to fight for the Hospitallers. Not Oliver Rideau. I persuaded this big bugger to join me and we slipped out of the castle that night and never stopped running until morning.'

'Eventually we ended up here, in Tyre. Conrad put us into his militia straight away. We have been here ever since.'

Bernard raised his glass to them. 'A strange adventure. But you survived.'

The two men nodded.

'What about you?' Jurgen asked. 'How did you end up in Tyre?'

'We went in search of the captives,' Bernard answered. 'The minute we were given our freedom. My wife and family were taken by the Saracens.'

Oliver put his hand to his mouth. 'Not Agnes?'

Bernard nodded.

'And the children? Gerard and Eleanor?'

'And my nephew, Claude-Yusuf.'

Jurgen put his hand upon Bernard's shoulder. 'Thank God that they are together, at least.'

Oliver frowned. 'Are they here then? Are they in Tyre?'

'No.'

'Have you searched for them?'

'We haven't,' John said. 'But our captain asked his friends to search high and low for them. They are not in the city.'

'Laurence is there,' Bernard said, beckoning the captain over. 'He has money from Conrad. Let him buy you a drink.'

Laurence began to make his way towards them. Before he got to them, however, there came a sound of a scuffle near the entrance.

Half a dozen nobles had forced their way into the tavern. They were drunk and looking for fun. They shouldered aside anyone in their path and made their way to the bar.

'Wine and food,' cried one. 'And not your usual slops. The best you've got.'

John tensed. It was Gilbert Vallon, the man responsible for their flogging.

The tavern-keeper ignored the man he was serving and hurried to get wine for the lords, yelling at the rest of his family to come and help serve. They must have sensed from his voice that something was amiss for they rushed out to help.

His wife and two sons brought platters of cold meat from the kitchen while his daughter joined her father and poured the best wine into clean goblets.

'Pretty wench,' said one of the lords. He leant over the bar and dragged the young girl half over, slobbering at her mouth to the cheers of his friends.

John tensed at this.

Bernard grabbed his arm. 'Don't be a fool.'

The girl broke free and retreated to her father, wiping her mouth as she did so.

'How much for the girl?' yelled the man.

'She's my daughter,' the tavern-keeper said.

The man shrugged. 'What difference does that make?'

'She's a good girl, Sir Henry.'

'Let me be the judge of that,' Henry cried. He made a lunge at the girl, grabbing her by the hair.

John watched in silence for a moment longer. Then he shrugged off Bernard's grip and walked across to the man.

Bernard turned to Matthew for help but it was already too late.

John clutched the nobleman by his arm.

'She is only a child,' he said. 'Be courteous, I beg you.'

Sir Henry's eyes widened as he stared at John. 'How dare you,' he began. He paused. John sensed that the knight half-recognised him and was struggling to recall from where.

Gilbert Vallon had no such difficulty.

'Look what we have here,' he said. He pushed his way towards John.

'Sir Peasant, the Knight of the gutter,' he cried with a mock bow to John.

His friends laughed at the words.

'Of course,' said Henry. 'Balian's ragged champion.'

'Balian's piece of shit,' said Vallon. 'Balian's ill-bred knight.'

John said nothing. Part of him wanted to avert his eyes, to cast them down. Yet a larger part made him refuse to do so. He blinked and gazed back directly at Vallon. Then he yawned, as if bored by the conversation.

'Insolent dog,' cried Vallon, slapping him on the cheek.

John tensed but forced himself to stay calm.

'Look over there, Gilbert,' said one of the others. 'Sir Gutter has his friend here. The Mule.'

Gilbert's eyes slid towards Matthew, thinking him equally good prey.

'I'll deal with you in a minute,' he murmured to John.

Vallon stared at Matthew for a long time, amusement building in his face.

'I can see why you were chosen to be a beast of burden,' he said at last. 'You look as strong as a brute and no doubt you've got the brains of one.'

Matthew fought to control his anger. He took a breath and turned his back on Vallon, picking up his wine. This was a mistake.

Vallon cried, 'Let's see how strong a mule he really is,' and leapt upon Matthew's back.

Matthew felt the man's legs lock around his chest and his strong hands jerk his head backward by his hair.

'Now it is I who ride the Mule,' Vallon yelled. His friends cheered with delight.

Matthew turned this way and that, desperately trying to dislodge Vallon. But the noble had ridden war-horses since his youth and it was no problem for him to tighten his legs and keep his seat. The more Matthew turned, the tighter he gripped. He swept out his sword and began to beat Matthew on his thigh.

'Ride Mule, ride. Show me your tricks.'

'Lord Vallon,' cried the tavern-keeper. 'Careful with your sword, you might wound him.'

Vallon disregarded him, or maybe not. The next beat of his sword cut into Matthew's arm and drew blood.

This was too much for John. He jumped towards them and dragged Vallon to the ground. Vallon did not move in time and John threw himself upon him, his knees landing on his chest with his full weight. The crowd watched in grim silence as John rained punch after punch upon Vallon's face.

Vallon's friends were too astonished to react for a moment. Then they attacked. Henry reached them first. He swept out his sword and held it high above John's head. He struck. But the sword did not.

Laurence had parried the blow with his sword.

Henry turned and stared speechless at the newcomer.

'You scum,' he cried and lunged towards Laurence with his sword.

Laurence blocked the blow and forced Henry back a step. He

recovered instantly and sliced low, seeking to cut Laurence's legs. Laurence leapt away just in time. Henry straightened and raised his sword in both hands. He cut at Laurence time and again, the weight of his battle sword forcing him back until he had reached the tavern wall. There was no where else to retreat to. Henry laughed and raised his sword for the killer blow. He glanced around, checking that his friends were watching. Laurence ducked and stabbed. It was a desperate blow and his sword thrust through the knight's chest. Henry staggered and stared down at the blade, a look of disbelief in his face. He slid to the ground.

Laurence stared at the fallen knight in horror, the enormity of what he had done racing into his brain.

He glanced up. The whole of the tavern stared at him in silence.

Bernard grabbed hold of John, dragging him off of Vallon. He turned towards Laurence and called out, 'Come with us, Laurence. We must flee.'

Laurence was dazed by what he had done. He felt Matthew grab him by the arm and hustle him towards the door. Two men stepped close behind.

'We're coming with you, Bernard,' called Oliver.

They pushed through the crowd.

The men moved aside to allow them free passage. Then in silence as one they turned towards the nobles, their faces grim and set, their arms crossed.

'You're going nowhere,' called a voice from the crowd.

The nobles took one look at them and edged back towards the wall.

'How about a drink?' one called out nervously.

The crowd did not answer.

The six friends raced out of the door and turned left towards the city walls. It was pitch black now, with the crescent moon giving little light. Bernard and the others were soon lost in the maze of streets.

He pressed his face close to Laurence's. 'Where the hell are we?'

Laurence shook his head, still in a daze. He glanced around, trying to discern the shape of the buildings.

'Near the fish-market,' he said. 'Where are we going?'

'We're escaping from Tyre,' Oliver said. 'John beat Gilbert Vallon to a pulp and you killed Henry Colville.'

Laurence held his hands over his eyes. 'I'm a dead man,' he muttered.

'You are if you remain in Tyre,' Bernard said. 'Come on.' He led the way down the street. He had his bearings now.

They had only gone two hundred yards when Laurence called to them to stop.

'What the hell for?' cried Bernard. 'They'll be after us in minutes.'

'We'll never escape on foot,' Laurence said. 'The stables are close by.'

They turned and followed Laurence down a narrow alley, stumbling into each other in the dark. After a few minutes it opened out into a small square. The smell of horses hit their noses.

Laurence led them into the stable. Silently, in a haste of panic, they selected six horses and saddled them up. 'Take a spare,' John whispered. 'We can't risk any going lame.'

'Then let's take three,' Bernard said.

Ten minutes later the six men walked the horses out of the stables. All was quiet.

'This is strange,' Jurgen said. 'I thought we would have been pursued by now.'

'I know why we aren't,' Oliver said. 'Our friends have prevented the lords from leaving. News of what happened in the tavern won't have got out yet.'

'Then let's go while we've got a chance,' Bernard said.

They were only a short distance from the walls. Laurence led them left, away from the main gate towards a smaller one which was normally used by traders coming in and out on foot.

'It will be guarded,' he said, 'but more lightly.'

He was right. Two soldiers lounged beside the gate, their supper spread out before them. They looked up in surprise at the sudden appearance of men and horses.

'Where are you going?' one cried, reaching for his sword.

'It's me, Laurence Dubois.'

The sentry stood up and raised a lantern to Laurence's face. 'Sorry sir,' he said. 'I didn't realise it was you. We have to challenge everyone.'

'Absolutely,' Laurence said. 'Well done.'

The man continued to stare at him, a questioning look on his face.

'We're on a mission to scout for Saracen war-bands,' Laurence explained.

'I thought Saladin had gone, sir.'

'There's rumour they're filtering back. Or so the Marquis thinks.'

The man stiffened at the mention of Conrad.

'It's a secret mission,' added Bernard. He glanced around. 'The Marquis fears there are spies in the city.'

The two guards looked around in alarm, as if expecting to see hooded figures spring out in the darkness.

'We won't breathe a word,' said the man quietly. He turned and opened the gate slowly, easing it open without a sound.

Laurence clapped him on the shoulder and led them out of the city.

They walked their horses for a couple of furlongs then mounted up and began to trot. It was only when they had covered the best part of a mile that anyone spoke again.

'There's still no sign of pursuit,' John said.

'Thank God,' Bernard said. 'Let's make the best of it. We can't ride fast in starlight but let's get on.'

They started off once again. All except Laurence. He turned in his saddle and looked back at the city.

'Come on, sir,' Bernard hissed. 'We've got to get a move on.'

'I'm not coming,' Laurence answered. 'I'm a captain in the city guard. I should go back.'

'If you go back you'll be dead.'

'It was a fair fight,' he said. 'Witnesses will testify that I killed in self-defence.'

'What witnesses?' John asked.

'The men in the tavern. The tavern-keeper and his family.'

'Do you really think their word will count for anything against Vallon's and his friends?' John was incredulous.

'Of course it will. There are dozens of them. And my word counts for something in the city.'

'You're fooling yourself if you think that. I was flogged merely for pushing at Vallon.'

'And for claiming to be a knight,' said Matthew.

'Whatever the reasons, I was flogged. So what do you imagine your punishment will be for murdering a knight?'

'It was not murder.'

'That's what they'll call it.'

Laurence said nothing, his gaze still fixed longingly upon the city.

'But I've never left Tyre,' he said. 'Where will I go? Tyre is my home.'

'You'll go with us,' said Bernard.

'And your home will be your horse,' added Matthew.

'And your kin will be us,' said John. We're the only kin any of us have got.'

He frowned, cursing himself for saying such a thing in Bernard's hearing. 'Until we find our loved ones,' he added quickly.

'So,' said Laurence. 'You poor souls are my new companions.' He paused. 'What did Gilbert Vallon call you?'

'Balian's ragged champions,' Bernard said.

'Ill-bred Knights,' said John.

'Ill-bred Knights,' echoed their voices in the darkness.

CHAPTER 46
WAR IN THE HAREM
Baghdad

Agnes gazed at the view from her window. A long sweep of lawn led down to the Palace walls. Peacocks strutted on the lawn. Soldiers strutted on the walls. Beyond the walls she could see nothing but a clear blue sky with a skein of clouds wafting slowly in a high breeze.

She forced herself back to her embroidery. Her fingers concentrated upon it but her mind wandered far away. She worried daily about Gerard and Claude-Yusuf. She knew that they were still alive and staying near to the Palace. Habib had left a message for her saying that they had been taken into the most important futuwwa. She had no idea what this meant but the messenger assured her that this was excellent news and Johara had confirmed this.

She was comforted that at least Eleanor was with her. In fact she had taken extremely well to the palace, loving its beauty and luxury. She had confided in her mother that she thought she was now a princess.

Most of Agnes' thoughts, however, concerned her husband. The last time she had seen Bernard had been outside the walls of Jerusalem. Wild rumours had swept among the captives, some even saying that Balian's knights were going to be crucified. She had almost fainted at the thought and wept inconsolably when it became clear that this was not going to be the case. Nevertheless, she knew that Bernard and John had been bought by Saladin's brother and that he was a man of diabolical reputation.

She heard a noise and glanced up. The Caliph was standing near the entrance watching her intently.

Agnes threw down her embroidery and knelt upon the floor.

'I am sorry, my lord,' she said, 'I had not seen you there.'

'There is nothing to be sorry about,' he answered. 'It is I who should apologise, for walking in to your chamber unannounced and for watching you as I have been.'

'Watching me?' A prickle of fear ran through her.

'Yes. Like some peasant from a village who gapes at a princess when she rides past, unable to believe that such a beauty can exist in the world.'

Agnes blushed. Al-Nasir stepped towards her and helped her to her feet.

'Are you comfortable here?' he asked. 'The chamber is small.'

'It is perfect, thank you, lord,' she said. 'I am very content with my chamber.'

She took him by the hand and led him over to a table where she had laid out a range of little objects.

'These are my gifts,' he said. He picked one up and examined it closely.

'You seem surprised,' she said.

'I always suspect that my gifts are hidden away in some cupboard and forgotten,' he said. 'I suspect Johara gets Dawud to sell them in the market. I swear I have bought the same brooch from there three times and given it anew to her each time I did so.'

Agnes laughed. 'Would she do such a thing?'

'Oh she would. And I forgive her each time.' He fell silent. 'I forgive in Johara things I would not forgive in anyone else.'

Agnes could not let this slip by. 'Not even Beatrice?'

For a fleeting moment the brightness in his eyes dimmed, or so Agnes thought. Her heart quickened. She touched the Caliph on his heart, a gesture she knew that he loved.

'But why am I talking of other ladies,' he said. 'I have come to visit you.'

Agnes lowered her head. 'And I am honoured.' She wanted to ask why but dare not. She had been told that members of the harem were always summoned to his chamber, never visited by him in their own.

He kissed her hand and walked around the room, sniffing at bottles of scent, playing with some wooden fruit which Johara had given to her, and finally picking up some of her embroidery and examining it carefully.

'You did this?' he asked.

'I did, my lord.' She walked towards him. 'Please take a piece that you like, as a gift from me.'

Al-Nasir looked at her in astonishment. He looked from her to the embroidery and back again. His lips tightened and he looked away, stroking his head time and time again.

She bit her lip, wondering what she had done wrong, wondering how she could put it right.

He turned back to her. 'Nobody has given me a gift since I was a boy,' he said. His eyes were wet.

She stepped towards him and held him close. Her heart beat faster but not, this time, with anxiety. Something had happened. Something had changed.

She took him by the hand and led him to her bed-chamber.

The next day Johara and Lalina hurried into her room. They

looked sick and scared.

'Whatever's the matter?' Agnes asked.

'Whatever have you done?' asked Johara.

'I don't know what you mean.'

'You must have done something,' Lalina said. 'You must have done.' She burst into tears and stroked Agnes' hand again and again.

Agnes put her hand to her mouth. This was terrifying. That her friends should be acting like this. Tears filled her eyes.

'Tell me what's wrong,' she whispered.

'Beatrice is in a rage,' said Johara.

'I've never seen anything like it,' said Lalina.

'Nor have I,' said Johara. 'And I've known the little hell-cat for years.'

'But what has this to do with me?' Agnes asked.

'That's what we came to find out,' said Lalina.

'But I've done nothing to Beatrice.'

'Whether you did or not, she thinks you have,' said Johara. 'You must appease her.'

'But how?'

'I don't know, but you must.'

No sooner had Johara said this than Beatrice's eunuch entered the chamber. Agnes took a step backward, uncertain what to do. He gave an urgent gesture for her to stay still and put his fingers to his lips. His face looked alarmed.

A moment later Beatrice swept into the chamber. She strode up to Agnes and slapped her hard across the face.

'You gutter-whore,' Beatrice cried. 'That a piece of filth like you thinks you can steal him away from me.'

Agnes opened her mouth to protest but Beatrice struck her

once again, even harder.

Agnes staggered then, without thinking, stepped back and slapped Beatrice across her cheek.

Beatrice held her hand to her face, her tirade cut short. Finally she overcame her astonishment and she found her voice again.

'You are dead,' she hissed. 'And so are all your family.'

She swept out of the room.

CHAPTER 47
THE POWER OF LUST
Antioch

Simon smiled and strode down the corridor which led to the main gate. He had only gone a dozen yards when he saw Princess Cybil watching him from the entrance to her chamber. Her bear cub was asleep in her lap and she toyed absently with its ear.

He immediately felt nervous and bowed low to her.

'Come here, Englishman,' she said.

Simon swallowed and looked about him before following her into the room.

'This is not my bed-chamber,' Cybil said, 'so you need have no fear. And perhaps not any hope.'

She smiled and he was once more reminded of a cat but this time one exotic and dreadfully dangerous.

'I've been watching you, Simon Ferrier,' she said.

'You have,' he mumbled. 'I hope I have not given any offence.'

'Oh we are hardly that intimate. Yet.' She sipped at a cup of wine.

'I have been watching you,' she continued, 'because you intrigue me. You are said to be one of the commoners that Balian knighted. Yet you don't serve him. Instead you serve that knave of a priest.'

Simon nodded. Her gaze terrified him so much that he did not know what to say.

Cybil touched him on the cheek. His fear was banished instantly and his lust aroused.

She laughed, a high and tinkling laugh like distant bells. 'So it is true. I have heard that you rut like a boar with some child from the gutter. But I look into your eyes Simon and know that you have had choicer meat by far.'

Simon did not answer. He saw Agnes lying naked on her bed; saw himself placing on her belly the eight dinars he had had used to buy her. Saw himself sneak back into the house in the night to steal the money in order to buy his own freedom.

Then he saw Cybil's eyes blazing into his. 'So. It is as I suspected. You are consumed by lust. That is not unusual in a man. But there is more to you than this. You combine lust with vengeance. You weave webs of hope and deceit; you gain what you most desire and then you betray. Oh what a fascinating man you are, Simon Ferrier. It is no wonder that Eraclius has seen your merits and seeks to use you.'

She brushed his cheek with her lips. 'But you, Simon, need to learn that there is a far, far greater power in Antioch than Eraclius.

'And one day she might just call upon you to serve her.'

CHAPTER 48
TRAINING REGIME
The Caliph's Palace

Sheik al-Djabbar's eyes narrowed as he watched Claude-Yusuf and Gerard sparring together. He was sitting in the shade on the edge of the training ground. The fringes of the field were lush with green grass but in the centre the movement of many boys had turned the area a dusty reddish brown.

Today, a dozen young boys fought with wooden swords, their feet slipping on the dry earth and making dust rise up like clouds of midges.

'The young Franks fight well considering their age,' came the bird-like squawk of al-Djabbar's friend.

'You are right, Bahir,' the sheik answered. 'And they have no experience of weapons at all.'

'You are a fool if you believe that,' Bahir answered. 'All boys know about weapons. Even boys from the gutter fight with swords made of wood or bone.'

Al-Djabbar pursed his lips and nodded. 'Once more you are right, my friend. I am so old I had forgotten it. You, presumably, know this from your boyfriends.'

Bahir laughed at the insult.

The two old men watched the fighting in silence for a while longer.

'The older boy is a clever fighter,' al-Djabbar said quietly.

'Not just in fighting,' Bahir answered. 'He has a tongue as fast as a cobra. And he is popular with the other boys.'

The sheik sniffed. 'He may go far in the Caliph's service. I shall push him.' He sipped at a glass of iced water. 'The younger boy? I forget his name.'

'Gerard.'

'What do you think of his promise?'

'He is not as intelligent as Claude-Yusuf, but there again, few are. He is bullied a little by the older boys.'

'That is good.'

'Yes, that is good. And he is learning how to stand up to them.'

'That is even better. I hear he rides well.'

'Like a Bedu.'

'And he has a gift with beasts?'

Bahir nodded. 'Yesterday I saw him quiet a stallion which even the grooms were finding difficult.'

Al-Djabbar laughed. 'I think he has inherited that from his mother. The eunuchs say she has quite beguiled the Caliph.'

'Has she, indeed?' said Bahir. 'I wonder what the bitch Beatrice will make of that.'

'And I wonder what she will do about such a rival,' said al-Djabbar. 'My suspicion is that Gerard will very soon become an orphan.'

Bahir took a drink of coffee. 'Have you seen his mother? Is she comely?'

'You old dog,' al-Djabbar said, swatting him with a cane. 'She is very comely. She has the innocent, everyday look that every man desires in his sister.'

'That is not so special.'

'Ah. But she also has something more, a rare beauty. She has the fleeting look of a fawn in the forest, delicate and fragile. A fawn which eagerly awaits the rutting stag.'

Bahir laughed aloud. 'Ah to be young again.'

'Ah to be a Caliph.'

'What do you think they're laughing about?' Claude-Yusuf said.

'Maybe somebody tickled them,' Gerard answered.

'I doubt that. Nobody would dare to get that close to them.'

Gerard nodded miserably. He was in dread of the two fierce old men.

The soldier who was training them blew upon a whistle. It was the signal to stop and go for food.

The Caliph's son hurried to join them in the scrum for food.

'Here, al-Dahir,' Claude-Yusuf called. 'We are at the front.'

Al-Dahir pushed his way towards them.

'I fought well, today,' he said. 'I got ten strikes on my opponents. How many did you get?'

'None,' said Gerard. 'Claude-Yusuf is bigger than me.'

'I got twenty,' said Claude-Yusuf. He saw the face of the prince fall. 'But that is because Gerard is smaller than me.'

Al-Dahir's face brightened. 'Of course it was.' He gave Claude-Yusuf a quizzical look. 'Although when you've had more practice you may prove a deadly swordsman.'

Claude-Yusuf blushed. 'What makes you say that?'

'I didn't,' the prince answered. 'Bahir did.'

Claude-Yusuf snorted. 'What does that old fool's opinion matter?'

'A lot,' said al-Dahir. 'He was the supreme general of the Caliph's armies. He is the only man that the sheik respects.'

'He was a general?' Gerard asked. This served to make him

loom even larger in is nightmares.

'Yes, to my great-great grand-father, al-Muqtafi. He was a mighty Caliph and defeated the Seljuk scum. Bahir was his General.'

'That must make Bahir hundreds of years old,' Gerard murmured.

The others nodded. He certainly looked it.

'If Bahir was a great general why isn't he in charge of the futuwwa?' Claude-Yusuf asked. 'Why Sheik al-Djabbar? Who is he?'

'He was one of al-Muqtafi's allies from the south. I don't know how he became head of the futuwwa.'

Claude-Yusuf glanced up at the old man. He could guess how.

Al-Djabbar pulled at his beard thoughtfully. 'You said that the younger Frank is standing up to bullying.'

Bahir nodded.

'How will he respond if we allow Suhail to return to the futuwwa?'

Bahir frowned. 'Ask Sinbad. But remember, Sinbad knew that a Jinni is best left in its bottle.'

Al-Djabbar chuckled and summoned a servant.

Towards the end of the day, after prayers, the boys of the futuwwa headed towards the refectory. Sitting on top of the table at the far end was a boy about fourteen years of age.

A loud cheer came from the rest of the boys and most rushed towards the figure. He did not move but allowed himself to give a contented smile. A couple of boys hung back for a moment then seemed to think better of it and chased after their peers.

Only Claude-Yusuf, Gerard and al-Dahir did not join the jubilant throng.

The boy climbed to his feet and walked along the table, kicking the carefully arranged dishes out of place. Gerard was shocked, imagining the sharp smack he would have received from his parents for doing such a thing. He glanced at the refectory orderly to see how he would respond but the man looked away and busied himself with some dishes on the side-board.

Gerard looked back at the table. The new boy had walked the length of the table and was now staring down at them.

'What do we have here?' he asked.

'They are Franks, Suhail,' said one of the boys quickly. He glanced up at the boy on the table as if to see how he might react to this information.

Suhail nodded. He stepped off of the table, onto the bench and then onto the ground. He did not look at where he was putting his feet because all the time his gaze was fixed firmly upon Claude-Yusuf.

Then he turned toward al-Dahir and gave an elaborate, courtly bow. 'Son of the Caliph,' he said. 'It is good to see you once more.'

Al-Dahir nodded but did not reply.

Suhail once again turned his attention to Claude-Yusuf. He walked around him several times, scrutinising him thoughtfully all the while. After two circles he stopped and stared into Claude-Yusuf's eyes.

'A Frank,' he said softly. 'How does a Frank come to be in Baghdad?'

'We were captured in Jerusalem,' Claude-Yusuf answered. 'My father is a captain in the army of the King. My uncle is a knight of Jerusalem.'

'That's my father,' began Gerard.

Suhail placed his hand over Gerard's mouth. 'I don't believe I was talking to you,' he said.

'Sorry,' Gerard mumbled. He suddenly felt alarmed.

Suhail continued to stare at Claude-Yusuf. 'You know that my name is Suhail,' he said. 'What is yours?'

'Claude-Yusuf,' he answered. 'And that is my cousin, Gerard.'

The boy surprised them by leaning back and giving a hearty grin. 'You are welcome Claude-Yusuf and Gerard. Even though you have such peculiar names.'

The atmosphere of the refectory changed instantly.

Claude-Yusuf grinned back at Suhail who clapped him on the shoulder. Gerard, however, continued to regard Suhail with suspicion. He could not tell why. He had felt this same tightening in his throat once before but could not recall when.

The boys were, as usual, famished after their day of training. They fell upon the food like wolves and were soon holding up their platters for more. The food was simple but of good quality and there was plenty of it.

Eventually every belly felt full and the room was filled with loud belching. The boys put their down their knives and waited impatiently. After a few minutes there came the sound of a gong. The boys leapt to their feet at once, pushing and shoving each other in the race for the exit.

They hurried out to get the last few minutes of daylight. It soon became clear that Suhail had decided to make a firm friend of Claude-Yusuf. He was waiting for him in the exercise yard and draped his arm around the younger boy's shoulder.

'I am sorry to hear that you were captured in Jerusalem,' Suhail said. 'Does this mean that you were sold as slaves?'

'Yes,' said Claude-Yusuf. 'We were brought to Baghdad by Habib and Dawud.'

Suhail laughed. 'Habib the Fat? I am surprised he is able to waddle outside of the palace.'

Claude-Yusuf laughed. 'He puffs and pants a lot.'

'He is a scoundrel,' Suhail said. 'Whatever you do, don't trust him.'

'I wouldn't. He played tricks on us from the first.'

'But he said that was part of our training,' Gerard said. 'And he was nice to us on the journey.'

'He did that to take you into his confidence,' Suhail said. 'You're lucky that you didn't wake up with your throat slit. Or worse.'

'Worse?'

'I hear from people that he likes boys.'

Claude-Yusuf looked concerned. 'I will remember that.'

'Do so.' Suhail pulled an apricot from inside his robe and offered it to Claude-Yusuf.

'Why haven't you been in the futuwwa until now?' Gerard asked him.

Suhail smiled. 'I was suspended for thirty days. I led an insurrection against the orderlies.'

Claude-Yusuf's face beamed. 'That must have been great fun.'

'It was. But I got caught and I got punished. I cannot complain. I am back here now.'

Claude-Yusuf's heart beat fast. He had been singled out for favour by a boy who was obviously one of the most important in the futuwwa.

He saw al-Dahir watching them out of the corner of his eye closely and gave him a cheery wave. The prince did not respond.

The next morning, at breakfast, Claude-Yusuf's place at the table was taken by another boy. Before he could ask why the boy nodded in Suhail's direction.

'Suhail wants you to sit next to him,' the boy said. 'Where I used to sit.' He was tight-lipped with anger.

Claude-Yusuf took his plate and strolled along the table towards Suhail. Gerard watched him go in silence, a sulky look upon his face.

'My friend, the Frank,' Suhail said as Claude-Yusuf approached. 'I want you to sit next to me from now on. It is important that we show generosity to our foreign friends. I know that your family fight against our people but they do so because of their own faith. I do not blame them for this.'

Claude-Yusuf smiled.

Suhail took a sip at his beaker before continuing. 'Did your father kill many Muslims?' he asked. His voice was curious.

'I don't know,' said Claude-Yusuf. 'I suppose he must have done.'

'And your uncle? You said he was a knight, a great warrior, a crusader.'

'He's really only an inn-keeper,' Claude-Yusuf answered. 'He was made a knight at the siege because there were not enough knights in the city.'

Gerard could just make out what they were saying from further down the table. 'My father was one of the leaders of the battle,' he called.

Suhail nodded. 'I'm sure he was. He must have killed many men in the siege.'

'Hundreds I think,' Gerard answered. 'He's very brave.'

'Crusaders are very brave,' Suhail said.

The other boys turned to listen, sensing something was different.

'I suppose your father fights from a huge horse and wears heavy chain armour?'

'I don't know,' Gerard answered. 'I don't think so.'

'I think he does,' said Suhail. 'Muslim warriors, on the other hand, like to ride fast as the desert winds so only wear a light breast-plate. They do not cloak themselves in iron.'

Gerard frowned. He sensed that Suhail's tone had changed but could not say how.

He raised his voice. 'Imagine what it's like to be Gerard's father,' he called. 'You are six feet above the ground, you have sharp weapons, you are safe behind your armour. He must have no fear when he attacks a Muslim soldier. No fear when he hunts down Muslim women and children.'

'He's not like that,' cried Gerard.

Suhail extended his hands in an innocent gesture. 'But he's a knight, you told us so yourself. A crusader.'

'But he's not like that.'

Suhail laughed. 'I don't suppose he has told you about the Muslim babies he must have butchered.'

Gerard flew out of his seat and sprang upon Suhail.

The older boy was surprised and for a moment struggled to push him away. He slapped Gerard around the ear, sending him reeling. But Gerard was up almost immediately and went for Suhail once again.

Suhail was ready for him this time. He towered above the younger boy, his face mocking, his frame thick and strong from greater years and hard training. It looked as if a waif were about to attack a full-grown man.

But attack Gerard did, ducking under Suhail's arms and head-butting him in the stomach. Suhail gasped and staggered back. He came back with a snarl, his face no longer scornful but full of rage. He punched Gerard full in the face, sending him crashing to the floor. He leapt upon him and continued to punch him in his face, time and again.

The other boys watched in amazement. It had all happened so quickly. Then Claude-Yusuf reached out for Suhail's hair and dragged him off his cousin.

Suhail lunged away and turned to Claude-Yusuf, his eyes sharp with fury.

'You Frankish scum,' he cried. 'You do this to me after I made a friend of you.' He threw a punch at him.

But Claude-Yusuf had seen it coming and leaned out of the way. He danced two steps to the left which meant that Suhail's second punch also failed to hit him. But he could not avoid the third.

He almost did so, turning his face in time. But the blow hit him on the ear. He was astonished how hard Suhail's fist was. The next moment, slightly stunned by it, he felt two more blows to his stomach. He doubled up and as he did so Suhail smashed two quick punches to his face. Blood spurted from his nose and he keeled over, his senses gone.

'Leave him alone,' cried Gerard. The little boy leapt upon Suhail's back, jabbing with his knees and biting at his neck.

Suhail threw him onto the ground. This blow was too much for Gerard. He was winded and he flopped onto his back. Suhail saw his chance and began to kick him violently in the side, sending his body this way and that as if he were a rag doll.

He was so intent that he did not see Claude-Yusuf stagger up and lurch towards him.

'You big coward,' he cried. Then he slapped Suhail

upon the cheek.

If it had been a punch Suhail would have reacted. But a slap. A slap was what an angry parent gave to a child. A slap was a sign of condemnation. A slap was an insult.

Suhail stood speechless, holding his cheek. The rest of the boys gasped.

Suhail stared at Claude-Yusuf for a moment longer. 'You are dead,' he said bitterly. Then he turned and hurried from the scene.

CHAPTER 49
THE FREE COMPANY
Niphin

John woke with a start. In a distant village a cockerel cried. Towards the east the rising sun had painted the sky a pale and streaky pink. A solitary star burned in the heavens.

John screwed up his eyes, trying to calculate how long they had slept. Too long, he thought. He kicked Bernard's foot.

'Agnes?' Bernard cried, sitting up with a blank look.

John shook his head. 'Sorry, friend, it's only me. We need to move on.'

Bernard stretched and gave a huge yawn. 'I've hardly slept.'

'Your snoring in the night says otherwise,' said John. 'Let's hope there's no pursuers near-by.'

The sound of their conversation woke the others.

Jurgen rose and stamped on the ground to warm his legs. 'I am famished,' he said. 'Did you bring any food, Oliver?'

The small man looked at him in disbelief. 'We fled for our lives, you big oaf. Forgive me for not stopping off at the market for bread and wine.'

'I was just wondering. My belly is groaning.'

'He's got a big frame,' Oliver explained to the others. 'He needs lots of fodder.'

'That's been concerning me as well,' said Bernard. 'We've got no food and no water. We need to find some.' He looked around, as if he might find a little cache upon the floor somewhere.

'How will we find it?' John asked.

'We could steal from the Saracens,' said Oliver.

'Or the Hospitallers,' added Oliver.

'If I had my leper's weeds I could beg,' said Matthew. Jurgen and Oliver shifted uncomfortably. They had been told that Matthew was not a leper but they were still suspicious. They discreetly kept their distance from him.

'There's no need for such extreme measures,' Laurence said. He took out a leather bag and rattled it. 'I've got the remainder of the money that Conrad gave me to buy wine.'

The others gathered around him while he counted it out. There were a dozen copper denier coins.

'Enough for some food,' said Bernard. 'Laurence, where is the nearest village?'

'We are close to Aadloun. It is a Saracen village but they have always been friendly with the people of Tyre.'

'They might not be now,' said Oliver. 'Not now that Saladin has defeated us.'

'If they are anything like me,' said Bernard, 'they will not care about the faith of a customer, just as long as he has money and doesn't cause trouble.'

'Then let's hope we find a merchant there who is as unprincipled as you,' said Oliver with a grin.

Aadloun was a few miles further north along the coast. It was a small settlement but the streets were busy with people gossiping and traders selling their wares. The villagers fell silent as the six men passed by but did not seem unfriendly.

They stopped at the market and dismounted, allowing their horses to drink in the water-trough provided. Bernard led the way to a stall which was well-stacked with bread. It was hot and smelt good. To one side of the counter were pastries and mounds of cheese.

He ordered half a dozen loaves, some flat-bread for the journey and a bag of soft cheese which would keep fresh in the sun. The merchant packed up the goods in a piece of cloth. He grinned. Travellers with appetites like this were few and far between.

'How much?' Bernard asked, holding three deniers on the palm of his hands.

The merchant bent to examine them and shook his head.

'Sorry, my friend,' he said. 'That is Frankish money. It is worthless now.' He shrugged apologetically and took back the food.

'How about gold?' Laurence asked.

The merchant looked at him shrewdly. 'Gold is always good. Arab, Jewish, Greek or Frankish. It is always good.'

Laurence pulled out a Byzantine hyperpyron and showed it to the merchant.

'That is very good, excellent in fact.'

Laurence placed the coin upon the counter and pulled out his knife. He placed the blade on one edge of the coin, cut it and then moved it along a tiny amount to make the second cut. He glanced up at the merchant. The man gestured with his hand for Laurence to make the cut a little larger. Laurence moved the blade the slightest fraction. 'That's as much as I will go,' he said.

The merchant shrugged and nodded his head.

Laurence pressed down carefully and pulled a sliver of gold from the coin.

The merchant took the gold, examined it and nodded with satisfaction. He gave Bernard the food once again. Then he reached out for half a dozen pastries and thrust these into the cloth as well.

'You are an honest man,' Laurence said.

'And you, I suspect, are a good one.'

The six friends rode out of the village. A few miles further along they found a small pool fringed by trees. The day was clear and bright with clouds flying high on the winds from the sea. It promised to be warm. They ate some of the bread and cheese. The water from the pool was dark and unpalatable but the horses were content to drink it so they did as well.

'I would feel happier if we all had weapons,' Laurence said. 'I am the only one with a sword.'

'Do you have enough money to buy weapons for us all?' Bernard asked.

Laurence shook his head. 'I have only the deniers and the one gold coin. This will keep us in food for a while but nothing more.'

'Then we shall have to steal some weapons,' said John. 'Or steal money so we can buy them.'

Bernard looked shocked. 'Who should we steal from, Saracen peasants or Frankish ones? I, for one, could not do such a thing.'

John felt fewer qualms over what he thought of as their own survival. He decided not to argue.

'The Hospitallers,' said Jurgen. 'I would love to steal from them.'

'I wouldn't advise that,' said Laurence. 'You'd have the wrath of Christendom fall upon you and besides, they are well-armed and folly to cross. The Templars even more so.'

He put the bread to his mouth and stopped. 'I've just had a thought,' he said. 'There is someone I would be more than happy to rob from.'

The others waited in silence.

Outcasts

'On the road north from Tyre,' Laurence continued, 'ten miles south of Tripoli, is a castle owned by Baron Raymond.'

'Raymond of Niphin?' Matthew asked. He leant forward eagerly.

'Yes,' answered Laurence. 'He's a vicious man, nothing more than a robber. He has a large retinue of knights and soldiers and plunders the land for miles around. He steals from anyone and everyone, Frank, Muslim or Syrian. Yes, he's one that I would be more than happy to lift some money from.'

'The robber robbed,' said John, rubbing his hands together. 'I love the sound of that.' For the first time since the siege of Jerusalem he felt himself filled with purpose.

He glanced around at the others. Matthew stared into space. A slow smile came to his lips. John decided not to ask what he was thinking, just yet.

The others were equally drawn to the idea. All except for Bernard.

'You don't look happy with the idea, old friend,' Oliver said.

'I'm not.' He took a deep breath. 'My wife and family are captive. My only desire is to rescue them. An adventure like this merely stops me going to their aid.'

John felt a surge of sympathy for his friend. An image of Agnes rose in his mind and he realised that Bernard was not alone in wishing to find her.

Laurence put his hand upon Bernard's shoulder. 'You will find such a task easier with money and weapons,' he said. 'You know I think your quest is well-nigh impossible as it is. Without weapons it will definitely be so.'

Bernard did not answer. He did not even want to think about what Laurence said. He feared that if he did so he might give up even the slender hope he still had.

'I suppose you're right,' he said at last. 'Let's seek out this Baron of Niphin and his den of thieves.'

They mounted their horses and cantered down the coast road to the north. They were all glad to have a new purpose to their lives.

Laurence reckoned it was a hundred miles or more to Niphin. 'We'll have to take care,' he said. 'The coast road might be dangerous, but it's the most direct route.' He reckoned it would take two days to get there.

The road, in fact, proved anything but dangerous. It was normally busy with Frankish knights and soldiers, travellers and merchants. Now the road was virtually deserted. Saladin's army was still rumoured to be in the vicinity and only those who had desperate need were willing to travel far from the safety of their homes.

They travelled the rest of the day without incident and set off just after dawn the next morning.

'One thing's been troubling me,' Oliver said as they trotted along the road. He looked at Laurence. 'You said that the Baron of Niphin had a large retinue. How are we going to attack them when we have only one sword between six of us?'

Laurence frowned. 'I have been thinking on that for all of the morning.'

'And?'

'And nothing. I haven't come up with an answer.'

'That is no good,' said Jurgen. 'You suggested robbing the Baron. Now you tell us that you don't know how.'

'I thought I might come up with an idea on the way,' Laurence answered.

Oliver and Jurgen exchanged a disgruntled look.

'It does no good to quarrel,' John said. 'And just because Laurence thought of the plan doesn't mean that he has to think of every last detail.'

'I agree,' said Matthew. 'We're in this together so we have to work together. Let us think about our choices as we ride.'

So they began a debate about how to steal money from the castle of Niphin. For an hour they argued this idea and that, dismissing the most ludicrous and eagerly pursuing the ones that seemed to be of most promise. Yet, the more they talked the more all suggestions appeared equally flawed and futile.

Finally, they fell silent. They were defeated.

John was riding at the front of the company. He reined in his horse and pointed. 'I can see a castle,' he said. 'Is that Niphin?'

Laurence joined him. 'No,' he said. 'That is Gibelet,'

'Is is safe to go there?' Matthew asked. 'Who controls the castle, Saracens or Franks?'

'Who can tell anymore,' Laurence answered. 'I think we would be best to skirt around it.'

They took a track which led into the hills to the east of the village, keeping out of sight of the castle. It took half an hour to return to the coast road. At this point it became better maintained and they were able to push their horses forward more swiftly.

It was an hour after noon. The company still debated how to steal from the knights of Niphin but the more they talked the more obvious it became that they had little chance of success. One by one each man decided for himself that the idea was impossible. Yet none wanted to be the first to admit it.

'I am famished,' announced Jurgen. He glanced up at the sun. 'It is almost noon. We should buy some more food.'

He pointed out a small village upon the shore.

Laurence swore to himself. 'We have come further than I thought,' he said. 'That is the village of Chekka. We must be cautious now. We're only a couple of miles from Niphin.'

'I cannot wait any longer,' said Jurgen. 'I must eat or die.'

'The next settlement is Niphin,' Laurence said. 'So we would be better to buy food from here.'

The company followed Laurence into the village. As they rode through the streets, scores of children crept out of their homes. They stretched out their hands to the strangers. They were skinny as cats, the skin of their heads tight upon their skulls. Their eyes bulged from dark sockets. Half of them wore nothing but filthy rags.

'What's happened here?' breathed John.

Laurence shook his head. 'Baron Raymond and his men,' I guess.

'They have robbed these poor villagers?'

'I don't suppose they were poor until they were robbed.' He turned towards Jurgen. 'I doubt we will find any food here.'

They continued down the street. They had seen no adults; presumably they were all in hiding. As they got to the edge of the village, however, they spied one adult. An old woman was hunched upon the ground, watching them intently.

As they approached her, Laurence reached inside his tunic and pulled out his purse. He handed it to her in silence. Her eyes flickered for a moment and then she bowed. 'Shukran.' She peered into the purse and clutched it to her chest in joy.

The road turned west towards a little bay a few hundred yards from the village. There were a few more adults here. Three aged men squatted in the dust watching a young man who was intently mending a fishing net.

As soon as he caught sight of the Franks the younger man attempted to hide the net. The older men bowed their heads and began to wail.

The company dismounted from their horses and approached.

'Don't be scared,' Bernard cried in Arabic. 'We will not harm you.'

The young man looked at them warily. 'Niphin?' he asked.

Bernard shook his head. 'We are from Jerusalem.'

The wailing calmed.

'My net is all I own,' said the young man. 'Please don't take it from me.'

'We have no desire for your net,' said Bernard. 'Do not worry.'

'Ask him if he has any fish?' Jurgen asked.

But before Bernard could translate, the young man gave a shrill laugh.

'I have no fish,' he said in clumsy French. 'My boat was stolen from me so I now can only fish close to land, as far as I can throw my net. There are few fish so close to shore.'

'Who stole it?'

'Who do you think? The Baron of Niphin, of course. He takes everything. He is squeezing us to death.'

'I am sorry,' Bernard answered.

Suddenly, one of the old men began to keen loudly. His head shook violently and he pointed back towards the village.

A solitary horseman came trotting down the road towards them. He was in full armour, armed with sword and mace. He held a spear in front of him and as he got closer they could see that Laurence's purse was skewered upon it.

'Baron Raymond,' cried the young fisherman. He leapt to his

feet and fled.

The horseman spurred his horse and charged towards them. They had no time to mount their own horses. Laurence drew out his sword and stood in the path of the Baron. It was courageous but suicidal. Raymond lowered his spear, aiming at Laurence's heart.

The others were all rooted to the ground.

An idea flashed into Bernard's head. 'Seize hold of the net,' he cried. His voice held such a tone of command that John hurried to do his bidding.

Bernard plucked up the other end and began to run towards the charging horse. He held one end of the net at shoulder height and gestured John to do the same.

Matthew saw what they were doing and leapt ahead, shouldering Laurence out of the way just in time. The horse thundered past, straight into the net.

The impact was so fierce that the net was torn from their hands. The horse reared, neighing in terror. Its hooves were caught fast in the net and it crashed to the ground, sending its rider rolling into the three old men.

Matthew was up in an instant and leapt upon Raymond. Despite his fall the knight turned quick as an eel, reaching out for his dagger as he did so. He plunged down with the blade but Matthew caught his arm and began to bend it back. The man cried out in pain and the dagger fell to the ground. Laurence reached the struggling men and placed the tip of his sword upon the man's neck.

'One thrust and you're dead,' he cried.

The man went limp. 'Mercy,' he cried, 'mercy.'

Laurence dragged the war-helmet off of the man, revealing the yellow, skull-like head of Baron Raymond of Niphin.

'Mercy,' Laurence said. 'It's a marvel that you know the

meaning of the word.'

Within minutes the whole of the village had descended upon them. They watched in jubilation as Jurgen stripped Raymond to his underclothes. They were of the finest silk.

'I'll have those as well,' said Matthew, tearing off the clothes to leave him completely naked. A loud cry of scorn came from the village.

'How dare you,' yelled Raymond.

Matthew plucked up the dagger from the ground and pressed it to his throat. 'The Mule dare do anything to the man who robbed me of everything.'

Raymond's eyes widened. 'You are the Mule.'

'Matthew nodded. 'Yes. And you are the bastard who stole all of the gold which King Baldwin gave to me for bearing him.'

Raymond laughed. His amusement at what he had done was even stronger than his fear. Matthew pressed the dagger hard, causing a pool of blood to seep out from his throat.

'Mercy,' Raymond said again. 'I am sorry for that. Come with me to my castle and I will recompense you five-fold.'

'Oh no,' said Matthew. 'We will come to your castle. But you will recompense me a hundred-fold and the same for these poor villagers.'

Matthew held up the under-clothes and threw them to the villagers. 'That will fetch a good price in Tripoli,' he murmured. 'Part recompense at least.'

'But we will keep his weapons and armour,' said Laurence.

The village cheered them on their way as the company trotted north once more. Baron Raymond was bound at the wrists and the cord looped around Jurgen's saddle.

'What made you think of using the net?' John asked Bernard

when they were a little down the road.

'My friend Alexius,' Bernard answered. 'The Greek moneylender. He used to tell us tales of how his ancestors watched men fight in the arena for the pleasure of the crowd. He claimed that a man with a short sword was often pitched against a man with a trident and fishing net. He would throw the net upon the swordsman and try to bring him down. I never believed the story, to be honest. But it came back to my mind just in time.'

'Thank God that it did.'

They rode at a good pace for a mile or so. Even when Raymond slipped, Jurgen refused to slow, dragging him in the dust until he somehow managed to stagger to his feet.

When they stopped at last the Baron was covered with dust except where steaks of blood seeped through.

'I will get my revenge,' he snarled up at them.

'Don't be so sure,' Matthew answered.

The Baron laughed. 'I am sure. That is my castle.' He gurgled with delight. 'And here come my men to deal with you.'

They turned and saw thirty horsemen galloping out of the castle and turning towards them.

'Thirty,' Oliver murmured nervously.

'We have the whip hand,' said Laurence. He climbed from his horse and approached the Baron.

Raymond turned venomous eyes upon him. Laurence smiled and brought out his dagger. 'Grab his hair, Matthew,' he said.

Matthew needed no second bidding. He leapt from his horse and grabbed Raymond by the hair, jerking his head back savagely to reveal his neck. Laurence placed the blade against it and turned to watch the approaching men.

The leader of the band caught sight of what was happening and signalled his men to halt.

'Stop there,' Laurence called, 'and he will come to no harm.'

The man lifted up the visor of his helmet and took in the situation. 'What do you want?' he asked.

'Money,' said Laurence. 'A thousand dinars.'

'What?' cried the man.

'Isn't your Baron worth that?' sneered Matthew.

'And that's not all,' continued Laurence. 'We want five sets of weapons: swords, knives, and spears. And five sets of chain-mail.'

'You ask for a lot.'

'We offer you your leader's life.'

Matthew bent Raymond's neck back even further. They all heard a sharp crack.

'Give it to them,' cried Raymond. 'Give them all they ask for.'

'And food,' said Jurgen. 'We want food and wine.'

One of the horsemen from the rear cocked his head and urged his horse forward. 'Is that Jurgen?' he called. He took of his helmet.

'Ralph Fishmonger,' cried Jurgen. 'What are you doing here?'

'It's a long story,' Ralph answered.

A dozen more men pushed forward towards them.

'Oliver's here as well,' Jurgen cried, 'and Bernard Montjoy and the mad young Englishman.'

'Who in heaven are these?' Matthew asked.

'Our fellow knights,' John answered. 'Some of the men Balian knighted at the siege.'

Laurence pushed the blade deeper into Raymond's neck. 'Enough of this chatter,' he said. 'You've heard what we want. Now go and get it.'

The leader of the band ordered half a dozen men to go back to the castle. The rest he ordered to dismount. He never took his eyes off of Laurence, waiting for him to relax his guard.

'Don't try anything,' Laurence said. 'Or he's a dead man.'

They waited in silence for a few minutes longer, watching until the knights had entered the castle.

Bernard walked over to Ralph Fishmonger. 'So what are you doing here?' he asked. 'Why are you with this crew of cut-purses?'

'They're the only ones who would take us,' Ralph answered. 'We offered our services to the Templars and the Hospitallers but they laughed in our faces. The same with Conrad of Tyre. Only Raymond of Niphin would accept us for what we were.'

'But at what cost?'

Ralph looked at the ground and did not answer.

'We get paid,' said another man. 'Paid well. That's all that matters.'

'I'm sorry to hear you say that, Etienne,' Bernard said. 'But it doesn't have to be that way.'

'What other way could it be?'

'You could join with us.' Bernard looked around at the others to see if they were in agreement. They nodded their heads.

'They are sworn to the Baron's service,' said the leader of their band.

'Such a promise is worthless,' said Bernard. 'They are sworn already, to Balian.'

'And Bernard is the most senior knight here,' said John. 'So really they are bound to follow him.'

The dozen men from Jerusalem looked at each other in consternation. They drew apart and began to talk amongst themselves.

A little later the knights who had been sent back to the castle returned leading a cart with all that Laurence had asked for.

The friends slipped on the armour and weapons, Oliver took charge of the money and Jurgen of the food.

'Thank you, my friends,' said Laurence. 'Keep hold of him, Matthew,' he said, before mounting his horse. He gestured quickly and Matthew heaved Raymond over Laurence's saddle.

'We had a bargain,' cried the leader of the knights.

Laurence pressed the dagger against the back of Raymond's neck. 'You don't think we'd be stupid enough to trust you, do you? We will release your Baron to Bohemond's son at Tripoli. I don't much like the idea of having wolves like you on our heels.'

He lent forward in his saddle. 'If we see any sign of you following us then Raymond will never reach Tripoli.'

He gestured to his friends to mount up.

'What about you, my friends?' said Bernard. 'Will you join us?'

Eight of the men from Jerusalem shook their heads but four climbed on their horses and joined them.

'Let's go,' Bernard cried.

They headed north on the road to Tripoli.

After a mile they glanced back. The Baron's men were still waiting by the road. A furlong after the road took a turn to the east and they were lost to sight. Laurence led them for a little while longer than abruptly took a turn up a path to the right.

'This isn't the way to Tripoli,' yelled Raymond.

'Who said we were going to Tripoli?' said Laurence.

'You did.'

'I beg pardon. I made a mistake.'

'Then where are we going?'

'To Damascus,' Bernard answered. 'And if need be to Baghdad.'

CHARACTERS IN OUTCASTS
Historical figures are in bold

John Ferrier
Simon Ferrier
Bernard Montjoy, owner of the Inn
Agnes Montjoy, his wife
Gerard, son of Bernard Montjoy
Claude-Yusuf, son of Robert and Farah
Eleanor, their daughter
Matthew of Jerusalem. The Mule
Alexius Kamateros, a Greek moneylender, friend of Bernard and Agnes
Guy of Lusignan, King of Jerusalem
Raymond, the old Count of Tripoli
Balian of Ibelin, noble of Jerusalem
Jerome Sospel, comrade and friend of Balian
Archbishop Eraclius, Patriarch of Jerusalem
Saladin, Sultan and conqueror of Jerusalem
Al-Adil, Saladin's brother and lieutenant
Herald of Saladin
William Esson, one of Balian's sergeants
Oliver of Provence, one of Bernard's friends, knighted by Balian
Jurgen of Saxony, Oliver's friend, also knighted
Yacob, Claude-Yusuf's grand-father
Terricus, Grand Preceptor of Jerusalem and Acting Grand

Master of the Knights of the Temple
William Borrel, acting Head of the Hospitallers
Pasque de Riveri, Eraclius' mistress and mother to their child, Constance
Walter, Eraclius' Deacon
Peter, a wine-maker from Tours
Khalid, an Emir in Saladin's army
Issam, a Muslim doctor in Khalid's troop
Habib, factotum of the Caliph
Dawud, Habib's friend
Al-Adfal, Saladin's elder son
Uthman, Saladin's younger son
William, the Marquis of Montferrat
Conrad of Montferrat, defender of Tyre
Raymond, robber Baron of Niphin
Raymond, eldest son of Bohemond, the new Count of Tripoli
Ermoul, Balian's squire
Bohemond the younger, second son of the Prince of Tyr
Armengol, Proviser of the Knights Hospitallers
Bohemond, Prince of Antioch
Cybil, Princess of Antioch, Bohemond's wife
Caliph al-Nasir, Spiritual Head of the Muslim world and ruler of Baghdad
Johara, one of the Caliph's wives.
Lalina, one of the Caliph's harem.
Beatrice, the Caliph's new favourite
Gabriella, the young prostitute, Simon's lover
Gregory, one of Simon's guards
William, another of his guards
Theo, the torch-boy

Al-Dahir, son of Caliph al-Nasir
Sheik al-Djabbar, head of the Caliph's futuwwa
Bahir, his friend and lieutenant
Gerard de Ridefort, Grand Master of the Templars
Emir Walid, one of Saladin's commanders
Laurence of Tyre, an officer of the city
Gilbert Vallon, an arrogant noble from Tyre
Sir Henry Colville, a Knight of Tyre, a friend of Gilbert Vallon
Suhail, one of the boys in the futuwwa

THANKS

Thanks to Janine Smith for her advice and skill in editing the novel. Also to Dr Stephen Carter, Nick Britten, Kevin Scott Day and Rembrandt Ten Hove for their help, advice and support.

BOOKS BY MARTIN LAKE

THE FLAME OF RESISTANCE

The Battle of Hastings is over. The Battle for England is about to begin. Edgar Atheling, the young heir to the throne must decide if he will battle William the Conqueror for the kingdom.

TRIUMPH AND CATASTROPHE

Edgar leads an English army into alliance with the Danes and war with the Normans. At first there is only triumph and glory. Then William returns and catastrophe ensues.

BLOOD OF IRONSIDE

Edgar is banished from Scotland and takes the war to the land of the Franks. But the death of his mother forces him to return. And there he faces death at the hands of the man who slew his father.

IN SEARCH OF GLORY

Edgar has been tricked into making peace with William. But when his old friend Cnut invades, Edgar takes up again the struggle against the Normans.

LAND OF BLOOD AND WATER

Warfare and warriors meant nothing to Brand and his family. But then King Alfred chose their home for his last-ditch defence against the Vikings.

BLOOD ENEMY

Ulf has risen high in King Alfred's service. But when he shows himself a berserker he loses everything. Can he redeem himself and return to favor?

WOLVES OF WAR

Leif Ormson is a Skald, a story-teller, renowned for his witty tales. His brother, Sigurd is a black-smith, making knives, scythes and horse-shoes. And magnificent weapons of war.

But one day, Ivar the Boneless, son of Ragnar Lothbrok, commands the brothers to make him a great sword. And he demands that they accompany his army to England.

Leif and Sigurd are thrown into a maelstrom of war and violence. The great Viking army blazes across England, murdering, plundering, killing kings and setting up puppet-rulers in their place. Until now the Vikings had come only to raid and plunder. Now they have come to conquer.

Leif and Sigurd face an agonising choice. Do they seek to return to their familiar lives? Or do they stay in England and embrace this uncertain new world of war, wealth and glory?

OUTCASTS: CRUSADES

Saladin is marching to conquer the city of Jerusalem. Within the city waits only one nobleman, Balian of Ibelin, and four knights. In desperation, Balian knights thirty ordinary men of the city in to lead the defence. History says nothing more of the men raised so far above their normal station. 'Outcasts' tells the story of how they fare in a world grown more bitter and fanatical.

A LOVE MOST DANGEROUS

Her beauty was a blessing…and a dangerous burden…

As a Maid of Honor at the Court of King Henry VIII, beautiful Alice Petherton receives her share of admirers. But when the powerful, philandering Sir Richard Rich attempts to seduce her, she knows she cannot thwart his advances for long. She turns to the most powerful man in England for protection: the King himself.

Reveling in her newfound power, Alice soon forgets that enemies lurk behind every corner at court…and there are some who are eagerly plotting her fall…

VERY LIKE A QUEEN.

The King's favor was her sanctuary—until his desire turned dangerous.

Alice Petherton is well practiced at using her beauty and wits to survive in the Court of King Henry VIII. As the King's favorite, she enjoys his protection but after seeing the downfall of three of his wives, she's determined to avoid the same fate. Alice must walk a fine line between mistress and wife.

She finds a powerful protector in Thomas Cromwell and Alice has every reason to believe that she will continue to enjoy a life of wealth and comfort at Court…until she puts everything at risk by falling in love with a Frenchman, Nicholas Bourbon.

When Cromwell is executed, Alice loses her only ally and flees to France. There she hopes to live in peace with Nicholas. But Alice is lured into a perilous game of treason and peace doesn't last long. Will Alice get back the life and love she's fought for? Or will she lose herself to the whims of a capricious monarch?

A DANCE OF PRIDE AND PERIL

Four thousand years ago, Crete is a land of contrasts. The mountains are wild and forbidding yet on the coast, a new world is arising.

Mulia is famous for its thrilling and deadly acrobatic displays, where young men face the fierce charges of giant bulls, leaping over them or dying in the attempt. Talita is sold to the owner of the arena and trains as a dancer, her job to entertain the audience and goad the raging bulls.

Yet she wants more than this. Even as a child, she protected her flock from bears and wolves and was undaunted by them. Now she yearns to be a bull-leaper, a role reserved for men. Her friends and lover believe she is foolish to have such dreams. Foolish, wilful and dangerously reckless.

When she realises that she has a bond with Torq, the mightiest of the bulls, her ambition grows even stronger. Yet her dreams are thwarted when priests arrive from Egypt and steal Torq. Her enemies accuse Talita of taking Torq and she and her lover Pellon are condemned to death.

Will she find the strength and courage to escape? Dare she voyage to the distant land of Egypt and challenge the powerful, cunning, High Priest? Can she liberate Torq, prove her innocence and save her life?

THE ARTFUL DODGER

After his trial Dodger is transported to New South Wales. He is taken in by a kindly family and learns to improve himself. But when he returns to England he finds himself stalked by a man who seeks to kill him.

PATHS OF TIME

We all live within the bounds of time and it marches on inexorably. Yet sometimes it has an elusive, subtle feel which makes us feel uneasy or perhaps exhilarated. On occasion time does not work at all as we expect. We are wrong-footed, confused, beguiled.

FOR KING AND COUNTRY

Three short stories set in the First World War.

NUGGETS

Fast fiction for quiet moments.

MR TOAD'S WEDDING

First prize winner in the competition to write a sequel story to The Wind in the Willows.

MR TOAD TO THE RESCUE

Mr Toad almost gets married but he has a lucky escape. The bride is kidnapped, not once but twice and Toad and his friends leave their familiar home to journey to the French Riviera on a desperate rescue mission.

THE BIG SCHOOL

Three light-hearted short stories about a boy's experience of growing up.

Printed in Great Britain
by Amazon